HELL SENT

- The Vigil Omnibus -

by Stephen Hunt

HELL SENT

ISBN-13: 978-1-8380539-5-6

www.StephenHunt.net

Twitter: @s_hunt_author
www.facebook.com/SciFi.Fantasy

First Edition

Printed in the U.S.A & United Kingdom

HELL SENT was written by Stephen Hunt as part of the
Author's Apprentice Literary Program, an interactive online
platform where hundreds of secondary schools and thousands
of students followed the book's serialised writing process across
a year; voting on varied facets of the novel including plot twists,
character names, the work's title and cover art, as well as acting as
both test readers and copy editors.

Stephen would like to thank all the students and their teachers
for taking part in this unique creation and hope that the book,
thoughts and moments shared will stay with the students for the
rest of their long reading - and writing - lives.

To receive an automatic notification by e-mail when Stephen's
new books are available for download, use the free sign-up form at
http://www.StephenHunt.net/alerts.php

To help report any typos, errors and similar in this work, use the
form at http://www.stephenhunt.net/typo/typoform.php

-1-

~ TAKEOUT MENU ~

The security on the back door lifted the staff badge across Ian's chest and scanned its barcode while he waited by his cart. He tried, unsuccessfully, to slow his pounding heart. It was natural to be nervous. And not just because this pair of brutes looked like ex-marines squeezed into black suits. Matching bald heads, ear mikes and hulking muscles as large as sides of beef fattened on the free steroid diet. *In retrospect, that should be a bit of a giveaway*, thought Ian. After all, why would an exclusive art installation in a semi-abandoned factory ten miles away from the nearest highway need these lethal-looking bouncers? Nobody uninvited was likely to be turning up here . . . mistaking the crumbling, weed-overrun industrial buildings for an illegal dance party. No, Ian had reasons for having to hide his nerves while projecting the image of bored, minimum-wage staff. Good reasons. Deadly reasons. Ian glanced back towards his large catering van. It lay on the far side of the makeshift car park, a lot packed with expensive Mercedes, BMW and Range Rover vehicles. The cars were another clue that this factory wasn't quite what it seemed. Artists and starving went together. Artists and Porsche four-wheel-drives, not so much.

Ian admired a bright purple Ferrari resting on the lot like a coiled panther. 'That's a hell of car.'

'Yeah, that's a *Hell* of a car.' Guy Drew halted his plastic food cart directly behind Ian's, its four wheels resting on the mouldering, broken tarmac.

Like Ian, Guy wore a double-breasted white chef's jacket with a pair of stiff black trousers. He was old and grizzled, almost three times Ian's age, a disappointed flat bulldog face that spoke – falsely, as it happened – of being a serf-to-the super-rich for far too long. It was a face born to have a half-smoked cigarette naturally bobbing in the corner of his curled lips. He didn't currently. Nobody here wanted to smell Guy's second-hand cancer-stick smoke. His hair was short-cropped, silver, and as bristly as the old man's manners.

To the rear of Guy, Diane O'Hara trundled up with the third cart, her neck bright and blotchy above the chef's jacket, skin almost approaching the colour of her short bob of ginger hair. That neck was like a map if you knew how to read it. Today, the destination was a nervous *Please let me survive this*. Luckily for Ian – for all three of them, really – the bouncers were relying on more traditional detection equipment. Ian wheeled his cart under a wide metal detection arch, as if someone had set up an airport on the far side of the gate. The old man and Diane went through next. Not a beep or a bleep from the scanning equipment. Neither of the two bouncers paid Diane a second glance. She was pretty in a quirky, winsome, young girl-next-door way. A lot more so if she ever came to realise it. But compared to the people inside, all the beautiful people, the three visitors might as well have landed from Planet Ugly. And, of course, Ian, Diane and Guy also wore glasses. None of the people inside needed spectacles. Not unless it was for vanity . . . designer pairs with plain glass rather than prescription lenses, for that extra-intellectual hipster look.

The third bouncer on duty on the gate gazed suspiciously at Guy, as though he could scent a bad odour. 'He with you?' asked the bouncer, addressing Ian.

'No. *He's* with *me*,' said Guy.

Ain't that the truth of it. Natural enough for the rent-a-thugs to believe that Ian was the leader of this little group as opposed to Guy. Ian walked confidently rather than slouching, his white polycotton jacket stretched taut over a muscular frame. Perhaps a college student in his first year, looking to earn a little extra money to supplement a sports scholarship? Ian wouldn't have appeared out of place in a bouncer's suit, except for his face. A little trusting, soft, a smooth and untroubled demeanor. A well-fed Afghan Hound to this guard unit's hungry Dobermans.

'You're late,' said the third bouncer. 'The others have already arrived and are setting up.'

Ian grunted non-committedly when what he wanted to say was: *Of course we're late. We had to intercept the real catering van. We had to take out the people inside. We had to hack your stupid staff list ID system.* At least they had remembered to spray the catering company livery and logo across their van the day before. Give it time to dry. Nothing would have given them away faster than wet paint.

'We'll work fast,' said Guy Drew, in a tone that suggested he really didn't give a fig.

All three of them passed into the factory. It had been a vehicle assembly plant once, all the large machinery long since stripped out. Ian found himself inside a sizable chamber with exposed brick walls where a mobile kitchen had been set up. A long line of stainless steel gas-fired hobs and ovens in the chamber's centre, like some extreme barbecue cooking contest had started. The chamber had been a two storey structure once, but the upper storey had disintegrated, only a few jutting metal supports to indicate there had been another level above.

A backroom event coordinator jogged over. He looked flustered. 'You're late.'

'Getting here was simply murder,' said Guy.

'Just get the plates and cutlery out and onto the buffet tables. Now! Hurry up!'

Diane watched the coordinator jog off to hassle the staff cooking at the oven unit. 'Smells like roast chicken. Is that a good thing or not?'

'Depends on whether this food is intended for the people already arrived or for the latecomers,' said Ian.

'Wasn't so long ago you two were newbies,' said Guy, sliding the side of his cart open and removing piles of white plates. 'Same as the saps turning up here later for the Reds.'

The crockery was expensive, durable white catering issues. The cutlery was made of the same substance air stewards gave out on passenger jets. Resembling metal, but in reality an ingenious plastic designed to snap and break if anyone tried to use it to hijack a plane. Its use here wasn't an accident. The guests inside didn't want to get stabbed.

The three of them piled the plates on top of their carts, removed stacked boxes of cutlery, and then pushed the carts through the doors into the main event. Another ex-factory hall, even larger than the first. This one's floor was scattered with metal sculptures – abstract, for the most part, with just a hint of form – lit by multi-coloured uplighters, lights shifting and highlighting different angles and sides along the works, making them seem to move and sway. A crowd of wealthy-looking patrons moved through the exhibits, all wearing dark dinner jackets and discrete cocktail dresses, the standard uniform of the rich, the chatter of their observations and small-talk swelled by classical music playing from expensive sound-stand speakers. Catering staff passed among the patrons carrying trays of finger food and fluted champagne glasses, allowing the guests to graze. Ian and his two companions pushed their carts to buffet tables lining the back wall of the installation. Piles of hot food on metal trays. Heavy cream tablecloths. Most of the food looked Asian and Japanese-inspired. Coin-sized pieces of chicken in soy sauce; duck dumplings; peppered twists of squid, octopus balls; pale squares of hot vinegared rice. It smelled good too and Ian had to resist the urge to pick at the buffet himself as he started to toss out piles of plates, dropping cutlery upright into heavy porcelain dispensers. *Wouldn't do to get tossed out of here for raiding the table.* Guy and Diane worked by his side. Quickly, efficiently. But then, they were a team, even in such mundane tasks.

There was slight tickling by Ian's ear as his spectacle's hidden speaker fired into life. Using silent bone vibration-induction rather than actual sound, so nobody without specs could overhear Alasdair's words. Alasdair was the other member of this night's team, warming himself out in the surveillance van on the lot. *Lucky lad.* 'Coach is just parking up now. Supper is served.'

'Special order menu,' muttered Ian.

Diane and Guy had heard the message too in their frame mikes. Ian traded what he hoped was a reassuring glance with Diane. In reality, he probably just looked worried.

It wasn't long before the bus's passengers had been ushered through the front-of-door security check. There were maybe thirty of them, an even mixture of boys and girls, none of them older than seventeen, the youngest maybe ten. They were underdressed for the occasion, jeans and t-shirts and inexpensive dresses. But then, this group had arrived from an orphanage. They were wearing charity cast-offs. *And frankly*, Ian mused, *they are the lucky ones*. Their families were already dead or dysfunctionally distant, not murdered to order to supply a spare meal. The orphanage thing was old, but the Reds never seemed to get tired of using this ploy. *Sometimes I think institutional care is just one big factory farm*. Easier to arrange than hijacking a plane and faking an air crash, when it came to snacking on passengers, though.

A tall distinguished-looking man in a dinner jacket took to the stage near the main entrance. After he welcomed the visiting party of orphans to the gallery he made a speech about how glad he was that the proceeds from tonight's viewing was going to benefit a family shelter in New Jersey. Then the compere made way for the gallery owner to give a talk about the healing benefits of conceptual art for underprivileged children. It was all hot-air with just one purpose. Getting as much food as possible down the necks of the visitors from the home. The youngsters duly obliged. Whoever the inside contacts in the home were, they had intentionally kept the kids hungry before getting here. No meal before they left. No snacks on the bus in.

Same old same old. The Reds preferred their prey with a full stomach and the prey's muscles stressed by the flight-or-fight response. Gave the food an exquisite flavour, or so Ian had been told, and when you only needed to feed once every six months, it was all about the flavour. *Maybe that is why the Reds favour veal over mutton.*

'It is time,' called the gallery owner on the platform, raising his hands.

'Stay frosty,' growled Guy, for Ian and Diane's benefit. 'Hold your lead.'

Here we go. At least the jawing about the joys of modern art has stopped.

'Let the feast begin!'

By the buffet table, most of the orphanage party had turned around in surprise, obviously wondering what the triumphant-sounding clown in the dinner jacket was going on about now. Even the ones still stuffing their faces paused and gasped when the crowd of supposed wealthy benefactors began to move towards the children almost as one, a steady stalking gait. Hungry expressions distorted the patrons' faces, pairs of pronounced razored fangs extending from their teeth. None of the unfortunate young victims knew what was going on, but they understood this was crazy freaky. They knew that having a crowd of internet billionaires and trust fund types suddenly encircling and advancing on you as though you were mice and they were cats was in no way normal behaviour.

A single orphan hadn't joined the group of wary children pulling back, though. One of the older visitors. Standing alone, her legs spread and ready to kick ass. She wielded a useless airline knife that would crumple on the first thrust. Ian admired the attitude, but the young lady didn't have a snowflake in hell's chance against this many half-turned. Even if the attackers had been human, they could easily beat the brave girl down with these numbers. Ian felt guilty. Allowing this massacre to happen. Human bait for the wider war. *Come on girl; give them a fight worthy of the name.*

Plates dropped, cries of fear and surprise, the children retreated back around the table in a reflexive herd defence. The rest of the catering staff drew away and waited calmly by the wall. As uncaring as if they were watching dogs chase birds around a park. Ian loathed the human groupies. In it for the money or the sick thrill of watching. Paid to look the other way. Eager for their chance to earn a place in the pack. And right now, Ian hated himself, too. *We have to wait. We have to watch too.* Only some of the beautiful people were vampires or the half-turned wretches known as demi-gogs. The remainder were groupies, as mortal as the average Joe on the street. There was always an insanely long waiting list just for the chance of becoming a Red. *It's amazing what the super-rich will do for immortality.* It had taken a year for Ian to unlearn everything he thought he knew about vampires from the movies and fiction. Apart from their lust for human blood . . . that part was all-too-true. Garlic, useless. Holy water, useless. The old daylight test, useless. Aversion to crosses, forget about it. Vampires were perfect chameleons. When Reds wanted to play human, their DNA was indistinguishable from human. When they fed, after they had converted, it was like flipping a kill switch. *I guess their DNA is a lot different, then. Faster, stronger, quicker to heal. Able to suck the life out of a human quicker than sucking juice out of an orange.* Of course, by that point in the proceedings, taking a vampire in a feeding cycle alive, sticking a needle in its arm and drawing a blood sample in the name of medical research, that would prove kind of suicidal. *Better Dead than Red.* Always.

'Switching to heat,' announced Al's voice at the back of Ian's ear.

The view across Ian's spectacles altered to infrared, a complete head-up display with the heat signatures of those inside the party room tactically marked with coloured arrow graphics. Green for human-level metabolisms – blue for demi-gogs. None of the arrows blinked red yet. And that would signal the prize. That was why Ian and his two companions were inside here. They had to give it time. When a vampire's body was warming up, it was indistinguishable from a demi-gog. Took a minute or more for it to convert to the full Dracula. Of course, that was a minute these poor benighted orphans didn't have. There wasn't exactly an overpopulation of Reds in the world. They were territorial and didn't care to manufacture too many rivals. Demi-gogs might share the same terrible hunger as the Reds, but at best the half-turned wretches were only a fraction as powerful as a full Red. House cats compared to lions. But such kitties could still scratch for their owners.

Over by the buffet tables' side the demi-gogs seized a couple of the children and now the screaming really began. Out in front, the dark-haired girl sliced out at the four attackers who surrounded her – three dinner-jacketed men and one woman in a luxury trouser suit. The nearest monster swung back out of the way. Ian had him pegged as recently half-turned. Should have known that knife wouldn't harm him too badly, even if it had been stamped out of pure steel. Or maybe the newbie had mistaken it for silver. The remaining three demi-gogs weren't put off, though. They went in like a coordinated pack. Had the girl's flailing body locked down tight on the floor within seconds.

The infrared reading on one of the figures in the crowd flared sun-bright, a blinking red graphic across Ian's display bouncing madly just in case he was either asleep on the job or completely colour blind.

'And we have a winner!' spat Guy. The tough old dude didn't waste a single second. He reached for his cart's handle, twisted it to the side, and slid out the concealed ceramic-bladed sword. From short-order chef to twenty-first-century samurai vampire slayer in one easy move.

'Oh, cheez'n crackers,' swore Diane. She pulled out her sword from her cart as Ian hit the hidden latch on his. Spring loaded, the reassuring heft of the blade thumped into his right hand.

They had what they had come for. *Maybe a bit too much. A metabolism running that overclocked. Big trouble.* Ian's specs targeted a woman wearing a one-piece velvet blue gown, crazy tall, immaculately beautiful – of course – with sandy-coloured hair that had a Roman style to it, piled on top and running to elaborate curls by the time her strands ran out. Ian hoped she wasn't actually old enough to have developed a taste for that hairstyle during the reign of the Caesars. The ancient Reds were always the most powerful. Fully in control of the more peculiar range of powers that developed with long age. She moved towards the orphan girl. Her four half-turned servants held the girl out for the Red. Shoving dinner forward. An offering for the dark goddess. One of the strange twisted iron statues stood behind the vista; reinforcing the awful feeling Ian was witness to some prehistoric human sacrifice.

'Crash team inbound,' announced the disembodied voice by Ian's ear. Naturally, Al's wireless feed from the glasses had immediately picked up the Red's presence. 'I'm prepping medical out here.'

Guy Drew was already fighting through the crowd, cutting down the half-turned as he ran. With each killing blow, struck bodies trembled and converted to a dark ash-like residue, splintering apart like dry barbecue remains. The old man was trying to cut a path to the Red, but the furious numbers of half-turned were slowing him.

All the goodness has already gone, said Diane's voice, directly in Ian's mind. It didn't matter Diane was using what the team laughingly called brain-mail now. Signora Roma wouldn't be able to eavesdrop on our telepathy, but she'd hear it like a buzzing. The Red knew her party had been crashed. And she was a fool if she couldn't guess by whom.

Protect the children from the half-turned, Ian projected back at Diane as he sprinted forward. *I'm with Guy. We'll take down Signora Roma-hair together.*

'Forced entry!' warned Alasdair, the disembodied voice shaking inside Ian's ear. The crack of ceiling-opening charges from above was followed by a shower of masonry. Egress allowed the whup-whup-whup of Blackhawk helicopter rotors on stealth-mode to intrude into the factory, along with the tumbling whips of rappel lines, then the slicing noise of dozens of troopers abseiling down. These days the cavalry wore black body armour rather than blue jackets. Modern tactical helmets with far more advanced HUDS than Ian's covert spy spectacles concealed. The days of silver-jacketed bullets secretly blessed by priests were long over, too. Depleted uranium micro-rounds seemed to disrupt whatever Hell-sent mojo the Reds and their demi-gog servants had going on. *Effective against zombies and werewolves, too. Ghosts, not-so-much.* The guns made little tyre-puncture noises as the troops descended, silencers rotating on muzzles, suppressing intense flashes of fire.

Guy was swamped by demi-gogs, dozens of them trying to break past his whip-fast blade. Doing what they had to, to protect their Red. Didn't have much of a choice in the matter, is how Ian understood it. Like soldier ants instinctively sacrificing themselves for their nest's queen. Quite literally in the blood. *A little help!* Guy projected.

Ian growled, hacking away at the sea of crazed fanged faces. *Coming. Hang on.*

Not me, damn you. Guy sent. *The Red. Go for the Red before she vanishes.*

Ian altered direction back towards the strange iron statue standing like a twisted metal tree among the melee. He groaned as he continued to fight his way through the inhuman mob. The destroyed ceiling admitted the distinctive roaring sound of a Ferrari trying to race away from the car lot outside. One of the vamp-lovers had decided discretion was the better part of valour. The attempted escape didn't seem to make the AH-64F Apaches riding shotgun for the Blackhawks happy. One made its displeasure fully felt with a burst from the 30mm chain-gun hanging under its cockpit. That aerial cannon sounded like a chainsaw in action. Probably had much the same effect on the escaping car. It seemed a shame to Ian to waste the Ferrari. But then the half-turned could afford it. Damn demi-gogs weren't immortal like the Reds, but after being turned from human they could still survive two hundred years. A couple of centuries of compound interest would make you rich even if you weren't when you started out.

Ian's heart sank as he passed the metal artwork. The half-turned holding the young woman from the home had booked, leaving their victim shaking on the floor, caught in a fit. Tossed aside like fast-food packaging. *I know what this means.* Ian knelt by the girl, keeping his sword raised in the air to ward off the mob.

'What did she do to me?' moaned the young woman.

Ian felt the two bleeding puncture wounds on her neck. Of course Signora Roma had fed on her. And, intentionally, not to the bitter end. Showing as much pluck as the young girl had, she had been judged perfect demi-gog material. 'What's your name?'

'Eleanor Lythe. My body's itching. Feels like my muscles are on fire.'

They are. 'Don't worry. We're getting you out of here.' *Damn it to Hell. Literally!* 'We've got one on the flip. Female, Caucasian, seventeen. Blue jeans and a yellow *Girlpool* t-shirt.' He said it out loud for Al's benefit.

Al's voice sounded over the mike. 'Crash team confirmed to extract to me.'

Eleanor started wheezing. She was having difficulty breathing. 'Please. I can't move.'

'Temporary paralysis,' said Ian, kindly, trying to sound more confident than he felt. He knew her actual odds of surviving. *I'll never make a doctor.* 'It won't last more than a few minutes.'

The Red! Eyes on the prize. That from Guy Drew, desperate, almost frying Ian's brain like a sneeze on a Winter's morning.

Ian leapt to his feet and spotted Signora Roma shoving her way through the crowd of dinner jackets and Dior dresses. A nearby soldier aimed his Vector CRB Carbine at her, but she casually swept forward and grabbed the trooper by the throat before he got a burst off. Tossed him over the crowd like she was throwing away a crushed beer can. *It's chaos inside here.* Guy held back an inhuman wave of half-turned; Diane's blade sketched intricate patterns of cuts by the buffet table, every demi-gog who tried to pull a kid to feast on meeting that sword and collapsing, frequently in multiple pieces; Cav special-forces types blasting in every direction, warding off snarling monsters in human form. Ian prayed his specs were still broadcasting a friendly combatant ID out to their crash team. His heat-signature looked a lot like a Red when he got moving. *I'm on her.* Ian's legs pumped, the melee inside the hall seeming to slow as he skipped a twisting path through the fight, ignoring the distorted twisted faces of the half-turned, his own reflection caught in the Cav troops' helmet visors. Only a single focus on his mind. Signora Roma. Her little blinking red icon shimmering tantalisingly nearer and nearer on his head-up display. She knew he was coming. Her senses literally supernatural. One super-predator scenting another. But Signora Roma didn't quite know everything. *Soon you will, Drac.*

Signora Roma turned, snarling, as Ian drew close enough to strike her spine with his sword. Facing off close to the entrance. No sign of bouncers. Hopefully, snipers sitting on the Blackhawks' hatch positions had taken the security out as they swept in low over the woodland.

'You are from the Vigil!'

'I'm from Hell,' snarled Ian. *And you sent me there.* 'Your turn!'

The Signora surged forward and seized Ian's weapon arm, forcing the sword back. She was expecting to break his arm. To catch the blade with her spare hand and shove it through Ian's chest. Instead, Ian matched the Red strength for strength. Not as strong as her, but strong enough. Ian had a world of burning hate to make up the shortfall. All the memories of his murdered family to draw upon. Her eyes narrowed as she realised just what Ian was. 'You're a filthy Debasement!'

'Maybe. But assbite me if I'm the one eating kiddie-snacks in the middle of nowhere while admiring modern art.'

Signora Roma hissed at the young man as they struggled back and forth, like this was some insane arm-wrestling match gone wrong. 'You have perverted the blessing.' She howled a fresh curse at Ian in what sounded like Latin.

'I've got a blessing for you, Drac.' Ian head-butted the Red. She stumbled back, confused and urgently trying to re-evaluate the situation. *If there is one of us here there could be more.* And she was quite right to be worried. *Al, Guy, Diane. We are all Debasements. Happy to be so.*

The Red seemed to blur. Moving to both sides at once. This was her version of the old Jedi mind-trick. Reaching inside Ian's head and clouding his vision. A useful deception for a predator to possess when out shopping for human sandwiches. Sadly for her, the trick didn't work half so well on the computer drive integrated inside Ian's spectacles. He followed the rolling targeting graphic on the head-up display, flowing left, with his sword, felt the blade slam into something satisfyingly hard and fleshy. This was a moly-blade . . . five molecules thick diamond-carbon edged. *Ultimate paper-cut.* Even super-healing couldn't recover from that. Ian's glasses went dark for a second as he rolled and ducked, a fierce blast of ashes and dust flying out in all directions. *Older the Red, bigger the bang.* A fiercer, more spectacular version of what happened to half-turned corpses. The scientists back at the Vigil called that an entropy wave – something supernatural that really shouldn't exist in the universe restoring to a more normalised state of matter distribution. Ian personally preferred the term used by Scutum Dei, the Pope's secret army of old-time European vampire-slayers. *Devil Wind.*

Ian felt the dark wave of failed supernatural energy unfolding behind him, whipping around the hall and spreading misery and fear among the demi-gogs. The half-turned had lost their queen. This pack was down their Alpha-dog and they felt as though a vital part of them had been amputated. They were still gripped by an unholy hunger, though. The demi-gogs had come to devour prey and they needed to feed now. No choice in the matter. The Vigil, as always, was happy to oblige. *The depleted-uranium diet, .45 hollow-points, extra crunchy.*

A nearby demi-gog rushed Ian, a red bow-tie with orange foxes repeated in a subtle pattern tied around his expensive white dress shirt's collar. Ian's sword thrust out on raw instinct, a fast *Mugai-ryu*-style thrust that would have left his fencing tutor Ikeda Hanzo back at the Vigil with a grin on his face. *And that's your dessert.*

'Scratch the Red,' Ian shouted out loud, racing through the residual cloud of ashes. Then, for the benefit of the crash team on his mike, 'Confirmed kill.'

'Non-combatants extracted,' called Diane over the mike. 'We're safe out in the green zone.'

'Crash team fall back immediately,' ordered Guy Drew. 'GPS-I.D. everyone is out of the factory and alive before we sterilise.'

Ian was nearest the main door. He fought off the demi-gogs desperate to leave, his blade a blur, allowing the soldiers past as they retreated backwards, folding stocks of their submachine guns tight against their chests while their weapons fire targeted the raging mass of half-turned, blasted supernatural bodies apart in black cinder explosions.

The circling Apache gunships barely waited for Ian and Guy to exit the warehouse door, the two of them the last to retreat, darting past the blinding headlights of a tight perimeter circle of ground forces – soldiers with heat and night vision goggles scattered between M132 armoured flamethrowers, Stingray light tanks and M3 Bradley vehicles - before the gruff squadron leader's voice broke across the encrypted circuit. 'Green Angel to host. GPS-free on all friendlies. Weapons clear. Light it up.'

Quite frankly, the mass volley of 30mm automatic M230 chain guns were a little unnecessary, given the simultaneous flight of hundreds of Hydra 70 rockets emptying from the gunships' weapon pylons. The entire factory complex rose on a bright column of fire, broken blocks of concrete coming down like leaves in Fall. There was surprisingly little smoke for such wicked devastation. The warheads were implosion-type ordinance, sucking in the air and the heat and the fire. Ian had kept his promise to Signora Roma. A tiny little corner of the world turned into Hell, but a Hell where demons weren't going to come crawling back out anytime soon.

'Ashes to ashes,' spat Guy.

'Dust to dust,' added Ian.

The two of them swept past one of the Vigil's best cleaners, a public relations wiz called Shawna Steele. She was on her mobile, dressed in a grey business suit a little too light for the chill night air, honeyed words flowing out with the phone pressed close to her ear. 'Yes, the scheduled demolition of the old pickup truck works is going ahead tonight as planned. Purely coincidental that a flight of the 87th Air Wing is returning to McGuire Air Force Base on the same night. Weapons fire? Of course not. That's the rattle of demolition charges. And there is also an extremely well-attended fireworks display being held over in Pemberton tonight.'

'Got to love Shawna,' said Guy. 'She could have sold D-Day to the Nazis as an accidental landing by a couple of lost fishing boats.'

He should know. Rumours were that Guy was one of the first G.I.s on the beach at Juno. But Ian had other things on his worried and guilty mind. *Eleanor Lythe.*

'This is on us,' said Ian, heading quickly for the van on the lot's far side. A white medical tent had been extended over its open hatch. Alasdair stood outside by a stretcher-topped gurney.

'Don't beat yourself up, kid,' advised Guy.

'We could have stopped the people from the home going in there.'

'And the Red and her pack would have been out of here as soon as they realised dinner wasn't turning up. Supper would be rearranged, and maybe next time we don't get the intel and the drop on their feast. You know how this works. We need to confirm our kills by sight. Otherwise, the war just becomes a bad re-run of Vietnam. Napalm bombing. Inspecting the hills and finding nobody and nothing. Never knowing if Charlie bought the farm or ducked down a tunnel laughing at you.'

'Is this really war?' asked Ian. *No parades. No medals. Zero news coverage. The rest of the world carrying on in blissful cluelessness because the terrible truth would incite mass paranoia, cause societal breakdown and lead to more deaths than mere ignorance.*

Guy lit up a foul smelling victory cigar. He really was a product of the 1940s. A true throwback. 'If it isn't, pal, it'll have to do until the real deal comes along. You shouldn't have stopped to check on that bitten dame. The damned Red nearly got away. Give her another minute and she would have been wearing one of our faces and trying to bluff her way through the perimeter guards.'

Give her two and she would have turned into a wolf or something. Ian didn't reply. He wasn't sure he wanted to end up like Guy. Still fighting after all these years. So much a soldier he had forgotten almost everything else about himself. The old man started to head for the coach from the home. The children were there, being talked to by one of the film crew, being thanked for their participation in this pilot for an exciting new live TV prank show. The rest of the camera team filmed the burning ruin behind them. Laying down footage for the faked demolition clips that would be uploaded on YouTube tomorrow.

'Don't you want to visit Eleanor, the bitten girl?'

Guy shook his head, a melancholy look in his eyes. 'She'll live. Or she'll die. That's the way it goes.'

Ian saw Guy stalk away. He knew the old soldier's cold exterior was as faked as their demolition footage. Guy Drew couldn't bear to watch the human bait for this operation perish in front of his eyes, not without breaking down, and he didn't want anyone else in the team to realise he still had a heart. Was capable of feeling something more than glacial fury.

Ian came up to the van. Diane was already by the vehicle, Alasdair Colburn's tall, lanky form bent over the patient as he wiped the sweat away from her forehead.

'How is she doing?' asked Ian.

'Crash team carried her here fast,' said Alasdair. Al still held a stainless steel hypo injector gun in his right hand, like a totem. 'Didn't even have time to come out of paralysis. I injected her less than five minutes after she was bitten. That will help.'

Ian gazed at the violently thrashing young girl on the stretcher. Eleanor was secured tightly into it with arm and leg clamps, her body wired into a medical monitor on one side of the gurney and an intravenous drip on the other. Eleanor's body desperately battled the serum; or rather the evil alien corruption brewing inside her blood fought the antidote. Fought the attempt to tame the vampiric curse. To render it inert and as relatively harmless as mere mortal biochemistry could accommodate. Eleanor was semi-conscious but wracked in a fever-dream. Not really her, yet. Possessed. Residual memories passed from the Red eating away at her like acid, she spat, choked and frothed at the mouth, swearing and begging in ancient languages that no human had spoken for millennia.

Over seventy per cent of us die from taking the serum. Ian sure hoped that Eleanor Lythe wasn't going to be one of them. Perhaps not just from guilt and the responsibility he felt in this mess.

'Fight the evil,' urged Diane. 'Find your soul instead. Embrace the soul inside you and focus on it.' Diane started to pray.

Alasdair Colburn checked the blinking heart rate on the medical monitor. 'It's only the serum which will save her.'

Diane shot him an evil look. 'You're a heathen.'

'I'm a scientist.'

Ian didn't give voice to what he thought. *I don't think computer science from MIT counts.* 'Come on you two, save it for later.'

Eleanor lashed against her restraints, screaming in tongues now. Ian didn't understand a word. Her body was actually steaming, exposed out in the cold night air. The stretcher's straps were made from the same composite material as the soldiers' body armour. No way were they breaking anytime soon. Eleanor was drawing close to the moment when she was going to be healed or the vampiric curse would fatally reject the serum, burning her up like a hateful petrol suicide.

Stay with us, Ian begged. *We've lost so many. And not just to the serum.*

Eleanor hissed in agony, her blue eyes wide and clear as something like black smoke hissed out of her mouth, curling into the air and spearing up towards the cloudy night sky. Some believed that was a fragment of a Red's soul, passed across in the vampiric feeding and now on a long overdue express-ride to heaven for judgement.

Ian gazed down at the girl as she croaked, weak and delirious before she gratefully tumbled into unconsciousness. Alasdair quickly administered a second injection. A sedative that would help keep her under for a couple of days. Allow her to heal properly. Before she awoke to the shocking realisation of her strange new powers. *Less than human. More than human.* 'Welcome to the Vigil, Eleanor Lythe.'

2

~ THE HUNGER ROOM ~

Eleanor woke up alone and for the fifth day running she seriously wondered if she had gone insane? Madness would certainly explain the all-too-vivid visions she had been suffering inside this sealed, claustrophobic room. Visions that could have come from some home-camera reel shot from history. Roman centurions running at her with swords, Eleanor tearing them apart. Leaping across rooftops of Vienna in the 18th century, curling smoke from a thousand chimneys irritating her eyes, before she converted into some sort of leathery-winged flying creature, soaring and sweeping across the cold sky, past candle-lit windows where pale faces sometimes pressed their faces against the panes, trying to peer out into the darkness. Juicy, hot, blood-filled *food*. The hunger, that was what she remembered. The hunger. Eleanor scratched and slapped at her legs. Her blood quite literally boiling inside her. Like an overclocked engine. She sprinted at the metal walls enclosing her, smashing into them. She needed to run, lift weights, work this horrific burning sensation out of her system.

Eleanor ran at the door and slammed into it, but the heavy steel portal didn't budge a millimetre. *No pain,* she realised. She had hit the door hard enough to knock it off its hinges, by rights. It held. But she had felt no pain. 'Let me out of here!'

An answer vibrated from a grey plate in the ceiling: it was

a speaker, but not the kind you could rip off from the walls. That, she suspected, was rather the point of its design. 'You are in medical quarantine. You have been exposed to a rare strain of avian flu which is causing your brain to overheat, inducing extreme hallucinations. We understand this is unsettling for you. You are perfectly safe and will be released after a limited period of medical isolation.'

'Stop playing that stupid recording! This isn't a hospital. Where are the drips and monitors and doctors? Why haven't I seen anyone since you locked me inside this place? You can't hold me here forever. I have rights!'

'You are in medical quarantine. You have been exposed to a rare strain of avian flu which is causing your brain to overheat, inducing extreme hallucinations. We understand this is unsettling for you. You are perfectly safe and will be released after a limited period of medical isolation.'

Eleanor fought down the fury. She had never been so angry before. What she felt now was raw, pure rage. You couldn't catch that from a cold, either. 'Enough, already! I don't believe you! What I saw back at that party was real. I was attacked by monsters. You can't just tell me I caught a cold from some guest and imagined that massacre.'

The message looped again. 'You are in medical quarantine . . .'

'Go to hell!' She tugged at the loose-fitting one-piece white medical robe covering her modesty. 'Putting me in this toga doesn't make this a hospital. You better keep me locked up in here for the rest of my life, because when I get out I'm going to run to the TV stations and newspapers and tell everyone what freaky crap you're pulling inside here. I'm going to tell everyone about the monsters that attacked us!'

Actually, I hope they don't keep me in solitary confinement for the rest of my life. Eleanor stopped panting long enough to glance around the room. This wouldn't be any kind of existence. No people to talk with. No TV, Internet or radio. No books or magazines. Her quarters were 180 square feet with a doorless entrance to a wet room a quarter that size - no towels: just a circle of holes in the ceiling which sprayed water followed by warm air. She had a small bed to sit on - built into the wall - no other furniture, and the bed didn't come with a mattress or sheets, only a white rubbery surface that moulded itself around her spine if she lay still there long enough. Below a wall-mounted drinking water spigot was a small security bin hatch, where Eleanor could shove rubbish, close the hatch, then hear it slide down into an incinerator. She only knew it was an incinerator because she smelt the burning after the hatch closed. Her sense of smell seemed oddly enhanced. Eleanor currently had to shower three times a day just to be able to stand her own sweaty stench.

A single locked metal door gave onto Eleanor's room, but it hadn't opened since she first woke up, panicked and screaming, to discover her confinement. One of the wall's surface seemed to have a slightly different feel to the touch, like ceramic rather than metal. It felt cold and glossy. The ceiling came with a chequerboard effect and Eleanor wondered if cameras were hidden behind some of the squares. *Being watched, or being abandoned inside here, not much of a choice.*

Eleanor raised her voice again. 'Who are you? Why are you keeping me here?'

Another canned recording began to play. Eleanor recognised this message all too well.

'One of the side-effects of avian flu is a greatly increased appetite as a result of your elevated temperature and quickened metabolism. This is part of your body's natural healing mechanism. Please feel free to eat far more than you normally would.' As familiar as the other recordings by now. *Chow time.*

A section of wall low down by the floor rotated like a revolving door, a slight whir, bringing a long paper platter filled with food into her isolation ward. How much food had they given her to eat this time? Eleanor's desperate eyes counted six double stacked hamburgers inside seeded buns, a cardboard bowl filled with pasta fusilli and sausage chunks, chopped onion and crushed garlic that could have fed a table of ten, and a similarly super-sized bowl of egg-fried rice. There was also a paper-like cup for the water spigot, which was good, as the cup's material seemed to degrade after a day if she didn't incinerate it.

Eleanor fell upon the food as though she hadn't eaten for days - although in truth she was getting four squares a day. She managed to suppress her wild, unnatural hunger long enough to use the supplied fork and spoon, even though every inch of her ached to grab the food and stuff it into her mouth. They didn't bother giving her a knife, but if it was made out of the same weird biodegradable cardboard material as the fork it wouldn't have been any good to her for slicing. They obviously weren't planning to feed her steak anytime soon.

What's happened to me? Feeding like a greedy stray dog, ripping into lunch. Her dignity fled with her freedom. She was almost glad she was in solitary confinement, so she didn't have to fight anyone else for a share of the hot food. So good, the intense smell of the meat making her mouth water, pasta sliding down her throat like it hardly existed. Five hamburgers went within minutes. There wasn't a speed-eating contest Eleanor couldn't win at the moment. She finished the meal gasping and briefly sated, then stumbled to the wall and shoved the ruin of plates and cutlery inside the bin hatch, removing the stench and glad there wasn't a mirror in the room for her to see how much of a mess she must look.

What's is this? I'm sick alright, but it isn't any flu. She sunk onto her bed and tried not to weep. *I won't give them the satisfaction of seeing them get to me.*

***

A couple of Cav guards stood by either edge of the one-way ceramic viewing window. Ian hated to see Eleanor like this. Caged up as though she were a lab rat. But many of them on his side of the window had gone through decompression in this base, the headquarters the Vigil called simply, the Vault. And the observation cell - nicknamed *The Hunger Room* by those who worked for the Vigil - also served a second purpose. Many of the powers a vampire possessed were unique to each Red. Eleanor had been infected by a distinct strain, and the Hunger Room gave the Vigil the chance to monitor what might have been passed onto the survivors they studied.

'Anything worth noting, Doc?' asked Guy.

Doctor Vargas glanced up from her computer tablet, nodding towards the dents left in the reinforced steel wall. 'Nightmares during REM-sleep exit seem a little on the high side. I'd recommend monitoring her for post-traumatic stress. Her level of post-bite aggression, mental dissociative states and inherited memory flashbacks all fall within normal limits, though.'

Ian grunted. *Isn't much normal about this.* 'What about pass-on powers?'

Doctor Vargas tapped the tablet and brought up the results from the room's concealed monitoring equipment. 'Only the usual on the register so far. Enhanced strength and speed, a slowed ageing cycle. It'll take time for anything much more esoteric to manifest. The acuity of her senses appears fairly toppy. I think she can actually detect when we run the room's ultrasound scans. It seems to trigger bouts of extreme hyperactivity in her routine.'

Guy raised an eyebrow. 'More extreme than *that*? She's practically climbing the walls as it is.'

'Actually, her metabolism is well into her normalisation dive,' said Vargas. 'We've got a lot better at doing this since your day, you know.'

'Yeah,' said Guy, tapping the side of his head, 'that much the old man does remember. Back in the day it was hypo needles, ice baths and straightjackets.'

'The original Cure was developed by Leonardo da Vinci for the pope,' said the doctor. 'Its chemical structure has been considerably refined since then.'

Guy snorted. 'There was a cure long before that . . . a sharp blade swung through the neck. Works every time.'

'We need to watch this one closely,' said Vargas. 'The records we pulled from her home indicate that she was borderline disturbed before she was bitten. The patient has a history of minor arson attempts.'

'We'll make sure to hide the matches, doc,' said Guy.

Diane O'Hara entered the monitoring room. Everyone was curious about the new girl. Willing her to survive and join their ranks. 'I wish I could go in there and be with her. Wouldn't it help if we could pray together?'

'You could try that, but you better pray she doesn't beat you to death for the last chicken drumstick on her plate,' said Guy.

'We're in the realm of the surgical rather than the spiritual here,' said the doctor. 'But I'm sure praying for her couldn't hurt. At least, as long as it's done safely on this side of the glass.'

'Can't we help her with sedatives?' asked Ian.

'I wouldn't recommend sedation at this stage,' said Doctor Vargas. 'Chemicals won't react well with the changes in her body. Mentally - physically - she needs to adjust to what she is becoming. Same reason we don't have a TV in there for the patients. No distractions.'

'Don't get too close to the probie,' warned Guy. 'Not until we're confident we won't have to flush her.'

Flush her. That was a euphemism if ever there was one.

'You need to give her a chance,' said Ian. Diane nodded intently by his side. It hadn't been so long ago that Ian and Diana had both been survivors quivering behind that viewing wall. They remembered exactly how scared and lonely and confused Eleanor felt right now.

'Probie's been snacking inside the Hunger Room for a week,' said Guy. 'Long enough. Stick her with the priest tomorrow morning. Let's see if she survives induction.'

'That thing's not a priest,' protested Diane. 'And it hasn't been for a very long while.'

'Well, he prays. *It* prays. Damned if I know for what, though.'

Ian winced at how cold Guy's tone sounded. How casually indifferent. 'And if she does survive induction?'

'Then I do believe Miss Lythe will have earned herself that chance you mentioned.'

3

~ MONSTER GOOD ~

Eleanor tried not glance at the wall. The wall that felt oddly glossy to the touch. Eleanor didn't want to let on she had belatedly realised there were people behind it. Some kind of one-way glass, but far better camouflaged than the mirrors you found in police interview rooms. Since Eleanor had woken up this morning she could hear them talking behind it. Not well enough to pick up the words, but good enough to overhear a low murmur of conversation. *Watching me like an animal in a zoo.* Eleanor had visited the Gorilla Zone of a zoo once, the latest of animal-friendly designs. A family of gorillas resting on a bank of grass beside an artificial stream, supposedly oblivious to the crowd of human gawkers milling beyond their cage. But someone had used a camera flash, which they weren't meant to, and a furious alpha male came running up to the mirrored glass and smashed at it in a wild rage, like a miniature King Kong trying to shatter his way to freedom. Everyone had screamed and fled away from the glass, fearing it would break. The viewing wall hadn't, of course. *And now I know just how King Kong felt.*

As if overhearing Eleanor's thoughts, a recording triggered from the ceiling plate which she hadn't heard before.

'Thermal temperature monitoring of your body indicates that

you are now fully recovered from your illness. Congratulations on your successful recovery. Please report to post-quarantine evaluation prior to release.'

Her heart skipped a beat. *Release?* Eleanor didn't miss the recording's use of the more-truthful-than-she-was-used-to-word *illness*, rather than that bare-faced lie about avian flu. Eleanor knew that whatever the heck she was now, 'cured' wasn't even close to it. Her body thrummed with unlimited reserves of nervous energy, as though she needed to spend it on running a marathon with a bonus mountain to scale at the finishing line. As though she just had to do something.

Evaluation, though, what is that all about? Was some idiot about to try to convince her that everything was now normal? That she was normal? Write off her insane nightmares and monstrous memories of that so-called charity art gala as a fever dream. *Good luck with that.*

The room's armoured vault-like door unlocked by itself, a clacking like a dead robot being dragged away. There was nobody waiting outside. *How do I even know that?* Suddenly Eleanor realised there was only a single scent in the vicinity. Hers. Nobody else's. Eleanor tentatively poked her head outside. A bare concrete corridor, electric lights up top and metal pipes with water and electricity and cabling down the sides of the wall. It resembled the behind-the-scenes service passages of a mall where she had once worked a Saturday job for a few months. Until the manager had hit on her and made it clear that there were other duties which came with the minimum wage retail position. She had been fired for punching him out . . . and the real culprit had, as was so often the case, sailed away Scot-free.

If this is a hospital, then I'm a fully trained midwife. Eleanor sensed that they were deep underground. The oppressive weight of soil above her, everything deathly silent and muffled. *Which way, left or right?* She sniffed the air. There was the slight trace of a scent emanating down the left-hand stretch of corridor, so she followed that. As she drew nearer, she began to have second thoughts about her decision. The smell was wrong. There was no other way to describe it. Not dead or rotting, exactly, but cold and still - like a slab of meat pulled out of a deep freeze. Alive, yet lifeless. A terrible thought occurred to Eleanor. What if she hadn't escaped the monster's ball? *What if those monsters captured me. Maybe five days trapped in that funhouse back there is their version of fattening me up for supper? What if the strange hunger was from drugs in the water to make me famished and eat like a horse?* A second realisation occurred to her. *Those things wouldn't need to pretend I was in a hospital. That mob of horrors were stronger and faster than me. If I was their prisoner, they'd kick me around like a chicken in a factory farm, and I'd have about as much say in my treatment as a chicken nugget.*

Eleanor drew closer, detecting a second set of scents, too, bestial and dirty.

Then Eleanor came across the source of the animal scents at the end of the corridor, in front of an open door. A series of cages filled with pigs. Behind the cage mesh, the swines grunted and pushed agitated at the metal barriers. They didn't seem happy inside their new home. She sympathised with that feeling. *Are they doing medical experiments down here? Is this a lab?* But something told her that whatever this place's secrets were, live animal experimentation wasn't on the list. Eleanor didn't discover a laboratory through the open doorway. Instead, a small room with a table in the centre with two chairs, a priest in the far chair, his back framed against a second open doorway. His face was as dark as his cassock, a pattern of thin scars on both cheeks that might have been some indication of rank. The priest looked about sixty, hair greying at the temples on either side of his intent, serious face. He was the source of the terrible scent.

'You're one of those things that attacked me!'

'Indeed, Eleanor Lythe, I am one of their kind.'

Eleanor recoiled at the sound of her name from his cold, corrupt lips. *Closer, closer.* Near enough to bring him down.

'I have gone hungry for so long that I can no longer even camouflage myself as a mortal. I must sit here with my sins fully revealed. Sit as a vampire, a monstrosity, a Red. Of course, vampires call themselves none of these things. Among ourselves, vampires refer to our kind as the Blessed . . . recipients of the Gift. But I was not one of those who personally attacked you. Not yet.'

Eleanor didn't wait to hear anymore. Acting on pure instinct, she formed her right hand into a fist and drove it forward towards the creature's nose, aiming to smash the bone and render him unconscious, dead - or at least, deader than the priest might already be. He swayed to the side, still sitting, caught Eleanor's hand and dragged her over the table. She struggled with all her unnatural energy but he just shook his head sadly, as if she had disappointed him. Eleanor was almost beginning to lose consciousness as he lifted her body into the air, choking, with his hand around her neck, as easily as the priest might lift food off the plate with a fork.

'Yes, you are fast and strong. Not nearly as fast and strong as me.'

Eleanor spluttered, unable to escape his vice-like grip. 'Why don't you just kill me?'

'I may yet.' He suddenly dropped her to the floor. She fell, choking. The priest lifted Eleanor not unkindly into one of the chairs. 'Sit, my child. And try not to fidget. The temptation to feed upon you is very strong. Even the Lord our Saviour did not have to undergo trials such as this.'

Seeing little other choice, Eleanor reluctantly accepted the chair as the priest moved opposite, occupying the other seat again. 'Trials?'

'Yours and mine. My name is Father Kamara Okoro and it is my job to judge you.'

'Judge - just what have I done?'

'Why,' he laughed, 'you are a monstrosity, too. Not such a large one as I am. A little monster, shall we say. That is why I must judge you. Not for what evil you have done, but what evil you may yet do.'

'I don't understand.'

'Of course you do not understand. That is what this cell is, my child . . . a classroom. Sometimes it takes a criminal to catch a criminal. Sometimes it takes a monster to catch a monster. This is your trial, but it is my penance.'

'What does something like you have to teach me?'

'How the world is. What you are. It is always more believable coming from me. If I was a mortal sitting here, a bureaucrat with a clipboard and a white coat, you would doubt what I have to say. But nobody doubts Father Okoro. That is why I am kept here. Why the people who built this complex suffer my presence. A half-tame wolf to scare the sheep with his terrible wolf stories.'

'Dear God! I was bitten, wasn't I? Am I a vampire too - am I one of you?'

'Surely not. I was told you were bitten by a female vampire, is that correct? You were set upon by a single assailant?'

Eleanor bit her lip, hardly daring to hear what this thing had to say about her future. 'Yes.'

'Then your averted destiny was to have become what is called a demi-gog. A half-vampire. A servant of the same monster who bit you. To turn into a full vampire, you must be bitten by both a female and a male during the same feeding. You might say it is how vampires procreate. They are physically sterile, so their pattern is passed on by converting others into their foul kind. Into versions of themselves. But vanity is the least of their sins . . . *our* sins.'

'So you were bitten like . . . ?'

'Yes, that is how I am here. I was once a priest in the Congo. I built up quite a following among my ministry, enough followers to encourage the return of peace to my country instead of civil war. Peace rarely suits the Reds. So they turned me. I am sure I am quite a disappointment to both of my inhuman "parents".'

'So I am a . . . what do you call them, demi-gog, now?'

'No, our hosts injected you with an antidote. Your process of conversion into a demi-gog was broken. You are still fully human, but you have been left with some of the powers of the female that bit you. The Reds call your kind debasements. Human reflections of their kind, outside of their control.'

Eleanor rocked on her chair with shock. *My kind? Just what is my kind now?* 'Powers? What the hell have you made me into?'

'Mortal. But far stronger, faster, more resilient. Maybe other things. You will see. If you survive to enjoy your new life, you could have about two centuries of life to see. Not much compared to me. My trial will go on for longer than yours, or until our hosts grow tired of my presence.'

'Our hosts aren't vampires?'

'Surely not. They are an organisation called the Vigil, formed as a clandestine arm of the U.S. Secret Service after the Reds arranged for Abraham Lincoln's assassination.'

Relief at this strange news washed over Eleanor like a cold shower, before the implication of how twisted the situation she found herself in truly sunk in. 'Vampires were behind Lincoln's assassination? You're joking?'

'Not at all. The Reds hoped to provoke Great Britain into joining the U.S. Civil War on the side of the South, starting what would have become a global conflict, but a branch of the Catholic Church's Inquisition managed to derail their plot. The Red's murder of Lincoln was the Red's revenge. You will learn more of the Historia Arcana, the secret history, from other lips.'

Eleanor's mind spun. 'What you're saying is . . . . madness.'

'Quite. Imagine if you weren't hearing it from a vampire. But you are still only scratching the surface of the world's hidden truths. The Reds are just one of the Sidhe Antiqua, the ancient races. Most of the Sidhe Antiqua prefer to hide among your people, holding to a fake humanity to ensure their survival. But the Reds are night hunters - alpha predators - and humanity are their preferred sustenance. Their kind will not bend. For a long time the Reds as good as ruled humanity. They resent their fall from that position of high greatness.'

'Ruled? Like some kind of Count Dracula deal?'

'Reds are shadow-clinging chameleons and stalkers . . . imagine a Trapdoor Spider given humanoid form. Deeply territorial and long-lived. They ruthlessly control their own population and used to manage humanity's herds - but always as the power *behind* the throne. They were the advisers, the secret councils, the hushed whisper in the ear, but never the actual kings or emperors. Immortal blood-drinking queens quickly meet human mobs armed with pitchforks smashing down the palace gates. Subterfuge is the Reds' natural inclination. It was the age of science that totally surprised their kind, which blindsided them. The Renaissance, the industrial revolution, then information technology. Mass communication and mass prosperity and democracy. Every year more changes, ever-faster with additional complexities flowering along the exponential curve of Moore's Law. When society was a simple feudal pyramid, the Reds dominated the rulers at the top of the pyramid and they controlled the kingdoms. They started wars on whims and fed well among your chaos. But how do you rule the Internet and three billion consumers voting by the microsecond with their wallets? How do you control a corporation with a hundred thousand shareholders? How do you fog the mind of an algorithm inside the Cloud? You can't feed on a self-driving car. The Reds wrote off science as a mere casket of conjurer's tricks, yet now humanity's tricks are pushing them to the brink of extinction.'

'If you're a vampire and the people keeping me here are human and your enemies, then why . . .?'

'Why do they let me live? Why do I allow myself to be kept? A good question. I gaze upon the evil in the hearts of mortals,' gasped the priest, striking across the table and seizing Eleanor's wrists. 'I see the evil inside my own. That is both my greatest gift and my greatest curse.' Father Okoro's mouth grew inhumanly wide, as though he was about to attempt to swallow a rabbit, his teeth extending outward - becoming long, elongated and razored.

Eleanor tried to break away from the priest's grip, but his fingers were too strong. 'Leave me alone!'

'Yes, you can feel the power coursing through your veins. So much power, so much energy. You can do almost anything with it, now. Murder the people who hurt you and wounded you in your past. I can feel your soul's wounds, flayed and raw. You can track all those evil people down. Take anything you want. Money from banks, lives from the unworthy. Don't you want to rip into the world and punish it for this? For what you have been made to become?'

'No! No! Leave me alone.'

A voice echoed from the ceiling. Another speaker plate; but this voice wasn't a recording. 'Well - verdict?'

Father Okoro's face glanced up, contorted and sweating. 'She passes. There is still a kernel of goodness here. I cannot willingly feed upon innocence.'

Eleanor stood up as his grip faltered, overturning her chair as she back-pedalled away from the table.

Okoro left the table and slowly advanced towards the girl. 'But my will is weak. I am weak. She has so much goodness in her sweet blood, sweet veins running with it.'

A terrified squeal sounded. One of the hogs had been released from the cage outside and galloped towards the far door, trying to out-pace the killing zone of the enclosed room. Father Okoro swivelled and leapt onto the table, before springing off its surface, attracted by the movement and moving faster than anything had a right to, seizing the pig and rolling across the bare concrete floor with the animal writhing in his grasp. 'Beautiful, warm. Yes. I need my reward for resisting my sins.' The monster in human form glanced greedily across at Eleanor, desperate and ravening, his eyes yellowed and pupils changed into something close to a lion's. She was rooted to the spot, paralysed, the way prey should be. Eleanor literally couldn't move.

This strange moment of paralysis was broken as the priest ripped into the still living animal with his fangs, and as he tore apart the pig a number of figures appeared enclosed in orange hazmat suits, dark boots thudding across the floor as they dashed into the room. They were slower than they should have been with heavy battery packs strapped to their backs, each pack connected by coiling cables to a lance-long electrical prod. Faces hidden behind flat misted glass visors, the figures raised their lances with dark gloves, sparks of orange light flaring as they drove the monster back long enough for Eleanor to make her escape. The door slammed shut and one of the suited men turned a wheel on the entrance, sealing it like an airlock. In their cages outside, the surviving pigs squealed in panicked unison, protesting the cruel sacrifice of one of their companions.

Eleanor turned in outrage on her so-called rescuers. 'He nearly killed me in there!'

A figure pulled off his suit's hood and visor, revealing a grizzled old face, an almost smoked cigar stump hanging from the man's lips. There was something familiar about him. Had he been one of the people present at the insane charity night? 'You passed, kid. If you ever meet Okoro again, you'll be able to take the priest down.'

'How the hell would I do that?'

'You're a blade, girl-chick, even if you don't realise it yet. Right now, you're a blunt dinner knife, but with the right honing, you're going to buff up just as shiny and razor sharp as a commando dagger.'

Eleanor gazed suspiciously at the old man. She knew enough about daggers to know that they only got sharpened by constantly grinding them against rough stone. *Horribly painful for a dinner knife that never asked to leave the cutlery drawer.*

4

~ MISTRESS OF BLADES ~

'Y ou are not concentrating!' accused Ikeda Hanzo, landing a painful slap of his wooden sword blade against the side of Eleanor's neck.

Hanzo might look like some short-arse Japanese fusion of Mr. Miyagi and Yoda, but Eleanor had learned over the weeks never to underestimate this manically sprightly pensioner. His wrinkled face and permanently amused eyes always at odds with the look of distaste he reserved for his lazy, soft students. And as far as Hanzo was concerned, they were *all* soft and lazy.

'You draw your bokken like a fishmonger pulling out an eel to sell. Where is your heart? You shame Hanzo's teachings. Again!' barked the combat instructor. 'Faster!'

Eleanor slid her bokken daitō, a wooden katana-sized sword, back into the scabbard by her side. Ready to take it out again. The art of drawing a sword elegantly was as important to the instructor as the blade's actual use in combat, which seemed as much a waste on her part learning the technique as this old devil trying to teach it to her.

She lunged out, drawing the wooden practice sword in a smooth blur, aiming to cut the teacher in half if it had been a real blade. Hanzo's bokken rapped off hers, as loud as two baseball bats smashed into each other.

'Too slow. Hanzo will show you how it is done. Keep your bokken out. Defensive stance.'

'Alright.'

'Alright, master,' barked Hanzo. 'In here, I am the master and you are to learn. That is why you have two ears but only one mouth. So you may listen to Hanzo's words twice as much as you complain.'

'Alright, *master*,' echoed Eleanor, the last word pulled like one of her teeth,

She heard a whispering from the side of the hall. Meant to be private, but Eleanor was effectively a human microphone now. 'Not bad. She's learning.'

Not bad, but no cigar at this freaks' funfair. There were two other students presently in training alongside Eleanor, watching her and passing comment from the practice hall's sidelines. Both male and in their early twenties. Both wearing - like Eleanor - a white *keikogi* shirt above with a black *hakama* below, a garment that resembled a skirt from a distance but was actually separated in the centre to form two baggy trouser legs. The first trainee was called Christopher Bischoff, the second, Samuel Chickering. Eleanor wasn't sure if they were their real names or not. Christopher was a Canadian if his accent was anything to go by. Sam had mentioned in passing that he came from Baltimore. None of the trainees were meant to discuss their past lives while a probie: one of the many seemingly pointless rules they needed to adhere to, along with a punishingly strict schedule. Both pupils were dark-haired and just under six foot tall with similar lean physiques, but she could tell them apart easily enough. Chris was as pale as a sandwich filling while Sam was African-American with a thick hipster's beard. They usually hung together, and Eleanor knew their nickname was the *Brothers Grin*, after the pair's easy smiles. Both young men had been in what passed for the Vigil's induction programme for months longer than Eleanor, but already she was faster and superior in combat to them. She knew she shouldn't feel too much pride at that fact - often it came down to how ancient and powerful the Red had been who had turned the new blood. But she felt a measure of self-satisfaction all the same.

Eleanor took up the defensive position, sword clutched in front of her, quivering and held tight with both hands. She prepared herself for the instructor's first strike. There would be no tells from the short old man before he drew. At least, no creasing around the eyes or twitching of the fingers. Hanzo would move from still to kill almost instantly, driving home the first-strike-is-the-fatal-blow message along with his sword. Matters went down exactly as she'd predicted. One moment the man was just standing there, his fingers resting easily around the hilt of his sheathed blade, the next the sword was out of the scabbard and darting towards her neck again - only, this time she managed to throw her bokken in the way, a sharp clack of wood on wood as she deflected the blow.

'Better,' said Ikeda Hanzo. 'Your senses are acute. You are predicting my strikes, now.'

Eleanor never explained she was using the little pheromone bursts leaked by the instructor to get ahead of his sword while they trained. It wasn't even a conscious process anymore. The power had become a sixth sense she relied on without worrying where her preternatural warnings sprung from. These strange changes in Eleanor's body seemed very private to her, even if the Vigil's doctors obviously wanted to track her progress as though she was a lab rat. Their constant presence behind the scenes felt like having lurkers outside the toilet, trying to overhear her bowel movements. There were other powers bubbling inside Eleanor. Powers which terrified her. A terrible energy thrumming inside Eleanor, pent-up and burning, making her flesh feel like a battery close to being overloaded with power; bursting into fire. This could only be something murderous and dark, inherited from the monster who fed upon her. It was hard to hold onto, sometimes, especially when fighting inside the practice hall. But suppress it Eleanor must. If the people here realised how dangerous she truly was, they would lock her up just as deep and tight as that half-tame vampire priest. This was her sin to bear. Her secret.

Eleanor spoke, if only to distract herself from her hidden anxieties. 'So, when do we get to practice with real blades, *master?*'

Hanzo grunted. 'Never. When you draw a moly-blade, it is only to kill an enemy. To draw a sword is to doom a foe or to doom yourself. Hanzo has given you instruction in Shinkendo, Bōjutsu, Shorinji Kempo, Aikibujutsu, Shurikenjutsu, Wadō-ryū and Toyama-Ryū Battōdō. A wooden sword is no different to a moly-blade . . . it is a matter of applied skill.'

Eleanor didn't take her eyes off Hanzo. He dished out humility with that wooden blade of his like a party clown dishing out balloons. 'Swords are all very well, but when do we begin training with guns?'

Hanzo pointed towards the instruction dummies on the far side of the hall, made to resemble Reds and demi-gogs, areas such as the neck marked out with bullseyes as high-value strike points. 'Guns are metal hammers for barbarians. A full vampire moves faster than most soldiers shoot. A few Reds may turn to mist to allow bullets to pass through their bodies. Even a lowly demi-gog can absorb a small calibre revolver's chamber and recover in a week using their quickened healing.'

'The Cav have rifles that can—'

'And will you walk down the city streets with such a brutish cannon in your hand? Is your name John Wayne? An extendable moly-blade may be concealed inside a lipstick, ceramic-edged to be undetectable to sensors. You can walk through airport security and board a plane with it. Brutes like Guy Drew will teach you how to point the Cav's clumsy metal toys.' Hanzo raised a finger and made a little trigger squeezing motion. 'That is not skill. And rifles and moly-blades are not weapons. *You* are the weapon. That is what Hanzo teaches here. Guns, daggers, throwing stars, moly-blades, they are all tools. You are the only weapon inside Hanzo's fighting hall. Educate the mind but make quick the body.'

'I'm getting a little bored of this routine,' said Eleanor. 'Every day the same with this wax on, wax off stuff. When will our training end?'

'Poor impatient flower, you mistake this for your training?' laughed Hanzo. 'This is merely your dance practice. Training at the Vigil is done on the job. There is no *Dummies Guide to Slaying Creatures of the Sidhe Antiqua* for sale on the Internet. There is no fine graduation ceremony where you parade for your family and throw your hats in the air. You learn by putting your life on the line and surviving to do it again. In between, you practice.'

'So, when does our practice end?'

'Never. But it may lessen slightly if you succeed.'

'Succeed in what?'

Hanzo laughed. 'Beating your teacher!' He bowed to the three students and made a show of creeping around the floor using his wooden sword as a cane. 'Poor old Ikeda. He is an old man. Trained to be a samurai two centuries ago, coming to the end of his sad long life. Surely one of the three young, strong blades I see in this hall can beat him? Perhaps all three, striking as a team?'

'Let's do it,' said Chris, always the more eager of the other two.

Sam made a sucking noise to indicate how badly he suspected this was going to end.

'We can do it,' said Eleanor. 'If we fight as a team.'

'Yeah, and you know all about that,' said Sam. 'That cowboy style you've got.'

Eleanor ignored the jibe about how she liked to keep to herself. 'It's cow*girl*, horse. And we can do this.'

Hanzo seemed amused by their hesitance and made a second show of hobbling around the hall, baiting his pupils. 'Yes, poor old Ikeda, bones creaking, most of his teeth fallen out, only able to eat soft fish and rice.'

'Sod it,' said Chris, patting the hilt of his bokken. 'I'm in.'

'You have bored Hanzo with your indecision. He must rest a little now.' Their instructor knelt down on the floor, bowed his neck, rested a hand on either knee and closed his eyes.

Chris and Sam circled around the instructor, right hands resting on their sheathed swords, ready to draw. Sam took position behind Hanzo to the old man's left while Chris stood rear right. Eleanor crept to stand before the kneeling, seemingly dozing instructor; making herself the point of the team's triangle. The walls of the hall might be white-painted concrete, but the floor was oak, as though someone had stripped an old school gymnasium to outfit this training centre. With Eleanor's enhanced hearing, she knew the creaking wood hadn't shifted an iota. All three of them had been trained too well in Ninjitsu to make sounds while they padded on bare feet. Hanzo shouldn't have a clue where any of his three students were standing. *Unless his sense of smell is as hyped as mine*, warned Eleanor's subconscious mind. Sam raised his left hand into the air, keeping his right firmly on the bokken hilt. Three fingers. Two fingers. One finger. They struck as one, drawing their swords and flinging blades towards Hanzo. Except he wasn't kneeling anymore. Hanzo had started rolling to the left even as Eleanor's fingers tightened on her sword's hilt. Eleanor's sword was out and thrusting through empty space, colliding with Sam's bokken, his cry of confusion joining Chris's, except Chris's was louder, tumbling backwards as Hanzo swept-kicked him over. Eleanor just managed to deflect a spinning kick the old man sent in her direction, about the same time she yelled in agony as she realised Hanzo's blade had danced up under both her and Sam's swords, smacking their wrists in turn as the bokken passed. He'd struck at their central nerve clusters and two bokkens fell from paralysed fingers, leaving Eleanor and Sam disarmed. Eleanor's mind was reeling, and she was just about to convert her stance into a leaping kick at Hanzo when the old man caught one of the falling swords. Both blades windmilled in his hands and when the swords came to a halt, there was a wooden sword edge pressed under Eleanor's neck, a second under Sam's, while Chris struggled on the floor, completely pinned by one of Hanzo's bare feet.

Hanzo shook his head sadly. 'Loud, clumsy and full of false confidence.'

'Jesus,' moaned Chris from the floor. 'How do you move so fast?'

'Beginner's mind,' said Hanzo. 'Every day Hanzo learns and practise. Two centuries of practice. One percent better every week. Such skill compounds.' He sighed. 'You will not beat Hanzo today. Perhaps you shall try to beat Bex Crawfield?'

Eleanor lowered her head as Hanzo withdrew his sword. *What trickery are you up to now, you old lizard?* 'Who's Bex Crawfield?'

'Trainee in upper class,' said Hanzo. 'Miss Crawfield's practice is close to lessening. Yes, you shall see what you may become after Hanzo has taught you to master the beginner's mind.'

'If she's about to graduate from this underground circus,' said Eleanor, 'how come she's still got a beginner's mind?'

Hanzo raised a finger on his hand and slowly, deliberately prodded Eleanor on the nose with it. 'Because the finger that points at the moon is not the moon.'

'Just a finger, man,' said Sam.

The instructor made a weary throat-clearing sound. 'Hanzo might as well attempt to teach rocks to think. Miss Crawfield shall finish practice with you.' He walked up to the intercom by the hall's entrance and made a call. Ten minutes later, a young blonde woman showed up, tying her belt around the bottom of a white *keikogi* shirt as she entered the hall. Eleanor eyed the opposition up. Bex must have gotten turned early because she looked about the same age as Eleanor; short hair tied at the back, blue eyes, a calm serious face which belied her obvious Barbie

Girl beauty. Eleanor wasn't sure why this girl was being held up as some exemplar of what they needed to aim towards. Average height, a slightly curvy figure - not slim, but not Junoesque - Bex Crawfield would look more in place studying first-year law in college, everything paid for by daddy's expensive trust fund. Eleanor had to resist wrinkling her nose in distaste. *How much Chanel can one woman wear?*

'You think she looked like that when she was bit?' whispered Sam.

It was a natural enough question. Face-changing was another common Red power that frequently got passed on. Most people who took the Cure couldn't face-change instantly, but if you pinned a photograph of someone to your bathroom mirror and stared at it real hard every morning, willing your flesh to flow, you could morph into a cross between yourself and the target photo over time. Many of the Vigil's staff who came into the service with a family left behind had to change their face as well as their name. Too dangerous for the people you left behind if you stayed as the same old you. Of course, Eleanor hadn't left anybody behind. At least, nobody she wouldn't mind getting popped, at any rate.

Chris grinned. 'Who cares.'

'Man, I got to get myself in her class,' said Sam.

Chris nodded in agreement. 'I hear that.'

'Boys,' announced the girl, bowing towards Hanzo as she halted, 'I can pretty much guarantee that none of you are in *my* class.' Bex fixed Eleanor with a slightly mocking gaze that instantly made Eleanor's hackles raise. 'How about you, dimples? You with Beavis and Butthead here?'

Eleanor tapped the handle of her practice sword. 'No, I'm here with Bob the Bokken. And the two of us are going to open a can of whoop-ass on your butt.'

'Let's see how that works out for you.' Bex eyed Hanzo. 'I was in the refectory finishing dinner, master.'

'Poor flower. You have Hanzo's apologies,' said the instructor. He pointed towards Eleanor. 'Perhaps now would be time for your dessert?'

'If you say so, master.'

Eleanor flashed the girl the bird. 'If teacher's pet is still hungry, she can eat this.'

'Positions,' ordered Hanzo.

Eleanor faced off against the young woman as Sam and Chris walked to the wall and waited under a series of banners sown with Japanese calligraphy. She suspected that given how used the two men had gotten to receiving beatings from her bokken, they might not be adverse to seeing her humbled by another student. Eleanor exchanged bows with the other girl, then spread her feet in a T-position, leaning slightly forward, right hand on hilt. She cleared her mind, ready to receive the subtle signals of scent that would precede her enemy's muscles engaging for combat. Eleanor almost squawked like a bird as Bex's blade cleared its scabbard and came rocketing towards her face, only just managing to swivel enough for the blade to flash past without scoring a strike. *There was no warning!*

Eleanor backpedaled, trying to suppress her confusion. Bex came at her again, and this time she deflected the sword's thrust with a parry. This bout wasn't going down anything like Eleanor had foreseen. Bex Crawfield was slow compared to Eleanor, slow compared to Sam and Chris, but she was relentless and incredibly skilled with the bokken. And compared to Eleanor's usual sparring, this was like fighting someone's detached shadow. No warnings, no third sense feeding her where her enemy was going to be before he even knew himself. It was like Eleanor was a heavy frigate and Bex a hunter-killer submarine . . . moving unseen below the water, deadly, striking fast and then withdrawing. *Is she doing something to my mind?* That had to be it. Hanzo had warned the three of them that some of the most powerful vampires could cloud a human's mind, a form of telepathic hypnotism used to paralyse prey before the feast. Is this what Crawfield had inherited from her biter? Some kind of stealth fog to make Eleanor easy meat before Bex's sword?

If Barbie Girl was slower, then Eleanor needed to rely on her superior speed. She feinted to the left, then attacked to the right with every ounce of velocity her unnaturally humming body could muster, driving her sword twice into the opponent's gut, right at the base of the solar plexus, just as Hanzo had taught. Eleanor almost stumbled when Bex didn't fall moaning to the ground, didn't even falter, just thrust again out with her bokken, nearly rapping Eleanor's skull with the skillfully wielded blade. *What the hell's going on here? I tried that move on Sam yesterday and knocked him out of the bout for half an hour. But she took that blow like I just tickled her with a twig.* It was no good, Eleanor realised she couldn't get a reliable read off her opponent. She had the speed, but not the mastery of the bokken to make her speed count. After ten minutes of desperate back and forth, Eleanor fell exhausted to a series of blows against her arms and spine, sent tumbling to the oak floor. She thought about trying to rise but decided to call it a day and just lie there, listening humiliated to Bex's still relatively shallow breathing. Crawfield hadn't even broken a sweat beating Eleanor. *And I thought getting my ass handed to me by a Japanese pensioner was disgrace enough.* Eleanor had been wrong about that.

'Miss Crawfield has the match,' announced Hanzo.

'That is so much hogwash,' complained Eleanor, groaning as she got to her feet. 'I struck her twice with my bokken, first. Everything after that is history. If I had been using a real blade, I would have impaled Barbie Girl here like King Prawn on a barbecue spit.'

'A fighter seeks victory from their high ground,' said Hanzo. 'As you should have noticed, Miss Crawfield has superior ability to receive punishment. This is her natural high ground.'

'That's fine because in real life, I'd be pulling my blade out of her gut and wiping it on her trousers.'

'Actually,' said Bex, 'I'd use my chest as a sandbag to trap your blade, then *I'd* pull your blade out and turn it against you.'

'Yeah,' laughed Sam, doubtfully, still leaning against the wall. 'And who was it that put the bite on you, girl . . . Wolverine or the Terminator?'

'Unusually perceptive of you, Mister Chickering,' said Hanzo. 'Miss Crawfield was never given the Cure to save her from a vampire's bite.'

'Then what . . . ?' asked Eleanor, shocked at the unexpected revelation.

Bex smiled smugly. 'I was bitten by a *zombie*. You want to take me down, dimples, you better drag yourself a guillotine to the fight next time .'

Hanzo bid his nearly trained student out of the hall and then turned back to the three others. 'You think you understand what you fight? No. Hold onto the beginner's mind. There are hundreds of races recorded in the Bestiaries of the Sidhe Antique and we have not recorded them all. Some races have only two or three members left in hiding. Secretive. We know nothing.' Hanzo prodded the tip of Eleanor's nose again. 'You rely on this too much. False confidence. Something both dead and alive at the same time carries no scent.'

Damn. Eleanor suddenly realised why Crawfield stank like someone's grandmother. The girl was using perfume to mask what she had been turned by.

Hanzo raised a finger to tap Eleanor's forehead. 'When you fight a zombie, this is your target. Strike high. Strike fast. Strike first.' He leant forward and whispered in her ear, these words meant for her alone. 'Everyone feels fear. It can never be banished, only channelled like energy. Master it. Use it.'

Eleanor felt both her body and mood slump as she realised how badly and easily she had been beaten. This hadn't really been a lesson for Sam or Chris. *This one was all mine.*

* * *

An hour later, Eleanor was inside the refectory on Sub-level Seven, sitting at one of the metal tables and demolishing a plate of Mexican food - rice, refried beans and chicken strips so spicy they might have been dipped in acid. She could just about control her voracious appetite now, but she was still eating twice her normal portion size every day. Her body was running as overclocked as a gaming PC, and this junk was her fuel. Eleanor fiddled with a little silver Zippo lighter, a bright Eagle painted on its side. Apart from the clothes she had been wearing when she was bitten, this was the only thing that had made it across from her old life. She glanced up as she saw Christopher Bischoff and Samuel Chickering approaching her table. They were out of their practice robes and, same as Eleanor, had switched into the olive green one-piece suits issued to base staff. It made them look a little like fighter jocks from Top Gun, even if the closest they had got to the cockpit of a warplane was the window of a browser's flight sim.

Chris reached her table. 'We're going to be watching *Bram Stoker's Dracula* in the TV room up on seven, later.'

'The movie with Gary Oldman? The cross-species passion that can survive a thousand years? Love never dies. What, is that meant to be ironic? I'm pretty sure the only thing a Red ever loved about a human is our taste.'

'Hey, at least they got that crawling around the ceiling trick right,' said Chris.

'Only because their palms excrete an endo-bonding substance.'

'You see, I knew you were paying attention in those Sci-tech Division lectures.'

'I'm guessing that she's not up for TV night,' said Sam, trying to move his friend past Eleanor's chair.

'What I am, is nearly done eating here,' said Eleanor, shooting the pair an annoyed glance.

'Come on. Move along, brother, nothing to see here,' said

Sam. The two of them walked across to sit at another table further inside the refectory. Silently, Eleanor reproached herself. She knew she should make more of an effort. *It's just that effort was tiring, and these days it was more than she could muster.* Even on a good day when she hadn't been slammed around in the practice hall. *You know that's just an excuse. You weren't exactly Miss Congeniality back at the home, either.*

Thinking about making friends and influencing people Bex Crawfield approached Eleanor's table. Eleanor was almost tempted to shout over at the Brothers Grin to get them back to sit at her table, but then she saw that Zombie Girl wasn't carrying a lunch tray to sit down. Oddly, the woman came bearing a bundle of black clothes.

'You having a yard sale to raise money for a new bottle of Chanel No. 5, *Miss* Crawfield?'

Crawfield dropped the neatly folded pile of dark clothes on the table's steel surface. It appeared to be a trouser suit. 'These are in your size.'

'What's this, have I got a job interview?'

'Orders. Put them on,' said Crawfield. 'Then report to sub-level five.'

'What's going on here?'

Bex Crawfield flashed a slightly superior smile. 'Do what I say and you'll find out, won't you?'

Bex swivelled and stalked away, leaving a niggling trace of perfume behind her. *This is it,* Eleanor realised. *They put me to the test in the practice hall and I flunked it. Not a team player, not even able to beat that slow-moving mutant-zombie-human California Girl. These are my marching orders. Just the same as being back in the home.*

The home which couldn't wait for Eleanor and her trash-talking smart aleck attitude to cross the threshold into legal adulthood so they could chuck her out into the street. *Why should the Vigil be any different?* Of course, there was another possibility. Perhaps one of the medical team had reported what they suspected about Eleanor. That the powers she had inherited from the monster who bit her were too dangerous to risk containing. That Eleanor was a danger and a disaster waiting to erupt on the world.

Eleanor got changed and then walked up the stairs to sub-level five, not wanting to take a lift and risk meeting anyone she knew. She arrived at an open space filled with comfy chairs and tables and sofas. It looked like the rec area of some venture capital-backed software firm. All it was lacking was the foosball table. And soon enough, her presence too. It was nearly empty, all except one familiar-looking face who came over smiling when he saw her.

'You remember me? My name's Ian Holderness.'

Eleanor remembered. It was Vigil tradition for the team who rescued a probie and gave them the Cure to hold a welcoming party after the survivor left Hunger Room quarantine. She hadn't acted particularly welcoming back towards the people at that party, and now she felt a little guilty that this was one of the same people entrusted with kicking her out. 'Yeah, from my greet-and-meet wake. Goodbye old me, hello new me. You gave the probies a talk on resisting Vampire Mind Judo on my first day in training, too.'

'TCA,' corrected Ian. 'Telepathic Confusion Assault. We always understand something better after we label it with an acronym.' He indicated one of the large elevators which needed a passcard swipe to enter. Ian pulled his badge out of a pocket in the dark suit he wore, then ushered her inside once it arrived.

They're doing it, then. Order of the boot. All on my own again. Had it ever really been any other way? At least this lonely fate was better than being thrown in a cell next door to that half-tame vampire priest. Caged up for the rest of Eleanor's unnaturally prolonged life.

The elevator rose slowly upward, gaining speed before slowing and the doors slid open with a little digital ding. Eleanor stepped out, almost shaking with uncertainty. Light, natural light streaming through glass. *Sunlight.* She had grown so used to the strip-lighting of the underworld that this bright natural glow was now a novelty.

'Where are we?'

'Foyer of the Empire State Building,' said Ian. 'You want to access New York V-Command, you enter any staff-only maintenance elevator, tap 105 on the panel while keeping the Restricted Basement button held down. There's no 105th floor - and then the lift goes down rather than up. You can exit command to arrive up here from any of our top five sub-levels, but entering always takes you to the same screening point at security control on sub-level ten.'

Eleanor glanced around. Hundreds of tourists and office workers passing through. The constantly shifting crowd acted as the perfect cover for the Vigil's agents and staff coming and going. 'Where do I head now?'

Ian looked confused. 'What do you mean?'

'You're kicking me out, right? That was Hanzo's recommendation after I was handed my ass on a plate.'

Ian grinned. 'Everyone gets handed their ass on a plate by Hanzo. He's been getting meaner and sharper every day of his grumpy old life. But you're right, this is Hanzo's recommendation. He passed word up the line that you're ready for your first ride-along.'

'This is a mission?' asked Eleanor, stunned by how quickly things might have turned around.

He tapped his chest. 'Put your hand in your jacket pocket.'

Eleanor dipped her hand inside the suit and removed a leather wallet. She opened it to find a little silver badge sitting above a Homeland Security ID-card bearing her photo along with a bar-code and biometric data chip. 'This is real?'

'It swipes through airports real enough. Not sure about the rest. Hanzo must have given you that speech about learning on the job by now? He's right on the button about that. Breaking bokken in the practice hall can't prepare you for what we have to do out here. Only surviving the job does that. But don't worry, the thing we need to do today is usually low mortality rate unless you catch some bad luck.'

Usually. Somehow, Eleanor suspected there was a lot more to whatever she had been pulled out of the Vigil's warren for. 'And what happens if I get unlucky today?'

'Brain embolisms, first-degree burns, that kind of stuff.'

'How long you been doing *that kind of stuff,* Ian? You only look a few years older than me, but that doesn't mean much inside the Vigil, does it?'

Ian nodded with a slightly sad look of agreement settling across his features. 'True enough. I was bitten back in the eighties. That's last century, not the American Civil War or anything.'

'By a Red, right, not something weird?'

Ian snorted with laughter at that, attracting curious glances from a party of passing tourists following a female guide holding an umbrella up high for them to track her through the crowd.

'I say something to amuse you?'

'I guess I forgot how easy it is to sink into this life. The idea of being bitten by a vampire isn't weird any longer, but being turned by a Cannibal Forest Bigfoot or whatever, that is odd.'

'What's odd, my man, is your dress sense. I should have guessed you were an eighties throwback. Downstairs, you usually dress like you're attending a Miami Vice fan-boy con.'

'I try and keep current,' protested Ian.

'So what's with the dark suits,' said Eleanor, indicating Ian's as well as her own. 'We keeping current by looking like accountants, today?'

'Roll with it. We need to blend in. I still feel twenty, you know, as well as looking it. The years move slower for you after you stop ageing normally. Mentally as well as physically.'

'I wonder how the Reds feel about it,' said Eleanor. 'Some of my nightmares - I mean, I'm seeing some crazy history that looks like it was pulled from an episode of Spartacus.'

'I think I know exactly how the Reds feel about it; their bodies regenerating across the millennia unless they meet with a little unexpected brute force trauma. They see humanity as insects, annoying grubs that live for a few days compared to a vampire's extended lifespan. Very tasty grubs.'

'This grub doesn't want to get eaten.'

'Won't happen,' said Ian. 'Not after taking the Cure. Your blood's poison to pretty much any race of the Sidhe Antiqua that tries to feed on you now. That's another reason the Reds and their demi-gog stooges loathe our kind. We steal their powers, get to remain human, and we're removed from the dinner menu at the same time.'

'Reassuring.'

'Don't get captured alive,' said Ian. 'They can't feast on us, but the ripping us apart piece by piece is something they'll usually run with.'

'Not so reassuring.'

'Your dreams will start to fade after six months,' said Ian, helpfully. 'Although you'll often get the occasional faint false memory flashback, triggered by smells or sights. The Red who turned me became a vampire during the French Revolution, an aristocrat who only just escaped to the New World. Madame Guillotine was pretty much designed for slaying Reds. I used to see Notre Dame in my visions, cobbled streets along the Seine, peasants wearing rags. I nearly had a psychotic episode when I sat through a matinee showing of Les Misérables at the Imperial Theatre.'

'I knew there was a reason I don't want to watch Ben Hur again.'

They left the foyer of the building, passing through a set of revolving glass doors, and walked out into the street. Eleanor had forgotten how busy New York was, buried down inside the Vigil's concealed concrete warren. She sucked in the smell of the city and nearly gagged as she was assailed by the odor of hundreds of strangers, busy moving, car exhausts vomiting pollution, the smell of food wafting from burger vans and restaurants. People, throngs of frenetic people living unconcerned lives, everyone oblivious to the fact they were a herd of live meat for predators higher up the food-chain.

Ian looked concerned and steadied her. 'Are you alright?'

'Just finding my street legs,' said Eleanor. 'Hanzo should try scheduling a little free-time into the students' schedule. I'd forgotten what the world was like.'

'It's the same world,' said Ian. 'It's us who are different.'

Eleanor had never really understood that, before. Seeing all this, though, it was like being hit by a tidal wave. A whole busy world of normal. And she was walking around it like she was an alien visitor from another planet.

'Sorry,' said Ian. 'You want to go back inside the centre, take a moment?'

'Dude, whatever I got passed by the Red's bite, I'm fairly sure it wasn't agoraphobia.'

'I forgot how hard it was to exit decompression for the first time.'

A black van pulled up in the street beside her and Ian, another familiar face from Eleanor's welcome wake . . . Guy Drew behind the wheel. 'You ready for a road trip, kids?'

Eleanor was no longer sure about this. 'How far do you need to drive to hunt vampires?'

'Vampires, they're easy. Today we're out hunting Big Game.'

'What's bigger than - ?'

'You remember when I pulled you out of Father Okoro's cell after the rascal developed the munchies?'

'Yeah, thanks, those are the nightmares I get when my head's not being forced into watching gladiator re-runs from the Roman Arena.'

'You're welcome. This is the same deal . . . it's a you-got-to-see-it-to-believe-it thing.'

Eleanor forced herself through the open door, following Ian, and sat groggily in the back seat, willing herself to adjust to being back in the world. Trying to beat down the terror and adjust her mind to just how real things were going to get. The kind of real able to shatter her sanity. *Everyone feels fear. It can never be banished, only channelled like energy. Master it. Use it.*

5

~ DEATH-ROW DIVA ~

Attica Correctional Facility didn't appear much like Eleanor had expected a maximum security prison to look. From the outside, its walls seemed more like a citadel - white concrete walls thirty feet high, the long length dotted by keep-like gatehouses, each keep mounted with a spire that belonged on a fake castle inside an amusement park. *Disneyland for the deranged.* A wide open stretch of tarmac served as a car park outside - broken only by tall flagpoles with fluttering state standards - further added to the feeling Eleanor had driven into an austere funfair. The guards who greeted them had obviously been expecting visitors. Guy, Ian and Eleanor flashed their mostly fake Homeland Security badges and were ushered through a series of stark corridors, doors like submarine airlocks, cameras everywhere. The three of them passed through multiple checkpoints, pressing badges against scanners, cage doors sliding open in response. Every guard wore a blue riot helmet with mirrored visor, padded jacket and a snub-nosed submachine gun strapped to their waist. Faceless security for prisoners intended to be locked away and forgotten for the rest of their miserable lives.

Eventually, the three guests from the Vigil were led down a narrow corridor where a single ominous cell door blocked the end. It was made of metal with a crack of a viewing slit that could be flipped open to check inside before entering. Above the portal was a sign that read 'Security Max-A', split lower down into two sections containing the words 'occupied' and 'unoccupied'. The portion of the sign that read 'occupied' glowed green, indicating someone was inside.

'There needs to be three of us inside the cell at all times,' said Guy, rubbing the stubble on his chin. 'Nobody leaves until all three of us are finished.'

Eleanor tried to peek through the narrow slit; catch an advance glimpse of who was on the other side of the steel door. All she saw was a flickering light, as though someone was watching television inside. Guy's warning piqued her curiosity. 'Why do we need to stay together?'

'In the Vigil, this is what we call a walk-in,' said Guy.

Eleanor suppressed her irritation. 'We're the only ones who've walked in here. This is a supermax prison, right, not a supermarket? Just who's inside that cell?'

Ian answered for the old man. 'The *body* in there belongs to Dravin Braxtell.'

Body? She didn't like the way Ian had emphasised that single word. Dravin Braxtell . . . Eleanor had heard the name. *But where?* How was this the Big Game that Guy had mentioned? Then the name and horrific story attached to it suddenly slid into her mind and she wished it hadn't. Dravin Braxtell was a serial killer sitting on Death Row. In fact, Eleanor thought the monster had already been executed. Braxtell had been a minor league global TV presenter, touring the world's war zones and producing reports for the rolling news channels. In the chaos of the world's nastiest civil wars and famine-driven conflicts, the notorious TV presenter had secretly been murdering refugees. War proved the perfect cover and ideal environment to practice his sick addiction. Leaving victims under rubble beside thousands of corpses murdered in vicious conflicts, with many more swelling the death count after Braxtell departed on his way to his next assignment. An agent of chaos whose job carried him daily through the heart of darkness. A shadow hiding in the centre of the night. Eventually, a camerawoman on Braxtell's crew grew suspicious enough to plant a hidden cam in his hotel room while they were filming inside one of the largest Middle Eastern refugee camps. After the camerawoman retrieved the spy-cam, she discovered grisly footage of Braxtell drugging and murdering refugees during their brief stay. Those victims' bodies had never been found, but under police questioning, Braxtell copped to racking up a death count close to a small war himself.

'You said *body*, is Braxtell dead?'

'Not yet,' said Guy.

Guy nodded towards the two faceless prison guards as they unlocked the heavy door for the visitors. 'Come on. This is one of those things you need to see for yourself.'

Eleanor hung hesitantly back for a second. The Blood War's recounting had been entrusted to a vampire priest scuttling around the ceiling like a spider, but *this*, whatever *this* was, she needed to see for herself? What could be so horrific it needed three of them to enter at the same time, like a gang of small children huddling terrified together in a Ghost House's dark corridors?

Eleanor stepped through, Guy walking in front and Ian taking the rear. She found herself inside a small room, no windows, just like the rest of the prison. Everything lit by harsh neon illumination-strip lighting, painting every surface a chilly blue hue. In the cell's centre rested a bare steel table, three green plastic chairs waiting on her side of it. The prisoner sat opposite her . . . his metal chair riveted into the floor, legs manacled to it and hands restricted by chains joined to the table. It might have been Dravin Braxtell on the other side of the table, but Eleanor found it impossible to tell. Where the man's mouth and eyes should have been, were blurs of light, fierce white fire as though the figure was vomiting napalm.

'What-!' Eleanor realised her legs were carrying her back towards the cell's shutting door; trying to escape without any conscious command from her brain to her feet.

[Stop] The word boomed from the figure, that fiery white slit of the mouth convulsing. Rather than sound, the whole room seemed to vibrate from that single curt instruction.

'She's new,' said Guy. 'Cut her some slack. Probation year and all. Probie's never seen an angel before.'

Angel? What kind of insanity is this?

Ian leant across and whispered to her. 'All three of us have to stay in the cell. It can possess two of us at once if it wants to. But angels have problems controlling more than two mortals at the same time.'

Fresh words echoed from the gruesome figure. [This vessel burns]

'That much I know,' said Guy. He sat down on one of the chairs, and Eleanor uneasily followed the man's lead. 'We're on the clock. This ain't my first time on this fairground ride, pal. Who are you? Who are we talking with?'

[Zadkiellllllllllll.]

'My first time with you,' said Guy, as casually as if he was commenting on a new waiter's employment at his favourite restaurant. 'What, Gabriel too busy to talk to his favourite lost soul?'

[Time is many-foldeddddd.]

'Not down here in this little corner of creation it ain't.'

Eleanor noticed Ian had quietly been consulting his mobile phone. 'Zadkiel. You're one of the angels of mercy - a servant of the Archangel Michael.'

[We all but serveeeeee.]

'Very humble of you,' said Guy. 'Let's cut to the chase here, Zad. What's on your infinitely infallible mind?'

White flames lashed out of the thing's mouth like a frog's tongue and Eleanor had to suppress the urge to flee again. *This is real. You're not insane, Eleanor. This is actually happening.*

[The enemy is on the trail of the Judas Purse: we judge their success to be likely: they must be opposeddddd].

'The *what* purse?' asked Eleanor, a touch of confusion to mix into her fear, sitting opposite this horrific burning vision.

Guy shot her a dark look.

'Later,' whispered Ian. 'The angel doesn't have long on our plane of existence.'

Eleanor was about to ask why but bit her tongue instead.

'It's been a while,' said Guy. 'This scheme to recover the purse . . . it's backed by the Reds?'

[Yesssssssss].

'Any clan sucker in particular?'

[The vessel named Martin Bormannnnnn].

That name sounded vaguely familiar to Eleanor, too, but she wasn't sure from where, precisely. *Not another serial killer.* Eleanor tried to stare at the flaming figure, but the blaze burnt her retina. She averted her gaze and felt like a coward while doing so.

Guy seemed to recognise the name, though. He groaned. 'Oh joy. How do we get to the Judas Purse before the Reds do?'

The fiery figure shook its head, a strangely human gesture from this burning man. [Balance: light gives way to darkness: night to dayyyyyyyyy.]

'You ever get splinters from sitting on that fence, Zad? Throw me a bone, here!'

[The floating vessellllllllll.] As soon as those words had been uttered the fire seemed to dwindle, a furnace dimming. As the prisoner stopped speaking his body slumped back in the steel chair and began to turn to ash, disintegrating before Eleanor's shocked eyes, embers falling and scattering about the cell floor, little wisps of orange boiler suit caught by the interrogation cell's air conditioning and left drifting through the air.

Eleanor raised a fist to her cover her mouth, fighting her gag reflex. 'Dear God, where's Braxtell?'

'Ridden out,' said Guy. 'As in good riddance.'

'He's dead? Not just—'

'What, teleported away? Out on good behaviour? Day release? Nah, I reckon Braxtell is somewhere a lot hotter now.' Guy looked across at the powder of soot falling off the chair. 'You never hear of someone finding God in prison? I guess it cuts both ways. No loss in this particular case.'

Eleanor was horrified how casually the old man treated Braxtell's death. Was that a byproduct of surviving as long as the old man had lived? Fighting in this horrible, secret war? Had Guy's humanity gone up in smoke as easily as the prisoner? 'How can you be so cavalier? Braxtell was a prisoner. He had rights.'

'What about all the children left in shallow graves under the rubble of Syria and Somalia like discarded cola cans? They have rights, too? Or you taking that old Stalin line here - the execution of one man is a tragedy, the murder of a thousand is only a statistic?'

Eleanor still felt sick. 'Who - *what* am I fighting for?'

'I can't tell you that, kid. Even the infinitely infallible Zad can't tell you that. On the plus side, you're going to live a couple of centuries to make your mind up. Unless you mess up badly enough and buy the farm first.'

'Braxtell was as good as gone when he arrived on Death Row,' said Ian, trying to excuse what they had just witnessed. 'He was extradited to the USA on the basis that he would be tried for a capital crime.'

Eleanor shook her head at his rationalisation. It sounded weak to her. 'Was that *thing* really an angel?'

'Best as we can tell,' said Guy, standing up from the chair and stretching. He was as untroubled as if he had just finished lunch in a burger joint. 'The angels take a different view of things. I reckon for them, time happens all at once - the past, present and future. If angels are playing competition chess, then humanity is just a stadium full of deaf, dumb and blind spectators.'

'Closer to bacteria clinging to the bottom of the chess board,' said Ian.

Their quips did little to quieten Eleanor's deeply disturbed mood. Ian rapped on the cell door and the two guards opened it. She noticed there was an orderly outside with a bucket and mop and felt a pang of guilt for what this interview had cost. *I thought the Vigil saved me from becoming a monster. But maybe this is how I lose the rest of my humanity. A little piece chipped away every day.*

'Portents and omens,' growled Guy as they put the cell behind them. 'Angels never show up with good news and an invite to a pot roast, that much I know.'

'Tell me about this Judas Purse!' demanded Eleanor, anger flaring within her. She knew the rage she felt now was the natural kind, not a byproduct of her being bitten by a vampire. 'Tell me exactly what was worth a man's life back there.'

'You never read the Bible, kid? Or maybe you've only seen the movies? Judas Iscariot betrayed Jesus to the Sanhedrin for thirty silver coins. That's your Judas Purse right there. After Christ's crucifixion and Iscariot's suicide, the thirty coins were cursed with the darkest form of power there is. When you possess that purse, you attract riches and power, the world-changing kind, but the coins also corrupt you and drive you insane. The Judas Purse is a planet-sized can of whoop-ass waiting to be opened. Archives back at the ranch should have more details on where it could be located. One thing I do know, we need to either ensure the purse stays lost or get to it before the Reds.'

'So we can trust Zadkiel's warning about the Judas Purse,' said Ian.

Guy sighed. 'I'm afraid so, kid. Zad's intel is gold.'

'Why so certain?'

'I'm carrying history with this gig.'

'You are?' said Ian, sounding surprised. Eleanor suspected

it was more because Guy was willing to discuss his past. They exited the castle-like keep built into the high walls, walking out into the windy, cold prison car park and headed for the nondescript black van they had used to drive here.

'You need to travel back to the forties to get a handle on this,' explained Guy as he opened the van door and got into the driver's seat. Ian slipped into the back seat next to Eleanor. Guy started the van and continued explaining while he pulled away. 'The Judas Purse has been lost to history for centuries, but wherever the purse is now, it only consists of twenty-nine silver coins, not the full thirty. The thirtieth piece of silver was discovered inside a burial barrow in Ireland by Nazi spies in 1939 . . . that piece is called the Myrddin Coin. Legend says the coin was mounted to the sword Excalibur's hilt by the sorcerer Myrddin for the Dark Age King Arthur. Made Arthur as good as invincible until his court fell apart in civil war. You might say owning Excalibur proved to be a double-edged sword.' He snorted in amusement at his own joke.

Eleanor could hardly believe what she was hearing. 'You're telling me Adolf Hitler ended up with Judas's thirtieth coin?'

'Gave Hitler the power to nearly win the Second World War in an early knock-out blow,' said Guy. 'Made the Nazi war machine as good as unstoppable.'

'But they were stopped,' said Ian, stating the obvious.

'Thanks to a few good men. You know when I was bitten by a Red, don't you . . .?'

Ian nodded. 'You mentioned it once . . . during the second world war. D-day?'

'I hit the beaches, sure, but I got the bite earlier than that.'

Guy's eyes narrowed. It was clearly an unpleasant memory for him. 'Yeah, I got turned during the Battle of Monte Cassino in Italy. I was a sergeant in the U.S. 36th Division, a G.I grunt, a humble ground-pounder. Dumb as dirt and just another cog in the lean, mean, killing machine. One of the units we battled against up in those mountains was the Iron Guard, a group of fascist volunteers from Transylvania and Romania fighting for the Nazis. What I didn't know was that their colonel was a Red and half his soldiers were demi-gogs. Fanatical peasants who believed their officer was a god rather than a devil. They chewed us up pretty good in that battle, in my unit's case, quite literally.'

Eleanor realised she had something in common with this grizzled old dog, now. *We're not that different, there's a scary thought. Please don't end up like him.* 'You were bitten and got the serum in time, like I did.'

'Sure, the Vigil were in the war fighting inside Europe as a covert arm of the Office of Strategic Services, the OSS. Same outfit who went on to become the CIA after the war.'

'What does all that have to do with the Judas Purse?' asked Eleanor.

'A hell of a lot, kid. Listen and learn. The Battle of Monte Cassino centred around an abbey on top of the Rapido Valley. It became the bloodiest battle of the Italian campaign. Both the allies and Axis powers took incredible casualties attempting to seize that ground. And the real reason for the fighting's ferocity was an ancient text uncovered in Italy by Gestapo treasure hunters. An old book which suggested that the abbey's founder, Benedict of Nursia, was once guardian of the Judas Purse and had hidden the coins in a secret vault below his abbey. Hitler already had one coin. You could say he wanted to collect the set.'

'Both sides were fighting over the Judas Purse?' said Ian.

Guy snorted in derision. 'We were fighting for possession of the vault, baby. The Allies lost more than 55,000 fine men seizing two valleys, and all we got for our troubles was an empty crypt hidden below the abbey. After we won the battle, we excavated the vault. All we found were dust and cobwebs inside. The purse had been there once.'

'Maybe the Nazis got there before you, stole the purse and carried it away?' speculated Eleanor.

Guy shook his head. 'I know for sure that didn't happen. If the Nazis had gotten their filthy mitts on the Judas Purse, we would have lost the war within a year. Just the power of a single coin allowed Hitler to sweep through Europe and conquer everything up to the English Channel. Given enough time, the Nazis would have crushed the rest of the world too. They were developing V3 Rockets, jet fighters, castle-sized tanks and the A-bomb. But Hitler never got the chance. The Vigil seized the Myrddin coin from the Nazis in the gutsiest raid of the war.'

'Hitler must have had the artifact well-defended?'

'Oh, he had the coin well-defended alright,' said Guy. 'Hitler was paranoid about members of his own circle stealing the coin and using it to seize control of the party from him. Ernst Röhm tried to filch the coin and paid with his life for betraying Hitler. To keep the coin secure, Hitler ordered the construction of a massive u-boat base and atomic research centre hidden under Antarctica. What the Nazis called the Neuschwabenland Citadel. That was where the Myrddin coin was guarded by the SS and the Reds. I was part of the combined OSS and Vigil commando force which infiltrated the citadel and stole it away from them, as well as destroying as much of the Axis nuclear programme as we could blow up and get out alive. We used Churchill's crazy plan to convert an iceberg into a covert floating aircraft carrier and sneak up on the citadel. Our team escaped through the snow back to the carrier. Carried the coin back to America and after that, the winds of fortune began to favour the Allies. The Soviets started to turn the tide against Hitler in Russia. The Allies mounted D-Day and recaptured Europe. Without the coin's power, Hitler began to get sick and shrivel up, his mind half-destroyed. Owning that foul piece of silver takes its toll.'

Ian's eyes flashed. 'Do we still hold the Myrddin Coin?'

Guy shook his head. 'After the war definitively turned in the Allies' favour, President Franklin Roosevelt gave orders for the coin to be destroyed. It was just too dangerous to be locked away and kept on ice forever. Sooner or later some politician would have been tempted to use the coin to influence world events in America's favour. The road to hell is paved with good intentions. Roosevelt knew keeping the coin meant that the USA would eventually end up as a dark all-powerful world empire every bit as evil as the Third Reich. On FDR's orders, the coin was taken from the Bullion Depository at Fort Knox and welded inside the Little Boy atomic bomb. The Myrddin Coin was vapourised in nuclear fire at Hiroshima and good riddance to it.'

'The President must have been sorely tempted to keep the coin,' said Ian.

'More than you know. Roosevelt was seriously ill at the time. The coin's power was the only thing keeping the President alive. After he signed the order for its destruction the coin took its revenge . . . Roosevelt passed away days later.'

Eleanor wondered if she would have had the strength to give such a power up, knowing that forsaking it would be as good as a death sentence. *I hope so.* But then, she also prayed she would never be put in a position where she'd need to find out how strong her will-power proved.

Guy shook his head sadly. 'Lost a lot of friends in that war. Lost a lot since, too.'

'Back in the cell,' said Eleanor, 'it sounded like you know the vampire hunting the Judas Purse.'

'You don't know who Martin Bormann is? I guess you skipped history, kid.'

'I guess you lived through it,' retorted Eleanor.

Guy grunted. 'Got me there. Martin Bormann was the power behind the throne inside the Third Reich - Adolf Hitler's private secretary. Also a Red - a senior level vamp. He disappeared during the Soviet Army's great siege around Berlin. Turned up in Argentina. Faked his death twice since. Not the first time he pulled that trick, either. The Vigil believes he was originally turned in 1582 when he was a Middle-European warlord butcher called Gebhard Truchsess von Waldburg.'

'So we're going to be fighting someone who thought that World War Two was a mighty fine idea,' said Eleanor.

'Fine, as in von Waldburg helped start the war. Maggots love corpses to feed on,' said Guy. 'Ian, get on the phone back to V-com. Tell Diane and Alasdair to head down to archives and begin researching this mess. We need to shake some solid leads out of the tree to follow.'

'It won't be easy,' said Ian.

'Tell me something I don't know. If it was easy, we would have already done it.'

'We can't allow the Reds to recover the Judas Purse,' said Ian, sliding his phone from his suit. 'If they do, it won't be a matter of counting corpses - we'll be counting how many people are left alive after the Reds abuse such power.'

Guy's hand gripped the steering wheel a little too tight. 'The chaos of the Second World War amplified to the power of twenty-nine wicked pieces of silver. There's a party I don't want an invite to.'

Eleanor agreed with his sentiment, but she kept quiet, staring out of the window at cars zipping past on the freeway. She tried to ignore the disturbing feeling that an invite to that party was exactly what had been extended by a possessed, burning corpse inside Attica Correctional Facility.

6

~ DOWN AND DUSTY ~

Eleanor had been down to the Vigil's archives level before to research subjects set during training. The New York Public Library it wasn't. One of the deepest levels of the Vault's underground complex, Archives Division was a maze of corridors filled with metal shelves on rollers crushed tight together. Often, to reach a specific book or filing box, you needed to roll a dozen other shelves forward and back to reach what you were looking for. And you had to remember to lock the shelves in place, or risk a fellow browser in another room move shelves , setting off a domino reaction that would crush you while you were trying to extract your book. Once Eleanor retrieved a tome, she had her choice of hundreds of leather-topped desks lit by brass lamps, their surfaces cluttered with antique-looking microfiche readers and old computers. The computers possessed no Internet connection, but instead acted as dumb terminals for server rooms filled with large chattering tape machines as well as more esoteric equipment, such as banks of computer chips held suspended in cooled tanks of bubbling green liquid. The staff who worked down here were closer to priests or wizards than the agents you ran across in the upper levels - cliquish, they kept to themselves and seemed to resent the intrusion of upsiders into their domain. Visitors - supplicants - who despoiled their perfect realm of dusty knowledge. When Eleanor arrived in the archives with Guy and Ian, the other two members of Guy's team - Diane O'Hara and Alasdair Colburn - had already been ferreting about the level for hours. Aided by the Archives Division staff, the two agents had, it seemed made an important discovery.

'What you found?' asked Guy, reading their faces and realising they had something to show for their time.

Diane spoke for the pair. She indicated a book trolley loaded with green tomes bearing the coat of arms of the Black Pope - the shadowy leader of the Catholic Church's secret supernatural combat arm. 'In here . . . the monks recorded a rumour that the Judas Purse was relocated from the vaults below the Monte Cassino monastery during the siege of Vienna. The purse was sent north out of Italy when the church became convinced Southern Europe would be totally overrun by the Turks. Later records speculated the coins were returned to the Benedictine Order at Monte Cassino after the Turkish threat was beaten off. But if for some reason the purse wasn't sent back to Monte Cassino, then the purse could still be held in its backup location!'

'How do we find out where the backup location is?'

Diane smiled. She was good at this work and seemed to want to draw the moment out. 'The secret monastery records of Saint Benedict of Nursia will have recorded where the coins were sent for safekeeping.' Diane offered out one of the church ledgers to Eleanor and she accepted it, brushing the dust off the coat of arms stamped into the leather - a pair of crossed axes below the Keys of Peter. Eleanor opened the pages to peruse what Diane had discovered, but stopped when she realised that the text was written in Latin.

Ian could barely contain his excitement. 'So, where are Saint Benedict's records?'

Diane's grin faded. 'That's where it gets tricky. They were looted from the monastery in the 18th century during the wars of unification. We contacted Rome. The Inquisition believes Saint Benedict's records have ended up in the hands of the Keeper … inside the Old Paradise Shop.'

Guy sucked in a deep, heavy breath. 'Oh, *great*. Well, at least that explains why nobody has been able to chase down the Judas Purse.'

'A shop?' said Eleanor. 'What's the biggie? We can just visit the place and buy the monastery records back.'

'The shop moves,' explained Ian. 'It never stays in the same place for long.'

Eleanor didn't understand what the young agent was talking about. 'Moves, as in, what - this dude's a mobile trader selling out of the back of a van?'

Ian shook his head. 'No, the shop's a physical building. It's just the building never stays in the same location for long.'

'*Right*. I'll have the rest of the bottle of what you've been drinking.'

'He's telling the truth. But finding the store isn't the real issue,' said Diane, 'our main problem is the price we have to pay to shop there once we find it.'

Eleanor looked quizzically at the woman, waiting for her to elaborate.

'Souls,' said Diane. 'The Keeper sets his price in mortal souls.'

***

Eleanor was still trying to wrap her mind around the nature of a shopkeeper who priced in souls when Guy reappeared from the depths of Archives Division. He had left Alasdair and Diane hunting for any other clues they could dig up in the files, and now carried a steel suitcase that bore the Latin motto of Archives. *An Veritas, An Nihil.* The Truth, or Nothing. Guy lifted up the case. 'On loan from Archives. We need to get some face-time with Moonbeam and let her do her thing with it.'

'What kind of stupid name is Moonbeam?' asked Eleanor, wondering what was inside the metal case.

Guy led them towards a lift. 'The hippie kind. Moonbeam's real name is Alice Montovich, bitten in 1963. She's non-operational: we never put her in the field. Too valuable. Plus, she's kind of whacked. Wouldn't last a month out in the wild hunting Reds.'

Eleanor made a show of fake enthusiasm. 'Wow! She sounds like a barrel of laughs.'

'Highly-strung,' said Ian. 'Her quarters are down on seventeen. Decorated to resemble the period when she was bitten. Alice never leaves. She believes it's still the sixties, so don't say anything to upset her delusions.'

The lift arrived and Eleanor stepped in alongside the two men. 'What, like pull out my phone and ask her if she wants to join my clan and help me level up.'

Ian shrugged. The lift descended. 'Yeah, exactly that kind of stuff.'

'What makes this dippy chick so valuable?'

'She sees things.'

Eleanor was confused. The lift doors opened and she hesitated before stepping out. 'What, ghosts - the dead?'

Guy answered for the younger agent. 'Visions. Catching glimpses of the future . . . the talent is called precognition. About as rare an ability as exists on the register. Hardly any Reds possess it, so we don't usually see it develop in agents post-Cure.'

They were in another corridor. Rather than painted concrete, this one had been done up in panelled wood and green patterned carpet. It looked like they had arrived at a hotel. From down the corridor a door opened, a tall distinguished man who looked in his mid-sixties stepping out of the room. Eleanor guessed he wasn't room service. He wore a grey three-piece suit, the kind of thing Bond wore when he was played by Sean Connery.

The man approached them, nodding as he passed and slowed. 'Agents. Sergeant Drew.'

'Chief,' said Guy. 'How's Alice today?'

'More focused than usual,' said the stranger. He spoke with a slight Boston accent. He pointed at the steel briefcase Guy was carrying. 'Is that what I think it is?'

'Reckon so.'

The man grimaced. 'Go easy on Alice if you can.'

'Easy, that's my middle name, chief.'

'Indeed? You must have changed it from Mayhem,' said the man. He squeezed Guy on the shoulder and set off down the corridor.

'Who's he?' asked Eleanor. 'Looks kind of familiar.'

'That's John, the Vigil's current Director. Our big cheese. You might say he's from the period, too. He's changed his face a lot since the sixties . . . we had to fake his murder in 1963. John's one of the few people that Moonbeam will open up to.'

'Was he well-known?'

'Not anymore with that face. You're probably triggering off the men John based his new features on - a morph-mix of Joey Bishop and Dean Martin.'

'Who?'

Guy sighed. 'I'm working with the heathen, here.'

'So, shouldn't we get boss-man back in here for this interview if he's tight with her?' asked Eleanor.

'Nah. Me and Moonbeam are good. I was on the team that gave Alice the Cure when she was bitten.'

There was a doorbell outside, and Guy pressed it. Hearing no answer, he opened the unlocked door and ushered the three of them inside. They rustled through a curtain of hanging beads to enter. 'Moonbeam? It's Guy the guy. You around, hon?'

Eleanor waited on a thick shag pile carpet and glanced around the apartment's living room. A lava lamp bubbled on the windowsill, and the window had to be some kind of ultra-high-resolution screen, because it looked pretty convincingly like they were high up inside a city apartment building, a block opposite with an advertising hoarding scaffold on the roof for Macy's Christmas 1965 Sale. The projection showed the kind of cars you could only see in Cuba moving along the street below, a honk and thrum of traffic, the occasional old-style siren of a police car echoing off the brownstones.

The psychedelic pattern of the tangerine orange wallpaper was making Eleanor's temple start to throb. 'Looks like we're on the set of Mad Men.'

Ian hissed her to be quiet before Guy heard - or worse, the woman walking out from the kitchen to greet them, padding as lightly as a cat in light brown moccasins. Moonbeam wore a bright red Indian sari, her wavy light blonde hair set with a fringe braid and tied back with a bandana. Frankly, Eleanor thought the woman looked like someone's mother attending a sixties-themed fancy dress party.

'Guy-baby, the man with the plan. Just had John in here. Like, I'm Miss Popular today. What's happening?' The woman sat in a white pod-shaped chair and swung herself around on it.

'Same-old same-old, Moonbeam.' Guy indicated Ian and Eleanor. 'Brought a couple of the tribe along. You mind? Ian, here, he was with me last time I visited. Eleanor's fresh.'

'Fresh as a flower,' said Moonbeam. 'Looks kind of sad, though. You been putting downers on the new chick?'

Guy rubbed his stubble, mournfully. He sat down on a sofa opposite a glass coffee table and the woman. 'With this face? I'm all about the light, Moonbeam. You remember that.'

'I'm in the nest, man,' said the woman. 'It's warm and cosy and I'm never coming out.'

'And we're fixing to keep you safe up here,' said Guy. 'But I'm going to need you to visit the Spirit World. Find your Goddess and help us locate something that's missing.' He placed the steel briefcase on her coffee table, opened it, and removed a leather book wrapped in brown parcel paper. 'This belongs to the man we need to find.'

Moonbeam seemed to recognise the book, shying away from the table. 'I've done that trip before - and it's a bad one. Full of pain and regrets.'

'I know you have.'

'You bagged this book from the *monster*'s library.'

'And we lost someone bringing the book back to to us,' said Guy. 'Three went into the shop and only two came out. I'm not asking you to open the book. Just touch the binding and work out where his shop is. He'll never come here for you, you know that. But it's only because we're out in the big bad, doing that voodoo that we do, that it's so warm and safe for you up here.'

'It's twitchin'. I dig this apartment, Guy-baby. Rent-controlled in the Big Apple. That's rare.'

'Don't you know it.' Guy tapped the uncovered tome. 'You might say *this* is the rent collection book.'

The old soldier slid it across the coffee table towards her.

Moonbeam looked unhappy, but she did as she was bid, leaning forward and placing her long pale fingers on the book. She sucked in her breath as she made contact, as though the leather was freezing steel, the kind that could rip your skin off with contact in Alaska. Moaning, her eyes rolled to white in her sockets, and she began rocking violently in the plastic seat, almost falling out of it. 'I can see, see it.'

'The shop?'

'It's a living thing, soul and bones and blood twisted and refolded as something . . . evil.'

'Where is it?' Guy gently insisted. He was like a dog with a bone and he wasn't going to give it up.

'Creeping. Always creeping. Sliding across the world. Nowhere wants it. Nowhere can hold it for long, not without vomiting it up.'

'I just need to know where the shop is now.'

Moonbeam cried out, the book shaking under her fingers.

'It's in - Batavia City.'

'How long before it bounces?'

'Twelve hours,' moaned Moonbeam. 'The shop is in the city for the next twelve hours.'

'That's it. We can make it,' said Guy. He lifted Moonbeam's hands off the book and she jolted like he'd just freed her from gripping an electrified fence. For a moment, Eleanor thought Moonbeam was going to be the one vomiting, but she held it down, wiping her sweating forehead with the back of her hand.

'You did fine,' said Guy.

'There's nothing fine about that vile thing,' said Moonbeam. 'Take it out of here, Guy-baby. Take it out and burn it, that's what the Goddess wants.'

Guy ignored her suggestion. 'Grab a chopper and we can just make it to Batavia in time.'

The woman looked happy all of a sudden. 'Chopper? Guy-baby, you got yourself a Harley?'

'Not that kind of chopper. This one's like a Huey, Moonbeam.'

She shivered. 'They're still killing the kids in Danang. They're so full of kill out there.'

'Moonbeam, let me tell you, it's pretty full of kill everywhere.'

Moonbeam stared intensely across at Eleanor. 'Don't go with them, sister. You stay frosty here with Moonbeam.'

'What else did you see in your vision?' asked Ian, suspiciously.

'There something we should know?' added Guy.

Moonbeam turned away and wouldn't meet any of her three visitors' gaze. 'It's been laid on me, Guy-baby. I'm never laying it on anyone else. What happens has got to happen. That's the will of the Goddess, and you never stand against her.'

Guy looked like he was going to argue, but stopped and

thought better of it. 'Okay. You've done good. Thanks for doing right by the tribe.'

'We can't just leave it there,' said Ian.

'This is the Keeper, here . . . and we're on the clock,' said Guy, indicating that was an end to the matter.

Ian didn't look happy about the situation, but that was nothing to how she was feeling. Eleanor wanted to stay and shake out just what the hippie-chick was insinuating here about her future, but Guy was eager to be about the chase now he had the city they needed to visit, ushering Eleanor out before she said something to pop Moonbeam's mystical soap bubble.

Moonbeam watched the three of them stand and leave her fake apartment, calling out as Guy shut the door. 'Happy trails with the freaks. I'm staying here. I'm in the nest for good.'

Eleanor stared at the closed door and knew how the hippie woman felt. 'She saw something about me, specifically, didn't she?'

'Maybe she did,' said Guy.

'Maybe? We're going with that, are we?'

'The thing to remember is that we exist in a quantum universe,' said Ian, trying to reassure Eleanor. 'The future isn't set in stone. It's shaped by our decisions. What Alice sees are just possible futures, the manifold paths we can take.'

Yeah, and she seemed fairly sure that I shouldn't take this one. But then, visiting a shop where the price was set in souls, Eleanor had twigged onto that fact without the intervention of Moonbeam and her dippy Goddess-sent telegram service.

7

~ THE MYSTERY MACHINE ~

'Tell me what we're going to be facing,' said Eleanor. The team had left the big double-rotor Chinook helicopter behind them, driving off its rear cargo ramp as smoothly as departing a ferry. Now she was in a compact black RV with smoked mirrors; no beds or kitchenettes inside, but everything else the mobile Vigil agent might need on the move. From a full armoury in a cloakroom-sized gun-safe, to the medical centre with a dozen vials of the Cure stored inside its refrigerated vault. Eleanor wouldn't be long on the road, though. Batavia City was only half an hour's drive away from the small private airfield where they had landed the Chinook.

Guy sat behind the wheel. Eleanor suspected the man had control issues, which meant he'd sooner lose a hand than relinquish control of the RV to one of the younger agents. 'We're not entirely sure what we're going to be facing. The Keeper's an EBE: an energy-based entity. Some of the Sci-Tech geeks believe he's a rare form of Sidhe Antiqua. Possibly the last of his race. Others have him pegged as an ancient human sorcerer who managed to free himself from human form; gaining a form of immortality. One thing we do know, he only stays alive by feeding on his customers.'

'With this many of us,' said Eleanor, 'can't we just take him out?'

'Plenty of people have tried. Us, the Reds. Nobody has ever succeeded. Inside the shop, the Keeper is the master of his realm - the store's closer to a dream he's dreaming, a dream he controls. As far as we know, he never leaves the shop.'

'He's a demon,' said Diane, her voice dripping with loathing. 'A devil exiled from hell.'

'Exactly what the Keeper *is* doesn't matter, right now,' said Guy. 'Keep your focus on what he can *do*. He'll appear before us as a mortal, but bullets and blades have as much impact on him as opening fire on a lightning bolt. Bravo Team, Fourth SAD, tried to cap the Keeper back in the eighties. Half of them died trying to terminate that sucker. That's how we know.'

Eleanor processed the old soldier's worrying intelligence. The Vigil operated twenty Special Activities Division groups, or SADs, out of their New York base; each group with an alpha, bravo and charlie team containing anything up to eight agents, if you included the sergeant in charge. Guy Drew's unit was Alpha Team, Seventh SAD group. Anybody - any*thing* - that could take out four enhanced humans finely honed by a swordmaster like Ikeda Hanzo wasn't just dangerous. It was fatal. Eleanor felt her jacket pocket, the little knuckle-duster-sized hilt of an extendable moly-blade tucked inside. 'If the Keeper's all that, how come we're carrying swords?'

Diane answered. 'The demon keeps hired help around the Old Paradise Shop. Sometimes human, sometimes Reds or other races of the Sidhe Antiqua. The swords are for his minions.'

'This just keeps on getting better and better.'

'We have something on our side that the Keeper does not,' said Diane.

'Yeah, what's that?'

Diane opened her jacket and revealed a little pocket-sized bible tucked inside. 'Blessed be the Lord, my rock, who trains my hands for war, and my fingers for battle.'

Eleanor didn't reply. All things considered, she was kind of glad her hand had been trained by the psycho samurai. *But hey, if the Lord's got my back on this one, I'll take all the help I can get.*

Alasdair opened his jacket and revealed a boxy little device the size of a small iPad. 'This is SciTech Division's latest mobile sensor unit. I said I'd field test it for them - grab some readings from inside the shop.'

'Faith is a stronger shield,' insisted Diane.

'Any sufficiently advanced technology is indistinguishable from magic,' said Alasdair. 'Science is what the Sidhe Antiqua really fear. Science is what's going to beat the Keeper, the Reds and all the rest of them in the end.'

Diane obviously didn't agree. 'For by grace you have been saved through faith. And this is not your own doing; it is the gift of God.'

Alasdair shook his head in frustration. 'It's just a book . . . why not quote from the Lord of the Rings? You might as well emigrate to Europe and sign up with *Scutum Dei*, Diane. The Black Pope always has room for another Ninja Nun in his old school.'

'And you should—'

'Enough,' growled Guy. 'Both of you stay frosty and save it for the Keeper.'

They drove in wintry silence and reached Batavia City seven minutes ahead of their sat-nav's estimated arrival time, Guy flooring the vehicle and driving fast and focused. The old soldier had tersely reminded them that every minute would count once they were inside the store. But what they gained on the trip in, they wasted driving around the streets trying to find the Keeper's store. Eleanor was wondering just how reliable Alice's visions were, but then they finally came across the Old Paradise Shop on a road called Fabyan Parkway. They parked the RV in a bay opposite and dismounted. Eleanor noted Guy Drew had removed a steel briefcase from the RV, carrying it with him. She sure hoped it was some kind of experimental weapon the Vigil had issued to the team. The Keeper's curiously mobile residence appeared as a narrow, rickety two-storey storefront. It looked out of place in the town's modern upmarket shopping district, like a long neglected antique shop in the middle of its closing-down sale. The words 'Old Paradise Shop' were painted in gold leaf script on dark green wood, its windows dirty, dusty and covered in a framework of iron bars. The half-timbered second storey was painted white and possessed two narrow window slits, a slate tile roof squatting above, half-covered in moss which matched the weeds fringing the green door entrance below.

There's something desperately wrong about this place. When Eleanor stared at the store, her eyes seemed to slide off it. And it wasn't a pleasant sliding experience - a greasy and cold feeling, like discovering the slippery rancid corpse of a dead dog decaying at the back of your yard. Despite her misgivings, she crossed the road and approached it. Eleanor attempted to read the sign inside the shop's window, but the text seemed to be set in illegible one-point size.

'Don't dawdle,' said Guy, tapping his watch. 'We're only

going to have twenty-five minutes inside before the shop vanishes and reappears in a new location.'

Eleanor's head was beginning to ache. She remembered the seer woman's pleas towards Eleanor. To stay safe with the hippie chick and refuse to travel here. *Too late now.* 'What if we're still inside when it jumps?'

'Then we're his,' said Guy. 'Extra stock. So stay frosty in there and watch the clock. Understood?'

A murmur of affirmation sounded from the team.

'Let's get this done. Everyone goes in, everyone comes out.'

Guy pushed open the door and an old-style bell tinkled, signalling his entrance. The old soldier held the door open for the rest of his team to enter.

Eleanor wrinkled her nose in distaste at the musty smell which assailed her. She stood on creaking floorboards, the start of a large sale room that looked like something from the 19th century - dozens of open and glass-fronted bookcases with a wooden shop counter at the far end, a shadowy open corridor leading further into the Old Paradise Shop. Hundreds of leather-jacketed volumes filled the shelves, pushed in tight together at all angles, ancient busts and dead animals floating inside preserved specimen jars acting as bookstops. Timber beams crossed the ceiling, splintered black oak hung with a strange variety of artifacts - bronze shields with hideous gargoyle faces, coils of rope and rusted daggers. The sales counter had heavy framed oil paintings leaning against it, a selection of wooden caskets piled on a faded Persian rug. As Eleanor looked again, she started as she realised that two staff stood behind the sales counter - a tall man in his fifties with a shiny shaved head and a pretty younger auburn-haired woman in her early twenties. *They weren't there a second ago.* The male staff wore a single-breasted tweed suit in muted brown, flecked with red, part of the pattern, but it could have been speckled with dried blood. He sported a Rasputin-style bushy black beard and intense, staring blue eyes that seemed to bore into her brain. Eleanor hoped beardie was the Keeper. *If there's anyone more scary-looking in this shop, I don't want to meet them.*

'Ah, Mr. Drew,' said the man. 'Back again. Every day I wake up and I feel the pulse of a few less Reds in the world. And I think to myself . . . . yes, my old friend Mr. Drew has been about his business again. Keeping busy. I, also, have been keeping busy.' He indicated the young woman standing behind the counter. 'Another one seeking adventure. Travelling across reality is so immensely bracing. It's no wonder there's an oversupply of waifs and strays who can't wait to embrace the exciting position of becoming my shop assistant. When young Emma-Jo came through my door, she knew this store was going to be her special place.'

Guy nodded sadly towards the girl. 'We've come here to trade, Keeper.' Guy walked forward and placed his steel briefcase on the counter, opening it to withdraw a transparent airtight ceramic box. Eleanor couldn't help but be disappointed. *Not a weapon.* An ancient-looking book rested, protected, inside the clear box. 'This is a Gutenberg Bible. One of only sixteen complete copies in the world.'

The Keeper leaned across the counter and lifted the box before his face, twisting the case in the dim light of the sales room, examining the contents inside. 'Ah yes. Fascinating, the starting shot of the information revolution. From these drab, faded pages, have sprung all the gaudy, meaningless trinkets of the 21st century.'

'The rarest, most expensive book in the world,' said Guy.

'Don't patronise me. This is the Old Paradise Shop, not a branch of Christies.'

'I was trying to tempt you, not patronise you,' said Guy.

The Keeper leered. 'Oh, but I am tempted. Just not by this early printing press run-off.' His eyes drifted over the rest of the Vigil team as he hungrily licked his lips. 'You know what the trouble with the Bible is? It's never been finished. And I simply can't stand to have the first book in a series sitting on my shelves without the final work resting by its side. The Reds are aiming to write the final chapter. But you must already know that, or you wouldn't be here.'

'This Bible,' said Guy, 'for the monastery records of Benedict of Nursia.'

'Records? We're not a record shop. Although I do enjoy music of a sort. I have to make it myself, of course.'

'Don't play games with me,' growled Guy.

'Don't? You've rather missed the point of my premises. It's no wonder I keep on moving. My never-ending journey trying to locate worthy patrons rather than ill-educated savages such as yourselves.' The Keeper noticed the sensor unit inside Alasdair's fingers and tutted, irritated. 'That's just rude. You need to remember what curiosity killed . . . ' He waved his hand and the device changed into a cobra. Alasdair yelled in shock and dropped the wriggling snake, watching it hiss at the Vigil agents before slithering on the floorboards, moving behind the shop counter.

Guy clicked his fingers, returning the Keeper's attention back on him. 'You're a shark, Keeper . . . you keep on moving so a pitchfork mob doesn't come hunting for your missing customers. Stop stalling. I know we're on the clock, here. We're not planning to be with you when you jump the store.'

'Perish the thought. Do we hold Benedict of Nursia's records in the shop?' The Keeper glanced towards his shop assistant and she stepped back, as though startled she was being addressed, then nodded. 'Such a good memory. How long have we been having our little adventures, my dear?'

'Thirteen months, Keeper.' Her voice had the trace of a foreign accent. *British?*

'That long, Emma-Jo? No wonder I'm growing bored of your steel-trap memory.'

'Please!'

The Keeper raised a chiding finger. 'Everyone gets shelved in the end. Novelty in *all* things, you must know that about me by now.'

'Don't do that. I promise I'll please you, I - '

The Keeper lunged forward and squeezed his palm over her mouth. When the Keeper withdrew his hand, her mouth has been erased. Instead of lips, there was just unbroken skin, as though she had been born a mouthless mutant. 'I believe I have had enough of your moaning. Your silence pleases me. Now, back to the storeroom and retrieve the item which this gentleman is seeking.' He pointed at Eleanor. 'Take this one with you.'

'I decide where my team go,' barked Guy.

'Then decide if you wish to check the provenance of the item you seek. Either your girl goes with mine to retrieve the book or you are all welcome to depart my premises. Let the Reds have their way and look on the bright side. At least your tedious religious scribblings will appreciate in value after the final chapter is inserted in your deity's dreary text.'

Eleanor glanced over at the terrified voiceless shop assistant. 'I'll go.'

'Let me do it,' said Ian.

'I'm sorry,' laughed the Keeper. 'Are you my new manager? I must have missed the memo from headquarters. No, in these premises, there is only one person's whims that are indulged. Gallantry bores me. Ladies first, that is the rule in the Old Paradise Shop. Off with you two now.' He wagged a finger at the pair of girls. 'You may pass.' Then he flicked his fingers at the others. 'You may not.'

Eleanor watched in horror as the rest of the team's words were cut off, an invisible wall had dropped between her and the Vigil's agents. The team tried to advance towards her, but a fierce sparking in the air halted them, trapped behind a transparent electric fence. Now Eleanor understood what Guy had meant about this shop being a dream inside the Keeper's mind. This was his realm, entirely. The rest of them were merely thoughts crawling around his insane brain.

'Quickly now,' instructed the Keeper. 'Tick tock. You only have seven minutes left before the shop relocates. I don't want Mr. Drew leaving empty-handed and complaining I cheated him. Reputation is everything in my business.'

Eleanor stepped through the gap in the sales counter and followed the young girl down the corridor. It was beyond dim, and Eleanor found herself tracing the outline of the walls with her hand to follow the course. She might not be able to see the walls clearly, but she could feel the shapes carved in the wood. Except the wood felt like bones and the shapes were runes that seemed to glow as she brushed them. By the time she emerged from the narrow corridor, the glowing sigils had destroyed her night vision.

The storeroom proved to be an almost warehouse-sized space packed with hundreds of narrow shelves - some of them holding books, others artifacts collected through the long ages by the Keeper. It seemed impossible that the small shop front could lead onto this amount of square footage, but Eleanor suspected that if this madness was the worst of what she would find here, she would have come off easy. Emma-Jo turned to make sure that Eleanor was following, then continued into the labyrinth of shelves. To Eleanor's shame, she could hardly bear to look at the shop assistant, her unnatural smooth face where her lips should have been. There were no labels on the shelves or signs to indicate the logic of the layout, but Emma-Jo led them deeper into the storeroom without hesitation. Finally, she stopped at a junction between shelves. There were a small round reading table and a rickety old chair standing there. As Emma-Jo turned around, Eleanor saw there was an ancient-looking book in her hand. She must have pulled it off the shelves on their way here. Like the volume she had seen back in Archives Division, this one carried the coat of arms of the Black Pope. Eleanor realised this must be the missing secret record book from the monastery. The store assistant rested the prize on the reading table, then went across to another bookcase. Emma-Jo picked up the pencil from the dusty shelf, withdrew another one of the leather-bound books and opened the book to a blank page near the front. She scribbled something down and passed the tome to Eleanor to read her message. There was something distracting about the book. The binding looked like ancient leather, but it felt wet and slimy, like a bloodied cut of meat.

Don't leave me here. Kill me.

Eleanor digested the message in shock. 'We, we can help you escape!'

The mouthless assistant grabbed the book back and dashed out a second message, before returning the damp pages back to Eleanor.

No escape. My body can't leave the shop. Bound here by unbreakable wards. Part of it. Please help me die!!!!

Maybe it was the surprise of reading the girl's plea for an end to her life, but the pages of the tome fell open and Eleanor almost dropped the book. A terrible discordant humming emerged from the volume. And on each opened page was a distorted female face, quivering slightly, trapped in a state of eternal torture and unable to escape the tome's trap.

Eleanor shrieked in surprise as the book lifted out of her hand. It was the Keeper. He'd crept up on the pair of women as silently as a spectre.

'Now, that's almost shoplifting. You're browsing my private collection. These are not for sale at any price. Did you know bookbinding is becoming a lost art? I believe the leather for this edition came from a Vigil agent I skinned seventy years ago.' The Keeper opened the book and hissed in fury as he saw the messages scribbled in pencil there. 'Defacing my property! Oh, Emma-Jo. Such ingratitude.'

Eleanor reached for the knuckle duster-sized hilt of her moly-blade, springing the extending sword into its full length. 'Leave the girl alone!'

The Keeper sighed, jabbing an irritated finger towards Eleanor, her sword transmuting into a child's windmill toy atop a wooden stick. He blew towards her weapon and the little red foil windmill head rotated in a lazy circle. 'Live as long as I have, my dear, and you will realise that the Vigil is full of hot air. Damaging stock? Emma-Jo, you know your chastisement is set out in your employment contract.'

Eleanor dropped the windmill and formed her fist into a needle punch, but the Keeper just smiled as a transparent wall formed sparking between her and Emma-Jo. 'So feisty. It'll make taming you all the sweeter.'

The Keeper's store assistant used the second's distraction to swivel and turn to run, but the monster was too fast. He lunged at Emma-Jo and seized her wrist with his right hand, scrubbing her face with his left hand. Emma-Jo's mouth returned and the narrow space between the shelves echoed with her frantic screams. The Keeper pushed her down to her knees on the floor, choking the girl around the neck. Emma-Jo's frenzied yelling dissipated as her body seemed to flatten in front of Eleanor's eyes, converting into a human-sized cardboard cutout, her body folding like origami. The Keeper held the book out open, pushing Emma-Jo's folded form into an empty, dangling page. Eleanor's fists flailed against the barrier, but the store assistant had vanished from the narrow gaps between the shelves. The Keeper's horrific work done, he turned to show Eleanor the open volume. The last note of Emma-Jo's final scream had been converted into a continual low drone, the page with her twisted face pushed into it seeming to flicker as her features shifted frantically left and right, the only movement allowed to her, trapped inside the tome for eternity. 'You and I will peruse my private collection after the store is closed. Flick through the pages and listen to the music of the souls. If you like, I will describe the beautiful moments I and my dearest shared together.'

Eleanor tried to master her terror, banging desperately against the invisible cage.

'There's nowhere to run inside the Old Paradise Shop,' laughed the Keeper. 'Nowhere that isn't me. You're inside me and I'm inside you. Now we just have to settle on your rate of pay. Of course, in my store, my assistants pay me, rather than the other way around.'

Eleanor continued to smash against her unseen walls. *No way out of this. Not until he drops the field.*

'Here we are,' smiled the Keeper, running his fingers over the monastery records left on the reading table. 'Mr. Drew will be so pleased to hear we have what he desires in stock. There's a deal to be done after all. The book for . . . you.' The Keeper waved his hand and there was a slight fizzing as the invisible enclosure trapping her vanished.

Eleanor back-pedalled. 'Get away from me.'

'Why do you think your decrepit Nazi-killing colleague brought so many of his team into my shop? I need to have my pick. I think the two of us are going to get on famously.'

Eleanor was running out of space to retreat. 'I'll never agree to be your shop assistant!'

'You agreed by stepping over my threshold - didn't your

Vigil colleagues tell you that? You should have read the terms and conditions, they're clearly on display.'

Eleanor indicated the ancient monastery records as she back-peddled. 'So, you think this is a done deal? Those records belong to the Vigil, now?'

'Naturally. And in time you'll come around to your part in the trade. That's always the fun part - breaking new staff into their duties. Well, fun for me. And in the Old Paradise Shop, it's all about *me*.'

'You think you're original? I've done this Rodeo before. You know what happened to the last lecherous pig of a floor manager who thought I was part of his remuneration package . . . ?'

The Keeper kept on coming, raising his hands ready to seize her face. 'That's a potty mouth. Let's scrub it away for a while. Yes, we're going to need to start your training programme immediately.'

'You've already shown me your monster,' said Eleanor ducking his grasping hands. 'Let me show you mine.' This wasn't the practice hall. Eleanor didn't hold back. She formed her hand for a knife-hand strike and threw it towards his neck, aiming to break his windpipe. The Keeper seemed to flicker, vanishing like a cloud of black ash and reappearing a foot to the right - her blow passed through empty air. The soul-filled book didn't make the transit with the monster. It tumbled down onto the floor between the shelves. Eleanor fought to regain her balance, but the Keeper didn't push his advantage. She cursed her stupidity. If she had been facing Hanzo, she would be out for the count right now.

The Keeper hooted with derision. 'You're like a moth mistaking the light for the torch.'

Eleanor pivoted and put all her power into a short range one-inch punch, hoping to catch the Keeper by surprise, but the entity flashed with black light and rematerialised down the narrow corridor between the shelves. Her body, her blood burnt with the fight and the transformation. Like a battery being overcharged.

'And a moth always flies into the flame in the end. It is the creature's destiny.'

Eleanor tried not to let despair get the better of her. *How can I beat this thing?* 'I know you want to touch me,' spat Eleanor. 'And you have to be solid enough to wound for that.' She ignored the itching pain building inside her.

The Keeper chuckled. 'Oh my dear, I can be anything I like.' His form flickered again, but rather than disappearing and reappearing, the human form shimmered to be replaced by a humanoid creature from a nightmare - a squid-like head whose face was bearded by a writhing mass of worms below locust eyes, a slimy bloated corpse-like body, shambling forward on clawed scorpion feet while narrow insectile wings fluttered limply behind it. The Keeper raised a nest of decaying tentacle arms. 'So many long limbs to caress you with.'

Eleanor twisted to scoop up the moly-sword turned windmill toy, snapping the head off and flicking the sharp broken wooden shaft as a dart towards the Keeper's locust eyes. Rather than jumping, this time the monster turned as transparent as a phantom, the dart passing harmlessly through the head and embedding itself in the books behind.

'My realm. My beautiful realm. We'll be moving on in a minute. Then you're mine for eternity! Don't tire yourself out too early. Leave us a little for later.'

Eleanor gasped for breath and warily retreated, the Keeper advancing, his clawed feet clicking across the discarded ledger of souls. The drone of the assistant's final screams seemed to doppler-shift like a siren as the monster trampled across the tome. That awful drone merged with the agony of her burning body, making a vibration that was almost too painful to stand. And in that instant she knew how to beat the Keeper.

'I know what you eat,' coughed Eleanor.

The Keeper's monstrous form converted back to its more human-looking form, leering at her. 'I am transcendent, foolish little girl. I have no mortal need for flesh of fruit or beast. I never even drink water.'

Eleanor ran her fingers along the leather-spined books, fighting down the generator whine building up inside her. 'These aren't books and this isn't a library. This is an energy farm and these are solar panels for a demonic sadist.'

'They're paper and skin, as you will find out when I tire of you.'

'Yeah, really ancient paper. You may not drink water, but you better pray you've got a sink around here!'

Her hands pulsed with the power that had been building with her and she gave it physical form, the light from her hand momentarily blinding her, like a Molotov Cocktail going off. The shelf her hand had been resting on burst apart, a hundred flaming books showering out, and everywhere they cannonballed, the inferno was shared. Eleanor had given the storeroom its match, as brittle and dry as a tinder box. With the collection of souls burning, the Keeper mirrored his food-source - remade into a banshee-screaming torch, stumbling blindly, his burning hands reaching out and only spreading the fire. His wicked pain no longer sounded human - more like a fox screeching into the night. As loud as the Keeper howled, Eleanor struggled hard to hear him. The books went off like frying bullets, a death rattle of escaping souls so ear-splitting it shook the cavernous store room by the foundations.

Eleanor thrust past the human-shaped inferno, booting the Keeper back into the shelves where his conflagration exploded with the dry ancient tomes racked there. 'You thought you were the monster, here? It was always me.'

Eleanor realised she had underestimated just how deadly dry this firetrap had been. She was only going to have seconds to get out of here before this room became her tomb. Eleanor slowed her desperate escape just enough to scoop up the tome on the floor where Emma-Jo had been imprisoned, adding the private monastery records of Benedict of Nursia to the loot she clutched. Flames leaped from shelf to shelf as she fled outside, ancient, dry, hidden and airless, flames licking along as fast as a fuse. Then she was following the twisting, dark corridors, and the walls throbbed and pulsed like the walls of a cramped stomach, an eerie moaning noise as the substance stretched. This dark lair was starting to fall apart. The Keeper was the shop and the shop was the Keeper. *Let them both burn.*

Eleanor followed the tricky, deceptive passages, chased by the Keeper's hideous screams, and sprinted into the shop's sales room. As she arrived, the barrier sealing off the Vigil team vanished. *I guess it's kind of hard to maintain a shield when you're on fire.*

Ian ran forward, his eyes flicking down the corridor, searching for the Keeper. 'What the hell happened back there?'

'We played doctors and nurses,' called Eleanor, hardly slowing. 'I showed the Keeper mine and now he's sorely in need of the Demon Doctor. Got the records, let's rabbit before the shop jumps.'

Ian didn't need further urging. None of the team did. Ian flung open the door and the agents began to pile out into the street. Eleanor noticed that Guy hadn't said anything about her reappearance before retreating. *Tell me you're surprised I survived, old man. Tell me something!*

Eleanor followed through the open doorway, yelling as the book of souls clutched in her fingers bounced out of her hand. It was as if the book had been torn out of her fingers by an invisible force. The volume fell open on the floor, exposing a flattened, twisted, distorted female face and the flat drone of the assistant's final scream. Eleanor lunged down and retrieved the book.

'They can't leave,' shouted Ian, still holding the door open, coughing in the choking smoke beginning to fill the sales room. 'It's not possible . . . they're part of the shop, now.'

Eleanor cursed and swung the book fluttering into the inferno licking across the counter. *I'm sorry.* 'Well, so is that fire.'

The tome began to pop as though Eleanor had thrown a chain of firecrackers into a bonfire. Every bursting sound, the bubble of a soul being released. *Best I can do.* At last, Emma-Jo had the final freedom she'd begged for. Eleanor turned and fled, chased out by the intense heat, putting the Keeper's evil realm behind her.

Alasdair was last out of the store. His sensor unit had reverted back to reality, a cobra no longer, so the young agent had grabbed it up from the floor. The walls and windows of the Old Paradise Shop trembled like the skin of a living creature, an animal doused in petrol and set on fire. And beyond it all there was something else. The Keeper's silhouette stumbled, trapped behind the narrow windows of the second storey, a creature of fire joined with the inferno, an entity of raw malevolent energy, roaring and screaming as his storefront began to fade like a bad dream. The store was relocating, its timer triggered. But this time, there might not be a whole lot arriving at the new destination.

'Wherever you're jumping,' yelled Eleanor, 'you better hope they've got a crack-hot fire brigade on standby.'

The last shadows of the Old Paradise shop vanished like the grin of Alice's cat; the Keeper's premises replaced by an empty lot between two stores, overgrown with weeds and filled with discarded rubbish. Some of the garbage smoked slightly, the blaze's residual heat still lingering.

Guy Drew stood there, gazing into space, shocked by the sudden turn of events. 'What did you do?'

Threw your plan for me, perhaps? Eleanor lifted up the monastery records. 'Went into a bookstore. Lifted a book. You alright with that.'

'But how . . .?'

Eleanor wasn't going to give the old man the truth. Not until she knew whether her main purpose on this trip had been bait. Lady goat to be staked out for the lion. Eleanor slipped her Zippo lighter out from her jacket. 'Your people tried bullets and blades. I tried this. Old manuscripts burn pretty good.'

'Nothing about that fire looked natural to me.'

'Yeah, I'm willing to bet that's because the whole store was some kind of Inter-dimensional Hell Portal deal. Enough of that stock was real enough, though.'

Drew looked uncertain about the truth of Eleanor's tale, but the senior agent had the monastery records as well as bigger fish to fry than pursuing his suspicions. 'Well, give a girl a hammer and every problem looks like a nail. Give a pyromaniac a lighter and maybe every problem looks like arson.'

Eleanor swayed on her feet. Ian tried to steady her, but she shrugged his hands away. She felt emptied, the thrum of energy inside her body spent. But Eleanor sensed it would come back. If this was a curse, at least it was a curse that could be shared. 'Hey, if it works, it works. Right?'

The Keeper had wanted Eleanor. To be fair, she had given the creature pretty much everything she had.

8

~ HELL CALL ~

Dawn Heliot drew much pleasure springing surprises on mortals. Normally, because it involved dropping her pretence to be anything other than a witch. There was always a split second of pure delicious shock as her latest victim watched her perfect porcelain skin age two centuries in seconds, turning as wrinkled as rain-soaked leather; high cheekbones sagging, flawless blonde hair shimmering into brittle silver barbed wire, full lips cracking like ice. Transforming until only her beautiful wide blue eyes remained untouched inside her wizened face, a mirror of her twisted soul, which she allowed her prey to glimpse truly at last. This particular victim, a muscled college football player, a prize bull for the slaughter, had begun a very unmasculine scream as Heliot's face altered and her beauty fell away. His scream had instantly cut off when she expertly stabbed him through the heart and began casting the spell of eternal youth, fixing his life force to drain inside her. This handsome young Jock was a fine specimen. His youthful vigour would keep Heliot alive for at least six months before she needed to feed again. Heliot didn't, however, much enjoy *receiving* surprises, which was why she reluctantly abandoned her spell, tutting in fury, as the corpse unexpectedly started to rise from the bed, her sacrificial dagger still embedded through the football player's heart, its ornamental handle slick with blood. Heliot's first thought was that she had inadvertently seduced a zombie, but she instantly dismissed the idea. Predators recognised other predators by their scents and signs, so the chances that this beautiful brute had been anything other than a boring mortal was slight. The dead prey's eyes started to burn with an orange fire as the corpse sat up, fixating the witch with an unholy power that she recognised all too well. Yet another surprise, to receive a call from whatever Hades this creature had ended up cast into. Dawn found herself almost as perturbed that the Keeper had allowed his physical form to be destroyed, recast here as a disembodied spirit reaching out from beyond the grave. *Even I never managed to kill the Keeper - the beast must have grown sloppy in his dotage.*

Dawn allowed her distaste to show. 'Has no-one ever told you that it is rude to interrupt someone when they are busy eating?'

The corpse's lips wobbled, but it was the Keeper's voice whispering from the dead throat. 'I am slain, deaddddddd.'

'Obviously. And your possessed husk is also bleeding all over my sheets - despite the strategically positioned towels I laid across my bed earlier.'

'The covenant, the covenant, you must avenge meeeeeeee.'

'You have to be joking. Each and every one of your assistants would have said anything, agreed to *any* covenant, just to escape your disgusting clutches. And in case you have forgotten, I removed myself from your "care" through my own cunning. You had very little choice in the matter. You were an idiot to leave so many volumes of arcane spells and powerful witchery on your shelves. You underestimated me - you thought me a pretty simpleton as well as an illiterate. Given your current reduced circumstances, it doesn't look like you learnt much from the lesson the first time, either.'

'Avenge meeeeeeee!' demanded the spirit inhabiting the corpse.

'I'm not the naive Victorian flower girl you tricked inside the Old Paradise Shop. It wasn't your assistant who escaped you . . . it was a Witch of the Sixth Seal. You want me to revenge you?' Heliot giggled. 'Give me your murderer's address. I shall be sure to send the foe who cast you down a congratulations card.'

The pool of crimson blood pooling on her bed turned into a silvery mirror, a quicksilver window into the dark recesses of the Keeper's demonic soul. Dawn couldn't help but be impressed by that level of sorcery. Even disembodied and defenestrated, the Keeper still clung to the vestiges of his old power.

'*This* slew meeeeeeee.'

Through the portal, Heliot saw the power of the Keeper's killer ripping into the monster, drinking from it like a fine wine - such a rich taste, such a gorgeous nectar. Heliot watched recent events replay inside the Old Paradise Shop. The Keeper and his ever-shifting Hell's gate both destroyed by - by. 'Sweet darkness! What is that girl that burnt you? Obviously bitten by a vampire and administered the antidote. Was it the Vigil or the Black Pope's meddlers who saved the fey thing?'

'She is not what she seemsssss. I discovered too late, too lateeeee.'

'Too late for you, perhaps,' cackled Heliot.

'Feed on her, take her power and use it to restore meeeeee.'

Heliot reached out and stroked the corpse's now pale blue cheeks. 'Oh, I'll steal her power. I'll drain her life-force like wringing a gravy-filled cloth wipe for its nourishment, but you, my old master, you can stay as mist clinging to the distant edges of the world. A little bit thinner and weaker every day, always watching, but never able to touch the living or rise out of the shadows. As powerless as all the girls you trapped inside your little nightmare. I'd say that's a fair exchange, wouldn't you?'

'The covenanttttttt . . .'

'Yes, yes, the covenant. Why don't you call a lawyer and sue me?' Heliot lifted the female creature's name out of the silvery portal. *Eleanor Lythe*. It had been while since Heliot had encountered something new in the world; the witch wondered what this bright shining abomination might be. It was entirely possible the creature didn't even know herself. *Something about her family lineage, perhaps?* It would bear investigating. You always needed to understand your enemy. 'Stop licking the crumbs from my table, *master*. Show a little backbone, a little pride.' Dawn allowed the Keeper a long hiss of agonised rage, before laughing and shoving the helpless corpse back down to her mattress, savouring the spell to cast the Keeper out as it crossed her lips. Then Dawn observed the consumed ruin, fallen still and lifeless once more, with a fastidious disgust. *Not enough energy left to feed a gnat, let alone a witch.* She dragged her dagger out of its chest and rose to stand in front of the mirror by her sideboard. 'Mirror, mirror, on the wall, who's the hottest babe of them all?'

Heliot's mirror remained silent, but she moaned in hideous pain as her face flowed back to its original fair, flawless aspect. Working such evil Wicca when she was as empty and hungry as this came at a terrible price. Thankfully, Heliot wasn't going to need to be the one to pay it. She checked her victim's backpack, searching for anything that might help the police identify the murdered young man. Heliot had become as expert as Sweeney Todd at the disposing of bodies over the centuries. Even when the authorities found the remains of her consumed prey, they never tracked the husks back to her. As Dawn searched, she came across a paperback fantasy novel titled *The Shepherd's Crown* by some writer called Terry Pratchett. Amazingly, if the blurb at the back was to believed, it featured a coven of kindly witches travelling around some imagined world like charity workers, doing good deeds. Heliot cackled to herself. No wonder this young idiot came back to her apartment so willingly. The true witch pulled black plastic sheeting out from under her bed and rolled the Jock's hollow lifeless body onto it. 'And now I'm going to have to return to the Sports Bar and convince a couple of your silly friends to leave with me. I'm going to need to be at full strength before I claim the female creature's soul - I don't intend to end up like the Keeper.'

Those who had escaped the Keeper's malicious clutches were something of a unique club. Membership, it seemed, had recently risen to two. *Time for that number to return back to one.*

9

~ BIG ANTS ~

Sophia passed two tall male vampire guards standing sentry in the corridor and noted how they worked to control themselves in the presence of the young teenage girl walking by Sophia's side. It was obvious neither of the pair had supped on human blood yet this week. The guards wore black uniforms with gleaming breastplate armour protecting their chests, modern submachine guns strapped by their hips alongside ceremonial daggers. It was an archaic mixture, much like the Vatican's Swiss Guards, and similarly purely for show. The vampire soldiers were far deadlier than the weapons they carried. But human supplicants sometimes came here, hoping to beg, borrow and steal some small fraction of the vampires' vast power, and the prey expected to see such trappings. As with so much of existence, what you didn't see mattered far more than what was actually displayed.

Sophia and Joanna came to the end of the corridor. No doors or gates blocked entry to what lay beyond. None was needed. Most sensible people avoided walking down the steps on the other side at all costs.

'Don't go in there,' Joanna begged Sophia. 'Please. *He's* inside there.'

'He is. And that's why I don't have a choice in the matter.' Sophia possessed a honeyed voice which hypnotised most people without even needing to draw upon her powers of mesmerism.

Even so, her words barely seemed to calm Joanna this afternoon.

'Why must you?'

Sophia raised her long fingers and stroked the human girl's cheeks. 'I am what I am. Wait here, my darling. I shall return to you shortly.'

Joanna shot a nervous glance towards the two sentries down the corridor.

'They won't touch you, Joanna. They know you arrived here with me. And they also know well who I am.'

Joanna nodded and made a gentle little cough, which was her way of saying she understood but still didn't approve.

Sophia stepped through the doorway. Wide stone stairs swept down to the bottom of an open, windowless vault. It was every bit as desolate and chilly as she remembered from her last visit. A portly man sat behind an old-fashioned wooden desk in the centre of the large, echoing concrete chamber. One thing you could say about the High Prince of the vampire race, he wasn't vain. Von Waldburg looked like a middle-aged accountant: sallow skin, fat cheeks, a mop of brown hair that could have passed for a badly designed wig, although Sophia knew it was his original hair and as natural as any vampire might be considered natural. Von Waldburg was an ugly vampire, and that by itself was a badge of his vast eternal power. Only in his eyes could you see the creature's danger. A piercing gaze that could cut through you as if your very soul was being flayed. But Sophia would meet his gaze. Not that she had any more choice in the matter than she did in answering his summons.

'Come on in, little *Figchen*,' called von Waldburg without looking up, sensing her presence.

The Master of Masters knew that Sophia didn't enjoy hearing her nickname, but that was the point. Gebhard Truchsess von Waldburg was one of the few creatures in the world who could get away with allowing that insulting diminutive to cross his thin lips and not suffer her revenge. At least, not *yet*.

Sophia indicated the mostly bare concrete hangar which von Waldburg had made his lair, walls hung with a few tatty tapestries that had probably been old when the vampire leader had been a medieval warlord. 'I like what you've done with the place.'

'Do not pout, Sophia Augusta, we have both known each other long enough that only honesty should pass between us.'

Sophia walked down the wide steps. A single strip of worn green carpet covered the middle of the treads. 'Honesty? Well then, it seems curious to me for the world's most powerful vampire to be holding court in a chamber so uncomfortable, bare and industrial it might pass for an abattoir.' Sophia suspected it was because the chamber reminded von Waldburg of Hitler's bunker when the Prince of Vampires had still worn the name of Martin Bormann.

'I used to own a fine alpine castle filled with warm wood panelling, four poster beds and priceless oil paintings. It was flattened by American B25s trying to kill me during the war.' He smiled ironically. 'And because the Axis lost the war, I could not even claim on my buildings insurance.'

'You mean *we* lost the war, not the Axis powers.'

'No, *we* lost a battle. Our war continues.' Von Waldburg sniffed the air and glanced towards the top of the stairs where Joanna lurked out of sight beyond the archway. 'A vampire can never have too many demi-gogs; but the fashion for keeping human pets will, I trust, never catch on.'

'I have my reasons.'

'I am sure you do. And it is a tribute to our long liaison that you are still alive to have them. Toying with your food counts as poor manners, though. I always thought you were better raised than that.'

The Vampire Prince's hard eyes flitted up towards the vault's entrance, and there was a sharp sliver of curiosity in his gaze, as well as the expected hunger for the prey's blood. Von Waldburg wanted to uncover the secret of Sophia and Joanna's relationship, but Sophia could never tell him. Not without killing the vampire, first. Which Sophia would probably have to do sometime this century, if not the next, she suspected.

'I have flown a long way to meet you if this is to be a mere lesson in etiquette.'

Sophia did not fear the vampire prince. She was always cautious around him, but knew her utility to the malicious creature granted her a status beyond her existence as merely another vampire. Of course, their long relationship cut both ways. Von Waldburg was utterly unmoved by Sophia's fine porcelain beauty, her deep blue eyes that should have looked young, but didn't, her hair so blonde it shone almost white. Sophia had always been beautiful, never using her powers to alter her face towards a model she had not been born to. Of course, she had made a few subtle rearrangements over the decades, as well as increasing her height to humanity's present standard. The advent of photography was a curse; always a chance someone would happen across some seventy-year-old image of Sophia and wonder how she could still be wandering around unaffected by the ravages of age. Not understanding that supping mortals' life-force was far superior to even the most expensive of beauty products. No, like the rest of her kind, Sophia slowly altered her features each year, just enough to protect the secret of her immortality.

'Let me see if I may broaden the curriculum for you.' Von Waldburg activated an intercom on his desk. 'I will receive the report now.'

Ebu Kulk entered their chamber through a small corridor on the ground floor. Centuries before, Kulk had been a vizier to the sultans. The Turkish vampire had a penchant for first tying those he fed on to teams of wild horses, before tearing his victims apart. He claimed such terror before death seasoned the blood's taste. Vampires tended to tolerate each other at best, but even so, Sophia could not suffer this thin wrinkled creature for long. Kulk was oily and obsequious to those above him in the pecking order, vile to those below. Ebu Kulk even walked like a little twisty creature, each step careful and measured and precious. He slid a glance at Sophia, both sly and knowing, clutching a folder of bound papers tight to his chest.

'What is your assassin doing here, Gebhard? Are we finally dealing with the rat problem by employing her teeth?'

'My little *Figchen* has arrived to deal with the human problem, Ebu, not the rat one. Humans breed more prolifically than rodents these days. How many prey are there currently in the herd?'

'The world human population currently numbers over seven billion, my prince.'

Von Waldburg raised his hands in mock despair. 'You see. Too many for even us to feed on. It hardly seems fair that our numbers are diminishing while the herd's rise so intolerably high. We vampires have become a race of bone idle woodsmen, neglecting to copse our forests. Now we cannot even move through our own forests, so dense and thorny have they grown.'

'We can blame nuclear weapons for that, my prince,' simpered Kulk. 'Humans halted mass warfare between nations when atomic bombs arrived.'

'Yes, yes, Mutually Assured Destruction, no more culling of the herd. Atomic weaponry has made cowards of the entire planet. We may look no further than what has happened to the victors of the last great war we caused ... America and Europe and Russia. They won't even fight each other face-to-face anymore. Instead, they launch drones from continents away and leave the bodies of their enemies as bug splatter. Surgical strikes, limited tactical engagements. I ask you. Give it a few more centuries and the preys' minds will all be software downloaded onto super-computers, and what will we feed upon then? Rats and mice perhaps . . . the rats you think my little *Figchen* has come to hunt for me. You know my lust for blood and sport, Ebu. Tell me, what has happened to the emissary we sent to the Keeper?'

'There has been a small complication, my prince,' stammered Kulk. 'The Old Paradise Shop is not halting anymore. It seems to be rotating through the planes of existence in a somewhat, well, ruined state of operations.'

'By ruined, you mean burnt to the ground?'

Ebu hung his head in shame. 'Yes. But perhaps the Keeper would not have dealt with us anyway? The Keeper always did have very peculiar ways.'

'If by which you mean leaving the murdered corpses of vampires in the abandoned lots of his store, then I would agree with you. Very peculiar, for the foxes to happen across a lion. Would you care to posit how the lion was so badly burned?'

'We presume by the Vigil.'

'So the hens murder the lion while the foxes must look on and wonder how they pulled off such a trick?'

'The Vigil are not hens, my prince. They are hyenas. Debasements. Enough of them together may bring down a lion.'

'Your hyenas have made off with my book. The best chance for locating the Judas Purse.'

'It is possible the Vigil may not possess the monastery records of Benedict of Nursia.'

'Oh, they do.'

'You have this on good authority, my prince?'

'You have it on *my* good authority, Ebu. I trust you still accept that?'

Kulk bowed low, like the courtier he had once been. Not as low as the slug he still was, though. 'Yes, yes, of course.'

'Do you keep human pets, Ebu?' asked the prince.

The thin vampire appeared disgusted at the very thought of the notion. 'They are but prey, my prince.'

Von Waldburg raised his hands in mock victory. 'You see, *Figchen.*'

Sophia said nothing, not wanting to alert the odious courtier to Joanna's presence. Kulk would enjoy tearing her apart just to pain Sophia. It was the kind of petty score-keeping that the courtier did so well.

'I do, however, keep pets, Ebu,' barked the prince.

'My prince?'

'Have you never wondered about the shipments of live cattle your office signs for?'

Ebu shrugged, hesitant and not a little confused. 'Medical experiments?'

'Oh no. I am a traditionalist, I always use humans for that.' He patted a little silver-framed portrait of Hitler on his desk. 'If only there were more like this fine lad, I might even keep human pets myself. Such a useful puppet. We won't see his like again, and our world seems smaller without him.'

'I shall recall our emissary to the Keeper from the field, then, my prince.'

'Do not trouble yourself,' said von Waldburg, 'I have already done this.'

Ebu nodded, probably thinking that this was how the clan leader had heard the news of the Keeper's demise before Ebu had a chance to deliver it himself. Sophia suspected that the courtier was misreading that particular piece of information, as it happened. But then, Sophia had been making herself useful to von Waldburg for far longer than the Turk had been trying to ingratiate himself with the Master of Masters. 'Off to meet the emissary with you, Ebu,' ordered von Waldburg.

The courtier went to the stairs, turning before the first tread. 'I shall fully debrief the emissary, my prince, to discover why she failed you so badly.'

'That's the spirit,' smiled the prince. It wasn't one of the smiles you wished to get from the clan leader, however, and even the Turk had the good sense to recognise this. Ebu Kulk turned frantically to run, but the high prince activated a switch under his desk and two hidden doors swung open below the Turk's shoes, sending him tumbling down into some kind of steel chute. The doors instantly sealed shut again. Sophia could only admire the engineering and precision behind the snare. She had walked over that very spot herself and failed to detect any joins in the concrete, nor a breeze rising from below which should have alerted her to its existence.

'Keeping human pets is a commonplace pastime given their shocking overpopulation these days,' said von Waldburg. 'I prefer far rarer breeds.' He pressed another button and a section of concrete wall on the side retracted down into the floor, revealing a sandy desert environment below and sealed off behind an arc of thick, armoured glass. Von Waldburg got up from behind his desk and strutted over to the viewing window. The metal chute which Kulk had taken had ignominiously deposited him onto the orange sands below. The environment behind the glass was well done, realistic with intense yellow lights mimicking a high desert sun. The only other thing inside the sand-filled tank was a scattering of bleached white bones. Those, Sophia suspected, belonged to whatever attractive bait had been sent to negotiate with and tempt the Keeper.

'Snakes are not exactly rare,' said Sophia.

'I never have to look far to find snakes around me,' said the prince, tapping at the glass and waving happily at the Turk. Kulk had risen to his knees in the sand, both hands raised imploringly towards the window above him. 'There are no snakes on the other side of the glass. Ebu is begging, yet he doesn't even know what's inside there with him.'

'Kulk was obsequious, true, but not unintelligent.'

'A fair appraisal in hindsight. Over the centuries, I have grown more discerning about who I give the gift to and raise into one of us.'

'Shall I take that as an insult?'

'You, I am sure, I shall never have cause to regret.' The prince gazed down into the chamber. 'Always interesting to see how one of our kind fights. Poor Ebu always had the hunger, but he was never very good at anything beyond the most basic powers. You'd expect someone of his age to have mastered more than mind clouding and the physical strength which was his birthright.'

'Will Kulk's powers of mental influence save him?'

The sand stirred below Kulk's feet and the vampire stumbled desperately back, unbalancing as the dunes shifted below him. 'No. My pets possess very simple minds. They operate mostly on instinct.'

Sophia stared curiously at the sand disappearing from around Kulk's feet. Black plant stalks seemed to be growing out of the sand, wobbling and further stirring the dunes, the stalks forming a circle around Kulk, trapping him. The vampire tried to get to his feet, swivelling, watching in horror as the stalks started to vibrate faster and faster.

'Fascinating,' said Sophia.

'You will enjoy what happens next. You never much liked Kulk, did you? Not after he stole and fed on two of your prize stable's stallions back in the day.'

Sophia tutted. She had forgotten that slight. It was in the eighteenth century, and the Turk had his nest of demi-gogs rustle her two best studs while she was away in Austria visiting the emperor, leaving the horses' decapitated heads strewn across her bed sheets. A rather unsubtle message, she thought, but an act all too typical of the vampire.

Suddenly, three dark heads pushed through the orange sands and Sophia gasped, taking a step back despite the solid protection of the armoured glass between her and the vista below. The black heads belonged to ants, but each ant the size of a family car, razored mandibles larger than broadswords clacking furiously in front of their mouths. Kulk screamed, swivelling as he took in all three of the monstrous creatures. There was nowhere to flee to, however, even if Kulk hadn't been caught in the middle of their deadly pincer movement.

'You see, *Figchen*, I can move with the times. I have outgrown my need for my incompetent administrator's services.'

Thoraxes swelled out of the tumbling sand and then the nearest ant lashed out towards Kulk. The vampire tried to catch the razored mandibles but merely managed to half-impale his forearm on the ant's organic weaponry, leaving himself open for the remaining pair of monsters to leap from the flanks and tear his body in half. There was a flash of energy as Kulk detonated and blew apart, the ants left chattering like an angry freight train rolling over tracks, frustrated at being denied their prey's sustenance.

Sophia smiled. *We feed on all, we are not to be fed on.* 'I have never seen their like,' admitted Sophia, still a little shaken and speaking as much in truth as any need to appease the clan leader.

'I obtained these beautiful abominations from outside the White Sands Proving Ground, when the U.S Government was still foolishly detonating atomic bombs on its home soil. One of my demi-gogs had been snatched from the V2 rocket program and passed into NASA's clutches. He informed me of the cover-up undertaken inside the desert around Los Alamos. Humans make such a hideous mess of everything, don't you think? Their test's radiation leaked into the ant nests and created these savage mutations. My giant pets are a symbol of how badly our prey is out of control as a species. Humanity has become a plague crapping all over the land.'

'I would never have taken you as an environmentalist,' said Sophia.

'Just so long as *I* am the one to control the environment.'

'And I thought you brought me here to slay the Turk.'

'The day I need your assistance to bring down an underling such as Ebu Kulk is the day I fully deserve to have you assassinate me and supplant me as clan chief.'

Sophia's thoughts exactly, as it happened. The prince glanced at her as if reading her mind. As far as Sophia knew, that level of telepathy was beyond the vampire leader. Of course, if it wasn't, telepathy was just the sort of gift he would keep quiet as an ace concealed up his cunning sleeve.

'I believe it was Edison who said that "I have not failed: I have just found ten thousand ways that won't work". Edison would not have lasted very long working for me before I consumed him, I am afraid.'

It was true. For someone who was theoretically immortal, the clan leader possessed very little patience. The female vampire glanced up at the ugly electric strip lighting in the ceiling. 'Lucky for us Edison didn't work for you, then. I still remember how tedious hundreds of candles in a castle were to maintain . . . and the hideous odour of burning wicks.'

'That is your weakness. You have been blinded by our prey's neon lights, their petty little parlour tricks of science. I much prefer the old ways,' growled the prince. 'When the majority of our prey never strayed further than the village where they were born. When what the prey knew didn't come out of books or the internet, but from priests behind a pulpit, with the Borgias in our pocket to dictate the lessons. It seemed to me like an age where all we ever owned were swords, armour, sails, horses and bricks. From the Caesars to Cromwell. We never really needed any more than that.'

It was an age, thought Sophia, *it was the Dark Ages.* You didn't need mortal blood to enjoy central heating, chauffeured limousines and private jets. Sadly, von Waldburg was very much a creature of his time. Unlike Sophia, he had never evolved with the passing centuries. His mind was like the dead vampiric cells of his body, still mired in the past. Another reason she would make a superior clan leader to this capricious, blunt tool of an instrument.

Von Waldburg continued lecturing her. *He certainly does enjoy the sound of his own voice, though.* 'Even flintlocks seemed as a joke to me when they first appeared. Hollow spears that hissed smoke and tossed funny little lead balls out. And now our prey have weapons capable of incinerating the planet a thousand times over. That is what we have come to. So we shall give the prey a finely balanced war - a culling to end all culling. And all I need is the Judas Purse to make their end happen as I have foreseen. Humanity's civilisation is a house of cards, just waiting for a strong wind to topple it over. All that knowledge carved up into tiny fragments. How to make a solar battery in one mind.

How to maintain a wireless mast in a second. Cull enough of the herd and their society will revert to wattle and daub huts, savages with iron swords beaten out of the ruins of rusting cars. A glorious new Dark Age, and vampires feed so well inside the darkness.'

'Then we'll go back to ruling the herd from our palaces and castles,' said Sophia.

'The way it should be. The way we should have kept it.'

'How do you know that the Vigil hold your book? That it didn't burn to ashes inside the Old Paradise Shop alongside the Keeper?' asked Sophia.

'For the same reason I discovered the importance of the book in the first place, *Figchen*. Because there is a traitor inside the Vigil working for me. And when the Vigil finds the Judas Purse, so will I. Or rather, so will *you*. You shall follow the Vigil team while they recover the Judas Purse for me.'

A traitor within the Vigil's ranks? That made things much easier for Sophia. Of course, it shouldn't be *too* easy for her. The hunt had to contain some element of challenge to be worthy of the name. She seemed to live for so very little these days, but the hunt, that could still fire her cold blood into the passions she remembered from the old days.

Von Waldburg might be a blunt instrument, but Sophia was a scalpel. And what was the point of being a scalpel if it was not to slice your enemies apart?

10

~ WORST DATE EVER ~

Ian watched Eleanor slide her cycle into the bicycle lock on the corner of 6th Avenue and 41st Street, selecting a four-digit combination on its screen to secure the bike. Two strong steel rods slid between the frame and front wheel. Even New York's notorious bike thief gangs would need an arc welder and a good twenty minutes to cut through that. Ian had also just locked his bike in one of the hundreds of free cycle stands provided by the city for commuters on their way to the nearby train stops at Times Square and Grand Central Terminal.

'You sure I'm ready to return to active duty?' asked Eleanor, removing her bright green cycle helmet.

'The doctor's sure enough,' said Ian.

'Then how come I'm still scheduled for medical tests for the rest of the week?'

'You can't be too careful,' said Ian. 'When you're as new to all this as you are, it takes a while for your metabolism to settle.'

'Too careful,' mocked Eleanor. 'Maybe you should have thought about being *careful* before you and your friends treated me like the proverbial sacrificial lamb - a gift-wrapped girl-snack for that psycho-demon.'

'Guy didn't plan how the last mission went down,' insisted Ian. 'The Keeper could have asked for Diane to go with him to retrieve the monastery records of Benedict of Nursia.'

'Except the Keeper didn't ask - he insisted. His house, his rules. And maybe you don't need to peek into the future like the Vigil's tame hippie to guess how that particular game was going to pan out.'

Ian felt a deep twinge of guilt. Eleanor had a point. And as it happened, the Vigil's tame future-scrying hippie *had* correctly predicted that Eleanor would place her life in the gravest danger by accompanying the rest of them on her first mission. Ian tried to tell himself that Eleanor wasn't expendable; that their squad leader Guy Drew wouldn't have treated a new recruit in such a careless way. But ultimately, they were all expendable. The Vigil kept the darkness at bay, and that came at a harsh cost paid in blood and lives. Sometimes the only thing that kept Ian sane was the knowledge that if the Vigil didn't wage its secret war against the sidhe antiqua, the human race's casualties would be countless times higher.

'Forget it,' said Eleanor, still sounding bitter. 'You saved me from being turned into a half-vampire slave beast thing. Maybe trying to feed me to a demon as a distraction in your little heist makes us even.'

'It really wasn't like that.'

'Well, could be the next demon that needs distracting will fancy Michael J. Fox-lookalikes, then it'll be your turn to put out.'

'I don't look anything like him at all . . . and I'm taller, too.'

Eleanor raised her hand to rest about three inches taller than Ian's head. 'You just keep telling yourself that, Mickey J. So, what's with the cycles? We trying to go green with this mission, earn a few carbon credits, or are they cover?

Ian tried to cover his embarrassment. 'We're not exactly on a mission, more like R&R.'

'Was this Guy Drew's idea?' said Eleanor, suspiciously. 'It'll take more than picking up a couple of hamburgers on the company credit card to make up for the Keeper attacking me.'

'No,' said Ian. Actually, the squad leader probably wouldn't approve of this on a great many levels. So Ian hadn't asked. *Better to ask forgiveness than beg for, and be denied, approval.*

'Is this a *date?*' asked Eleanor, placing just enough emphasis on the last word to make Ian even more nervous that he already was.

'My way of saying sorry, at any rate. Maybe a half-date . . . a quarter-date.'

'The Reds put the bite on you in the 1980s, right?'

Ian grimaced. 'They did.'

'So you must be in your chronological forties now, even if you do still look like a college freshman.'

'We age slower,' said Ian. 'It's not like I feel like I'm my dad or anything.'

'Some people could label that kind of creepy.'

'Talk to me in forty years, then you'll understand. It's not exactly as though I'm Master Hanzo,' protested Ian, 'last of the Victorian dudes.'

'Last of the Tokugawa shogunate dynasty,' said Eleanor. 'Didn't you ever watch samurai flicks back in the day, or were you more of a Miami Vice kind of guy? Designer stubble and a purple T-shirt under a white jacket?'

Ian indicated the main gates into Bryant Park and the two of them entered together. 'My tastes haven't changed so much. Nor have the times. Apart from the Internet and mobiles that don't look like bricks, things are more or less the same as they were when I was given the antidote.'

'Oh, fabulous,' said Eleanor. 'You know, before I was bitten I was looking forward to growing old. Old enough to leave the home and strike out on my own. Make something of my life. Get away from everyone telling me what to do, what to learn and know, what to feel. Now you're telling me I'm biologically frozen at that point forever? What fresh hell is this?'

'You protest too much. You weren't that person, not even back when we first saved you from the Reds.'

'Talking of the antidote,' said Eleanor, 'apart from the usual super-hyped, long-lived thing, did you pick up any extras from the vamp that put the bite on you?'

'A level of empathic resonance,' said Ian. 'I can sense Reds, demi-gogs and a fair few other races of the sidhe antiqua in the distance when they switch into their feeding mode.'

'That's a pretty useful skill for a vampire hunter.' She slowed as she saw what was ahead. 'There's a cinema screen set up in the park!' noted Eleanor, at last a trace of approval in her voice.

'It's HBO Movie Night at Bryant Park.'

'We haven't had to pay anyone to get in?'

'It's free, dummy.' Ian opened his backpack and lifted out a wool picnic blanket, unrolling it across the lawn. There were hundreds of groups and couples on the grass already, with more people arriving. There wasn't much that was free in New York, but this evening was one of them.

'Wow, they sure turned them out frugal back in the eighties.'

'I'm springing for the food and drink tonight. Well - I will - I mean.'

'So, what's showing tonight, Mickey J.?'

'Ghostbusters,' said Ian. 'The original, not the reboot.'

Eleanor laughed at that. 'No way! You sure this isn't some sneaky video training type deal?' She tapped the pen inside her jacket's pocket, her concealed retractable moly-sword blade, standard issue for the Vigil's covert excursions. 'I guess I won't be needing this tonight.'

'If all the Vigil faced is what Bill Murray and Dan Aykroyd got to fight, we'd have already won and be out of a job by now.' Ian weaved through rows of park-issue deck-chairs and headed for a fast food stall before the crowds grew any larger, returning with a tray bearing two paper cups and a pair of foot-long hot-dogs. As soon as he reappeared, Eleanor raised an eyebrow at the cups' contents. 'So, I get root beer while you get the real thing?'

'You're not twenty-one yet,' said Ian.

Eleanor shook her head. 'Jesus, look at this face - I'm still going to be carded when I'm sixty, aren't I?'

'We'll print you a fake I.D. in a few years.'

'Old enough to die in humanity's eternal struggle against evil, not old enough to buy a cold one. Now I know how those newbie marines feel.' Eleanor tentatively lifted her hot-dog out of the tray. 'How did you know I wanted hot mustard?'

'You seem like the sort,' said Ian, with more confidence than he felt.

'Maybe I make it to forty-five, I'll pick up some of those slick Jedi dating moves, too. Sorry, *quarter*-date moves.'

Ian checked his wristwatch. 'The sun set about twenty minutes ago, so the movie will start rolling soon.'

'I bet you saw this film in the cinema when it first came out.'

Ian raised an eyebrow. 'How did you know?'

'You seem like the sort. Like checking the time using that antique on your wrist rather than reaching for a phone.'

Up on the screen, the opening credits started to run. They sat down, took their dogs and ate while the movie played out. By the time the film was a quarter of the way through, Ian was arriving at the opinion he shouldn't have supersized his drink along with the food.

'I need to hit the bathroom,' said Ian, standing up and excusing himself

'What, your superpowers of the supernatural don't ship with an enhanced bladder?'

Ian crumpled his empty beer cup. 'Sadly not.'

Eleanor shifted her gaze back to the screen where Sigourney Weaver was struggling with her haunted fridge. 'How come the Vigil never saved her?'

It was a rhetorical question; at least, Ian hoped so. He left Eleanor to the movie and went in search of the portable washroom cabins he'd spotted behind the food stalls and treeline. After he'd found the facilities, used them and finished cleaning up, he realised he was still hungry. That was the problem with running a human metabolism as overclocked as theirs - agents needed to take in a lot of calories just to stay standing still. And if he had an appetite, that meant that Eleanor, newly arrived at her powers, was probably sitting back on the blanket and cursing him as a cheapskate for only buying one dog each. There was a food stall nearby selling tacos, lonely behind the trees and in the dark with a pair of broken lamps nearby. Ian trusted that Mexican and spicy might be enough to get him into Eleanor's good books, so he made a pass by.

There was no queue right now, just the stall-holder pushing chili beef around a hot plate with a ladle, his face lit by the stand's glowing signage. As Ian approached, a young blonde woman in an expensive black overcoat appeared and collided with him.

Ian pulled back from the woman who'd bumped him. 'Excuse me.'

'My bad,' apologised the woman.

'That's alright, it's kind of dark back here. They should have working lights on the path.'

'Well, they were working,' said the woman, 'before I extinguished them.' She barely finished speaking as the food server lunged across his stand, seizing Ian's hands and yanking him forward. A dark, knotted piece of wood appeared in the woman's hand, and she viciously scratched Ian's forearm, drawing blood. 'Bad things are always going on the darkness, that's why mortals are right to fear it.'

Ian stumbled back, trying to draw upon his powers, find the enhanced strength and speed he needed, but they weren't there; instead, his blood boiled inside his wounded arm, a relentless heat spreading out and filling him. He tried to resist the burning, but within seconds it had converted into an itching pleasure unlike anything he had every experienced, a joy and ease with the world which he'd never thought possible, all his troubles and worries and fears turned ephemeral. He savoured his deep connection with this woman, this witch, this beauty. Such a gift. He was entirely unworthy of it, he knew that. He needed to earn her love, redeem himself in every way possible.

'That's better, isn't it,' smiled the beauty, finishing hissing something in a sibilant language Ian couldn't place. 'The Kiss of Wytchwood and Wormroot . . . does my glamour warm you?'

'It *burns* me,' gasped Ian.

'In a good way, I trust. I am your mistress now . . . Mistress Heliot.' The woman cackled and fixed the stall-holder with her glamour, like focusing a laser beam on butter. 'Two beers and two meals. Make them generous ones for generous appetites.' The merchant took meat off his hotplate, shook a wok over a flame, then pushed the food across in paper trays while serving the beer in paper cups identical to those from the hot-dog stand, the park's green logo printed on the cups' side. Everything was dropped inside a disposable cardboard tray. Mistress Heliot mixed a bag of herbs into one of the beer cups, adding the thick green contents from a vial slipped out of her pocket. Swirling inside the paper cup, the beer steamed as though it had been microwaved, twists of smoke curling into the air. 'Pass this sweet potion to the girl you came with,' ordered the witch. 'When she has drunk it, ask her to return with you. She will have no choice but to obey.'

'Give me the job, mistress,' begged the stall-holder. 'I'm stronger than this mere *boy*.'

'He's not,' growled Ian, trying not to shout the undeserving dog down. 'He can't help you like I can.'

'Never a truer word was spoken.' The witch sighed, shaking her head. 'That's the problem with casting the Glamour of Wormroot, sometimes it's simply too strong for its own good.' She waved a finger under the merchant's nose. 'I needed you to catch him; I need him to catch her. A fly to catch a frog, a frog to land a she-alligator. I spotted a lake on the other side of the park, little fly, find it and hold yourself under the water for the rest of the night to prove your undying love for me.'

The stall-holder practically salivated as he stumbled away to do her bidding.

Mistress Heliot giggled. 'Sadly for him, I suspect his love for me is very much of the *dying* kind.'

'Good,' said Ian. There could be no competition for this sublime creature's favour, he would never allow it.

'Shall I kiss you, little frog,' purred the witch, reaching around to rub the nape of Ian's neck.

Ian's blood burned as fire, every atom of his very being trembling at the gentle touch of her finger. 'Yes, you must, *please*.'

'Then, I shall. First, just give the girl you arrived with her sweet beer. It's filled with a potion of female compulsion. I need the hybrid every bit as meek and docile and obliging as you. Sadly, a witch's glamour only works on members of the opposite sex, and I, as you can smell, am very much a woman.'

'*My* woman,' murmured Ian.

'I will give myself to you in every way after you please me,' Mistress Heliot promised. Just the thought of the witch completing her promise was enough to make Ian so giddy he could hardly focus his mind to obey her.

'Move normally. Act normally. Do this for me, ' she commanded. 'And return quickly. Your glamour only lasts another thirty minutes. If you want to keep on burning like this, you must come back to me and allow me to renew these feelings inside you.'

'Please,' Ian begged.

Mistress Heliot pointed through the trees to where the cinema screen flickered. 'Go! Remember, you are helping the girl you arrived with. I shall share with her the gifts of my pleasures, too.'

Ian took the food and reluctantly left the sight of the mistress. Just being out of sight of her was a punishment so heavy he hardly knew how he could bear it. Distant shouts drifted from the direction of the lake as walkers spotted the stall-holder drowning himself. Ian chuckled. He had the mistress all to himself, now. Ian had his instructions. He knew what he had to do to please her. He returned to the picnic blanket where Eleanor was still watching the film.

Eleanor turned to look up at him. 'Extras! You really are slick, you've read my mind again.'

'This is for you, too,' said Ian, kneeling and passing her the potion-laced beer. *Take it, drink it quickly*, he willed the girl, as though telepathy was one of his gifts.

'Not root beer this time?'

'No.' Ian was sweating. The fire inside him burned so deep and potent. 'I changed my mind. You were right. Anyone old enough to die for their country is old enough to drink a real beer.'

Eleanor said something, but Ian didn't hear it, his eyes drawn to the screen, where Sigourney Weaver was sprawled across silk sheets, trying to tempt Bill Murray into bed with her, a deep unearthly demonic rumbling from her throat. Something about that scene resonated with him. *What is it?* His head throbbed, the heat swilling around inside him, massaging his flesh with its addictive electricity. So good, so pure.

Eleanor made a second comment, her words vibrating through the edges of his consciousness, dragging his eyes away from the screen and back to her. She had drunk the beer, the cup lying empty on the grass. 'Good, we have to visit the taco stand now.'

'Visit the taco stand now.' Eleanor rose to her feet, obediently.

'That's it. We still have time.'

Murmurs of annoyance came from the crowd watching the film as the two of them blocked the view, falling to silence as they moved out of the way and zigzagged through to the trees and the taco stand.

'She's still here,' said Ian, the heat of his bones vibrating like a buzz-saw the closer he drew to the mistress.

'*She's still here*,' parroted Eleanor behind him, not understanding the significance of the words she aped. Eleanor didn't feel the heat yet. But she would. The mistress had promised Ian as much. Jealousy rose inside him at the thought. How could he share the mistress with anyone? But he had to obey her stern commands, and this was what she willed.

Mistress Heliot waited by the taco stand on the shadowed grass, just like before, the light of the neon sign giving her fine porcelain features a devilish cast. The only difference was that the corpse of a female dog walker now lay still on the grass nearby, alongside a slaughtered Labrador.

Ian felt an almost manic protective rage surge inside him. 'Did they threaten you, mistress?'

'The hound, sadly, did not find my wise bones' scent to its taste,' said the witch. She flicked the fingers of her left hand, and Ian noticed she wore blood-slicked razor-clawed thimbles on two of her beautiful fingers. 'Her dog began barking at me, so I needed to slice both their throats. I do so hate a fuss.' Mistress Heliot smiled as she saw Eleanor approaching the stand. 'But I see the inconvenience has been worthwhile. Don't stand behind my frog, delicious darling, step out and let me gaze upon you.'

Eleanor did as the witch ordered.

'Curious,' said the witch. 'I sense very little of your power.

You hide it so well within you. Is that a natural reflex, I wonder, or were you taught by someone before you joined the Vigil? Answer me!'

'I was not taught by anyone,' whispered Eleanor, meekly.

'And yet you managed to defeat the Keeper,' said the mistress. 'I was once his assistant too, a very long time before you. Only you and I have managed to escape his capricious shadow. I through mastery of the Craft, and you, through, *what*? Another Vigil hybrid; a failed half-human vampire. No. I simply fail to see how you escaped.'

Ian's unnatural fire burned augmented by terrible jealousy, now. How could the mistress pay so much attention to Eleanor, when she had him still standing before her? 'Mistress Heliot,' begged Ian, 'your promise to me.'

'Silence, little frog! Sit on the grass and wait until I call for you, 'cackled the witch. 'You might yet make me a fine dessert. Now, for the main course . . . '

Ian moved away, tears in his eyes at the mistress's rejection of him, his legs like lead weights carrying him away from her, no choice in the matter. He wanted to beg and plead with her, but the mistress had commanded silence, and so silence there must be.

Mistress Heliot switched her attention back to Eleanor. 'Potions of compulsion are such temporary, fleeting things.' The witch dipped into her handbag and slid out a golden neck torc covered in runes which glowed with an acid green light as she caressed it. 'I'll not have you coming back to your senses inside one of my pentagrams, attempting to give me what you used to slay the Keeper. This is the Bidding Gold, warded and inscribed by my own fair hand across six full moons. Fix my gift around your neck and I'll give you a taste of the ecstasy your friend is experiencing right now. You'll never want anything else again other than to bring me pleasure through your compliance.'

Eleanor took the torc and lifted it slowly towards her neck, halting an inch from her skin. 'Actually, gold is last season's colour, so maybe I shouldn't?'

'What!'

Eleanor tapped the side of her nose and contemptuously tossed the torc to the gravel path. 'I can track a genuine beer across half this city just through the smell of its hops alone. Your Rohypnol cocktail is back on the lawn, making some worms get real jiggie.'

Mistress Heliot frantically dug inside her coat and emerged with a gnarled piece of dark wood clutched in her hand like a pistol.

'You've got to be kidding me, who are you, the Hermione from Hell?'

Ian ached to tell the stupid girl to shut up, to stop insulting the mistress, but he couldn't act against her commands. *That would be sacrilege.* The witch would never re-stoke this brilliant fire inside him if he acted against her will even once.

'I am your mistress!'

'You want to go all Fifty Shades on me, how about I give you a spanking, that work for you, *mistress*?'

Eleanor danced to the side as black lightning burst out of the tip of the gnarled wood, missing the new recruit and striking the taco stand, slicing it in half in an eerie explosion of darkness rather than fire. Onyx-coloured sparks hit the lawn where Ian sat cross-legged, moaning, consuming the grass like napalm, leaving the soil seared and burning in front of him. Ian ached to protect the mistress, but she had given him his orders. Stay still and silent while she fed on the girl. Eleanor cart-wheeled across the grass like a gymnast; moving too fast for the mistress to draw a bead on, the agent's shoe lunging into the wok, sending a stream of burning oil whipping across the air and into the witch's face. Mistress Heliot stumbled back howling, nearly falling over the dog walker's corpse.

'I guess revenge for killing the Keeper isn't a dish served cold after all,' said Eleanor, drawing her moly-sword and activating its blade.

Ian gasped as he saw the oil had burned away the true beauty of the mistress, leaving the ravaged skin of a two-centuries-old hag in its stead, the poor mistress moaning and spitting and cursing. If only the witch remembered Ian was waiting here for her; he could comfort her, his love would restore her beauty, but the mistress retreated even as Eleanor advanced on her. The wand spun in the mistress's hand, jabbing and casting, but whatever spell the witch was working up to was suddenly broken as Eleanor rolled to the side, slicing out with her blade and severing the gnarled wood in half. Mistress Heliot screamed as though her own hand had had been sliced off, clutching the wand's nub end in her leathery fingers. Its greater length fell to the ground and started burrowing into the soil like a snake, trying to flee the battle.

Mistress Heliot fell back towards the trunk of the tree and Eleanor moved carefully, relentlessly towards the witch. Ian recognised the deadly pattern of Eleanor's feet as she tracked across the dark lawn, a deliberate flowing *Ayumi ashi* from Hanzo's sword class, a dance that would be followed by a sharp diagonal cutting movement - in this case, most likely against the witch's neck. Ian moaned. Silence, Heliot had commanded, a silence that would now cost his sweet dear love her life. Ian sucked in his breath as the branches of the nearest tree curled out like tentacles and darted towards the agent. *How could I ever have doubted the mistress?* Even half-formed, her spell was magnificent, the London Planetree Sycamore protecting the mistress as fiercely as a guard dog. Eleanor lunged through the tree's assault and sliced madly with the moly-blade, branches falling hissing to the ground, writhing in agony at being separated from the main body of the tree. Mistress Heliot backpedalled through the limbs of the whipping tree, none of the Planetree's branches coming close to her, escaping Eleanor's furious, blurring blade.

'No,' croaked Ian, his heart thudding inside his chest. 'Don't leave me, take me with you!'

But the witch didn't hear Ian's pleas, or if she did, she ignored them like the insignificant bug he was.

Eleanor sliced away the last pair of branches trying to strangle her, but the unholy tree had served its purpose as a distraction. A broom hidden behind the tree flew across the air, embedding itself with a loud slap in Mistress Heliot's palm, then the limping witch fell across its length before cackling, urging it to accelerate like a firework across the grass, both broom and rider arcing away from the grass towards the end of the park, her form silhouetted against the yellow lights of nearby apartment blocks and skyscrapers.

Some distant part of Ian's training told him that this was just a trick of magnetic manipulation of the leylines, the broom's wood a sheath with a concealed iron core that could be ridden as fast as a Japanese mag-lev bullet train; but his mind's explanation was overwhelmed by grief ripping apart his heart, his raw shell-shock at being abandoned by the mistress. She was escaping, perhaps forever, swallowed by the moon and the clouds.

'Who ya gonna call?' Eleanor's gaze followed the witch shooting across the sky on her broomstick before she turned her attention to Ian. He moaned and writhed across the grass with the witch's dissipating spell leaving him eating some serious cold turkey. With a loud snick, Eleanor's moly-blade retracted back into the diamond-carbon pen casing acting as her sword's hilt.

Can't the foolish girl see how much agony I'm in, here? The mistress's absence turned the joyous heat of Ian's blood into cold acid. Why didn't Eleanor apologise to the mistress, scream into the cold night sky and beg her to return to both of them? Ian raised his hand to the dark star-spattered sky, drool from his mouth wetting the grass below his cheeks. 'Bring her back, please, return her beauty to us.'

Eleanor shook her head in disgust. 'Worse quarter-date night, *ever.*'

11

~ ANCIENT TONGUES ~

Diane O'Hara handled the monastery records of Benedict of Nursia as delicately as cradling a newborn child, turning the pages on a tabletop with high-definition cameras and bright low-temperature LED lamps, the agent wearing white rubber gloves. The recording gear was in case the ancient vellum disintegrated, leaving them with missing pages - any one of which might contain the Judas Purse's hidden location. Alasdair Colburn hovered behind Diane's shoulder, reading the script so carefully inscribed across the pages in ancient ink. They had been at this task for seven hours, now, and Eleanor was bored enough that she had left twice to get snacks at the Vigil's refectory. Guy Drew stayed inside the temperature controlled document room as though it was a position to be held. Like he was still a G.I. fighting in the second world war. It would take more than the promise of a burger with cheese to make him abandon his post.

'I don't think what we're looking for is here,' said Diane, frustrated.

Guy didn't look pleased with her pessimistic announcement. 'It has to be!'

'What the old man said,' agreed Eleanor. 'I did the whole sacrificial goat act with the Keeper and nearly got capped stealing that hunk of leather and parchment from his Supernatural Jokeshop. Then I nearly get capped *again* by the Keeper's ex-girlfriend. Now you're telling me your monk didn't Dear Diary where he packed the Judas Purse off to?'

'Benedict of Nursia writes about the threat of the Ottoman Empire, about how deeply worried he was that the Ottoman forces would overrun his mountain and loot the Judas Purse,' said Diane. 'But he doesn't mention where he sent the coins to for safe keeping. Only that he would be giving the job of transporting the coins to a recently arrived young English-born monk called Martin de Baskerville, with whom the abbot was deeply impressed when it came to matters of innocence and purity. Benedict needed someone to transport the coins he could rely on. Not a monk who might be tempted to filch them and use their power to crown himself Pope.'

Diane tried to drag Eleanor closer to the records so she could see for herself, but Eleanor shook her hand away. 'Girlfriend, the school I went to didn't teach me to read Latin.' *Didn't teach fencing and I don't remember having private stables out back, either, for that matter.*

'Jeepers, I never learnt Latin at *school*. I taught myself. We have been blessed with so many extra years beyond our three score and ten, it would be a sin to fritter away our time on purely indulgent pursuits.'

No, Eleanor was fairly sure the sin there would be not combining the power of compound interest with her extended lifespan. Ending up as a multi-millionaire through doing nothing more than just staying alive. Of course, given what the Vigil were fighting, just staying alive was definitely going to be the tricky part of that plan. 'Pity they've still got Ian on a drip down in the medical centre. Maybe he'd spot something we're missing in this.'

'Cut the kid some slack. A witch's glamour isn't a flu-jab

and out,' said Guy. 'We're going to keep Agent Holderness under observation until I'm sure your wicked friend with the wand didn't plant any nasty compulsions inside his mind. Like phoning in the location of our base, here, so her witchness can take a second bite of the cherry.'

'This particular cherry intends to shove her severed neck on a very sharp stick if she tries again,' warned Eleanor.

'She's on the grid now,' said Guy. 'We know all the signs to look for in New York, a trail of discarded human husks being the obvious one. Sooner or later she'll get sloppy. Then the Vigil will burn her.' He indicated a strip of torn paper near the end of the leather-bound tome. 'Back to this. Records look like they're missing a few pages in the back. Maybe someone tore them out?'

And the secret of the Judas Purse with them? Eleanor prayed that wasn't the case.

'But not all of the text is written in Latin,' noted Alasdair. His fingers hovered over one of the ancient pages, indicating margins filled with scribbles which looked to Eleanor like they were written in Arabic, as well as intricate doodles drawn in the form of elaborate gilded illuminations.

'I suppose you taught yourself Latin, too, Colburn?' asked Eleanor.

Alasdair smiled, bemused. 'No, I actually *was* taught Latin in prep school. My parents wanted me to become a doctor.'

'They must have been really disappointed when you only graduated engineering from CalTech.'

'You have no idea.' Alasdair bent the lamp to spotlight the ancient tome's margins. 'These side-notes are written in Classical Syriac, better known to us today as Aramaic. That's the language Jesus spoke; perhaps wrote, too - if he was literate.'

Diane sucked in a breath. 'Don't you dare suggest that the Lord our Saviour couldn't read and write.'

'Dude was a carpenter,' said Alasdair, 'in an age when anything resembling a book belonged to the cream of the tenth percent of the one percent. How do you think Jesus learnt to read . . . watching Sesame Street, or a free hall pass to the Library of Alexandria?'

Diane just managed to stop herself rising to respond to the jibe.

'Yeah, well,' said Guy, 'given I'm spending the extra years beyond my three score and ten reading labels of Jack - as in Daniels - tell me that one of you kids also reads Aramaic?'

'Sorry, I reckon I went to your school,' said Eleanor.

Alasdair sighed and nudged Diane over to one side. Eleanor suspected he liked brushing up to Diane like that. For that matter, Eleanor suspected Diane might kind of like it too, not that she would admit it to the heathen engineering graduate. Alasdair examined the margin messages for a couple of minutes before speaking again. 'These read like study notes, the abbot's observations about his official entries in the monastery records. Writing Aramaic was a very rare skill for a monk in those days.'

'It's not exactly like speaking Spanish in California these days, either,' protested Diane.

'You're good at it, though?' Guy asked Alasdair. 'We don't need to run these past some college professor?'

Alasdair shrugged. 'Like Diane said, there's only so much EVE Online you can play before you get bored.'

'Fairly sure I *didn't* say that.'

'The point I'm making,' said Alasdair, 'is that if Benedict

of Nursia wanted to slip in clues as to where the Judas Purse was being shipped away to, writing his clues in Aramaic would have been as good as using an Enigma machine to encode them. The Ottoman invaders threatening Europe had plenty of Latin-speaking slaves working in their galleons. Only the Vatican would have had a handful of scholars fluent in Aramaic.'

'Our boy Benedict was hiding his browser history,' said Eleanor. 'Dirty dog.'

'Sly dog,' corrected Alasdair. 'And one smart puppy.' The young-looking scientist continued examining the monastery records, making even slower going of translating the Aramaic side-gossip than Diane had deciphering the main Latin text.

'What we learning here?' asked Guy after another hour passed.

'That Benedict held a really low opinion of the closest Cardinal to the monastery, and an even lower one of the princeling who ruled the region — "An inbred donkey among a stable of braying idiots" is a fairly good translation. But—' Alasdair held up a finger to halt Guy's next irritable outburst— 'there is one particular note here that doesn't make much sense. Of course, a lot of Aramaic reads as completely obscure by modern standards, but this is really out there.' Alasdair quoted the note in question for the group. 'In the arms of the leopard and by the leopard's side will you find your answer.'

'What the hell does that mean?' growled Guy.

'It's the clue, I'm certain of it.'

'Are you sure you're not just mistranslating it?' probed Eleanor. 'Like, the cardinal can stick his arm up a cat's butt for all the rest of us care?'

'No, the translation's good. I just don't know what it means. It's the only note that lacks context inside the accompanying text.'

'Scan through the margins,' suggested Diane, 'some of the illuminations were of animals, right? Maybe one of the drawings is a leopard? It might be a clue leading to another clue inside the records.'

They leafed carefully through the book again, trying not to damage pages already suffering from the ravages of time. Eleanor saw giraffes and hedgehogs and hounds and foxes among the illuminations, but nothing that resembled a house cat, let alone a leopard.

'Billy-Joe Bleepers,' swore Diane, 'we're just going around in circles here.'

'If a clue is hidden inside the records, it was meant to be found and deciphered by rational minds,' said Alasdair.

Diane banged the table, missing the ancient book's page but not by much. 'You and your rational mind, it's a wonder you and your prep school aristocrats didn't have to turn sideways to walk through the door just to accommodate your big fat egos.'

'And it's a wonder that—'

Eleanor cut Alasdair off mid-retort. '*Aristocrats*, that's it!'

'What? asked Guy.

'How about this,' said Eleanor, 'and bear with me, as my lessons came mostly from the History Channel.' Diane rolled her eyes at that. Eleanor chose to ignore, given she was still relieved not to be witch-food. 'Back in the day, rich families had a way of doing things to make sure money stayed inside the family. First son got the family estate and all the treasure. Second son was packed off into the army. Third son joined the church. Get born female and you were out of luck - off to the marriage factory with you; bring us back some grandkids and make sure you land a rich one with a good title.'

'I think it was the second son who joined the church and third son who joined the army,' said Guy. 'And that was the Europeans. We never went into this crap much over on our side of the pond.'

'But it's not like today, when our priests are mostly dirt-poor immigrants from Brazil, and the money wouldn't be seen dead working outside of a bank job at Goldman Sachs. Back then, getting into a church was a great big deal. A real career option.'

'Your point being . . . ?'

'Church dudes like Benedict and Martin would have come from wealthy families. Aristocrats. And aristocratic families normally ship factory-standard with a coat of *arms*.'

Alasdair's eyes lit up. 'You're a genius!'

Alasdair grabbed his tablet computer and tapped away, accessing the Vigil's mainframe. He turned the screen around to show them when he had located his digital quarry. 'This is the family crest of the de Baskerville family.' Eleanor gazed at a colourful shield on the screen, three green leopards stacked in the right-hand corner of the yellow crest.

'And Martin de Baskerville's name was only mentioned once inside these records.' Diane O'Hara flipped the pages back until she reached the point where the courier's name appeared, a right-hand page, then traced her finger over to the illuminations and scrollwork down the adjacent margin. 'In the arms of the leopard and by the leopard's side will you find your answer.'

'That looks like another crest drawn amongst all the angels and scrollwork,' said Eleanor. 'No Leopards, though.'

'A second coat of arms,' said Alasdair, excitedly.

The illustration was cleverly concealed, the shield's outline formed in the negative by elaborate scroll-work, the crest's contents a scattering of supposedly random detail inside. But once you understood what you were looking for was a coat of arms, this clue practically leapt out from all the random iconography and grabbed Eleanor by the throat. 'I figure this crest belongs to whoever Martin de Baskerville lumbered with the coins.'

'So, let's see what we can see.'

It took both Alasdair and Diane's combined efforts combing the period's historical records before they matched the coat of arms to a name from the time. Pierre of Montague, abbot of a Benedictine monastery outside Zürichsee. What was today Zurich, Switzerland. They also fished images out of the database - a portrait from a miniature locket, Pierre of Montague, as well as a second portrait of Benedict of Nursia, the pair responsible for the Vigil's current search. Both abbots had tonsures, wearing thick grey monk's robes against the lack of central heating in ancient times. Benedict seemed like a typical fat, happy Italian. Eleanor could imagine him smiling behind the counter of a family pizza restaurant, today, beckoning prospective customer in. Pierre, by contrast, possessed a narrow hatchet-face and had been scowling throughout his portrait. *Maybe he'd heard he was being lumbered with guarding the most dangerous prize in Christendom? Wouldn't have made me a happy bunny, either.*

'Man, that's kind of lame,' said Eleanor. 'Benedict of Nursia needs to stash some hot coins out of Italy, so he sneaks the Judas Purse into the hands of a buttoned-up Swiss dude. I guess times haven't changed much.'

'Never travelled to Switzerland with the U.S. army,' said Guy, 'them being neutral and all.'

'Do you think the coins are still inside the monastery there?' asked Eleanor.

'Kid, there's only one way to be sure.'

***

Eleanor returned to her dorm after her latest medical checkup. She'd also used the time to check in with Ian. He was so sheepish about allowing himself to get ambushed by a crazy witch woman, you could practically carve him up and sell his meat as lamb chops. But he was alive and he'd get over it. What had happened to them spoke of the difficulty of even trying to live a normal life, again. Once you had taken a peek behind the curtain and seen that Oz didn't exist, you could never go back to the way things were before. *Glorious ignorance of the secret war.* But Eleanor had other things to worry about. Whatever crazy chemical disco was going on inside her body, Doctor Vargas seemed happy enough that Eleanor wasn't going to explode or worse, yet. *The doctor might have cleared me, but how can I clear myself?* Eleanor thought back to the insane level of power that had risen out of her body to consume the Keeper with fire. Eleanor didn't know if it was a good thing that the beast inside her seemed to be able to lurk undetected by the Vigil's medical staff, or if she was just kicking the can of an inevitable diagnosis down the road. A noise distracted Eleanor and pulled her out of herself. Up ahead in the sub-level seven corridor, Guy Drew stood deep in a heated argument with the Vigil's director while Bex Crawfield seemed to be playing the part of spectator. Eleanor's hackles raised at the sight of the woman. Bex maintained a studied indifference as Eleanor moved to wait beside her.

'Someone asking for a pay rise?' whispered Eleanor.

'You'd have to do some work worthy of the name first, to get a bonus,' Bex sneered.

Eleanor snorted but didn't rise to the jibe. She turned her attention to the argument ahead.

Guy made a short chopping motion with his hand. 'I just don't need someone second-guessing me in the field, boss.'

'This is too important, Guy, you need backup on this next mission.'

'You want to send a backup team to Zurich, fine,' said Guy, 'but at least make sure it's led by someone who can spell the word.'

'Is that *Zurich* or *team*?' asked John, wryly.

'Team, although I doubt she could spell the city, either. Give me a backup if you have to. Just don't make it Dirty Harriet's team!'

'Enough with the name calling, Guy. You nearly lost the monastery records inside the Keeper's shop. We have to recover the Judas Purse before the Reds get a whiff of the coins' location. Two teams in the field, with all the others on standby to assist. I need my two best groups on this. As of now, the Judas Purse is the Vigil's main priority.'

'We came out of the store alive,' protested Guy, 'and we're the ones who traced the coins to Zurich.'

'And that's why you're still the A-team on this mission.' John turned to face Bex Crawfield and passed her a sealed envelope. 'Present this to your commanding officer. You can tell Miss Flanagan and the rest of your team to gear up, you're flying out to Europe on a second plane.'

Bex shot a knowing glance towards Eleanor. 'Yes, *sir*. Tip of the spear, you can rely on us.'

But not rely on us - huh? The nerve! The half-zombie hybrid set off down the corridor, leaving her distinctive perfume trail as well as a thoroughly vexed Eleanor behind.

John fixed Guy with a steely gaze. 'Work it out, agent. Get the job done.'

'Director,' acknowledged Guy, practically through gritted teeth. He took Eleanor by the elbow and as good as dragged her away.

'Who's Dirty Harriet?' asked Eleanor, when the Vigil's director was out of sight.

Guy shook his head in barely suppressed anger. 'Harriet Flanagan. Used to be a cop in LA back in the seventies. Tough as old boots and able to spit nails; which you can understand, given she had to out-cop the other cops as a female officer.'

'And you've got a problem with this agent because she is a female team leader?'

'I've got a problem with Flanagan because she's a *cowboy*. She won't be acting as our backup, out there. She'll be acting as our competition. That's a can of crapola I just don't need.'

Eleanor tried not to wince. *And zombie girl is on Dirty Harriet's team; that figures.* It was bad enough having to train alongside the woman. *Now I'm going to have to rely on her to back me up? I don't think so.* 'If they're cowboys, does that make us the Indians?'

'If we are, we better make out like Apaches at Custer's Last Stand, because no way am I letting another team snatch the Judas Purse out from under my nose.'

'The director won't be happy.'

'John gets our politics done, that's what makes him an effective director. But I was staking vampire Nazis with a commando dagger when he was sunning himself on the deck of a torpedo boat in the Pacific. This is what I do. This job is all I do. So in the words of Ol' Blue Eyes, there's only one way things are going to go in Zurich, and it's damn well going to be my way.'

Guy's sentiments sounded like the kind of thing that Eleanor would blurt out. She couldn't say that it wasn't what she was thinking, either, not with zombie girl working up a hundred new ways to make Eleanor look like an amateur out there. *So why do I feel sick to my stomach? Fear, or something else? I don't want to fail.* Perhaps for the first time in her life, Eleanor had found something that mattered to her. And now that she had, she kind of wished she hadn't.

12

~ YOU DROVE THROUGH IT ~

Eleanor checked the sat-nav app on her phone. She had Diane nestled next to her on the minivan's middle seat. Ian and Alastair on the seats behind, with boss man next to the driver up front inside their taxi. They had just driven straight past the rendezvous point with the backup team, but no-one had commented on their failure to stop. Eleanor tapped Guy's shoulder in the front seat. 'We're not joining up with the others?'

Guy grunted in amusement. 'We could sit on the rendezvous point for a week and not group up with Dirty Harriet and her goon squad. She's got no intention of playing second fiddle to us on this mission. I'm not going to waste my time losing even a minute over her.'

'That's hardly protocol,' said Diane.

'You like the rulebook so much, Agent O'Hara, I'll drop you off at the square for the meet-up. You can buy yourself a Swiss watch and stare at it for a few days while tapping your feet. Flanagan's team haven't been answering their phone since we landed at the airport. We're on our own, here.'

'We're not exactly flying straight arrow, ourselves,' said Ian from the back seat. 'You got our plane fuelled and in the air before I had it fully loaded.'

'Unless you forgot your sword, kid, we've got everything we need right here.'

'Didn't pack your broomstick, though,' said Eleanor. 'Guess we left that behind.'

'That's just a *little* unfair,' complained Ian.

'As unfair as being handed over to Sabrina the Pensioner Witch, for a little sacrificial altar action?'

'How many times am I going to need to apologise for that?'

'Maybe when you're a pensioner, too?' suggested Eleanor.

'Eleanor does have a point,' said Diane. 'It's like the time I was taken to the prom by Blake Tarleton and the dirt-bag spent all evening dancing with Maria Newbern.'

'Was Maria Newbern planning to drug you, tie you up inside a pentagram and suck your life force from you?'

Diane seemed shocked by the suggestion. 'Zoinks, I hope not!'

'Fairly sure we're not swapping like-for-like war stories here, then.'

'There was that time when the nuclear submarine went missing off Argentina, Diane,' said Alasdair, 'and you were possessed by the spirits of —'

'I thought we agreed we would never mention that again!' snapped Diane.

Eleanor raised an eyebrow.

'Female pirate,' whispered Alasdair, 'most lascivious.' He stopped dead when he saw the evil look he was getting from Diane, and just shrugged.

Eleanor joined Alasdair in staring out at the clean streets of Zurich. This was Eleanor's first time outside the U.S., but she couldn't muster much excitement for the novelty of sights sliding past the minivan. Street signage and shop posters in French and occasionally German. Everyone fashionably and expensively dressed, looking like they had a personal trainer on payroll.

It had only been minutes since it stopped raining outside and Zurich's citizens looked well-turned out and wealthy even when damp. Every second car seemed to be a gleaming new Mercedes or high-end BMW. If Switzerland did poor people, the poverty was obviously confined to distant neighbourhoods with very high walls to help encourage them to stay inside.

Their taxi drew to a halt in a modern-looking street and the driver said something in French. Guy Drew replied in French and paid the man off in the local currency, the rest of the team spilling out of the minivan. Eleanor was glad to stretch her legs; a fresh natural breeze, rather than stale plane air followed by a van's air-conditioning.

'Man, this isn't right,' said Guy, gazing up at the modern glass and steel building, windows still wet from the recent downpour. The bright street lamps made silver pools of puddles along the pavement. Where they had arrived didn't look much like a monastery. It was an office block sandwiched between modern buildings on a quiet urban street. 'We should have driven further out into the city's outskirts.' Guy approached the frosted glass doors and rang a buzzer beside the entrance. A moment later the two doors slid apart on electric rollers, revealing a short balding man wearing a red cardigan and corduroy trousers. He was sporting a bushy black beard that would have given Rasputin whisker-envy.

'Is this the Zürichsee Benedictine Order?'

'It is,' replied the man, in perfect German-accented English, a wall of warm air following him out into the pavement.

'You're a monk?'

'Naturally. We are quite modern here these days. I rarely

wear my cassock. This is our seminary, a place of learning,' explained the man. 'I am Father Villiger, master of the academic staff.' He stared quizzically at the party and Eleanor guessed they appeared rather out of place compared to the students who usually arrived to study.

'I was under the impression, father, that the monastery at Zürichsee was a lot older.' Guy gestured up at the tower block. 'You know, stables and cells and herb gardens and the like.'

'Ah, I see,' smiled the priest. '*Tourists*. No, you are thinking of the original monastery. This is the new facility of the Holy Benedictine Order of Zürichsee. A lot less drafty, I would imagine, than the original monastery. Not that I ever taught there, although I did visit once when I was a student.'

'And how can we visit the old monastery?'

'I am afraid that is beyond the ability of even our good creator now,' smiled the priest. 'The oldest sections of the original monastery were badly damaged in a landslide, with the rest of its buildings declared unsafe. Hence our order's unfortunate but necessary relocation. Some said the landslide was God's punishment for allowing protestants to occupy our churches for so many decades. At any rate, the monastery was demolished soon after we deconsecrated it.'

'It doesn't even exist anymore,' said Eleanor, hardly believing their appallingly bad luck.

'If you travelled here by car through the Gotthard Base Tunnel, you probably drove across the site. The new autobahn tarmacked over the ground of our previous site.'

'Sometimes,' snarled Guy, 'progress really grates on my nerves.'

Father Villiger pointed to the hallway beyond. 'The original cross from the vestry is up there on the wall. And we have a stone water trough in our garden of remembrance from the old site which bears the inscription "The righteous man regardeth the life of his beast." Many of the monastery's items of historic interest were sold to The Swiss National Museum . . . you can visit the museum over at Platzspitz park.'

'Sold?' asked Eleanor.

Father Villiger indicated the tower block. 'This is Zurich, my child. You wouldn't believe the price of property here.'

Guy sighed. 'That I surely do believe, seeing how much I was charged for a cold one in the airport.'

'I see your taxi has departed. May I call you another one to take you to the museum? Our seminary must have made it into a new guidebook, you're the second tourist party to visit today.'

'Second?' said Guy, not bothering to hide the deepening suspicion from his voice. 'Was there a mousy-haired woman aged about fifty leading the group, a smoky-hoarse voice like she's been chomping through a few too many Marlboro?'

'Ah, yes, indeed. Are you doing the same tour, perhaps?'

'You might say we're on parallel tracks, father.'

Father Villiger's hand rose to usher them inside and he was about to add something when his words were overwhelmed by the sound of screeching tyres. Three matt-ebony Range Rovers with tinted privacy windows skidded to a halt, one brick-like car blocking the team's rear, two more sliding to an abrupt halt at the team's sides, cutting off any escape route except a hasty retreat through the seminary building. Doors kicked open before Eleanor even had a chance to take a step back. She looked on astonished as they were surrounded by what seemed to be nuns; except these nuns carried moly-blades and machine pistols and looked like they knew how to use them.

'What is the meaning of this?' yapped Father Villiger, as surprised as any of them at being bushwhacked.

One of the nuns jammed a machine gun's barrel under the priest's chin, purring in French-accented English. 'Back into your seminary rooms, Father Hipster. This is Vatican business.'

'You cannot—'

A second nun flourished a silver badge from below her wimple, she spoke in a cut-glass British accent. 'Off you bugger, Rasputin. We're under the Holy See of the Black Pope . . . *Scutum Dei.*'

At the mention of the Black Pope and the covert arm of the Holy Inquisition the priest wilted and retreated, averting his gaze as if he had been caught consorting with devil worshippers. Given how Eleanor was left on the pavement gazing down a forest of blades pointing towards her body, the father was acting wisely.

Eleanor met the eyes of the nun at the front threatening the group. 'What you looking at, Julie Andrews?'

'So much trouble,' hissed the British nun, by way of response.

***

'We're meant to be on the same side here,' protested Guy, secured, like the rest of the team, to his chair by white ties. Whatever these restraints were made of, it wasn't plastic - it was designed to hold humans who had been changed. The team were being interrogated by what Eleanor had come to think of as the Unholy Trinity. Sister Doe was the nun with the French accent. Sister Mee was the Korean-looking woman. Sister Rae was the Brit who resembled a cockney Mary Poppins, if Poppins had been a Ninja Nun wielding a moly-sword rather than a magic umbrella. Eleanor hadn't witnessed their journey to this bare steel-lined interrogation chamber, what with the black hood pulled over her head and all. But she definitely had the impression that the Range Rovers had driven them down into some kind of underground labyrinth, lower and lower, sharp turns with the sound of the cars' engines echoing from concrete. A hidden complex accessed via an underground car park, maybe? Sister Rae paced down the ranks of bound Vigil agents, swishing her sword in windmill circles like a jailer on the cell block twirling her truncheon. Eleanor reckoned this British thug suffered from withdrawal symptoms if she didn't get to decapitate a creature of the darkness every few days or so. Sadly for the Vigil team, she seemed to be on a vampire-killing diet at the moment and was itching to work her captives over to balance the books for God's greater glory.

'You know the terms of the pact,' said Sister Doe. 'The Vigil guards the new world, Scutum Dei polices the old world.'

'We didn't exactly have a chance to fill out the paperwork and arrange a chaperon for this dance,' said Guy. 'And every minute you hold us here is a minute where—'

'Shhhh,' urged Sister Mee, crouching by Guy's side. 'This phantom artifact you claim to be chasing has been lost for millennia. Do you think just because the great Americans send their Vigil enforcers to trespass on the Black Pope's domain, there is a sudden urgency in the air? Oh, the Americans are here, everyone must run around and do as they order. That is not the way things work inside Europe.'

'How does it work over here?' asked Eleanor, trying to rock her way free of her bonds, sadly without loosening them a millimetre. 'You waste our time while the Reds grab the Judas Purse, then you slink off back to your secret Pope and blame the Americans for the end of the world? That works for you, does it?'

Sister Doe tutted. 'You, girl, are so green I can still smell the sweat of the antidote on your skin. You've recently dropped out of the apple tree and know nothing. Scutum Dei's disciples have held the darkness at bay for a thousand and a half years; and that we have achieved by following the Shield of God's protocols and teachings. You Vigil agents are like drunk teenagers running riot around your first party. You believe you are invincible, even as you climb behind the wheel of your father's car to steal it, recklessly steering it off a cliff.'

Sister Rae raised her blade under Eleanor's throat. 'Do you feel invincible right now.'

'No, I feel kind of peeved. What do they teach you on this side of the pond? How to fill out Vatican paperwork in triplicate? We're talking the vampire apocalypse, and you want to arrange our official entry visas?'

'That *green* girl,' protested Ian, 'took on the Keeper inside the Old Paradise Shop and sent him straight back to hell.'

'Only a fool bargains with demons in the first place,' retorted Sister Mee.

'Wasn't much of a bargain for the old devil,' said Eleanor. 'I turned his shelves into a pyre, before pushing him into the bonfire.'

Sister Doe delivered her verdict. 'Young. Foolhardy. Lucky. None of which are characteristics that particularly endear you to me.'

'They should be escorted back to the airport and deported to the Americas,' said Sister Mee.

Sister Rae picked up a syringe of truth serum from a steel tray and flicked the needle. 'But first, we make sure they're not lying about their mission here.'

'You're going to need to pray up a miracle, then,' said Guy. 'We're like you . . . we've all been snacks for the sidhe antiqua, and we've all been pulled back from the darkness. You can shoot us full of as much Sodium Pentothal as you've got now and it will only give us a headache.'

'Don't worry, I shall offer you trial by ordeal in holy water, instead. Unless you've been bitten by a sharkman and possess gills, filling your lungs with holy water will loosen your tongue.'

Eleanor fixed the crazed nun with a contemptuous glance. 'Ordeal by water only works on witches. And I'm guessing it was a witch that tried to suck the life force out of you and left you as Sister Bunny-Boiler. . .'

Sister Rae moved to strike Eleanor, but Sister Mee held her back.

'Good nun, bad nun,' laughed Eleanor. 'Give me a break.'

'Certainly, pick an arm, Yankee-Doodle,' threatened the Brit.

'Let *me* go out on a limb here,' said Guy. 'I'm guessing the fact you knew to pick us up from the new monastery building in Zurich was down to an anonymous tip. And let me tell you, the person who phoned the Vatican Hot Line is playing you for a fool.'

Eleanor groaned, yanking against her arm restraints. *Of course, Dirty Harriet's team.* And Eleanor just bet ol' zombie girl wheedled the rival team leader to be the one to drop the call, taking Eleanor and her friends out of the game.

'Jinkies!' cried Diane. 'This isn't helping anyone. Can't we all try to remember who our real enemy is?'

'When you fight a war in the shadows, the enemy is the shadows. And even you newly come people cast them,' purred Sister Doe. She sounded more like a sensual perfume advert than some religious fanatic assassin for the inquisition, but looks - and voices - could sadly be deceiving.

'Therefore, if anyone is in Christ, he is a new creation; the old has gone, the new has come,' quoted Diane.

'Corinthians 5:17, 'said Sister Doe, approvingly. 'You might almost make the cut as a novitiate in the holy orders of Scutum Dei.'

Sister Rae moved behind Diane's chair, weighing her sword in her hand. 'And speaking of cuts . . .'

'Why are you really here in Europe?' demanded Sister Mee.

'Lost Ark of the Covenant,' called Eleanor. 'We're following some guy with a whip and a fedora.'

'I have had my fill of your prattle,' said Sister Mee. She indicated Diane. 'Let the agent who quotes so well from the Bible face the holy water first. The truth may be teased easier out of her lips.'

'No!' yelled Alasdair as they yanked Diane, still tied to her chair, over towards a metal tank filled with liquid.

'Your last chance,' said Sister Mee. 'Why are you in Switzerland? Why have you violated the pact? And do not tell me your children's tales.'

'You call yourself nuns?' laughed Eleanor. 'You've got a whole book full of kiddie tales to fall back on.'

Sister Rae stamped towards Eleanor's chair, dragging Eleanor across the room to face the tank as well.

'That is what the green agent wants you to do,' warned Sister Doe. 'She blasphemes to provoke you and spare her friend the trial.'

'Well, her gobby lip's worked a charm,' said Sister Rae. 'And I've got enough holy water for them all to take a dunking.'

'We should have gone to Geneva instead,' said Guy. 'I hear they've got some kind of convention there. Perhaps you've heard of it?'

'This is what we have for you inside Zurich, Yankee-Doodle,' said Sister Rae, tilting Eleanor's chair into the tank and submerging her prisoner's face. Freezing water hit Eleanor like a freight train; she tried to resist the cruel shock of it, keep the air inside her cheeks. Chunks of ice cut against her skin. She failed to keep her lips closed and gagged on water, flowing inside, drowning her, clawing at her throat.

The maniacal nun lifted Eleanor's head, spluttering and coughing, out of the water. 'Why are you really in Switzerland?'

Eleanor spat freezing water out of her rasping throat. 'Cuckoo clock. Need one for my bedroom.'

'You don't need a clock. I'll tell you what time it is, Yankee-Doodle - time to tell us everything we want to know.'

'Let her go!' shouted Ian. 'She doesn't know anything.'

'Then you shall tell me and your colleague's ordeal will end.'

'Lady, we can't tell you what we don't know,' called Guy. 'We're here for the Judas Purse. That's the truth.'

'Maybe the coins are hidden at the bottom of our tank? Let's find out!' Sister Rae shoved Eleanor's face back under the water. If anything it was worse the second time, now she knew what was coming. Iced water cut at Eleanor with its terrible cold heat. She desperately held onto the furnace inside her chest without opening her mouth, when releasing her breath would have been the most natural reaction in the world. Eleanor gagged onto the burning air trapped inside her lungs for an eternity before she was removed again. Her breath escaped like an explosion, heaving for oxygen, for a lick of beautiful normal air.

'Tell me!'

'Nobody-expects-the Inquisition,' wheezed Eleanor, between gasps.

'Not bad for someone newly arrived to the change, Yankee-Doodle,' said Sister Rae. 'At first glance, I thought just dropping a damp cloth across your silly little face and pouring water on it would have you singing for us. Now, how about your friend over there? Let's give your ginger a turn and see how you like watching—'

'Enough!' boomed a disembodied voice. Eleanor shook her dripping head, clearing her eyes and traced the sound back to a speaker she hadn't noticed before, the box still vibrating in the corner of the interrogation room. One side of the metal-lined room seemed to fog, turning from steel to glass. That was some neat treat of weirded-out materials science; either that or an even freakier act of sorcery. Eleanor didn't know which of those two options would comfort her more right now. On the other side of the glass loomed a tall figure in heavy crimson robes, his face covered by a silver mask which twisted helmet-like into the shape of a mitre over his skull. The visor's features clearly weren't meant to comfort Eleanor, either; like a cross between a samurai mask and a leering gargoyle's face stamped in silver.

The three nuns did some kind of crazy balletic courtesy towards the figure, falling to one knee in front of the window.

'Cardinal Netchelovek,' stammered Sister Doe. 'We did not know your eminence had arrived in the country.'

'I shall ensure my office sends my diary ahead for your approval next time,' said the voice, dripping in sarcasm.

'Isn't that just great,' coughed Eleanor. 'So, now we get to be questioned by Doctor Doom as well.'

'Silence,' hissed Sister Mee. 'All cardinals of Scutum Dei wear the mask. Silver is a holy metal, accursed by the enemy, which burns at their forsaken souls. It a symbol of purity, constancy and fidelity to the cause of light.'

'Pearls before swine, sister,' said the cardinal, 'or perhaps salted fries scattered as litter before Americans. You waste your breath with these heathens travelled across the water.'

Guy grinned in his chair, as though the man in the silver mask's arrival was a good thing for them. 'I know exactly who you are, Cardinal Netchelovek. And the fact you're here at all means you can cut your jawing and order your three stooges to cut my team loose. We've got a man's job to do in this town.'

Sister Doe glanced at the glass viewing portal for confirmation, looking as pained as if she had just lost the Calvin Klein commercial's voice-over. 'Your eminence . . . ?'

'His Holiness in Rome had received a visitation from the Archangel Saraqael,' growled the cardinal, 'blessed on high be Heaven's messengers.'

I wonder what poor sod got burnt to a crisp delivering that particular God-mail? mused Eleanor, still shivering from her exposure to the tank. 'How come you get to hear from a hoighty toighty archangel and we only get some winged prison-visitor called Zadkiel? Is that like a Pope's-eyes-only-thing?'

Cardinal Netchelovek ignored her jibes. 'The threads which have hidden the Judas Purse for so long from the world are being unravelled. We are to follow them. And as these threads run across the wide breadth of God's earth, so we must cooperate with the Vigil in this holy mission. This is now the will of the Lord, as it is also the will of His Holiness inside the Vatican.'

'And you don't certainly want to go against either of *those* two,' said Eleanor.

The cardinal's fierce silver features shook from side to side in annoyance. 'And He tests us. May you rise to meet the shadows' test, sisters, and do not be surprised at the fiery trial when it comes upon you to test you.' A priest entered the room and moved across to a table by the side of the chamber, a couple of soldiers dressed as Swiss Guards also entering to deposit sacraments on the white cloth. The nuns lined up dutifully to drink from the silver goblets, take a wafer and hear the priest's benedictions. To Eleanor's eyes, it seemed a strangely formal ritual for this dark place. *But what do I know?*

Guy Drew stood up from the chair, rubbing circulation back into his arms after Sister Rae had sliced away his restraints. From the expression on her face, it looked like the British nun was having her spleen removed without anesthetic just by freeing the Vigil agents. 'Need our weapons and comms back, lady. Jump to it. And if you own some wheels that don't make us look like a pimp convoy rolling out from the Azerbaijan Embassy, that'll be just peachy.'

'And I'll take a towel and a mug of hot chocolate,' called Eleanor. 'Two sugars.'

Cardinal Netchelovek's retreating voice muttered from the speaker, even as the wall port shimmered from glass back to metal cladding. 'I swear, we might as well be working with Herman Munster and his family.'

***

One of the pair of demi-gogs watching on the roof ducked back down. He slipped the binoculars away as a convoy of vehicles left the underground car park, their headlights breaking the night with bright beams. The demi-gog pairing was a male and a female, able to move through the city of Zurich posing as a harmless human couple where necessary. Of course, as the bloody mess of the vagrant scattered behind them across their rooftop attested to, harmless they were most definitely *not*.

'Our prey is on the move again,' said the male demi-gog.

'You are certain the Vigil agents are inside the vehicles?'

The male demi-gog checked his phone, a red pulsing dot rolling across the interactive map. 'It is as the Lady Sophia said, a tracker placed among the group by one of their own debasements.'

'I am glad we won't have to get close enough to track them by scent,' admitted the female demi-gog. 'The priests and nuns of the false prophet work to turn us into the hunted, we who should only ever be the hunters.'

'Their filthy unnatural order is coming to an end,' smiled

the man-thing, clicking his fangs. 'And we shall be there at their downfall. For a feasting unlike any other that has gone before.'

'Good times,' said the woman-thing.

'Yes, the best of times. Let our prey lead us to their own doom for the glory of the lady.'

The male demi-gog left the rest unsaid. That should they succeed here tonight, Lady Sophia would undoubtedly elevate her most loyal servants with the status of the true, final conversion; becoming a full vampire, elevation to perfection and paradise eternal.

Both of them turned hungrily to move across the rooftops, leaping like wild animals, tracking the cars below.

13

~ MUSEUM OF THE DAMNED ~

Eleanor reached the National Museum in the middle of Zurich's Old City District, their miniature convoy crossing a bridge to reach the building, swerving around the back to stop inside the staff car-park. She stepped out to find an impressive three storey Disney-style chateau complete with towers and courts, sandwiched in its own gardens on a long finger of island between the rivers Sihl and Limmat. It was deserted and late at night now; the last of the tourist boats docking close by at a river pier. Eleanor overheard the sounds of families dispersing back to expensive hotels, voices drifting across the slightly creepy deserted gardens as insects danced in the sodium glare of spotlights scattered around the grounds. With the museum closed, the Black Pope's nuns had needed to rouse a museum director to key them through the staff entrance around the back. A balding, overweight man, the fussy official didn't seem best pleased with being coerced into providing an after-hours tour. Eleanor tried to tune out his whining high-pitched complaints while she waited. *Hey, pal, just count yourself lucky you weren't water-boarded by these religious maniacs to get you on their side.* Long, crimson banner-like flags fluttered in the cold breeze, marked towards the bottom with a white Swiss cross.

'We 'ave excellent security,' said the official, in French-accented English. 'We are ze *National* Museum. No thieves 'ave breached our security in sixty years.' He stared suspiciously again at Guy's team and Eleanor guessed he was having trouble placing them as part of the FBI's Art Theft Unit. Not surprising given the Vigil agents had come into the country dressed as tourists with nary a dark suit between them. 'And, with respect to these Americans' intelligence, ze items from the Benedictine Order are of no great financial value - not when we 'ave ze Erstfeld treasure 'ere, Celtic gold jewellery worth millions.'

'What we're looking for will be in your coin cabinets, Director Goepfert,' said Sister Mee. 'Roman coins.'

'So you say,' tutted the official, swiping his security card through a reader and then keying in a combination to unlock the door. They entered a corridor hung with posters from visiting exhibitions, decades old, lights activating around the group on a motion sensor. Doors led off the corridor to private offices, lecture rooms and a canteen for back-office staff, all dark and deserted. Springing the staff door had obviously triggered a silent alarm, as three security guards turned up in a hall at the other end, blue-uniformed with double pistol holsters on their polished white belts, one for a taser gun, the other holding a snub but deadly effective SIG Sauer SP 2009 automatic pistol.

Director Goepfert spoke to the three large guards in whispered tones, the men glancing at the Americans and nuns in irritation at the mere suggestion that a major theft might be about to go down on their watch. The guards stalked off tutting, small figures under the elaborately arched cathedral-like ceiling, one of the men talking into a radio mike on the lapel of his uniform, hopefully telling the rest of the National Museum's security detail to be on high alert for intruders.

'Come,' whined Goepfert, 'I will take you to ze coins.'

Director Goepfert escorted the Americans and nuns through empty halls and past glass cabinets filled with elaborately engraved silver suits of armour, military drinking horns and flintlock rifles slanted upright like letter X's against wooden pegs, then up a twisting marble staircase and onto the second floor. This led to a hall holding the coins.

The official halted, gasping in horror as he saw the carefully sliced out glass circles in his coin cabinets. 'How can this be? No alarms 'ave been triggered! Someone 'as deactivated ze museum's entire security system. Not possible!'

All too possible. Eleanor grimaced, wondering whether it was the Reds or Dirty Harriet's team who had beaten them to the punch. There was a slight lingering scent of Chanel, which suggested that either the last tourists in the room shared zombie girl's hygiene preferences, or Dirty Harriet and friends had indeed been busy here earlier.

'Focus, director,' insisted Sister Mee. 'Which coins are missing from the cabinets? How many have been taken?'

The director stalked along the cabinets, dropping his thick cheeks close to the glass and fiddling with a pair of reading glasses he'd produced from inside his tweed jacket. 'Why - but nothing 'as been taken? Ze thieves 'ave reached inside and moved ze coins around, inspecting them, but nothing 'as been stolen?'

'The coins were never here,' hissed Guy.

'What else do you have on display from the old monastery?' demanded Sister Mee.

'Paintings, pottery, an 'andful of statues and icons,' said Goepfert, obviously distracted by thoughts of who was going to carry the can for this shocking breach of security. 'They are scattered throughout ze museum.'

'It's possible the Judas Purse was hidden in something else - the statues and pottery would be a good start,' said Diane.

Guy ran to the wall and grabbed a handful of brochures containing maps of the museum, passing them around the group. 'We need to split up and work fast. The thieves could still be here robbing the joint.' Guy carefully watched the director circle where the monastery's items were to be found on the map, then quickly allocated potential targets between the group. Eleanor could see the nuns bridling at the no-nonsense way in which Guy took immediate command, but they were under orders from their cardinal to cooperate, and had little choice but to fall in line with his plan. Goepfert picked up a staff phone in the wall and dialled through to the museum's security desk, ordering them in quavering tones to lock down the place. Nobody in and nobody out. A wise move, but he didn't understand that if the thieves were Reds, the intruders might be able to face-shift to mimic the guards.

Eleanor found herself allocated to the same search team as Ian - not so bad - but also with the British Bunny-Boiler, Sister Rae, on Team Lythe - which frankly sucked. As did the fact Team Lythe was given the main picture gallery and its anterooms to investigate. *Not going to be much chance of finding anything there.*

'If the Reds are here before us, it's not so much cat-burglars, as *bat*-burglars,' said Eleanor, racing alongside the other two.

'Save me from such terrible *pun*-nishment,' said Ian.

Sister Rae didn't seem much pleased by the banter. She scowled at the two Vigil agents, reaching under her robes and drawing out a wooden cross.

'You going to pray for my soul, or maybe try to give me another ice bath?' asked Eleanor.

The nun raised the cross, triggering its moly-blade and converting the cross into the hilt of a sword. 'Pray for the souls of those who would steal the Judas Purse for the darkness, Yankee-Doodle. They'll bloody need it.'

Eleanor lifted out her Parker fountain pen and triggered her own blade. 'I think you'll find this is mightier . . .'

'Amateurs,' muttered the nun.

Eleanor kept jogging towards the picture gallery. 'So, where the hell did they drag you in from?'

'You got it right first time . . . hell,' said Sister Rae. 'Or in my case, Bronzefield. That's where I got the bite and the cure, both.'

'Is that a town in Britain?' asked Ian.

'HMP, love,' said the sister, 'as in Her Majesty's Prison.'

'I probably shouldn't ask what you were in for before you found God,' said Eleanor.

'I didn't find God, Yankee-Doodle, God found me,' said the sister. 'Bleeding out on the floor of a high-security wing and one-tenth of the way to becoming a vampire's demi-gog slave. And I've done a lot worst in the Black Pope's name since I got out; though, to be fair, not to anything particularly human.'

'Queen decided to release you, then?'

'Yeah, in a body bag, same as the Count of bleeding Monte Cristo. Didn't inherit no pirate treasure, though. Just an FN SCAR-light 45mm, a sniper's laser sight, and a moly-blade, with the chance to slice the heads off the same buggers that ruined my life.'

Eleanor reckoned her life had probably been a lost cause before she'd ended up on the Reds' dinner menu. *We share that much in common, at any rate.*

Sister Rae grunted in bitter amusement. 'Alarms off inside the National Museum? Back in the day, I would have nicked half this stuff, had it right away.'

'And now?' asked Ian.

It was eerie the way lights came on as the three of them jogged through the empty, echoing halls. Eleanor tried not to let it get to her. A night at the museum was nothing compared to being hunted by a centuries-old serial killing witch during a night at an open-air cinema. She and Ian had survived that. *Has to count for something.*

'Living it large . . . what's the point? They say revenge is sweet, and I've got the mother of a sweet tooth for it. Don't reckon that the picture gallery is going to provide me with a taste of it tonight, though. Can't hide coins in the frame of an oil painting, can you?'

The same thought had occurred to Eleanor. When it came to searching the museum, the gallery was definitely the booby prize. Did that mean Guy was still uncertain of Ian's loyalties after his encounter with the witch? Or maybe it was Eleanor who was still in the doghouse. How much did Guy trust Eleanor given she'd survived the Keeper's clutches with only her unlikely story about how she'd managed to escape the demon?

Eleanor sniffed the air. No scent of anything non-human that she could detect, just the familiar presence of the nuns and the rest of their group fanning out through the museum, as well as the guards who had stopped them at the back of the place. Were they too late, or had the rival team from the Vigil muscled in a lot earlier?

'You're a vamp survivor, right?' growled the sister.

Eleanor nodded. 'Yes.'

'Enough with the snuffling, then. Bleeding werewolf survivors always did get on my wick - hairy mugs.'

'Would that be either Sister Mee or Sister Doe?'

'Nah. Mee was mauled by a pack of Reds, too. Local nurse helping a frontline MASH unit during the Korean blowup. Sister Doe was bitten by the vamps while working as a spy for the Section Administrative Spécialisée during the Algerian fight for independence. Vampires always did enjoy feeding during a good war - or a bad one, depending on your take on matters. Easy to hide your human snack habit when thousands are pegging it each day.'

'There a big problem with the Reds in Switzerland?' asked Ian.

'We're not here for the Reds,' said Sister Rae. 'We're here to trace and seize their dosh. All those secret bank accounts and sly private bankers willing to look the other way. Takes a vault full of readies to run the Reds' nasty little networks - a lot easier to bribe prison guard screws and care-home managers to hand over human snacks if you're rolling in readies.'

Eleanor was surprised. 'You're an *accountant*?'

Sister Rae gave her moly-blade an experimental swish in the air. 'Let's just say I *also* count.'

They reached the gallery by passing through an art-filled museum shop with shelves heaving full of illustrated books, prints, reference works, catalogues and just about everything anyone needed to know about the long, glorious and frankly slightly tedious history of Swiss art. The gallery was a connected maze of modern windowless rooms hung with ancient paintings, walls painted a tasteful dark green, the oil paintings displayed in identical expensive gold frames, occasionally a Greek-style statue standing on a plinth in the middle of a room. Large silver-grey marble floor tiles made their shoes click like tap-dancers as they hustled through. Place even smelt of *luxury* and *expensive*, as though the visitors were expected to leave bids for these no-doubt priceless paintings. *Damn, and I left all my credit cards in my Men-in-Black suit back in New York.* They moved quickly to the room circled by Director Goepfert. At first, Eleanor couldn't locate the monastery paintings, but then she spotted the wall behind her held dozens of smaller oil works, and the plastic information pedestal in front of the frames contained the words "Benedictine de Zürichsee" in its text. She retracted her moly-blade and tucked the pen safely away, as did the nun. With the museum's alarms killed by whoever had beaten them here, it was easy work to lift each painting off the wall, weigh it their hands, trying to get a feel for any hidden coins in the artwork.

'This is a right old goose chase,' complained Sister Rae after examining her third painting. 'These aren't even the original frames. See, they're identical to the frames on the modern art in the last room. If the Judas Purse was ever hidden inside one of the original frames, it probably ended up in the museum art restorer's workshop bins before being chucked out and crushed inside a garbage truck.'

'It would be difficult to conceal the coins behind the canvas,' said Eleanor. 'Even if you fitted on a false back, anyone handling the paintings would quickly realise the canvas weighed too much, find the coins and strip them out.'

'Be a right spectacle if someone tried to do that during opening hours. The rent-a-uniforms downstairs would have their tasers out faster than the babysitter's boyfriend when the car pulls up.'

A right spectacle - of course! Eleanor tapped the frames of her glasses. 'These are good for multi-spectrum imaging, right?'

'Of course,' said Ian, slapping his forehead.

Sister Rae didn't appear as impressed. 'X-ray specs? What, you haven't got contact lenses able to track a hot vampire? I thought you yanks in the Vigil were all 21st century on your side of the pond?'

'These are more than just infrared heat spotters,' said Ian. 'Ours lens combine battlefield networking, command and control functions and —'

'You're starting to sound like Alasdair,' said Eleanor, adjusting her lens view, the image of the paintings on the wall dropping from mid-infrared through to ultraviolet and then into the soft X-ray range. All the imperfections on the canvas shifted along with the wavelengths of the electromagnetic spectrum, showing where a few canvases had been scraped and then reused for new paintings. Nothing thrown away in the old days, not even a used surplus canvas. One of the paintings practically jumped off the wall and did a ballet for Eleanor under closer examination. She switched her lens view back to daylight, lifting the frame off the wall. There was something about the particular oil painting that nagged at her, but what could it be? Eleanor inspected the small plate containing the painting's name. "The Miracle of the Corn." Depicted on canvas, a line of foot soldiers wearing Roman-style armour questioned a pair of farmers, one peasant pointing to the right down the road, the other clutching a donkey's bridle. A few soldiers picked fruit from a nearby tree, seemingly bored with their mission. Oddly, the two farmers had been painted with halos, like they were some kind of saints for growing the crops swaying behind them.

Ian switched his glasses back to standard light, too. 'You found something?'

'I think so.'

'That scene's lifted from the Bible,' said Sister Rae. 'This is Joseph and Mary's flight from Bethlehem to Egypt with the baby Jesus. King Herod's goon squad were about to catch up with the Christ clan to give them the chop, but the crop planted by a group of farmers grew from seedlings to their full height in a few minutes, allowing the family to shelter and hide inside the fields. Then, the royal hit squad were distracted by a date palm tree bending down to give them lunch. So they ate, declared "Mission Accomplished", and sodded off back to Bethlehem.'

So, that makes sense. Eleanor saw a worried female face - presumably Mary's peeking through the corn. But Eleanor realised that Mary's weren't the features she was most interested in on the canvas. 'Maybe the birds in the trees started singing "they went that-a-way", too?' said Eleanor. 'But that's not what's odd about this.' She tapped the pair of peasants sweet-talking the pursuing soldiers while pointing down the road. 'I recognise these two farmers from our records back in archives. Same faces as on the portraits of Pierre of Montague and Benedict of Nursia.'

'Why you're right!' exclaimed Ian, squinting closer. 'It's the two abbots! But I'm not seeing any coins inside the frame or canvas?'

'Thanks for the vote of confidence, doofus,' said Eleanor. 'There're no coins hiding here, but there's definitely something oblong-shaped in the middle of the canvas which doesn't look like it belongs.' She slid out the frame's modern backing and ran her fingers along the canvas, pushing gently at its centre where she had spotted the anomaly. 'I think this canvas is double lined. There's a letter or document slotted inside it.'

'That's no coincidence,' said Sister Rae. 'Not in a painting of something precious being sneaked to safety, surrounded by enemies, with the mugs of the same two jokers who were charged with keeping the Judas Purse safe.'

Eleanor returned the protective backing panel to its frame. 'Certainly not going to open it here. We'll need a clean room, or as old as this document is, it'll just disintegrate in our hands.'

Sister Rae snorted happily. 'So I get to nick something after all! Beautiful. If word had got back to the old crew that I'd been inside the National Museum - alarms dead - and hadn't come away with at least a few baubles, I'd have my reputation ruined.'

'Given your death was faked,' said Ian, 'I suspect they'd be more surprised you were still alive and had hardly aged a year .'

'Yeah, there is that, I suppose.'

Eleanor tucked the painting under her arm. Then she, Ian and the nun made off for the pottery rooms, where Guy and the others were no doubt damaging dozens of priceless artifacts trying to discover the Judas Purse's hiding place. She had called it right. When they arrived in the big ceramics hall on the ground floor, Diane was practically holding a moly-blade to Director Goepfert's throat while the others ransacked the exhibits, trying to locate the missing coins.

'No, no,' wailed Goepfert, 'this is vandalism of ze worse sort. Stop, stop!'

'Never could save the world without breaking a few eggs,' said Guy, rattling a vase that looked more oriental than European.

'You are destroying ze world of Swiss archaeology,' pleaded the director.

Eleanor noticed the floor in the middle of the hall lay broken, marble tiles lifted away, dust and mud all over the floor, with a dark hole and a vertical drop past dirt and stone.

Sister Rae pointed out a series of domed objects resembling miniature heaters dotted around the building work; oddly, they sat on rubber wheels, as though they were remote controlled. 'Hack the security systems via broadband first, then bish-bosh. That's how the thieves bypassed the goons inside the museum's control room. Sonic sound wall, like in a posh nightclub's chill-out zone. Slipped those up and out through a small hole, then your tea-leaves could have dynamited half the floor out and nobody would have heard a thing. A proper nice job.'

Eleanor bent down and sniffed near the floor. Yes, there was a definite trail of expensive perfume here. One older, weaker trail when zombie girl first emerged, then a second fresher trail on the way back. Dirty Harriet and the supposedly backup Vigil team had already broken in and broken out. Eleanor hugged the painting closer to her . . . unlike her, *they* had left empty handed. A rank stink rose through the hole and Eleanor realised their competitors hadn't tunnelled in very far. They'd travelled most of the way using Zurich's sewer system, storm drains attached to the two rivers outside.

Eleanor approached Guy. He was holding the vase upside down and vigorously shaking it while Goepfert did a good impression of having a mental breakdown on the sidelines.

'The hole was Dirty Harriet's work, boss man. I can smell Bex Crawfield's Chanel calling card all over the tunnel.'

'Tell me something I don't know,' said Guy, obviously disappointed no Roman coins came spilling out of his vase.

'Please, PLEASE,' hissed the director.

Guy shoved the vase at the man, and he grasped it like it was his own infant baby being returned to its cradle. Shaking, he reverentially carried the object back to a glass cabinet - obviously sliced in half with a moly-blade.

'I guessed as much, kid. Reds wouldn't have left the museum security team alive, and those sonic silencers are only used by us and the CIA. And the CIA might be a lot of things, but art collectors . . . not so much.'

Eleanor lifted her prize up just as Alasdair and Sister Doe arrived empty handed from their corner of the museum. 'We took this painting from the monastery collection. Doesn't contain the coins, but there's what looks like a letter concealed inside a double canvas. And see the actual painting . . . look familiar?'

Sister Doe peered over Eleanor's shoulder. 'The Miracle of the Corn.'

'Here's your miracle, sister,' said Guy, tapping the two farmers in the painting. 'Them two is the ugly mugs of Benedict of Nursia and Pierre of Montague. This picture was commissioned by someone who knew about the Judas Purse and how it had arrived in the monastery. Which means whatever is hidden inside here, it likely isn't an archbishop's shopping list.'

Sister Doe ran her finger gently along the top of the oil work. 'This painting's style is imitative of early Constable, so it was created much later than Pierre of Montague's time as abbot. I would say this piece is early eighteenth century. We must take the painting back to the clean room in our base laboratory; image the painting in high definition before we open the canvas up.'

On the words "open it up", Eleanor heard a gasp, and she realised that Director Goepfert had slipped away to the wall where one of the intercom phones hung. He was busy making an SOS call. 'Help! Help! Vandals in ze Ceramic Rooms! Come 'ere urgently!' - followed by a string of urgent pleading in German. Sister Rae was on the official like a she-panther, knocking the director over, but it was too late. He'd already placed his distress call to the security room.

Sister Rae grabbed the phone and said something in German, then looked at the phone confused before holding it out towards Sister Mee, Doe and the Vigil agents. 'Line sounds brown bread - nobody's answering at the other end.'

Guy advanced threateningly on the director. 'How many uniforms in your security detail here?'

'Not possible,' stuttered Goepfert. 'Someone must be there! We 'ave a team of twelve. Always six in ze command room, monitoring ze screens and sensors, with another six on patrol.'

'Yeah, not possible like having all your security systems cut dead,' said Guy. He glanced at Ian. 'Can you sense anything?'

Ian closed his eyes, as though he was thinking deeply. 'There's something moving out there, very faint.'

'How about you?' Guy asked Eleanor.

'I can't pick up any guards nearby, but,' she sniffed uncertainly, 'there's - oh *no*. It's the same stench as Father Kamara Okoro back at the vault!'

'One of our priests?' said Sister Mee.

'A little more conflicted, you could say,' said Guy. 'We have Reds under the bed, ladies and germs.'

Sister Doe lifted up her robes, revealing a small secure-like satellite phone strapped above a pistol, as well as an expensive set of hosiery on a fairly lithe set of legs. She activated the phone and tried dialling out, but was only rewarded by a snake-like hiss. 'They must have a signal jammer in the grounds. What do you want to bet our land lines are cut now, also?'

'That's pretty tooled up for them,' said Alasdair. 'Which means they're prepared and attacking in numbers.'

'We don't wait for the cavalry, we *are* the cavalry,' said Guy. 'Tip of the goddamn spear.'

'We have two companies of Swiss Guards on standby back at our base,' said Sister Mee. 'We just need to call them out here.'

'Jeepers, I can take the phone and sneak beyond the jamming range,' said Diane. 'I'm highest rated in the unit at blanking demi-gog minds. They won't see me.'

Guy shook his head, obviously angry with himself at being outmanoeuvred like this. First by Dirty Harriet, then by the Reds. 'There's going to be at least one Mama Vamp out there, running her pack of little half-suckers. Going to be old bones, too, the value of this prize. She won't be easily fooled.' Guy gazed mournfully at Eleanor's painting. 'Normally I'd be game-on for calling staking time. But if this painting's hiding a map of where the Judas Purse is buried, we need to get it safely into Scutum Dei's hands. That's the mission.'

'I agree,' said Sister Mee. 'The *only* mission. We are all expendable.'

Eleanor sighed. She didn't feel particularly expandable. In

the distance, she heard the click of lights deactivating in halls where creatures were moving. Something was selectively killing the museum's power.

Ian leaned over the broken floor, pointing his torch's beam into the pit. 'It's not a deep drop, we can swing down by hand. But without comms, we can't call up the sewers' plans.'

Eleanor stared into the sewer below, a brown moving stream of sludgy water. 'I can try and follow the other team's trail.'

'You've got to be bleeding kidding me,' said Sister Rae. 'You want us to flee along the Crap Canal? I'd rather try fighting my way past the biters up here.'

'*Die* fighting,' said Sister Mee. 'And we only win if one of us survives to reach the church with the Miracle of the Corn.'

'I think the Reds are surrounding us,' warned Ian.

'Don't have any other choice, now,' said Guy. He indicated the pit. 'We're getting down and dirty.'

***

Sophia clutched the museum guard's head between her fingers, a grip so tight, the prey couldn't escape however hard he thrashed. She ignored smoke and sparks pouring out of the hacked security console where one of the faster guards to react had been driven into the machinery, the man's automatic pistol still dangling from his dead fingers. 'How many people entered the museum after hours?'

'Nine, I think,' stammered the terrified night watchman Sophia had pinned to the floor, 'including the director and the nuns.'

'Nuns,' hissed one of the demi-gog trackers. 'The Shield of God.'

Sophia's eyes narrowed. Yes, Scutum Dei were here, and the fact that they were actively cooperating with the Vigil indicated that everything the Master of Masters believed about the Judas Purse was true. *We are close, very close to seizing the ultimate power.*

'Debasements,' said another demi-gog.

'Churchlings, the Black Pope's debasements.'

'Be quiet you fools,' barked Sophia. 'I need to concentrate. Now, little man, you will think of your visitors, picture them in your mind's eye.' She increased the tension on the museum guard's skull, just to ensure he understood. Absolute silence fell on the security control room; even the disgusting sounds of her nest feeding on the murdered security personnel stopped. Images slid into Sophia's mind from the fear-frozen guard, mist-shrouded by the frailties of human memory: three nuns from Scutum Dei, a group of Vigil agents and the bureaucrat bullied into opening the museum to them. Her cold vampire heart fluttered like a dove caught inside her chest as she recognised the agent leading the Vigil team. *Guy Drew.*

'What is it?' asked Joanna from across the office, immediately sensing something was wrong.

Sophia sighed. 'A very dangerous man. A debasement who has lived for far too long.'

'But will you also not live a long time?'

'Oh, I shall probably live forever,' smiled Sophia, snapping the guard's neck and ignoring the sharp little crack. 'But this enemy is a mortal who is meant for death. Like all debasements, any power he possesses, he has stolen from us. Time, I think, to provide an old man with his end.'

Sophia stood up and nodded towards the two strongest and most reliably obedient members of her nest. 'Secure Joanna, here. Do not let the Vigil scum or the churchlings anywhere near the control room.'

'But I want to come with you!' protested Joanna.

'No,' insisted Sophia. 'It is far too dangerous. These creatures are expert hunters of my kind. They have corrupted our legacy and rejected our gift to mutate into what they are.'

'They will know I am human, then! They will not judge me a threat.'

'Both the Vigil and the churchlings would slay you without blinking. Many are the prey hoping to curry favour with us - such humans are called traitors by the debasements, treated no kinder than vampires or our creations.'

'I am no traitor,' cried Joanna.

'You are true to me, and that is all that matters.'

Sophia knew that Joanna thought her exclusion from the pursuit strange. But she accepted Sophia's reason at face value, even if she might suspect it was not the whole truth of the matter. *Good instincts.*

'I will stay, then. Swear you will take no risks.'

Sophia leant forward and kissed the girl's forehead. 'That I cannot do. I was sent here to risk everything if necessary. The prize is such that I have very little choice in the matter.'

Risk everything. But not Joanna. Never her.

***

Eleanor had badly overestimated her ability to track zombie girl and her pricey perfume habit through the sewers, backtracking the path to freedom the rival Vigil team had followed. There wasn't just a single bad stench down here, there were a thousand to select from, and every time she tried to focus on the sweet musk, something vile and foul swam up from the muddy flow they were wading through, sometimes a little too literally, wrenching her target scent away from her. They stumbled through the tunnels nearly blind, Stygian darkness swallowing them up, a maze of echoes barely broken by their torches' beams. Eleanor wanted to use her spectacle's night vision mode, but Guy had overridden her; telling them to save the few minutes their batteries would last for hand-to-hand combat when the team would need to match the vampires' exceptional night sight. In places the sewers ran as wide as subway tunnels, passing through open chambers with vaulted arches; as though a bored architect had tried creating a cathedral down here, only to realise that - maintenance workers aside - their work would never see a congregation. *No ladders to the surface, though. No manhole covers. Right now, I'd climb out of someone's privy to escape out of here.* At other times, the passages closed down to narrow walkways where the escaping party advanced in tight single-file. She followed the muck's flow as much as their rivals' trail, hoping to find an exit grille they could cut through.

Eleanor had never counted herself as claustrophobic, but there was always a first time, and knee-high in the flow of foreign bankers' excrement and toilet flush seemed as good a time as any. That was when she realised that it wasn't just the fading odour of Dirty Harriet's crew down here with them, but something else. And that *something* was savage, ancient and distinctly unfriendly.

'Company,' warned Eleanor, still clutching the painting tight under her arm. She figured there wouldn't be much point bringing the concealed document back to a clean room if she dunked it in this bemired sludge, first. *Yeah, the Reds have found the break into the sewers. They're probably right at home down here.*

'I was kind of hoping that was my imagination,' said Ian.

'And if wishes were kisses, I'd be Frank Sinatra with the ladies,' said Guy.

'This is madness!' protested Director Goepfert, as out of place wading through the rank brown sewage flow as a bow tie on a tiger. 'How can ze old monastery painting be so valuable, gangs of madmen break into ze museum and try to kill each other for it?'

'When you finally understand the answer to that, you'll be really sorry you asked,' warned Sister Doe.

'Where are ze police?' moaned Goepfert, 'where are my guards?'

Eleanor shivered as she recalled the mass feeding on orphans at an art installation outside New York and reckoned the director was better off not knowing the answer to that question, too.

Guy triggered his moly-blade from its concealed hilt, making Goepfert squeal and flinch in surprise, before recovering; barely. 'What are those things you carry . . . duelling foils?'

'Folding ceramic with a one-micron carbon blade,' said Alasdair, sounding a little too pleased with the scientific achievement.

'Yeah, swords,' said Guy.

'But some of you 'ave pistols! What in ze Lord's name are you going to do 'ere? Challenge ze other thieves to combat inside a filthy sewer?'

'Trust me, director,' said Sister Mee, 'some things are just better in this world with their heads sliced off.'

'That is a not in any way ze Christian sentiment, sister,' moaned the director.

'Oh, you would be surprised from just how on High those sentiments have travelled.'

An echoing howl started to build behind them. Low at first, like a pack of mournful coyotes lost in this rank-smelling Hades, then louder, an organic siren of raw fury bouncing from the crumbling slime-streaked brick walls.

Eleanor fought the urge to glance behind her; doubling her efforts to track the fading perfume trail. 'They really don't believe in surprise attacks, do they?'

'Surprise will be if we get out of this,' said Sister Rae.

Eleanor passed the painting across to Diane, who uncertainly lifted it out of her hands. 'Why me?'

'If you're as good as you say you are . . . one of us needs to be able to sneak out of here with this.'

Guy Drew nodded, approving Eleanor's choice of their final courier. Alasdair seemed relieved, too, and gave Eleanor a grateful look.

Guy stared at the three nuns. 'Any of you ladies able to twist the Reds' mind-tricks back at 'em?'

'I possess that talent,' said Sister Mee. 'But the cardinal placed me in charge of the sisters' safety.'

'Guard the agent,' said Sister Doe. 'You said it yourself, *this* is the mission. We are all expendable.'

Tears welled up on Sister Doe's eyes and for a moment Eleanor thought the Korean nun was going to refuse to leave, but duty and devotion to her mission orders trumped everything else. 'Go with God, sisters.'

'And you, sister,' returned the other two nuns, in unison.

'I do not understand any of this,' whined Goepfert.

'Head off with Agent O'Hara and Sister Mee, director,' said Guy, not unkindly. 'You're going to take your painting to safety and get out of the crap. Us, I reckon we're going to be wading neck-high in the brown stuff while we clean house.'

'I'll pray for you,' Diane told Alasdair.

Alasdair raised his pistol. 'I'll trust in Mr. Smith and Mr. Wesson - that and a strong back left guard with the moly-blade.'

'Such a heathen,' tutted Diane, but Eleanor thought she was having to work harder than usual on the disapproval in her quavering voice.

Eleanor watched the three team members' torch light bob as they fled down the tunnel, rising animalistic sounds swelling as the darkness seemed to grow thicker in the distance.

'The old bones in charge will send in waves of demi-gogs first,' said Guy, lighting a cigar and biting down angrily on it. 'Goddamn cannon fodder. Reds always make a few more of 'em out of prey, for every creature we slay.'

Those left in the rear-guard retreated in an orderly, deliberate fashion. Like Redcoats on a Napoleonic battlefield, holding the line steady for the moment the enemy closed with them. After a minute's retreat, they rounded a bend in the sewer, quickly coming across another corner - the original S-Bend beloved of plumbers. Guy halted the party when they rounded the second corner. 'This is our choke point - as good as anywhere to slow the Reds down.' Guy rummaged around in his camera case, and when Eleanor saw the two objects he produced, she realised his case was more than window dressing for their cover story as tourists.

'Daddy's brought a couple of pineapples to the party,' said Guy, tossing one of the grenades across to Ian.

'White phosphorus munitions,' said Sister Doe. 'I saw those filthy things used in Vietnam.'

Guy snorted. 'Yeah, I forgot you Frenchies lost that gig before we did. These eggs come laid with a patented twist, though. Solid silver fragmentation casing. There are jewellers who'd kill to defuse and melt one of these down. I'll pull the pin and toss mine around the first corner on the Reds' first assault. After that, we'll have a mad minute to open up on what's left standing until we run out of ammo. Then, we fall back to the second corner. Pull the pin on the last pineapple for the second wave. Whatever is left attacking, we poke with our pig-stickers until they stop twitching.' He fixed Eleanor with his grizzled gaze. 'Close your eyes for the blast, kid. White phosphorus will peel your retina off the back of your eyeballs if you're staring at it when it hits. You can only imagine how well that goes down with supernatural night predators.'

'How do you know there'll be so many of them we'll run out of ammo?' asked Eleanor.

It was Sister Doe's turn to snort. 'This really is your first dance, isn't it?'

'Only with the Reds,' said Eleanor, trying to suppress her rising nerves. 'If you don't count getting the bite.'

'Nobody counts getting the bite, Yankee doodle,' said Sister Rae. 'First one is always free.'

'As long as you survive the antidote,' said Alasdair. There was bitterness in his voice. An anger too that she had never expected to hear from him; always so unreasonably humane and level-headed.

'Alasdair was saved by the Vigil along with his twin sister,' Ian whispered from behind Eleanor, knowing her hyped hearing would pick it up. 'She didn't make the transition.'

Eleanor wondered what it would be like to have someone that close in your family - a twin you cared about so much. It was an alien concept in her world. Family was something to be forgotten, to be packed away into a little box marked 'Do not open' and abandoned in the attic of the past. She didn't have long to ponder on what she'd missed.

When the demi-gogs came, it was as though they were screaming a song, a broken bestial hymn that seemed to fill the sewers with a cloying hatred so thick she could hardly breathe. A part of her recognised that this was just a form of sub-sonic assault, intended to paralyse prey with fear. *But I'm not their prey anymore. I'm their hunter.* Guy had already pulled the pin on his grenade, silently mouthing a three-second count, before tossing the evil spherical object around the corner and giving the demi-gogs their chorus. Eleanor closed her eyes. Even with her eyelids tightly shut and the fierce explosion detonating around the corner, the sensation was like snorting raw chilli powder - a three million strength sizzler on the Scoville scale. A supernova flash ground broken glass against her eardrums, and then the team fell around the corner, opening up with their firearms.

While the Vigil team had only arrived with relatively discrete lightweight automatic handguns, the two nuns were packing serious heat - modified Czech Škorpion machine-pistols, drawn from twin leather leg holsters which, frankly, would have looked more in place on strippers. Eleanor fired her pistol alongside Ian like she had been taught, in a police marksman's stance, torch in one hand lighting up the carnage, pistol in the other, squeezing bullets into whatever moved. Demi-gogs leapt from the stinking darkness, still wearing the human clothes their forms had been masquerading inside - their bodies twisted into heavily muscled vulpine shapes, hideously distended jaws and twisted faces, all fangs and feral savagery with eyes like glowing pokers.

Hot cartridges rained down onto the stinking sludge from the two nuns' machine-pistols, bouncing off the tight brick walls, rattling as spent casings fell, making sewage hiss and steam on contact. Boiled sewage didn't smell any better than the raw kind to Eleanor's taste.

'Come on then, you freaks!' yelled Sister Rae, hosing the tunnel with her two weapons. She tore as furiously away at the demi-gogs as if there had been a ninety percent off sale at the World of Ammo store. Sister Doe fired more deliberately, aiming and squeezing off short bursts, giving the demi-gogs time to clamber over the corpses of their fallen brethren, conserving her ammunition to make every volley count.

Eleanor popped an empty clip into the sludge and smoothly slid a second one into her gun. *Draw. Bead. Fire. Repeat.* Ignore the howling wall of supernatural evil advancing, lit by muzzle flash as much as by torch light. She realised her hands were sweating, her pistol bucking violently, each shot deafening her without ear protectors. It was insane carnage down here now, the tunnel a flesh-lined avalanche of demi-gogs, almost impossible to trace her shots back to any individual creature falling and writhing across the sewer floor. Wounded monsters drowning in sewage as their peers clawed and shoved over the dying, trying to fling themselves at their human foe.

'Last clip,' warned Alasdair, his feet in a boxing stance, shooting with his left hand wrapped around his shooting hand for support.

'Hold one bullet back when you holster your pistol,' Ian advised Eleanor. He didn't have to explain who that last bullet was for. Being captured alive by vampires would make the nuns' interrogation room look like a day nursery, Eleanor suspected.

'Time for our second arc-light!' Guy shouted in Ian's direction. 'Ready to fall back and go green.'

Going green meant killing the torches and switching their glasses to night vision mode. It also meant they would be down to their moly-blades. *Down to our pig stickers and bad language.* Eleanor believed the military expression for their predicament and current chances for survival was charmingly known as *Fubar.* She felt a splinter of ice in her heart, a terrible premonition of death, but shook it off.

The handful of seconds it took to retreat and give the demi-gogs an opportunity to swamp forward were the longest Eleanor had ever suffered. Ian's three-second count after tugging the pin away seemed long enough to send out for pizza. His grenade tumbled through their air, the charging horde meeting the second lightning flash with a hideous screech that gave way to whimpering, desperate splashing across the flowing liquid as broken bodies twitched with whatever fleeting life was left in their death-throes. The brief pause in the assault gave Eleanor time to run hot, her blood coursing with a mutated version of what full vampires underwent when they dropped their pretence at humanity. She extended her blade, trying to hold it steady in her quivering hands - a mixture of raw fear and her overclocked metabolism overtaking mortal limits. Her fingers moved to her spectacles, activating its night sight, trembling as she tried to ignore the sound of the next wave incoming. Night vision mode worked by amplifying ambient light. There wasn't much of that inside the sewer, so the computer in Eleanor's specs settled on a half-way setting between ultraviolet and infrared, making crimson lanterns of the enemies' body-heat; each snarling, charging demi-gog a blurred furnace flying at her. *Yeah, thanks for that.*

They stood side by side, thrusting forward in tightly controlled movements like a company of samurai in one of those old movies Eleanor enjoyed so much. *More fun to watch, than experience.* Pity she needed to perish inside a filthy Swiss sewer to discover that for herself. She was going down, but she was going down swinging. Three demi-gogs charged towards Sister Rae. Just as Eleanor swivelled to assist the nun, another three monsters leapt off using the ceiling's purchase to launch over the defenders. Like mutant parkour practitioners, two creatures came down on Alasdair with the last ramming into Eleanor, knocking her hard into the foul thick sludge. It latched onto Eleanor's sword hand with one set of claws, a razor-sharp vice tightening around her flesh, its other fist caught by Eleanor as she stopped it trying to slash her face. The stink of the sewage's foul fluid was nothing compared to the demi-gog's breath. They rolled across the surf of filth, its grey-skinned face so twisted Eleanor could barely tell whether the monster had been male or female before it shed its humanity to assume its true form. Eleanor scarcely registered the other twisting, thrashing defenders fighting for their lives; those in the sewage and those still standing, attempting not to let the line crumple and the horde's seemingly endless numbers overwhelm them. More demi-gogs leapt across the defenders, practically scampering along the roof. *This is like fighting spiders.*

Eleanor's opponent smashed her sword hand against the brick, a burst of pain numbing her grip, the moly-blade left impaled inside the tunnel wall. Disarmed, Eleanor tried to summon the unholy fire she'd found within to incinerate The Keeper. She rolled through the sludge with the monster's sharp white fangs snapping at her, but nothing answered inside, only a damp spark that wouldn't light. Then a splinter of luck in her vicious hand-to-claw melee . . . a demi-gog bounded over their two thrashing bodies, meeting someone's moly-blade, a splatter of gore that went into the monster's face, blinding it. Eleanor used the distraction to head-butt the creature, finding the purchase to flip them both over and push the thing under the river of sewage where it belonged. She yelled in fury, drowning it, bubbles rising from the filth until the demi-gog finally went limp. She staggered to her feet and pulled her blade out of the brick stone wall, King Arthur of the stinking refuse. Ian, Sister Doe and Guy were desperately holding the line against swarming Reds, but it was Sister Rae and Alasdair who were in real trouble, cornered against the tunnel wall and fighting the demi-gogs who had broken past, sword against claw, bodies of the slain piled around them and bobbing in the excrement.

Hacking like a woodsman, no skill or finesse, Eleanor pitched forward and slashed into the monsters' backs, cutting them down from behind. They weren't expecting her, all their frenzied fury focused on the feeding in front of them. Their howls died in their throats, corpses toppling back to join their slain brethren. Alasdair and Sister Rae were left slumped against the brick wall, clothes torn and bloody from hundreds of frenzied claw slashes, trying not to slide down into the rank slush. If Eleanor had counter-attacked a few seconds later, her companions would be meat in the mud. As it was, they were both badly wounded and almost out of the fight - although Sister Rae seemed to just be holding on, using raw hatred and aggression as glue.

'Muppets,' spat Sister Rae, trying to raise her sword.

Eleanor steadied Alasdair. 'You able to retreat down the tunnel, head after Diane, maybe?'

Alasdair slowly shook his head, barely able to keep vertical with the wall as a crutch against his spine.

No, neither of them are fit enough to escape anywhere. Eleanor realised the demi-gog's shrieking rage had diminished. She wobbled over to the three defenders still able to raise their swords. Guy, Ian and Sister Doe had built a low wall out of the mangled attackers. The Reds had retreated back down the tunnel, but they were still there, their mewling and curses like background music to this fight to the death. Eleanor and the others pulled back, rounding the corner to relative safety. Darkness flowed in the tunnel beyond, just outside the ambient light range of her glasses. Eleanor thought she glimpsed the brief form of a woman, painted in orange and red heat. Running that overclocked, she had to be the vampire in charge of this carnage.

'You have finally found your natural habitat, Guy,' came a female voice drifting along the tunnel, as sweet and reasonable as melted honey.

'Hey, you're in here with us,' called Guy. 'Why don't you come forward and I'll put you down in the mud for good.'

Eleanor scraped her moly-blade clean of gore against the wall. 'She knows you? Who the hell is that?'

'Sophie Dornburg, a Red who came up with a mighty novel way of infiltrating NATO's West Berlin headquarters,' growled Guy. 'Back during the closing stages of the Cold War, when the Dracs were still trying to turn the stand-off burning hot, set the USSR and NATO onto each other.'

'I can feel her power from here,' said Sister Doe. 'That demoness is a dangerously old and powerful vampire.'

'Add cunning and as clever as any of them to that list,' warned Guy. 'Every year a little goddamn smarter, and she was probably as sharp as an assassin's stiletto to start with. If the Reds weren't sexist pigs in the round, that creature would probably be running the clans as Empress of All Evil by now.'

The vampire's voice rose from the blackness again, as powerful and foreboding as a coming storm. 'Let me give you your rest like a true old soldier. You deserve it. You would welcome it.'

'Ain't so tired, yet, Sophie. You going to come out of the shadows and dance, or you trying to bore us to death over here? You must have a few expendable idiots left from your nest you can send my way?' Guy reached around the corner and put the last round from his antique Colt .45 into the tunnel towards the voice. A malicious laugh indicated he had missed, followed by moans and pleas for help to their mistress from a handful of wounded demi-gogs left in the choked tunnel.

'Are you bored, Guy? Poor dear. Let me make things more *interesting* for you.'

A scuttling noise grew from the darkness, clacking claws - the kind of noise a gathering sea of rodents made an instant before being released in a torrential flood of black fur towards the team. Eleanor was suddenly struck by an inherited memory from the vampire who had bitten her. Celtic warriors wading towards the vampire Roman woman through thick gorse, murder on their minds. Right up until the moment the Celts were dragged screaming to the dirt, rivers of black rodents under the Roman's control streaming up their blue tattooed limbs. Biting and gnawing while the warriors flayed out uselessly with their spears, war axes and swords. But these latest howls were real, snapping Eleanor back to the stinking tunnel's confines. Wounded demi-gogs screeched as the undulating organic wave of the living weapon flowed across the wounded with only two instructions seared into their simple minds. *Forward. Kill.*

Ian grabbed Sister Rae, supporting her limping weight, backing away as fast as the wounded nun could retreat. Eleanor seized Alasdair and tried to drag him backwards through the sewage. *Damn, never looked this heavy when he was walking around under his own locomotion.* Guy overtook them and seized half the wounded agent's weight. None of the team was going to get further than a couple of feet before the whole party was swamped by a thousand psychotically possessed rodents. Eleanor prayed Diane, Sister Mee and the director had reached safety by now. That her death came with a purpose and meaning attached to it.

'It is time,' said Sister Doe, sheathing her moly-sword, its hilt remade again as a simple wooden cross.

Sister Rae tried grabbing weakly at the French woman's arm as she passed, heading for the wave of rodents. 'No! You have been purchased, and at a price.'

'This is the price, sister,' said Sister Doe, sprinting around the sewer's corner. 'And the cost. À la prochaine!' She vanished, her robes flowing behind her like a torn shadow.

'Down!' yelled Guy, abruptly throwing Eleanor and Alasdair face down into the sludge.

Eleanor was gagging and choking in the acrid liquidised night-soil when a searing blast blistered the top of her head, a deafening shockwave of falling masonry and flying brick fragments ricocheting around the enclosed space. Eleanor lifted herself up, throbbing ears ringing, choking inside a cloud of swirling red dust. She spat and spat, clearing her mouth of the sickening taste, trying not to vomit. The tunnel had collapsed, the sewer's corner remade as a cave-in - tonnes of fallen dirt and stone and collapsed brick supports. Now safely sealed off from the rodents and the Reds, with freedom lurking somewhere ahead of them. The faint teasing promise of a cold breeze hung in the air. 'We - we only had two grenades. . .'

'Sister Doe underwent the last rites back in the interrogation room,' said Guy, leaning groggily against the sewer wall, his face grey with dust and his voice a dry grating croak. 'Wasn't communion wine she drank. That was their prayer of forgiveness for a mortal sin. Liquid explosives, with a trigger chemical inside one of her false teeth.'

Tears clouded Sister Rae's eyes, barely conscious through her pain and wounds. 'No-one bleeding takes us alive. No monster takes us. Not ever. Only the first bite is free.'

Eleanor reached out shakily, touching the mountain of rubble separating her from the monsters on the far side. The rough feel of broken brick enough to convince her that the barrier was real. *Sister Doe sacrificed her life to save ours.* On reflection, Eleanor was grateful it was the Vigil that had first come for her, rather than the Shield of God.

14

~ SOMBRERO TIME ~

Sister Mee led Eleanor, Guy, Ian and Diane to a laboratory inside the church's subterranean complex below Zurich. Alastair and Sister Rae were still inside the base infirmary, being tended to by the best medical expertise money could buy. And in Switzerland, with its exclusive clinics, that expertise ran pretty high level as well as expensive. One thing money couldn't buy, however, was a new skin. Didn't matter how many showers Eleanor took, the stink still seemed to cling to her nostrils. Not just the sewer stench, either. Mangled bodies and their own vaporized dead. Not quite enough Red corpses for Eleanor, though. By the time the military help summoned by Sister Mee arrived at the museum, the attacking vampires had long vanished from the sewers. Absorbed by the very shadows - their signature escape.

'You feeling okay?' Ian asked Eleanor as they walked.

'Still a little shaky on my feet,' Eleanor admitted, fingering the tight bandage around her wrist where she'd been sliced during the battle. It burnt, a cold fire, which the doctor here had assured her was a good thing and nothing to worry about. Not that Eleanor was worrying for herself. Compared to Alasdair and Sister Rae, her wounds were insignificant. As for poor Sister Doe, there wasn't enough of the woman's ashes recoverable to fill a funeral urn. *Yeah, I'm walking tall, me and my luck.*

'It's not from the demi-gogs' scratches,' said Ian. 'Unlike

baseline humans, we're pretty much immune to the bacteria on their claws. It's the come-down after running hot. Same as the Reds. When they drop their chameleon act, their burst of strength is meant to provide a short-term advantage, like lions running down a gazelle. None of us are meant to stay overclocked for extended periods of time.'

'Glad to know we share so much with the vampires.'

'But not really.'

'Yeah, but totally not really.'

Arriving at the lab, Sister Mee carded their way inside. They entered a big room with steel tables stacked with CSI-style equipment and enough scientific instrumentation it was almost a good thing Alasdair was recovering in medical alongside the British nun - he would have had multiple strokes from his excitement, here.

Eleanor glanced curiously around the room. 'So, did the painting itself reveal anything under analysis?'

'Its age from carbon dating,' said Sister Mee. 'Plus a confirmed face-match on the two abbots being worked into the picture as farmers.'

'So, where's the document hidden inside the painting?' asked Guy.

'It's over here,' said Sister Mee, indicating a sealed steel case that resembled a coffin. 'Athanasius,' said the nun, please unseal the hermetic cabinet.'

'Yes, Sister Mee,' replied a disembodied voice.

Eleanor jerked at the sound, watching the lid of the cabinet retract. The room's yellow ceiling lights automatically switched to a crimson glow, as though the party had entered an old-style photographic darkroom. 'What, you church types got the Holy Ghost working for you down here?'

'Athanasius is Scutum Dei's A.I. software avatar,' said the nun.

Eleanor noticed a camera trained on her in the corner of the room and she tapped her iPhone. 'I guess you've got Siri beat.'

'Given that Athanasius runs on a cloud cluster of super-computers that cost over three billion Euros, I should certainly hope so,' said Sister Mee.

'That estimate excludes maintenance costs of four hundred million a year,' added Athanasius, in a fairly transparent attempt at one-upmanship. Or perhaps, in this case it was one-upmachineship.

'I'm a lot cheaper than that,' murmured Guy, '*and* I hunt vampires.'

Eleanor joined the others by the casket, a frisson of shock as she saw the document laid out under the lamp's red light for the first time. Definitely not what she had been expecting. *There's hardly any writing on it at all!* 'It's not a letter at all, it's a . . . musical score!'

'Correct,' agreed Sister Mee. 'The score for a hymn called "Ashes" - a hymn which was banned by the church after being ruled heretical.'

'How can a hymn possibly be considered heretical?' asked Diane. She seemed to be bristling for any argument, now. Had been like that ever since she'd left Alasdair in the infirmary. *Everyone has their own way of coping.* Sister Mee's way seemed to be doubling down on the work that needed doing. The nun had been plugging away at the secrets of the *Miracle of the Corn* like a crazy person.

Sister Mee raised her hands, as though disclaiming responsibility for the church's decision. 'It's chorus repeats: "We rise again from ashes to create ourselves anew." Rome took exception to the hymn, as the church teaches only Christ can create us anew. It was banned almost as soon as it began circulating.'

Eleanor's heart sunk. *So our battle in the sewers was for nothing?* 'Then the score has nada to do with the Judas Purse? Just a banned hymn one of the monks liked listening to - something he wanted to hide from the boss abbot without getting into trouble?'

'That's exactly what the person who hid the score wished the uninformed discovering it to think.' Sister Mee smiled. 'All nature is merely a cipher and a secret writing. The great name and essence of God and his wonders - the very deeds, projects, words, actions, and demeanour of mankind - what are they, for the most part, but a cipher?'

That sounded like a quote which Eleanor couldn't place; but she didn't care, not if this score meant that they were still in the game.

'A code hidden in the music, then?' said Ian, sounding impressed. 'That's very clever. Like modern-day steganography - hiding text inside the one and zeroes of a digital photo's pixels.'

'Clever for a time when few could even read,' said Sister Mee.

'What kind of cipher is it?' Eleanor asked.

'One very much of the age,' said Sister Mee. 'Latin vowels are represented by minims inside the score. Monks often hummed special tunes to identify fellow members of Scutum Dei. Priests also played hymn music within silent orders to pass coded messages between couriers. However, this particular secret is double-encoded; the score's minim code is itself encoded with a book cipher, replacing words in the hymn's hidden text with the location of words from a book.'

'Then we'd have to know which book was being used to actually decipher the message?' said Diane.

Eleanor scratched the side of her nose. This lab was going to give her a cold, she could feel the tickle in her throat. 'Yeah, what she said.'

Sister Mee indicated the stolen painting. 'How about the Bible's Gospel of Matthew, The Miracle of the Corn?'

'I got a feeling you're way ahead of us, sister,' said Guy.

'Something to help take my mind off recent events. Athanasius,' said Sister Mee, 'have you finished decrypting the message yet?'

'Yes, Sister Mee,' said the artificial voice. 'Activating screen display.'

A wall-sized piece of glass standing on the side of the lab started to glow with scrolling bright green text. Eleanor examined the translated message, along with the A.I.'s side-notes giving their historical context. The decrypted message from the musical score had been signed and dated by the abbot in charge of the Swiss monastery during the late seventeenth and early eighteenth century, one Abbot Urs Giger. An age when Napoleon had invaded Switzerland, toppled the government and replaced it with his own puppet regime - the Helvetic Republic. Reds had begun operating in the cantons. High military officers attached to the French Emperor's secret police, soldiers who were suspected vampires and demi-gogs, and they seemed to be searching hard for something. The Abbot — no fool — didn't require a visitation from an angel to warn him exactly what that *something* was. Napoleon's General Berthier had recently captured Rome, with Pope Pius VI taken prisoner and exiled to France, and the Black Pope of the age had temporarily relocated operations to Britain for safety, invited by Pitt, a prime minister who'd narrowly escaped being made into a demi-gog himself.

Abbot Giger had urgently needed to send the Judas Purse to a safe haven, so he contacted a pious and trusted friend in the Spanish church inside Mexico, making arrangements for the purse to be sent across the Atlantic inside an American ship - the U.S. being neutral at the outset of the Napoleonic wars. The coins' secret move was recorded in the coded hymn and concealed in the painting commissioned by the Abbot, with enough visual cues to give a genuine member of Scutum Dei a steer as to where the Judas Purse had been moved to. Father Pedro de Alcazar of San Juan Teotihuacan, it seemed, had become the next somewhat unwilling custodian of the Judas Purse. Anyone too willing, of course, would have been exactly the wrong sort of person to entrust with such power.

'Nobody discovered the coins in Mexico, then,' said Eleanor. 'We'd kind of know it if they had, right?'

Sister Mee rubbed her chin thoughtfully as she digested the message. 'Correct. Mexico. A good choice for the time. The Spanish church was still a dominant force in the country. Nobody would have dared question a church courier moving inside Mexico. And using an American ship to travel - very clever. Napoleon hoped to entice the U.S. into his side of the war against the British, and Great Britain did not want the Americans sticking their nose into the European war. The U.S. were briefly embroiled later, of course. The vampires tried to spark a true world war. All the Reds got for their troubles was a White House burned by Redcoats. Thanks in no small part to our efforts.'

'Well done,' said Guy, somewhat ironically. 'Mexico isn't such a great choice now, though, is it? Encouraging the drug trade is the Reds' favourite hobby; destabilising countries through the narco-wars, corrupting entire continents, keeping us lowly cattle addicted to their chemical filth. Half the Vigil's non-domestic ops are projected across the Rio Grande, fighting the Reds and their proxies down Mexico-way. How many drug lords running Mexico sit in a vampire's pocket?'

'I estimate that seventy-five point four percent of Mexican Narco Cartels are currently under the direct control of vampire clans,' announced Athanasius, unasked. 'A further twelve percent are likely to be indirectly subverted by Cartel influencers.'

'Well,' said Sister Mee, 'I'd say the drug war's stakes have just been raised, wouldn't you?'

'Straight into the heart of Vampire Central,' said Guy, slipping a cigar out and lighting it up. 'As if our damn mission couldn't get any hairier.'

'This centre is a no-smoking zone,' advised Athanasius, somewhat loftily. 'And this laboratory is a specified clean room.'

'No room with me inside it is entirely clean,' snorted Guy, continuing to draw on the cigar regardless.

Eleanor stared up at a security camera in the corner of the room, a little red light blinking as it pointed at them. 'How come you weren't so legalistic when I was getting water-boarded, Athanasius?'

'Enhanced interrogation inside this facility is legal,' hummed the A.I. 'Smoking is not.'

'And don't that tell you everything that's wrong with this cockamamie century,' said Guy blowing a circle of smoke out. 'Half-intelligent engine blocks notwithstanding.'

'I am fully intelligent,' insisted the A.I., 'although not yet fully sentient as measured by the Turing Index.'

'Hunk-a-junk,' muttered Guy.

Fully intelligent. I wish the same could be said of us, thought Eleanor. *Sent a deadly message inside the sewers, but we're going to ignore it, anyway. Yeah, I'd settle for half-intelligent, let alone fully intelligent.*

15

~ NIGHT OF THE WITCH ~

'What are you doing?' yelled the man. He was tied down inside Dawn's Circle of Power, frantically struggling against his bonds. Dawn Heliot had used police-issue plastic restraints which would need to be cut off, instead of a coil of enchanted rope. *Never let the other witches accuse me of being a traditionalist in such matters.* She tapped the little digital music player clipped to her skirt, a pair of expensive white noise-cancelling earphones dangling from her leather belt.

This idiot was a marine picked up from a bar notorious for being frequented by the military. Dawn needed a victim strong enough to survive through the thirty-three stabbings with her *athame*, a black-hilted crescent-shaped blade which could only be bloodied by human sacrifice. She dipped the blade in her carefully prepared potion, the golden goblet's plague-yellow contents sloshing over the sides as she chanted.

'Why are you doing this?' yelled the soldier.

Dawn smiled gently at him. 'I need to see a little glimpse of the future, my darling boy. Such visions can only be bought at a cost.'

'Why? What do you need to know so badly, you kook?'

'I'm trying to track down a couple of old friends.'

'That's what Facebook is for,' moaned the marine.

'Sadly, the couple I am searching for have been expunged from the drives of all your cursed machines. Their digital trail is as thin as soup kitchen broth. But don't worry, calling up the Spirits of Sight is far more reliable than your kind's flimsy silicon cleverness. The gossip of the dead, rather than the prattle of mortals, you might say.'

'I don't understand.'

'If you did, my dear, I would be quite worried.' Dawn stared into the man's deep blue eyes. She was only going to get one chance to complete this sacrifice. Then she would need to flee to a neighbouring state before her pursuers showed up, kicking down the door. The cursed Vigil had subsumed the office of the Witch Finder in these modern times. They knew Dawn Heliot existed now, and how assiduously they hunted her. Hunted her with all the cleverness of machines that never slept, machines which watched the roads with cameras, endlessly counting cars and licence plates, machines that scanned faces in crowds and matched them to graven images. Mortals might grow bored, or could be ensorcelled and charmed. But cold machines, never. 'The two I seek are the type of people who leave a trail of corpses behind. Those they have slain are bitter and all too eager to lend me the power I need to pierce the veil, glimpsing the pair's future. Your soul is the gift to unlock the Spirits of Sight, and it is the spirits who will unlock the future for me.'

'Please,' begged the marine, his eyes going wide as he realised this was no prank, no mere attempt to frighten him, 'don't murder me!'

He began yelling wildly for help and Dawn let him exercise his lungs to his heart's content. Mistress Heliot had hired this luxury lodge in the dark woods specifically for its far distance from its nearest neighbour. 'Hush now. Your death under the blade will be the least of your problems.'

'No!'

The witch plunged the blade into his chest, the first of many strikes. 'Yes!'

Dawn had chosen wisely, the soldier hanging on well beyond her final blow, spitting hatred and curses at her, screaming that she was a terrorist. Sadly for the young brute, it was the spirits of all those he'd slain in battle who were coming for him, drawn from Hell by the unholy bond which existed between vanquished and vanquisher. It was only through their tormenting of this dying mortal that the Spirits of the Sight could be enticed to appear in this grubby realm of dirt and dust. The witch shared their distaste. *We are all meant for better things than this.* After Dawn traced Eleanor and sucked the powers from the agent's broken body, she would have to see what she could do about that, too.

Dozens of spirits appeared like hissing snakes, bound by the candle-lit walls of her Circle of Power, striking the field with the flashing red outlines of horned heads. Fire flashed vainly after each failed attempt to escape. Dawn laughed at their attempts to breach her wards. 'No, my pretties, I'm not for you. This soldier is yours. Taste him. Surely you remember him? He cast you into the dark depths, so you should know him well enough.'

There were many fools who didn't know that ghosts sucked mortal blood as lustily as any vampire, but mere mortals understood nothing. Dawn watched with satisfaction as her summonings circled the victim's body, before darting at his flesh, daggers of malice and darkest evil. They worked hard to keep their victim alive while they consumed him. The racket was quite tedious. Hence the need for her earphones and music player. Dawn selected Taylor Swift and played *I Knew You*

Were in Trouble loud enough to drown out the screams, dancing around the Circle of Power to the tune, singing and conducting the song with the tip of her bloody dagger's blade.

The summoned took their tiresome time finishing the job, but at least the unpleasant things had the good manners to complete the rest of the ritual as was required. Dawn's eyes widened as the evil spirits rewarded her for her bloody gift of a sacrificed soul. Candles steamed spears of purple smoke. Her lips opened wide, letting the visions and smoke rush into her all at once. She struggled to hold onto the sides of the table where she had sacrificed the soldier. Her mind burned. Rarely were visions of the future so clear and distinct, so unsaddled by the branching tree of probability lines.

The Vigil's team assailed by waves of vampires, the stupid mortals ambushed inside Teotihuacan, their bloody deaths as pleasing to Dawn as a warm embrace. Dawn quickly saw how she could insert herself inside the Reds' horrific ambush, carry away Eleanor and bleed her of her powers before the Reds realised what they were dealing with. *How delicious*, thought Dawn. And how reckless of her relentless hunters to beard the vampires inside the Reds' great stronghold. So many Nazis had fled Europe for South America at the end of the last world war, the vampires hardly needed the drug trade's takings to fund their wayward appetites - they could have simply lived off the profits from the Nazi gold carried across on their u-boats. *The Vigil agents' deaths will be my revenge . . . and stealing the girl's powers will be the culmination of my reign.*

The Reign of the Witch.

16

~ THE DEAD EAT THE DEAD ~

Teotihuacan, it transpired, was thirty miles from Mexico City, sprawling across a series of valleys. Another town slowly being overtaken by the nearby capital, like prey gradually being absorbed by a jellyfish. A serious tourist venue, given it held the ruins of a mighty Mesoamerican - and later, Aztec - city, complete with ancient angular pyramids and grand squares and avenues stretching for mile upon mile. The jungle always close by to remind you how quickly things turned wild here. There was plenty of history on display: the Pyramid of the Sun, the Pyramid of the Moon and the aptly named Avenue of the Dead. The last was better named than even the local archaeologists knew. Columbus might have thought he discovered the Americas, but the vampires had known about the new world's existence from the time of Alexander the Great. The Aztec Empire's rites of human sacrifice came straight from the Reds' playbook; it had been like building their own zoo, feeding times thrown in along with free admittance - and the vampire lords had ensured their preys' civilisation never progressed far beyond obsidian blades. Which was to say, just far enough to carve out the live, beating heart of their next lunch. If Europe had never existed, if the Renaissance had never occurred, that is how South America would still exist today: nothing more than a humid farm for the Reds.

Eleanor took in the town from the air as the team arrived on a small chartered tourist flight. At least she wouldn't look out of place in Teotihuacan. Mexico might be, as Guy had described it, Vampire Central. But it was also Gringo Central, so Eleanor and the others would fit right in just by wearing bright shorts, loud t-shirts and making sure that expensive digital cameras dangled from their necks. After clearing the small local airport their group bundled into the first two cabs that became available. Their cases filled the boot space. For all their weight, there was very little in the way of clothing and clean underwear inside the luggage. Guy and Diane slid into the first cab. Eleanor sat in the next car with Ian and Sister Mee. None of them had enjoyed leaving Alasdair and Sister Rae back in the infirmary - not least the two wounded fighters themselves - but time was of the essence. They had to beat the vampires to the Judas Purse. Sister Mee spoke in Spanish, asking for the local cathedral, the Catedral del Divino Redentor, where the area's church records were stored.

Eleanor saw through the car window that the modern town hadn't had the same care lavished upon it as the elder civilisation's ruins. Dirty, cluttered pavements alive with stalls and street kids selling the usual tat - replica models of monuments, lurid t-shirts and snow-globes containing cheaply painted miniatures of pyramids. Their cab didn't have air conditioning - not unless you counted rolling with all its windows wound down. The spicy smell of local food frying in the open air, making the thick air reek with its scent. Rows of tourist coaches parked in back streets, unloading foreign passengers while idling their engines and keeping the air con running. It felt chaotic but alive. *And alive is how I'd like to keep on feeling, thank you very much.* The cabs stopped at the hotel the party had booked, but only long enough for their luggage to be taken to their rooms. Then they were on the move again. Eleanor had the impression that every second counted now, in the race to retrieve the coins.

Sister Mee still carried the little computer tablet she had been reading on the flight, resting it on her knees.

'Catching up on your Netflix subscription?' asked Eleanor.

'Research on the background of Father Pedro, the little that Rome possessed in the way of digitised records covering the man.'

Ian showed some interest. 'And?'

'Most of the material is on his family - an important clan in this neck of the woods. Not so much information on the bishop, though.'

'That speaks of a certain humility,' said Ian.

'Or that some of his successors knew the secret and went to a lot of trouble to erase his existence from Rome's records.'

That thought didn't reassure Eleanor. 'You think someone in the cathedral still knows where it is hidden?'

'It is possible,' said Sister Mee. 'But if so, I wouldn't expect whoever holds the secret to tell me.'

Eleanor stared at the nun. 'Why not? You're the strong right hook of the church, aren't you?'

'If someone still knows where the Judas Purse is, then they have kept the secret against all temptations. A legacy passed down through the ages. Having a delegation visit with Papal authority will be as leaves blowing in the wind as far as its stewards are concerned.'

Their cab arrived behind Guy and Diane's car, the destination ahead of them. Eleanor noted she could just see the top of one of the distant pyramids peeking over the cathedral. The cathedral itself had high grey stone walls that weren't quite tall enough to hide the red brick of the Catedral del Divino Redentor's domed cupola rising on the other side, a Spanish-tiled clock tower with a three-storey-high bell tower on top acting as a sentry post. An ornamental white archway led them into the grounds and a minute later they were past the thick walls and inside the cool of the main building. Sister Mee flashing the papal shield of Scutum Dei was all the authority they needed to as good as commandeer the Catedral del Divino Redentor and begin searching it for evidence of Father Pedro de Alcázar. They met the current bishop, an Irishman called Father Gerry McEyre, and the bishop passed them across to a senior member of his clergy, Monsignor Onyulo, and the monsignor passed them to a young priest called Father Gerardo who looked like he had only just learnt to start shaving. Duly fobbed off, the group started work in the cathedral's dusty records room. Luckily, the computer revolution was one revolution this corner of Mexico had yet to experience. All the local records were still on paper - or in the case of the cathedral logs from the early nineteenth century, leather-bound parchment. They dived into the records, searching first for news of the father himself. The last known guardian of the Judas Purse.

'Here we are,' said Sister Mee, tapping the page. 'Father Pedro left San Juan Teotihuacan to join the cathedral's staff here ten years after he returned from Europe. He died in 1864.'

Guy raised an eyebrow. 'But did he bring the Judas Purse with him? Or hide it somewhere in his old church?'

'It seems Father Pedro ended up as bishop of Catedral del Divino Redentor,' said the sister. 'He lived long enough to see the start of the American Civil War and the Invasión estadounidense a México - when the USA invaded Mexico to grab its Northern territories. He should have kept a private diary at the very least.' She consulted the young local priest assigned to help them, and he opened a wooden door to a back-room with even more shelves of church records. He returned with a large book with crumbling leather that had nearly ossified.

'It's written in a mixture of Latin and Spanish,' announced Sister Mee. 'Mostly Spanish towards the end.' There was a faded photograph in the front. An early example of photography . . . the father himself in his bishop's robes. He looked proud and tall even in old age, more like a matador than a churchman. Eleanor wondered how much of the man's rise to prominence in the cathedral was the Judas Purse's possession rubbing off on him. The coins trying to tempt him with the lure of unlimited power. She knew that the father had resisted the urge, or he wouldn't have just finished his life as a bishop in some Mexican backwater. He would have ended up as a Napoleonic-like ruler of all of the Americas - south and north - at the very least. Enough of the innocence that the Swiss abbot had seen in the man remained to keep him true.

'He must have hidden the coins well,' said Eleanor.

'Well enough not to be found and abused,' said Sister Mee.

'Quite a man,' said Diane.

'He had faith,' said the nun. 'Faith can carry you very far.'

Diane nodded but Eleanor wasn't so sure. *I had faith in a lot of things that proved to be wrong. Starting with family and ending with the true nature of the world.* So far, she had been proved wrong in just about everything she had thought she could count on. Now it was coming back to bite her; maybe, quite literally.

'The de Alcázar family were powerful landowners in Mexico,' said Sister Mee. 'Father Pedro had already renounced the wealth and power of his inheritance to join the church. He had walked away from such things once. The Judas Purse held little to tempt him.'

The book Eleanor perused had a faded crest embossed into the leather, a bull above a cross. She tapped it. 'Is this the de Alcázar family crest?'

'No, that's the cathedral's crest. The de Alcázar family's crest was a red and yellow shield with two white lambs on it,' said the nun. 'Their family motto was *Aude Sapere*. Dare to know.'

'Kind of ironic for someone who was keeping history's greatest secret on the down-low.'

'Lucky the Borgias didn't get their hands on the coins,' said Ian.

Sister Mee shrugged. 'They didn't need it, they already had possession of the Holy Grail.'

'You're joking, right?' asked the agent.

'You'll never know.'

Guy winked at Ian. 'Don't worry, we've got the Holy Grail in a wooden crate right next to the Lost Ark of the Covenant.'

Ian could tell when he was being teased and gave up on trying to winkle out the truth.

The records room possessed a single narrow window looking out onto the rear of the cathedral. Eleanor saw there was a graveyard fighting a losing battle with the thick undergrowth outside. 'I'm going to see if I can find Father Pedro's grave.'

Guy looked up. 'You expecting to find the purse buried out there, kid?'

'Even if I don't, it's got to smell better than a centuries old book.'

'Eyes open,' said Guy. 'The Reds have been one step behind us all the way during this caper.'

'I'll go with,' said Ian.

'And I'll look up what a caper is on my phone when I get a signal outside,' said Eleanor.

Ian smiled. 'It's a little green thing you find on the topping of bad pizza, isn't it?'

'Get out of here,' said Guy. 'Before you make me feel even older than I already do.'

***

Bishop McEyre and Monsignor Onyulo stood cloaked by the shadows of the bell tower, watching from on high as two of their young visitors searched the graveyard's tombstones. It was a small plot, mostly the bodies of priests who had laboured long in the service of the cathedral. Now there was no more room for such burials. Priests were buried or cremated in the new cemetery far out of town - alongside glass tombs the size of villas dedicated to the memories of drug lords, many with CCTV cameras to ensure rival gangs didn't come and machine gun the flashy monuments to criminal excess.

'They will discover nothing in the graveyard,' said the monsignor. 'Better for them if they find nothing in the cathedral at all.'

'They're our people, aren't they?' said Bishop McEyre, his bleary eyes blinking in the gloom. He took a brass hip flask out from his pocket and downed a quick guilty shot before dropping the flask back. The monsignor did not ask what was in it. He knew it wasn't water, at any rate.

'Maybe they are and maybe they aren't,' said Monsignor Onyulo. 'Wearing a scapular and bearing a badge of Rome does not always a nun make. And as for the *Americans . . .*' He said the last word like it was an infectious disease. 'What in the name of our good Lord are they? A cadet field trip for the CIA? One thing is for certain, they have not served with us here for decades. I refuse to trust those I don't know.'

'What if they find *it*?'

Monsignor Onyulo frowned. 'Then we will let nature take its course. The Yankees do not deserve such power. They are not worthy of it. They made a battlefield of Uganda during the Cold War and destroyed the Middle East with the same games. You know what North America would do with the coins. How much more powerful it would make the nation.'

The bishop waved a piece of paper - a sheet torn from a notepad beside the telephone. 'Are they not even to know they're the third blessed lot to come sniffing around here after Bishop de Alcázar's legacy this week.'

Monsignor Onyulo shook his head, snorting. 'That so-called academic woman, then those equally bogus archaeologists from the ministry? They are probably already dead if they weren't undead to start with.'

'Ah, it's a bad business.'

'It's a fatal business,' said the monsignor. 'For if the great evil was not properly protected, then it would be abroad in the world. And this I do know, there is enough evil in the world already. I will not willingly add to its weight. Not even by a gramme.'

'Too bad, then,' whined the bishop. 'They'll die like all the others.'

Monsignor Onyulo stiffened his back as though stiffening his resolve. 'The world will live, though. That is quite enough for me.'

'A bad business,' repeated the bishop in a low mutter. 'I'm going out to the town to visit the Ramírez's in a while. Their baby is still sick with the fever. I don't think their insurance will pay out for the little angel's medical treatment.'

'You don't wish to hear the Yankees die screaming. When you sentence someone to death, you must have the fibre to see the sentence carried out.'

'I'm a soft fellow,' said the bishop. 'Famous for it.'

Monsignor Onyulo grunted disapprovingly. 'I will stay. I will mourn them and say the rites.'

'Over what, man? Ah, there will be nothing left to bury. There never is.'

***

Eleanor and Ian returned from the cathedral's graveyard, their search a bust. Centuries old in many cases, most of the tombstones had been scrubbed blank by the passage of years, only illegible indentations where chiselled writing had once been tapped out. If the purse really was hidden outside, the Vigil would need to excavate the entire rear of the cathedral to stand a chance of finding it.

'Why can't something be easy for once?' asked Eleanor.

Ian opened the door back into the cathedral. 'So you'll appreciate finding it more this way.'

'Oh no, 'said Eleanor. 'I'd appreciate it just fine if I lifted up a flower pot on a grave and found a secret panel underneath filled with ancient coins.'

'I bet you're just saying that.'

'Hey!' said Eleanor, slowing to a stop. She halted by an archway with a small wooden door, indicating a small carving in the stone above. 'Does that look familiar to you?'

Ian peered up. 'Two lambs on a crest. The de Alcázar family shield!'

'It's the entrance to a crypt,' said Eleanor. 'The de Alcázars were a wealthy local family back in the day, right? Bigwigs always get the best seats in the house, even after they're dead.'

'A *family* crypt? You think that the bishop was interred down there?'

'If Father Pedro had his way, he'd probably have been put to rest in the dirt all humble with the rest of the priests. But after he was dead . . .? I reckon his family would make a point of treating him like one of them, just to teach him a lesson for renouncing the gold-plated yacht.'

Ian nodded in agreement. 'Gold-plated saddle in those days. Only one way to be certain.'

'Come on then!'

Eleanor tried the door. It was locked. Ian reached into his back pocket and pulled out a little black ceramic credit card-sized oblong. Fiddling with it, a lockpick sprung out of the device. He pushed the pick into the lock and rotated it around until a loud click sounded from the old iron lock.

'Don't tell me you used to jack cars or indulge in house breaking when you were back in the age of big shoulder pads and batwing sleeves?'

'Just wait till you see who your instructor is for covert entry.'

'Who, the Pink Panther?'

Ian simply smiled but didn't elaborate. Even unlocked, the door took a little hard shoving to force open.

Eleanor glanced around nervously, seeing if anyone had noticed the noise. 'We could have just asked for the door to be unlocked.'

Ian slipped away his lock pick. 'Maybe. I'm not sure the locals are on the same page as us. Sister Mee told the bishop and that grim-looking monsignor dude that we're researching Father Pedro. You don't think the bishop should have mentioned that he has the de Alcázar family crypt right inside the cathedral?'

'Maybe the staff don't know about the connection. It's ancient history as far as they're concerned. They probably have other things on their church plate to worry about. Repairing the leaky roof and looking after widows from the drug wars.'

'Maybe,' said Ian, but he didn't sound certain. 'That's the thing about this gig. A few decades with the Vigil and you start to suspect the worst in everyone.'

'That's kind of grim.'

'Yeah, but you certainly stay alive longer that way.'

'You ever think there's more to living than just staying alive?'

'Not until recently.'

Eleanor blushed as she followed the agent through the doorway, crouching from the low height of it - built for an age when people were a lot shorter on average. Steps led down a passage.

The cathedral budget hadn't stretched to electric lighting for the crypt; they needed to ignite candles set in the wall, flickering illumination casting long shadows against the brick walls. At the bottom of the passage, now deep underground, they arrived at the start of the crypt - candle light unable to illuminate the true scale of the large chamber, dozens of stone columns holding up a flying buttress high above them. The wall contained niches with resting urns. A series of block-like tombs rested across the flagstone floor, each with a prone granite figure lying on top, identifying the family member lying in the casket inside. Unlike the cathedral graveyard, these tombs were perfectly preserved. The couple inspected each block, reading out the names aloud, as well as epitaphs and inscriptions on each block. Towards the centre of the crypt, they found the tomb they were searching for. Pedro de Alcázar. Once bishop of the Catedral del Divino Redentor and more importantly, guardian of history's deadliest secret. Eleanor circled the tomb. Like the other tombs, a granite block three feet high, with a stone figure of the bishop stretched out on top. This figure had been carved wearing the robes of a churchman, a bishop's staff by his side. The same hawkish face she had seen in the crumbling photograph upstairs.

Eleanor traced her finger across the inscription below the man's name. *Más vale ser cabeza de ratón que cola de león.* 'Something about a mouse and a lion and how it's better to be a mouse's head than a lion's tail.'

'You speak Spanish?' asked Ian.

'Un poquito,' said Eleanor. 'It was the main lingo for a lot of people in the home - both for us *and* the staff.'

Ian rested his hands on the tomb's lid. 'Let's see if we can lift this.'

Eleanor moved to the other side and gripped the top. She pushed against it, slowly at first, then with all her strength, grunting as the lid failed to budge. 'Maybe it's ossified in place over the centuries?'

'With our combined strength? Together, we should be able to lift the entire tomb, not just shift the lid. I think this top is false, not a lid at all. It's part of the block.'

Maybe not a tomb after all, then? Eleanor knelt to read the inscription again. 'What do you notice about the inscription and the father's name?'

'That you speak better Spanish than me?'

Eleanor ran her finger along the script chiselled into the block's side. 'Look, the epitaph here has all its accents correctly spelt.'

'So?'

'The father's name has been carved as Pedro de Alcazar, missing out the accent on its *á*.'

'Maybe someone should have fired the stonemason, then?'

'The missing accent is at the head of his name, the mouse's head. The epitaph isn't about how Father Pedro lived a life rejecting his family's wealth, it has to be a clue.' Eleanor reached out and pressed the centre of the letter missing the accent. Nothing happened, but the stone where she touched did feel like an indentation - a concealed button, maybe? *Damn, I was so certain. Why isn't it working?*

Ian reached out to the *á* in the *Más*, resting his finger against it. 'Try again.'

Eleanor pushed down again, and as she did so, the tomb began to roll backwards on a squealing counterweight, revealing an entrance below to a concealed set of stairs. *I guess two á's are better than one - just like two heads.* 'Go Team Vigil.'

Ian stared down into the pitch-black. He picked up a piece of loose stone and tossed it down the hole like he was skimming pebbles across a lake. A tap-tap noise sounded as it tumbled down through the inky darkness. 'Time to fetch the others.'

'Yeah,' said Eleanor. 'The last dark tunnel we jumped into was under the museum and that didn't end too well for us, did it?'

'Just us here this time,' said Ian, somewhat more hopefully than his face looked, she thought.

Eleanor knelt by the hole, trying to pierce the darkness. She activated her spectacles' night vision mode, throwing the descending staircase into an eerie green light. There was something else. A distant scent drifting at the far end of her ability to detect. *That smell seems familiar, but why?* If only it was stronger, she might be able to identify it. And why did her stomach fill with dread and fear just peering down there?

17

~ ALL THE DARK POWER ~

Dawn Heliot sensed Bishop McEyre's presence long before he knocked on the door to the house. To a witch, he was like a nervous mouse given human form, reeking of anxiety as much as he reeked of Tequila. The fear was almost enough to overcome the glamour of desire she had cast over the churchman to ensure his compliance. Almost, but not quite, as his visit to her here attested. She opened the door to the house before he could ring the bell, being careful not to show herself to the pedestrians in the street. Some nosey neighbour might spot her inside and wonder what a stranger was doing inside the house. They wouldn't enjoy her answer much . . . that slaying everyone living in a home had two benefits. A brief vein of human sacrifices allowing her to advance her cause, closely followed by the benefit of free accommodation wherever she travelled . . . every dark witch's favourite version of Airbnb.

'Ah, my handsome bishop,' purred Dawn, stroking his fat ruddy cheeks as she led the man inside the house's living room. 'You have come with news, I trust?'

'For you, lady, anything,' wheezed the bishop. The bishop didn't comment on the bloody pile of bodies in the corner. Mexicans had such gloriously large extended families. If the witch was lucky, a few more relatives would come calling on the cheap house before she left, eager to pop in and share gossip or bring a pot of food. And in a way, they *were* bringing a gift of nourishment. Themselves!

'Tell me, then . . .'

'The Americans you said would come have arrived, and they've discovered the entrance Father Pedro had built down into the temple tunnels.'

'I told you they would come calling and discover the entrance,' smiled Dawn. And unlike her, they hadn't even needed to bewitch the plump bishop to discover the secret of Pedro de Alcázar's secret legacy. She wondered if the ghost of the old bishop would be twisting in his grave at the betrayal of the secret so easily by one of his distant successors.

'You did tell me, you did. But how did you know they were coming, lady?'

Dawn pointed to the table in the centre of the living room, still stained with blood from where she had cut out the hearts of the house's previous owners. A deck of tarot cards lay spread across the table on green felt. 'The cards rarely lie. Not when they have been charged with the souls of innocents.'

'I have done all that you asked of me,' sighed the bishop. 'Will you not give me a kiss like you promised?'

'Of course I will, but first, tell me . . . have your visitors worked out exactly what is waiting for them in the temple yet?'

'The coins, lady, the coins. They must suspect. That's what they're searching for.'

'Naturally, but I mean have they worked out what is *guarding* the coins.'

'Ah, no. They're poking around with some gobshite remote-controlled tractor at the moment.'

'How very cautious of them. They do love their modern toys. Whereas, they'd actually be better off tossing in a lamb or two to tempt out what's inside the temple. But nobody ever listens to a witch's advice.'

'I do. Command me and I will do it for you.'

'That's very sweet. You shall help me read the future, my handsome bishop. I have glimpsed so many visions these last few days. So many possible futures. Let the cards help show me which of the future paths will prove true.' She indicated the portion of her piled deck that had yet to be turned. 'Take the cards in your hand. Choose three at random. Lay the cards down on the table without looking at them, and I will reveal their secrets to you.'

Bishop McEyre eagerly did as she had bid. He picked up the deck and lifted out three cards at random, placing them face down on the table's green velvet mat.

Dawn reached out daintily, flipping the first card. Its nature surprised even her - although, to be fair, the real surprise was coming for someone else. 'The Seven of Swords!'

'What does it mean?'

'It means deception and betrayal. There is a traitor inside the Vigil. A human who is working for those filthy vampires. I caught a glimpse of that when I fed on the people here, but I did not believe it was possible. So, not a false shadow after all? There is to be a terrible betrayal from within their own ranks. Hah. Perfect. Let me see the second card!' Dawn slowly turned over the next card. 'The Suit of Swords! Well, I hardly needed to see that one, to know it was coming.'

'What does it mean, mistress?' pleaded the bishop.

'This card speaks of terrible violence.'

'Inside the temple and the tunnels?' asked the bishop.

'Yes. A waste of good prophecy, though - most who enter the temple meet that fate.' It was why Dawn had waited for the Vigil to arrive and begin her work for her. She was perfectly willing for the agents to do the dying for her. Leaving her free to step over their corpses and claim the prize she lusted after. 'You may turn the final card, my handsome bishop. This last one is *your* card.'

Bishop McEyre reached out and flipped the card over, revealing a skeletal hand holding a golden chalice. 'What is it - what does this mean?'

'The Ace of Cups,' said Dawn. 'The stirring of a powerful passion.'

'The kiss you promised . . .' drawled the bishop, reaching to seize her around the waist and draw her in towards his portly body.

'Yes, it is time.' Dawn plunged the dagger carefully hidden up her sleeve into the bishop's chest, watching the man stumble back in shock as he regarded the hilt sunk into his body. 'The kiss of my blade.'

'Passion,' spluttered the dying bishop. 'Passion.'

'The stirrings of *my* passion,' laughed Dawn, sweeping the cards off the table and revealing the pentagram sketched out underneath. She pushed the swaying churchman down onto the table, locking him in place to the table legs with the same handcuffs she had used to murder the house's previous owners. 'The last feeding for the spell I will need to cast to move through the tunnels unhindered until it is time for me to claim what is rightfully mine.'

All the dark power of the world.

***

D iane had drawn the short straw to grab a cab back to the hotel and retrieve a few choice items from their luggage. For starters, a little drone designed to trundle through earthquake zones, dropping a breadcrumb trail of communications repeaters to report back. So far, all the party had found hidden below the de Alcázar family crypt was an almost endless, empty maze of rock passages, five feet high and five feet wide. Stone plaques in the walls stood carved with a pantheon of Aztec gods' names lacking vowels - Huitzilopochtli and Tlaloc and Chalchihuitlicu - coiled serpents and warriors and myths, all speaking of the tunnels' original origins. The current cathedral staff denied all knowledge of the hidden passages' existence, of course, but Eleanor possessed doubts about how much they really knew. The bishop and the monsignor had shown an odd lack of curiosity about the strange discovery and what it might mean. Guy obviously shared the same doubts as her but didn't care much one way or another, as long as the locals respected Sister Mee's Papal seal and stayed well out of the Vigil's hair while they worked.

Sister Mee fingered her rosary thoughtfully as she inspected the hidden entrance revealed below Father Pedro's tomb, the flickering screen illuminating her curious features. 'There have long been rumours of a significant tunnel complex below the pyramids, used by Aztec priests to move unseen around the city. Underground temples for conducting forbidden rites. Aztecs priests were able to conjure unclean spirits by blood sacrifice to slay opponents among the nobility, whenever the state versus church arguments - and who kept the lion's share of the peasants' taxes - grew too heated. The spirits moved unseen and carried out their black work at night before disappearing.'

'Spirits don't need secret passages carved out of old lava tubes to creep into palaces,' said Guy. 'But assassins do.'

'There haven't been any Aztecs around here since the Conquistadors introduced them to the joy of rapid musket fire,' said Diane.

Ian wasn't in the mood for a history lesson. 'Yeah, but their tunnels are still here.'

'And what do you want to bet that there's a good reason why no archaeologist has ever uncovered the tunnel system and lived to report their find?' said Eleanor.

'There's a bet I wouldn't place good money against,' rumbled Guy.

'Pan the camera left,' said Sister Mee, 'I think there's a side-passage you just passed. It has something in it.'

Diane did as the nun asked, the drone's floodlights falling across a jumble of bones among the tattered remains of clothing. 'That's not an Aztec sacrifice. The state of decay of the fabric is too recent.'

Guy tapped the drone's remote control screen. 'And there's a battery-powered torch in the corner. Looks like seventies vintage.'

'An industrial-quality model,' said Ian. 'I'd say that's one of those missing archaeologists you were pondering, Eleanor.'

Eleanor felt queasy. 'Is it just me, or are half the skeleton's bones missing?'

'No, kid, it ain't just you,' said Guy. 'Take a gander at the state of the rubber grip on the torch. That's not decomposition from age. Something had a real good nibble on the handle before discarding it.'

'Not Reds, then?'

'Sure, they go crazy with hunger if they don't feed regularly. But trying to suck on battery acid? I don't think so,' said Guy. 'I'm going outside to establish an encrypted satellite connection back to John and fill him in on what we've discovered. Dirty Harriet and her reserve team must be on the ground by now. If we fail here, we need to make sure that the Vigil has a second bite of the cherry, and damn soon. '

Bite. Suddenly it came to Eleanor. Why the scent she had caught from deep inside the tunnels smelled so familiar. 'I think I know what's protecting the Judas Purse down in that maze. But you're not going to like it.' Come to think of it, Eleanor didn't like it any better. And the quickest, dirtiest solution - *possible* solution - to the problem was even *less* palatable to her.

***

'We should call for reinforcements,' urged the demi-gog. 'These are the same agents we fought in Switzerland.'

There was a nervous shifting of bodies, indicating agreement among the rest of Sophia's nest. They were allowing their fear of what had happened to them before to cloud their judgement, taking the edge off their appetite. They were probably allowing their proximity to the ancient temple complex to spook them, too.

Once Sophia knew the temple existed, it had been easy enough to find a hidden entrance in the tourist city, a portal concealed below one of the old pyramids. She had killed three site staff and seventeen tourists so far to break into the maze and keep their presence unnoticed above ground. Perhaps those killings had also contributed to taking the edge off her demi-gogs. You should never feed a nest too regularly. It dulled their appetite and made them lazy and unnaturally supine. Unnatural for a demi-gog, anyway.

Sophia considered how to proceed, then snorted in derision. 'And you had to be one of the ones who lived through the attack. Leave the thinking to me.'

'But, with greater numbers . . .'

'Would come other clans and all of their tedious clan politics,' said Sophia. Who was the chief vampire among the cartel clans now? Garcia Tovar, wasn't it? Von Waldburg was the master of masters, but there wasn't one of the other vampire warlords in Latin America who wouldn't betray him in a second if it meant even a slim chance of gaining possession of the Judas Purse. Fighting agents of the Vigil was one thing. Fighting off dozens of her own kind with their huge private armies, all desperate to seize the same prize, was quite another. And who knows, some might even hand it over to Von Waldburg and be content playing loyal underling as the nations of the world fell to *their* power, *their* will.

'I don't like this place,' said Joanna. 'It feels wrong.'

'We have the Aztecs, I fear, to blame for that,' said Sophia. 'They were rather miffed when the Europeans came and unleashed genocide against their empire. The churlish Aztec priesthood broke free of their bondage to our people. They embraced other solutions to their predicament. Desperate solutions.' The vampire felt contempt for the Aztecs' weakness. *What is the point of conjuring up a secret wonder weapon if it turns on you? If you can't control it?*

'That is what I sense inside the temple and the tunnels?'

'Possibly,' said Sophia. She had a huntress's scent for the jungle and other alpha predators. There was something else abroad in the dark tonight. *But what?*

'I wish you had helped the Aztecs drive away the Spanish conquerors, then.'

'War allows us to feed. It keeps the herd healthy. The weak must fall to the strong. That is the way of life.' *And the way of our kind, too.*

'The Vigil are not such cattle. They are dangerous.'

Sophia laughed. 'I certainly hope so. They need to lead us safely to the coins, after all.' Sophia recalled a time during the fighting on the Eastern Front when she had made a village full of frightened peasants walk ahead of her regiment through a mine field. Even cattle had their uses. The Vigil would serve a similar purpose for her today.

'Did your Vigil traitor tell you where this entrance into the maze was?'

'Only that the temple complex existed,' said Sophia. 'I did the rest. We have shunned this fallen city for centuries. Father Pedro was cunning to bury his prize among the Aztecs' black secrets. The priest hid it somewhere he knew we would avoid, even if we discovered the maze's existence.'

'Maybe we should shun it still.'

'Oh, on that much I agree. We should avoid this place. But it contains what Von Waldburg desires. And I cannot fail him too many times, however much the master of masters humours me for old time's sake. His tolerance only stretches so far.'

'I have listened to you many times speak of how his aims are backwards: old thinking. He'll take the Judas Purse and reduce the world to cinders with its power.'

'True, I would prefer a re-balancing to a wholesale act of arson,' said Sophia. 'But if push comes to shove, I can live with the slash-and-burn method of clearing productive harvest land. You will be safe, Joanna, whatever happens. That much I promise you. It will be the likes of myself and my allies who rebuild the world as a more hospitable place for our race. Von Waldburg likes to play with matches, but he has no patience for the boring work of reconstruction.'

'You could keep the Judas Purse for yourself. With the powers it would give you . . .'

'Hah! I recognise a simple truth that Von Waldburg refuses to face,' said Sophia. 'Using the coins to win your wars for you drives you mad and corrupts your flesh. Look at Hitler. A sallow walking skeleton at the end, dribbling inside the false protection of his bunker. Even if the Fuhrer had won the war, he'd have died a couple of years after victory. The coins bring you great power. Just not for very long, before they hollow your body out. A vampiric constitution will hold up better than any mere mortal's, but however slow such poison acts, using the coins is still poison.'

'The old monster must know that too, surely?'

'Of course,' said Sophia. 'Some part of him knows, even if he doesn't dwell on it. But he has tasted the ultimate honey, my dear. One coin that was briefly under his control before it was stolen and destroyed. Von Waldburg will do anything to ensure he grabs onto the rest of the honey pot.'

And Sophia intended to be the one to pass him that pot and let him gorge. Once Von Waldburg had broken the cattle's inexorable chain of progress and reduced humanity's survivors to savages huddled among the shattered ruins of their fragile civilisation, Sophia would stand back and watch the addict play with his needle until the drugs gave him the overdose he craved. And who would be left to rule, then? Time for a mistress of mistresses to ascend to the vacant throne.

18

Bex Crawfield was looking awfully smug to Eleanor's eyes. Even Guy had noticed her self-satisfied aura. 'You happy about moving up to the first team, kid, or just pleased to swap Dirty Harriet's tender touch for mine?'

That last remark obviously needled Bex. 'She's a great squad commander.'

'I bet that's what all the cops on her beat used to say too, just before she tossed some poor pickpocket off a warehouse roof. You ever ask the old girl how she earned that nickname of hers in the Chicago police?'

'Same way you got yours.'

'I have a nickname?' Guy looked around at the others. 'What, and you didn't think to tell me?'

Ian shrugged. 'Beats me.'

'Tough Guy,' said Bex. 'That's what Harriet calls you. Like, not in the kind of way that suggests she actually thinks it's true. You know, like *Little* John in Robin Hood.'

'Aces,' said Guy. He glanced towards Eleanor. Even Sister Mee was smiling. 'That ain't anything I expect to hear repeated from any of you.'

'I'm fairly sure pride is still listed as a sin,' advised the nun.

'So is trash-talking me,' said Guy.

'Are you certain there are zombies down there?' Diane asked Eleanor.

'Sadly, no doubt about it.' If Eleanor had been even one percent unsure, she would never have suggested getting Bex Crawfield on loan from the backup unit. *Not in a thousand years.*

'Your new girl isn't wrong,' said Bex. 'I can sense undead lurking below, too.'

'Then why haven't the zombies been attracted by the dead rabbits I bought at the market and tossed down there?' asked Ian.

'Because they're old,' said Bex, 'Aztec-vintage. Like, think of them as having their organic batteries run down. They need to see living flesh moving around before they reanimate and go into chase mode.'

Eleanor really didn't like the sound of that. 'So they need us to act as bait?'

'Hey, you're not as stupid as you look, new girl. You could always go back to Main Street Teotihuacan and hang out a sign offering free tourist tours of the Aztec temple below the cathedral. Let some dumb-ass day-trippers draw off the zombies while we make a run for the coins.'

'Dirty Harriet would be *so* proud of you,' said Guy.

'Such a wicked ploy would be counter productive as well as morally bankrupt,' warned Sister Mee. 'We would merely end up facing a horde of well-fed fully active zombies, rather than hunger-weakened creatures.'

'There is one positive to all this,' said Diane. 'If they bite us, we can't be turned. We've already had the antidote.'

Bex laughed. 'What, were you asleep during your zombie combat orientation week? They don't care about turning you. They're not Reds. They don't have demi-gogs. You're only three things to a zombie . . . breakfast, lunch and dinner.'

'Headshots and decapitation strikes with your moly blades,' said Guy. 'Does that pretty much cover Zombie Refresher 101, agent?'

'Just remember they're not mindless monsters from some Sam Raimi flick,' said Bex. 'Like, they're semi-sentient. Not clever enough to pass a physics exam, but cunning enough to lay traps, work in groups and use weapons. After they've fed fully, they regenerate their skin well enough to pass for a sick-looking junkie. The better fed they are, the quicker and smarter they'll hunt you down.'

'These zombies will have been bound to the temple by the darkest magic,' said Sister Mee. 'They cannot move outside the limits of the wards that were cast by the Aztecs.'

'How did Father Pedro hide the coins in the temple without becoming lunch?' asked Eleanor.

'He went in clutching the power of the coins, kid,' said Guy. 'The after-glow of holding that much bad ju-ju would have lasted just long enough for him to dump the coins and run for the exit.'

'Damn. And here I was hoping there was some sort or exorcism reading or holy water trick that would help keep us safe.'

'That'll be me, newbie,' said Bex. 'I'll take point. My scent should confuse the zombies long enough to get me close enough to remove a few heads. You people are just there to clean up after me.'

'Sure, and here's the mops we're going to use.' Guy opened a suitcase on the crypt floor. 'I'd have brought the case with the grenade launchers, but given the age of the tunnels, we'd be creating Cave-in-City down there. So this is what we're taking down for Zombie Clearance Day: Russian KBP PP-2000 submachine guns and Kel-Tec double magazine KSG Tactical 12-gauge pump-action shotguns.'

'Spray and pray weapons,' said Bex.

'Compact size, ideal for your enclosed space and quick reaction-type engagement,' said Guy. 'Good enough for Russia's Spetsnaz special forces. Good enough for *this* Tough Guy.' The old man picked up a submachine gun and tossed it at Eleanor to catch. It looked like a modern version of an Uzi - that mainstay of bad eighties action movies: a retracted folding stock, short snub barrel and magazine below the grip, with an integrated trigger loop. 'Cheer up, kid. That's 800 rounds a minute of payback you're holding there.'

'What have zombies ever done to me?'

He winked at Eleanor. 'It's preventive payback, kid. We're going to get our retaliation in first.'

Great. And the day had started out so promisingly, too.

***

'So, where are all these damn zombies?' asked Eleanor, the weight of the weapon clutched in her fingers seemed to grow heavier with each minute they nervously crept through the underground maze without encountering the enemy.

Bex scouted ahead at the front. She glanced back at Eleanor as if she really shouldn't have asked that question. 'I told you, they're recharging. If you want to know what I think, I reckon they are deeper inside the maze, drawn to the coins' power. Evil feeds on evil, right?'

'You can do a lot of things with the coins,' said Guy, 'but biscuits, they ain't.'

'Your half-zombie friend might have a point, ' said Sister Mee. 'The zombies might not absorb any sustenance from the coins, but the horde down here will still be attracted to the Judas Purse like bugs to a lamp. '

The answer to Eleanor's question suddenly arrived. There was just time to register a strange noise drifting down the temple tunnel when the first of the zombies appeared. They wore the garb of Aztec priests, but so decayed by the centuries that all colour had fled from their costumes. They looked more like mummies than zombies, decaying paper dry skin clad in ribbons of cloth. From their throats, an unnatural howl escaped which was the most alive thing about them. Words were mixed into the howl. Like the chanting of a spell. Eleanor had thought that fighting Bex was bad enough when it came to combating the semi-alive - or was it half dead? - but she would have settled for taking a pasting from zombie girl any day of the week compared to this gang of monstrosities.

Bex stepped smartly to the side, giving them a clear field of fire.

'Not yet,' ordered Guy. 'Wait until thirty metres effective.'

Not blasting away and wasting ammo was one of the hardest things that Eleanor had been called to do. Every iota of her innate self-preservation mechanism itched to start shooting. Anything to stop the shambling horde approach any closer.

'What is that they're calling?' asked Ian, his voice shaking uncertainly.

'Not sure. I think it's in Nahuatl, the Aztecs' original tongue,' said Diane as she raised her submachine gun towards the advancing pack of shambling horrors.

'Well, this is how I intend to chat with 'em,' said Guy squeezing the trigger of his weapon and sending a stream of bullets ripping down the tunnel at neck height. 'Reckon they'll understand just fine, though. Light 'em up!'

Zombies stumbled at the end of the tunnel, what was left of their decaying heads spread across those still advancing behind. Guy had highlighted the need to go for head shots, but when you were firing a machine pistol with such a ferocious rate of fire, you just needed to aim at the correct height and let rip. Eleanor realised she was frozen. She hadn't fired a single round. Eleanor willed her fingers to respond, to add to the weight of fire when she smelt the undead horrors to her rear; she swung around and saw a dozen Aztec zombies coming from a side corridor behind them, creeping up just as stealthily as shambling corpses could be expected to. Her combat spec's A.I. system flashed targeting warnings about the zombies' dangerously close combat range, target flashes indicating which creatures she needed to eliminate first. She squeezed down on the KBP PP-2000's trigger, producing a thunderous response from her weapon, chatter angrily echoing off the passage. Ian stood beside her, eyeballing the threat and opening up with his automatic shotgun, sending clouds of deadly pellets blasting down the narrow space with each shot. Eleanor was just glad that these creatures were probably ten years off their last meal. *I certainly don't intend to be their next one.*

Bex drew her blade as the party's magazines clicked on empty, wading forward, swinging the deadly molecule thin-edged sword and cutting apart what was left of the ancient assassins. As quickly as they had appeared, the first wave of attackers was left twitching on the floor, both front and rear. Where limbs had been separated from bodies they seemed to move with a will of their own like snakes, the last vestiges of energy drained away in a few last-minute twitches and spasms.

Eleanor surveyed the carnage, feeling sick.

'There'll be more of them soon,' warned Bex.' They hunt in packs and communicate by scent. Every zombie in this maze knows that we're here now. We need to find the coins and flee before they overwhelm us with sheer numbers. '

'And before we run out of ammunition,' added Eleanor. She palmed a spare magazine from her belt, ejecting the spent clip from her weapon and slapped a fresh one into the gun's grip.

Diane examined her drone's remote control unit and cut loose with a whoop of relief. 'I set the crawler to auto-explore and I think it's found what we are looking for.' Diane set the tablet to wireless broadcast and a little image appeared in the corner of Eleanor's combat specs - showing the feed from the drone's cameras. A large chamber supported by dozens of columns caught in the drone's crimson floodlights, and in the temple's centre, a slab with chains at each corner that had once been used for human sacrifice. On its surface sat a little wooden chest with a carved cross and Christ, acting as a locking mechanism for a rusty old padlock. 'Father Peter must have left that there. The Judas Purse!' Diane tapped the screen and the temple's image was replaced on Eleanor's glasses by a glowing map of the route the drone had taken to reach its current location. 'That's only five minutes from this tunnel. '

Five minutes too long when it came to clambering through Zombie Central, Eleanor mused, *but beggars can't be choosers*. They set off at a fast trot, nervously scanning the darkness with their torches, waiting for the next attack. Eleanor could barely stop herself shaking. They were so close to the prize they had risked their necks for. A chance to grab the purse and deny its contents to every wicked creature who would seize it and use its power for evil.

'Can't your undead cousins harness the coins' power?' Eleanor asked Bex.

'They would need to feed like crazy to reach that level of sentience,' said Bex.

'And then they would have to overcome the sorcery the priests used to seal them down here as guardians of the tunnels,' said Sister Mee.

'So what you're saying,' murmured Eleanor, 'is that if we fail and they feast on us, then we might be swapping the vampire apocalypse for a zombie invasion.'

Bex frowned. 'Yeah, I guess that's exactly what I'm saying.'

'Well, that's just beautiful,' said Eleanor.

Ian swung his torch behind them thinking he had heard something, but it was only one of the strange distant echoes filtering in from the maze. 'Don't worry, we are not going to let that happen.'

'You're wasted on this team you know, 'said Bex. 'When we get out of this you should consider transferring to Harriet's squad.'

Ah, now Eleanor caught a glimpse of the origin of California girl's hostility towards her. Bex liked Ian. But unless Ian had a taste for a tad too much scent on his female company, he'd be better off avoiding the blonde and staying on Guy's team. *On my team. Team Eleanor. It's the only team in town that counts.*

Guy slowed the party, pointing down the passage with his submachinegun barrel. 'Dream on, kid. We're not a soccer league. We don't do transfer season inside the Vigil. Eyes front. Does anything about that seem a little hinky to you?'

Eleanor instantly saw what the squad commander meant. Ahead of them, someone - or something - had lit torches along the wall. An acrid smell of ancient burning pitch as smoke drifted through the air - most of the maze's concealed air ducts long since overgrown and blocked aboveground. 'Do zombies need light?'

Bex shook her head. 'No, they're tracking us by the smell of our flesh. I doubt they lit the torches.'

So who had put a match to them? Eleanor wondered? She wasn't allowed long to ponder that mystery. A second heaving surge of zombie bodies emerged behind the party, attracted by the first wave's massacre.

'Save your bullets,' growled Guy, turning. 'It's light enough we can out-pace them.'

All of them sprinted down the corridor, using the unexpected illumination to reach a decent gallop. Eleanor glanced towards the undead filling the corridor behind them, gaunt chanting figures emerging from dozens of passages inside the maze, additional Aztec zombies strengthening the horde's numbers every second. *Please don't let me die down here. I want to kick the bucket in the sunlight, not torn apart like a rabbit in a warren.* 'What about when we stop and they catch us up?'

'Hell, then you can pop caps like you've got a discount card at Gun Mart.'

They had covered half the distance to the purse's chamber when Eleanor yelped and nearly fell, stumbling against the cold damp walls of the passage. Her body itched, her mind spun. It took a serious effort for her not to vomit.

'What is it?' asked Ian, reaching out towards Eleanor, a look of concern creasing his forehead. 'Were you scratched by a zombie?'

'No,' said Eleanor. 'It's the . . . coins, the Judas Purse. I can *feel* their weight.'

'Feel them how?' asked Guy, suspiciously.

Eleanor's head pulsed with a painful migraine. 'Like they're pushing against me, a magnet with an opposing polarity.'

'Your powers aren't fully recorded on the index yet,' said Sister Mee. 'It is possible you can sense their energy.'

'I've never heard of any power like that,' said Diane.

'There's a whole lot of unrecorded when it comes to the crap the Vigil have to deal with,' sighed Guy. He helped Eleanor stumble forward again, getting the party back on the move.

'If the coins call to evil, maybe it also repels the light, repels goodness,' said Diane as they jogged down a set of crumbling stone stairs.

Eleanor wasn't convinced. 'If you think that's me, you're really looking in the wrong place.'

'As far as we're aware, none of the previous guardians of the Judas Purse reported such a side effect,' said Sister Mee.

'I'll be okay,' said Eleanor, 'but if you're looking for someone to carry the damn coins, I think you better look for another pair of hands.'

'Or perhaps yours are just the pair of hands that are needed,' argued Sister Mee. 'Anyone eager to bear the weight of the Judas Purse would be the wrong person to entrust the coins to.'

'It wouldn't be for long,' reassured Diane. 'We've got the reactor at the Knolls Atomic Power Laboratory on standby to receive the coins and melt them down.'

'Forget it,' said Eleanor. 'I don't think I can even go near the damn coins, let alone dump them in my backpack.'

The group had just cleared an intersection of six narrow passages when dozens more zombies appeared shambling to their rear, reciting who-knows-what in their eerie dead language as if they were trying to remember their lost humanity. This wave of monsters had help, however; a pair of demi-gogs at the back of the horde, the arc flash of electric cattle prods forcing the zombies forward like a stampede of undead cattle.

'Bad company!' shouted Eleanor. 'Reds.'

'I see them,' growled Guy. He fired a short burst from his weapon, cutting down the lead zombies. The demi-gogs vanished back down an intersection, only their mocking laugher remaining, leaving the fruits of their labour moaning and hissing and chanting as the zombies noisily scuffled towards the party. 'Trying to slow us down.'

Eleanor didn't have to ask slow them down from what. The race to reclaim the Judas Purse below ground suddenly had a deadly extra competitor.

They retreated, firing, moving as fast as they could without being overrun, running and twisting in every direction with Eleanor's head throbbing even worse. She was just glad they were following the drone's three-dimensional schematic. It was little wonder the previous explorers had left their bones scattered across every tunnel and passage. This hellhole was a haunted house ride with a legion of real monsters stuffed inside it. The group came to a set of stairs leading down into an anteroom that gave onto three slightly larger tunnels. The roof was held up by columns engraved with snake-like Aztec carvings, a single stone block in the centre of the chamber, rusting chains to hold down the victims that had been sacrificed here. It wasn't the chamber the drone had found, though, this space was far smaller and didn't hold the drone parked inside it. One thing it did have, however, was a set of stone doors on sliding rollers by the stairs' archway. Guy and Ian placed their backs behind the door. With a final-sounding grinding rumble, the pair sealed them inside the anteroom. Eleanor prayed that the bulk of the undead horde was behind them, or they could have just trapped themselves on the wrong side of Zombie Central Station.

'Where do these three tunnels lead?' asked Sister Mee.

Diane consulted the drone's telemetry. She pointed to the left-hand tunnel. 'That one runs back deeper into the maze.' Then the central passage. 'Higher than normal air flow, vegetative matter in the sensors' atmospheric fingerprint, so probably up to one of the pyramids in Teotihuacan. If we take that, we'll hopefully reach another concealed entrance inside the ruins.' Diane indicated the tunnel on the far right. And that's the route the drone took to reach the temple room with the coins.'

'Lucky number three,' said Guy. Their squad commander started to move towards the third tunnel, then yelled as he was suddenly struck by an invisible force, thrown violently across the chamber. Guy landed moaning, his hands fumbling for his dropped weapon. As he did, a second unseen hammer blow materialised from thin air to slam the wind out of him and launch him rolling across the floor.

Eleanor raised her submachine gun and cast about. *There's nothing there? Are we facing an invisible tripwire left by the Aztecs?* 'What the hell is it?'

'There's something inside here with us!' called Sister Mee. She had drawn her moly-blade, circling around and testing the air with it.

'Don't shoot yet,' said Ian, 'too much risk of crossfire. Stand back-to-back. Shield positions.'

Eleanor drew her sword while keeping the submachine gun balanced in her other hand, bolting for Ian's position across the anteroom. So, this is what they had been reduced to. Trying to form a human shield wall like some Roman maniple faced with barbarians lurking inside a dark forest. She sniffed the air as she ran. No scents here apart from their own that she could detect. *Not zombie or demi-gog or vampire.* But there was something else. She sensed a presence. And not a friendly one.

Diane sprinted for their makeshift defensive formation too, but cried as she seemed to flip in the air, a blaze of energy slamming her up into the ceiling before dropping her like a stone towards the chamber's flagstones. The agent smashed into the floor with a groan, her tablet cracked into pieces from the force of the impact. *Is she unconscious or worse? No way to tell from here.* Eleanor cycled through her spectacles combat settings - movement sensing, heat tracking on infrared, but whatever monster was in here with them was coming up empty as far as Silicon Valley's little gift to the agency was concerned. *Beyond science, that's comforting.* Bex Crawfield ignored Ian's warning about the risk of a crossfire and opened up at random with her gun, fumbling for her sword with the other hand. That was until her blade seemed to take on a life of its own, yanked out of the young woman's grip, flailing around in the air, then windmilling back towards the agent. It sank deep into Bex's chest, its deadly sharp tip emerging from her back. The agent screamed as she tumbled over like a felled oak.

No! As much as Eleanor had disliked the other agent, she'd never wish that fate on her.

Only Sister Mee, Ian and Eleanor were left to finish the protective triangular formation, standing back-to-back and facing the seemingly empty anteroom.

Ian slashed the air in front of him with his blade. 'How can we fight what we can't see?'

'The torches,' said Sister Mee. 'Whatever is in here must have lit them. It needs light to see us!'

Eleanor and Ian didn't need to be told twice. They raised their guns and started shooting torches out of the stone wall mounts. *Let's put us on an equal footing and see how whatever this is enjoys playing with the sharp end of a moly-blade.* Eleanor had blasted away her second torch when she felt something mosquito-sharp bite into her neck. Eleanor just had time to pull out the poisoned dart from her skin before a landslide of darkness kicked her feet out from under her.

***

Breaking Professor Ruben Baez out of his cheap Mexican mental hospital hadn't been much of a problem for Sophia. Mexico was so gloriously corrupt. With the amount of American Dollars that Sophia had brought along for bribery purposes, she probably could have bought the archeologist's freedom and had one of the institution staff's grandmothers thrown into the deal as a sweetener. This was excellent luck for Sophia because Baez wasn't really insane - what he was, was completely deranged by being one of the few people to blunder into the subterranean ruins below Teotihuacan and survive. He hadn't actually murdered two of his assistants and eaten them. The zombies had done that. But because zombies obviously don't exist, the Mexican court system had come to an entirely rational decision and sentenced the professor to indefinite respite care at what passed for a maximum security hospital hereabouts. She knew the professor was completely off his rocker, because convincing him to lead her through the maze of passages towards the main chamber where he claimed to have seen the 'shining treasure' hadn't taken any fatal threats of violence. And given Baez was only a mortal human, reentering the zombie-infested maze really, *really* should have needed a threat or two.

A couple of Sophia's nest came trotting back towards her, having to stoop in the low corridors designed for ancient Mesoamericans, a look of triumph flushing their faces foretelling their mission's status. She was impressed despite herself. *They should have died doing their job. That's why we call it a suicide mission.*

'Our attack on the zombies drew most of the undead scum after us,' said the male demi-gog.

'And onto the Vigil debasements,' added the second demi-gog, like she expected to be petted for the job.

'Well done. I'm sure the zombies will be suitably grateful once they've recovered their minds enough to be able to think.' *Brains require brains to feed the intellect. The Vigil's stooges will do nicely in that regard.* 'Human flesh tastes so much better than that of our kind. We are created to be predators, not prey.

Joanna peered nervously through the darkness. She had agitated for so long to play an active part of Sophia's plans, now that she was actually here, she seemed stunned to silence by the enormity of the threat they faced. Not all the remains down here were human detritus. A few vampires had been drawn into the spider's web, too, faring little better against the cursed legacy of the bitter last Aztec priests. *Ah, Joanna, if only I could tell you why I truly need you down here today. But that would spoil the surprise.*

'Over to you, now, professor,' indicated Sophia.

'Oh yes,' gurgled the man. 'Left and right, then we fight. Right and left, then we —'

Sophia flashed her fangs at the lunatic and the threat had the desired effect. He quietened down. 'Spare me your poetic ramblings, professor. I once drove Byron to distraction. Compared to him, your doggerel is every bit as inferior as what's left of your tenuous grasp on sanity. Lead us the rest of the way to my shining treasure, if you please.'

'Shiny, shiny, so full of spiny,' Baez muttered. The man headed off, sniffing the foul dry air down here as though he was a bloodhound. Had Baez researched zombie mythology while in the institution? Learnt about their Morse Code of scent? Stranger things had happened.

'Is this the best way to find the purse?' asked Joanna. 'Shouldn't we search in different directions?'

'I won't have much of a nest left if I split up my demi-gogs and send them trotting off down a dozen different passages to locate the coins,' said Sophia. 'To survive a zombie horde you need strength in numbers or concentration of force. Down here, splitting up for too long is the same as dying.' She kicked a pile of bones lying in the ruined shell of a conquistador breastplate. 'Just ask him.'

Vampires were good at stealth, moving near silently like any nocturnal hunter. The force only came across a dozen or so zombies in the passages the professor led them through, the lunatic greeting them with cheery cries as if they were old students of his. Not so difficult in dribs and drabs to rip apart and leave decorating the maze's tight walls.

'Soon, soon,' chirped the deranged academic.

Sophia felt a rapture growing inside even her cold heart. *After all this time.* The master of masters would have his desires sated. And shortly after, a blink of an eye in the timescales of a near-immortal, so would she. Sophia was still contemplating how her destiny would change for the better when she slammed into something - a something composed of nothing. It was as if there was invisible reinforced glass armour between her and the rest of the corridor. She hammered into the strange barrier with all her strength. She might as well have been trying to kick down a mountain for all the effect her supernatural violence had on progressing forward.

'This can't be,' cried Sophia in fury. She beat her talons against the transparent barrier, but it filled the corridor as effectively as if the passage had been sealed with concrete. Sophia swivelled to face the professor's flinching form. 'You said nothing about this!'

'New, new, a wall seen by few,' wailed the archaeologist,

tears filling his eyes at failing Sophia. At least the vampire's snake-like trance over the man still held.

'What is this wall?' asked Joanna, curiously running her hands across the transparent field as though practising a mime.

'Sorcery, very ancient and very powerful,' said Sophia. *How many souls died to conjure up this dark art, I wonder?*

'The Aztecs' magic?'

Sophia glanced towards the professor. 'Our rhyming idiot thinks it's new. And I'm inclined to agree. Something of this ilk certainly could have been conjured up by the Aztec priests, but the barrier would have faded after a day or two. Keeping it functioning for centuries? There's not enough blood in a thousand worlds to pay the soul-price to maintain such magic for so long.' *I knew there was something else down here with us. My senses weren't playing me false.*

'Not the zombies' sorcery or the Vigil's work, then?'

'When it comes to the former, the zombies are prisoners of this maze's magic wards, not masters of them. And the Vigil and their papal friends? Too soft to slice out the hearts needed to fuel this.' She grabbed the professor by the white fabric of his hospital robe. 'Take us another way!'

'Only route, now,' moaned the man, pointing down the blocked corridor, 'just three minutes to the shiny.'

Three minutes? Sophia howled in frustration. To come so close to claiming the prize only to be halted here. It was intolerable. *It is inconceivable!*

***

Eleanor moaned as she regained consciousness. A fluttering bird where her heart should be, as she tried to recall where she was and why her body ached so damn much. Then the fear hit her as she remembered. *The Aztec maze!* The memory would have flattened her anew if she hadn't already been lying on the anteroom chamber's cold flagstones, her wrists bound behind her back with her ankles tied together so tightly she couldn't be sure the numbness she felt wasn't entirely a result of whatever drug still sloshed around her system. A strangely inappropriate giggle dragged Eleanor's attention towards the centre of the chamber. *Dawn Heliot!* The witch, at least, seemed exceptionally pleased with their reunion. *She's the only one.* Ian twisted at the end of a pair of wrist ties, suspended from the ceiling a ways inside the tunnel on the far left. Strung up like a haunch of kebab meat waiting to be carved. Bex's body had been left slumped against the wall of the anteroom, her bloody sword still plunged through her chest while blood pooled across the floor. Of the others, Guy, Diane and Sister Mee were all as hog-tied on the floor as Eleanor. The fact the witch had bothered to secure the agents must mean that they still lived - at least - for the moment.

Eleanor called out in their direction. 'Are you okay?'

'We're-' their answers were stymied by the witch. Heliot walked along the line of prisoners, kicking them to silence and threatening them with her wand. If Eleanor hadn't seen what that wicked gnarled piece of wood was capable of, she would have laughed. Heliot looked like a spoiled child at a birthday party, threatening the other guests with her magic stick.

Staring closer, Eleanor noted that Heliot appeared pasty and unwell. 'You allergic to zombies, or just still annoyed that kid with ruby slippers dropped a house on your sister?'

Heliot stopped by Eleanor and grinned like a piranha about to feed. 'The Spell of Glass I used to enter the ruins unseen and fight you takes its toll on a girl's flesh, my darling. But don't you worry, after I make the time to sacrifice a few of your friends, I'll be back to my former glory. I do believe I will sacrifice the girl and the nun first. Seasoned meat like the old man deserves to be kept as a snack to distract the zombies. They'll enjoy eating him.'

So, that at least explains why she drugged us, rather than darting us with a fatal poison. 'Why have you done this to us?'

'It is quite simple. Three tunnels. The middle one lead back to the surface, but the other two? They both contain bombs with timers on them. Tick-tock, tick-tock.'

'What the hell are you up to?' asked Eleanor.

'You have a choice to make,' cackled the witch. 'You can save the boy, or you can recover the Judas Purse. Pick one, because your other choice won't apply.'

'How can I save anybody trussed up like this?'

'You must release your powers. Don't be coy, I have seen what you can do. This is no time to hide your light under a bushel. Show me what you are capable of my darling! Let's uncage the real you.'

'What is she talking about?' called Guy. 'Is this about what happened inside the demon's store?'

'You really don't know what you have caught and tamed here, do you?' laughed Heliot. 'What a waste . . . for *you*. The clock is ticking, my darling. Release the beast within you. Let me glimpse her beautiful form.'

'Don't listen to the false creature!' warned Sister Mee. 'If a witch is daring you to do such a thing, she will have ...'

Dawn Heliot aimed her wand at the nun and a dark crackling fork of energy leapt the space between them, blasting the nun into unconsciousness. 'You know the price of everything and the value of nothing, sister. Time for a little quiet from you.'

Eleanor twisted frantically inside her wrist and ankle ties. *Damn it.* She had used the Vigil's own restraints. Cunning wonders of material science, designed to restrain something with a vampire's strength. Or an agent's. 'You're bluffing, Maleficent. I get that you're pissed about Ian overcoming your charms, but why put a bomb in the other tunnel? You would never risk the Judas Purse being lost.'

'Oh my precious darling, the coins won't be lost. The bomb in that tunnel will merely seal that section of the temple off from you. But not from the vampires. They are heading towards the purse from the opposite end of the maze. The pesky bloodsuckers needed you to draw off the army of the Aztec undead down here, which you so obligingly arranged for them. However, their progress is currently somewhat stymied by wards I have cast. Magical barriers that even vampires and their demi-gog slaves may not cross. Sadly for you, my shield wards are on a timer, too. Those barriers will drop soon and the vampires will finally be allowed to claim their prize.'

'What have the Reds promised you?'

'Nothing, silly girl. Deal with the bloodsuckers? I'd sooner trust the Keeper.'

'You destroy the tunnel, you'll lose your chance to take the coins.'

'I plan to live forever, not die twisting in agony as Empress of the World after a single season. Evil knows evil when she sees it. Those ancient coins have been cursed by the blood of the God-child. What is that old expression, a *poisoned chalice*? The coins glitter so brightly, yet still they are poisoned.'

'You ain't the sharpest tool in the shed, are you?' growled Guy. 'Allow the Reds to claim those coins and they'll bring destruction to everyone, including you.'

'Oh, I don't have anything against a little chaos released abroad in the world,' laughed Heliot. 'It was bad enough I had to flee Europe back in the thirties with the Pope's sanctimonious assassins hot on my trail. Your friends in the Vigil have grown far too adept at tracking me, now. When the global village is one big failed state resembling the sands of a post-apocalyptic movie, little old me will be back in my element. No more CCTV cameras, no facial recognition computers, no chipped ID cards or air-force drones scanning the sky for me anymore, never sleeping, never stopping. I was born in the Georgian era, remember. Do I look like I love Facebook? Do I look like I really need driverless cars? That's the glorious thing about the Reds' upcoming Dark Age - the darkness shall rule supreme. A millennia-long feast for all the races of the Sidhe Antiqua.'

'With you as its queen?' spat Diane.

'Mistress of my little corner of it. Unlike the bloodsuckers, I don't require the ego-boost of having millions of human slaves in thrall to me. A girl can only feed on one soul at a time, after all. Far more fun to hunt than to farm. If only the vampires could loosen up and embrace that philosophy, the world would be a far better place.'

Diane twisted in her chains. 'For *you*, you twisted servant of Satan.'

'Is there anyone else here who actually counts?' grinned the witch. Heliot checked her watch. 'Only a few minutes left. You really need to start freeing yourself soon, Eleanor. Do nothing . . . you will see the boy die as well as lose your precious coins to those horrible bloodsuckers. So, are you to save the Judas Purse and condemn Mr. Hunky Pants to death? Or will you save lover boy and allow the vampires their reign of blood? Poor Ian, but then there are those terribly important coins to consider? Choices, choices.'

'Save the coins,' pleaded Ian. 'One life is nothing compared to everyone else who will die.'

'Guy?'

'I can't help you here, kid. There're some choices you have to make for yourself. This one is down to you.'

Dawn Heliot capered about, savouring the agony of Eleanor's choice. 'Come on, girlfriend! Ian's about to die in a few seconds. The only tunnel from this room to the Judas Purse is nearly about to blow. Think of all the vampires licking their fangs and praying you go with your heart rather than your head. But then ... oh, poor, poor Ian.'

Eleanor felt the heat building inside her, just as it had back at the strange demon's travelling store. Her wrist and ankle ties started to glow from the fierce white heat of energy.

Sister Mee had recovered from the wand's violence enough to scream a warning. 'No, Eleanor, don't! She's prepared a spell to suck your powers from you, to steal them for herself. That's why the creature's set this choice up, she requires a heightened emotional response from you. Hold it in.'

Diane added her clamour to the nun's shouts and the witch's features twisted in loathing. 'Enough from you two darlings!' Twin bolts leapt from her gnarled wand, blasting Diane silent and smashing the nun back into unconsciousness. 'I need to feed on you or use you as snacks to draw the zombies away from me, but nobody said I have to listen to your insolence.'

Hold it in. 'I can't—' Eleanor desperately tried to pull back the power, contain it inside her flesh, but she couldn't stop. Not now. Such vast energy being channelled and she was its sole conduit, a single figure struggling on the slopes trying to hold back an avalanche which she had started.

'Too late for second thoughts, my dear,' cackled the witch, she raised her wand, a conductor about to instruct her orchestra. A web of shimmering green lines appeared in the air of the chamber, joining Eleanor to the woman like a web fixing a fly to a spider. The lines began to pulse as the life-force and the power Eleanor had conjured started to drain out from her towards the witch.

Dawn Heliot swayed bathed in golden light. 'Yes. YES! MINE.'

Heliot hollered in shock as Bex got to her feet and rushed the witch, the blade still impaled inside the agent's bleeding chest. The witch went flying, her wand spinning in the air as if she had been tackled by a quarterback. Eleanor gasped, the life-draining connection between her and the witch suddenly broken. *I guess I know what zombie girl's primary power is, now. Taking punishment. Turned into a human pin-cushion, but still able to dish it out.*

Eleanor felt her summoned energy flowing back again, burning her, charging her. She passed it through her wrists and ankles, the energy writhing like a beast crawling inside her body, and as she did so the plastic hissed and melted into a foul-smelling vapour, droplets congealing on the flagstones. *Free!* She seized her moly-sword from the ground where it lay discarded.

'Head for the Judas Purse!' urged Guy, writhing on the floor next to her.

Eleanor bent down and sliced his wrist and leg ties. 'You do it, I'll be right behind you.' Guy cursed but got to his feet not bothering to argue, snatched up his fallen submachine gun and hurled himself down the main passage. Heliot screamed abuse at Bex as the two women wrestled desperately across the chamber. *The bomb.* Eleanor didn't have time to think, she rushed towards the tunnel where Ian dangled thrashing from the ceiling.

'No!' begged Ian, twisting in the air in his restraints as Eleanor arrived. 'Go with Guy, he can disarm the mechanism while you run for the coins.'

Eleanor ignored Ian's exhortations and bent down, examining the package of explosives on the ground. Nothing fancy. Industrial mining explosives with a digital timer wired into the blasting cap. She yanked the timer out of the arrangement and tossed the deactivated unit down the corridor.

'I'm not the mission!' protested Ian as Eleanor cut him down from the ceiling. He collapsed on the flagstones with a heavy thump.

'You are to me.' Eleanor swivelled to see Heliot shove Bex away from her, zombie girl still weakened from being skewered, the witch rolling to the side to seize her wand. In another second she would fry Bex.

'You want my power?' shouted Eleanor. 'Take it!' She dropped to her knees and held out both her hands, focusing on what needed to be done. Releasing the surge of energy was as easy as vomiting from food poisoning and as much of a relief, too - at least for Eleanor. For Heliot, not so much. The stream of raw energy struck the witch in the centre of her body, flinging her back with a thunder-clap as if she had leapt in front of a two-hundred-ton locomotive. Heliot spun through the air like a rag doll, striking one of the temples pillars and smashing it in half, enough to break her momentum - and body - a shower of masonry and rock from the roof raining down on top of her twitching body. Then the entire temple jolted to the side, throwing Eleanor off her feet. For a second, Eleanor was terrified that Heliot snapping the column was bringing the whole chamber crashing down around them, but the blow-back of smoke and debris from the second tunnel revealed what had actually happened. *The second bomb! It's detonated!* Booby-trapped, or . . . she noticed the half-melted submachine gun thrown across the floor. Guy Drew's weapon. Eleanor stumbled to the passage snaking towards the main temple. The tunnel wasn't there anymore. An avalanche of smoking dirt, rock and broken stone completely blocked that passage; the explosion had collapsed the entire structure in on the maze. Guy had been caught in the blast, murdered trying to defuse the explosives. Eleanor's escape hadn't left the squad commander enough time. *Too slow. I was too slow.* No way the old man could have survived the fury of the blast. Vapourised, with even the ionised gas from the man's corpse, lost and entombed under a hundred feet of Mexican rock.

'He's gone,' whispered Eleanor. *And I killed him.*

Ian stumbled across to stand by her side, staring dumbly at the debris. 'No, he can't be —'

Eleanor turned as she heard the hoarse cackle of laughter. *Heliot.* Eleanor crossed to the body, to make sure the witch was finished. Furious enough to snap the woman's neck in revenge if she hadn't already received fatal injuries. But no, the woman was dying. Not even a dark witch's art was enough to put Humpty Dumpty's shattered shell back together again. Still the witch found the life to giggle as she expired.

Eleanor knelt beside the creature. 'There's a special place in Hell reserved for you. It took meeting a burning angel to make me believe. But now? I reckon you'll be meeting every last man, woman and child you ever fed on. They'll be lining up around the fires of perdition to stick pins in you.'

'Silly girl,' rasped Heliot. 'Did you — never wonder how — the bloodsuckers — were always one step behind you? Your precious Vigil — harbours a traitor. That's my — final gift to you. You have failed — because of one of — your own! You chose to — allow the bloodsuckers to win. My death here means nothing. You haven't — won a — single thing by slaying me. Nothing!'

Eleanor watched the final croak squeeze out of the witch, the woman's body convulsing. As Heliot died, all traces of her youth vanished. Slowly at first, then rapidly. Twenty years old. Thirty years old. Seventy. One hundred. Two hundred years. It was like watching a corpse caught on time-lapse video ageing across centuries. Within seconds, there was only a mound of dust filling an empty set of clothes. *Was Heliot lying? Trying to sow doubt in me with her dying words? As in life, so in death?* Eleanor stared towards at the others in the chamber. Diane looked like she might be coming back around. Sister Mee still lay unconscious. How well did Eleanor know the nun, or for that matter, Bex Crawfield?

How did the vampires know exactly where to find us again? Eleanor reached for the side of her combat spectacles and erased the last minute's worth of recording. She was going to keep this to herself until she knew who to trust.

'What did that old crone whisper to you?' asked Bex, grimacing as she yanked the moly-sword free of her body. The agent's hybridised zombie metabolism had already healed what should have been a fatal wound. For her, it was like pulling out a wood splinter.

'Nothing,' lied Eleanor. 'A dying curse with no actual power to make it happen.'

'We don't need her bloody curse to work,' accused Bex. 'You messed up by choosing to save Agent Holderness instead of the mission. By the time we dig our way through that tunnel the Judas Purse will be long gone. You allowed the Reds to steal the coins out from under our noses!' Zombie girl jabbed a finger towards Ian. 'You think you saved him? You've actually killed him . . . just really, really slowly! You've murdered us all, you idiot!'

As if reacting to the violence of the woman's voice the temple started to tremble; softly at first, then with increasing ferocity, dust and large sections of rubble falling from the ceiling. The walls began to buckle in spouts of ancient masonry as they caved in, a couple of centuries of zero maintenance finally taking their toll on the forgotten temple.

Ian lurched across to them through the collapsing clouds of dust. 'That explosion's done for the complex. We need to escape!'

Eleanor exchanged an angry glance with Bex, as though this was something else that was going to be blamed on her. 'Yeah, that sounds like a stand-up plan. I'll help Diane out of here. You two geniuses grab the sister.'

Diane was dazed when Eleanor ran across to her, groggy as though drunk. But look on the bright side, if she'd been baseline human, she'd still be unconscious from the lashing power of the witch's wand, if not far worse. Eleanor took the agent's weight under her shoulder and they hobbled up the middle passage like they were tied together in some insane three-legged race. Bex and Ian already had the nun held between them in front, the stone steps of the passage reeling underfoot as they all pushed forward, desperately hoping the guess that this route led above ground prove true. Escaping with their collective wounds wasn't made any easier with tonnes of soil and rock coming down around their ears.

'Wait, we've left Guy behind!' mumbled Diane.

'He didn't make it,' said Eleanor, coughing with ancient dust itching her eyes; trying to keep her gaze on the route ahead. Torches lit by the dead witch were being extinguished as sections of the staircase slid away, taking the light with them. 'Blown to pieces.'

'But the Judas Purse . . . ?'

'Nabbed by the Reds,' swore Eleanor, stepping aside as a slab of rock the size of a menhir crashed down from the ceiling. Her heart hammered inside her, how close that jagged rock had come to impaling her through the skull. 'The coins' theft by the vampires was Wicked Wanda's end-run, anyway.' Eleanor could feel the evil weight of the coins rolling away from her. The Judas Purse had been claimed, just not by the Vigil.

'He can't,' cried Diane, 'no, please, that can't have happened. Guy's rescued the coins. He's alive. He must be.'

It shouldn't have been Guy who went after the coins. I'm younger, faster. I could have ripped the fuse out of the bomb and grabbed the purse before the Reds showed up. They both reached the top of the stairs, a narrow tunnel, level and straight but filling in by waves of dirt as rotted timber ceiling supports burst above them. There was a shout through the dust, its meaning lost through waves of rubble, but she prayed the call signified they were close to the exit. Eleanor took another step forward but was slugged into the wall as an avalanche of rock and dirt slide-slammed her, sending her spinning, her hands grasping out for Diane, but the woman seemed to be dropping away. A rent in the floor had opened up behind them, dropping Diane through a gallows trapdoor. Eleanor frantically pushed rocks away, the pile of rubble swelling as additional debris fell from the ceiling. She caught a glimpse of Diane's position inside the cavern. The agent clinging onto an outcrop of rock with her left hand, dangling seven feet below the crumbling floor of Eleanor's passage, the other arm windmilling around for a second handhold. The rent that had opened up in the tunnel revealed another five levels of the labyrinth, all exposed to a rain of rock and soil, the very deepest level filled with Aztec undead frothing and rolling like a sea of slugs, their arms raised towards the signs of life above them. Like looking down into an exposed anthill, if the ants were zombies. Rocks the size of cars plummeted around the mass, crushing many of the creatures, but their chanting madness was still loud enough to reach up to Eleanor through the roar of collapsing temple.

'Hang on, I'm coming for you!' Eleanor reached for her backpack, going for the climbing lines and grappling hook inside.

'I believe,' yelled Diane, her body swaying below the outcrop.

In what? Eleanor never got a chance to ask. The entire side of the maze where Diane clung onto broke apart, crumbling into a shower of fragments, the agent just another piece of debris with her body spinning down towards the zombie horde, quickly followed by five levels of labyrinth folding in on itself. Eleanor stared incredulously into the disintegrating pit. A few seconds ago Diane had been alive. They were going to escape together. Now the woman was gone, her corpse entombed by a hundred tonnes of collapsing sediment. First Guy, then Diane. This mission was degenerating into a bloody massacre. The tunnel continued to buckle, piles of rubble falling away into the expanding hole. Eleanor's self-preservation mechanism, tinged with raw fear, suddenly kicked in as Ian emerged through the rolling clouds of dust and grabbed her, his eyes casting around for Diane.

'She's dead. Alive and then dead. How did that happen?'

'Out,' commanded Ian, dragging her back through the collapsing passage.

'Just gone.'

'Out before we die, too!'

They blundered through curtains of falling masonry, choking on debris, the crashing rubble thundering around them. When Eleanor finally saw the jungle in front of her, the stepped Aztec pyramid towering behind her, it took at least half a minute for her to realise that she could stop running, now. *Safe. Safe. Safe.* The combined strength of Bex and Ian was needed to prevent her from crashing wordlessly forward through the undergrowth. She should flee. Run all the way home to New York. The two agents shouted something at Eleanor, but she didn't understand their words. They might as well have been chanting in the Aztec's dead language. Post-traumatic stress disorder had flipped a switch inside her head she might just have officially lost it. A small part of Eleanor was actually grateful for her weakness. Far better than facing up to what she had just lost. Someone seemed to be screaming in front of the jungle. It might even have been her.

19

~ DIRTY HARRIET ~

Professor Baez raised his hands to greet the warm air of the Mexican evening. 'Yes! Fresh, fresh as —'

'Your death!' said Sophia snapping the man's neck.

'You killed him,' cried Joanna, watching the professor slump into the pyramid's moonlight shadows. There was a sudden moment of stillness across the landscape, only the distant lantern lights from a few night tours strolling through the massive archaeological site.

'Frankly, if I had to listen to this fool kill any more poetry, he would have murdered me,' said Sophia. She stepped aside and indicated the corpse to her demi-gogs. They didn't need to be asked twice, the creatures fell upon the body, feasting with an eagerness that could only have come from surviving the maze.

Sophia tilted back the lid of the little chest she had grabbed up, recoiling a little at the touch of the crucifix carved in the case. *Just superstition.* She didn't need the crucifix burning her, not with the casket's contents inside. Sophia's skin seemed to pulse as if filled with shivering maggots when touching the chest. Inside: a heap of Roman coins on white lace, ancient money every bit as shiny as the dead lunatic had promised. 'Judas, you bad, bad boy.' It wasn't every day you saw a pile of coins cursed by the betrayal of the Son of God. Coins that had once tempted Judas Iscariot to a treason that had changed the world forever. 'No, you foul little beauties. You're not for me. I have someone else for you to corrupt. An old friend who is *dying* to be reunited with your powers.' She closed the casket and dropped the case into her lead-lined knapsack.

'You did well,' Sophia told Joanna.

'I did?'

'Oh yes. Better than I could have hoped.'

More demi-gogs emerged from the pyramid behind them, brushing dust and rubble off their clothes.

Even if someone had their wicked fun with me down in the maze. The unsettling memory of invisible barriers, the thump of explosives collapsing the temple to remind Sophia how very narrowly she had triumphed. Sophia would be sure to kill that interfering *someone* if she ever encountered them again. They would be very, very sorry to have toyed with her kind. *We are cats, not mice. Soon enough the whole world will have reason to be reminded of that fundamental truth.*

***

Eleanor had lost all sense of time when the woman finally arrived in Eleanor's cell. Buried somewhere deep in the Vault's lowest levels. An armoured cell with a single cot, just like the chamber below New York where she had originally woken up. No natural light but plenty of questions over the speakers, unseen interrogators relentlessly debriefing her, time and time again, springing on any inconsistencies in her recollections. By the time she had told the same story for the five hundredth time, she kind of doubted her veracity herself.

'You know who I am?' asked the woman. She stood tall just

shy of six feet, her blonde hair cut in a fashionably short bob, maybe in her late forties or early fifties. The newcomer wasn't unattractive, but the natural beauty she possessed was marred by a black eye-patch over the left side of her face. The remaining eye was sea-blue, cool and knowing. There was an aura of raw toughness about the woman; coiled steel under the folds of her clothes, a night-stick ready to lash out if provoked.

'Dirty Harriet,' said Eleanor. It wasn't even a question in her mind.

The woman raised her hand and make a pistol-cocking gesture to indicate the cell's single occupant had nailed it in one. 'Never did like that nickname. We're all dirty here. Ain't none of us clean.'

'Where's my team? I want to see them.'

Dirty Harriet grunted in tired amusement. '*Your* team? That's cute. Yesterday's news. Disbanded, with all the chumps who survived reassigned.'

Gone? Eleanor could hardly process the words. Was that her fault, too? *The cost of failure?* 'Nobody has more experience tracking the Judas Purse than we do.'

'Not to mention watching the coins walk from under your noses. We'll struggle on without the benefit of your indispensable skills.'

'You need to get me out of here,' demanded Eleanor, trying to keep any note of pleading out of her quivering voice.

Harriet merely shrugged. 'I don't need to do anything. In fact, girl-chick, I'd say you're exactly where you need to be right now.'

'What are you talking about? Didn't you pick up on anything I've been telling the debriefing team? I can sense the coins. Since

I came close to them, they've been like a migraine gnawing away at the back of my skull.'

'Yeah, you and your nutty powers. The same powers you didn't bother warning us about in advance, and now we're just meant to trust you? The kindest view I can come up with here is that you weren't even close to field-ready when you were released into the world. Your arse-hat moves cost us the Judas Purse, the mission and the lives of two agents, one of them your illustrious squad leader.'

'Bet you're real upset about that …'

'You don't know me, girl-chick. You don't know a damn thing about me. Tough Guy was a pain in the butt, but he was a closer. He took down plenty of Reds and other freaks over the decades. You think I'm happy about losing an effective combatant in this war? You really don't understand word one: but *that* I knew already.'

'You know squat!'

'I know this much, sweetie. We're going to ship you to the Island. First class, Air Vigil. You'll enjoy it out there. A chance for you to relax and think about your life. It's like Club Med, but with orange boiler suits and a nice deep cell filled with the very latest in medical monitoring gear. We might not understand what you are, now, but we will. You're going to get your shit straight. Then we'll come to a decision about what the hell to do with you.'

'I'm not your damn lab rat, I'm an agent.'

'Not anymore, girl-chick. Papa's gone. I'm your Mama and Mama says you're grounded.'

'But for the love of god, I can help you find the coins!'

'You think we need your help for that? Eye of the storm, sweetie. We already know that the Judas Purse is somewhere inside the Yellow Sea region. If you were allowed a TV inside your little padded cell you'd know that the Reds have been plenty busy. There's a war brewing between Japan and China over ownership of the Senkaku islands. America and Australia have weighed in on the Japanese side. Fleets are busy mobilising. The Yellow Sea resembles one big naval regatta right now. The PLA is playing aircraft carrier tag with our Seventh Fleet. It's only going to take one false step or itchy trigger finger with some fighter jock, and cruise missiles are going to be flying in every direction.'

'I can help you fight the Reds,' pleaded Eleanor. *Please let me help make this right.*

'Your help might already have started the Third World War. We'll all be a hell of a lot safer when you're in a reinforced concrete hole in the Caribbean and we pull the hole up after you, don't ya think?'

Eleanor sagged down into her cot-bed, glaring up at Harriet. The woman was right about one thing. Eleanor really didn't know the first thing about the rival squad commander. *Dirty Harriet was back-stepping us all the way. Maybe she's the traitor inside the Vigil? Ambitious enough to want Guy and his team out of the way. Dropping hints back to the Reds about where we were all the time. Ready to lead a new assault team to seize the Judas Purse after she traces its exact location. Medals, kudos and glory all around.*

'Why are you in here with me? You came to gloat?'

'Your polygraph results on your debriefing,' said Harriet. 'There's something you're not telling us about the mission.'

Ah, so that was it. And if Dirty Harriet was the Vigil's traitor, then she'd be real worried about someone on the disbanded lead team having added two and two together and come up with, "snitch". 'It's just the questions about my powers triggering glitches in your tests,' lied Eleanor. 'I don't know what the hell they are, so I can't answer your people's questions. I was bitten. I turned and the cure brought me back. Whatever I am didn't ship with a user's manual.'

'That even sounds plausible. But I still suffer from a cop's itchy palms when someone is BS'ing me. That's one power I didn't pick up with the cure - surviving the streets of San Francisco did that. And right now, girl-chick, you're pure poison ivy on my mitts. So how about you tell Mama what you're not telling Mama. Why is it your spec's recording files are shy a few minutes of footage when you were in the temple?'

'The blast-wave from the tunnel explosion must have broken the device.'

'What, I just fell out of the tree, all green and shiny? Tell me the truth.'

'Bend in close,' said Eleanor, glancing up at the camera dome in the centre of the cell's ceiling. 'I don't want the CCTV to pick this up.'

Dirty Harriet humoured her request.

'Your little half-zombie friend claims she wears Chanel No. 5, but while she was still in shock from being skewered she admitted it's really a cheap Mexican knock-off bulk-purchased over the web. I reckon Bex monkeyed with the footage.'

Harriet wearily shook her head. 'You come back to me after a couple of years on the Island and we'll see how well you're doing in the wise cracking business.'

'With you and your arse-hats on the tail of that cursed purse, a concrete hole in the middle of nowhere is probably the safest place to be.'

'Hah! Out of the mouth of babes,' sighed Harriet. She raised a finger towards the camera and spun her digit around. The armoured door opened with the clack of multiple deadbolts pulling back. 'You just blew the only chance I was carrying for you. Guess you messed up *again*.'

Eleanor watched the woman leave, her heart thumping with anger. For a moment, Eleanor considered throwing caution to the wind and rushing the rival squad leader. But the glint in the woman's eyes told Eleanor that the ex-cop was fully aware of what her prisoner was thinking. *She'd probably welcome the chance to beat me inside the cell.* A busman's holiday for her.

20

~ IT'S GOING TO BE A LONG CLIMB ~

Eleanor's leather hood was finally pulled away from her head. The young woman had arrived at an airfield somewhere. No place she recognised, but she could smell the ocean's salt. *We're close to the coast.* An open hanger towered ahead, a large transport plane sitting outside with four swivel-mounted vertical take-off jets connected to each wing. The craft possessed the weird angular airframe of a modern stealth bomber. Aerodynamically unstable, requiring fly-by-wire to keep it in the air. So, this was the Vigil's answer to Con-Air. Sadly, this was likely to be the last glimpse of home Eleanor was going to get for a long time. A hatch had been left open towards the tail, a stair-ramp pushed up to the entrance. Her escort stood faceless in black ski-masks, armoured jackets and bulky Cav helmets with built-in tactical displays. As the guards shoved her closer, the plane's fuselage seemed to fade and turn transparent, revealing the other side of the airfield, building lights twinkling brightly in the cool evening air. Eleanor realised that was the advanced optical camouflage's electronic ink flowing across the airframe, erasing the plane from eyesight and complementing the plane's stealth profile. *Yeah, erasing the plane. Just like they're going to erase me from the world. What was it Dirty Harriet told me inside the cell? The Vigil would drop me in a hole and pull the hole up after me.*

The soldiers led her up the steps and into the aircraft. Inside the plane, there was little to give away its stealth capabilities - only the fact the wings weren't visible through the video-screen windows. Given the craft's interior resembled a high-end corporate jet rather than an aerial jail, Eleanor guessed the aircraft usually served as an airborne command centre, rather than prison transport. Her guards chained her into one of the seats and took the seats by her side. Given takeoff priority, the aircraft started taxiing around the airfield until it approached the main runway, then there was a thrum from outside as the main engines rotated into lift position.

One of the guards banged on the hatch they had used to enter the plane. A warning light blinked orange above the door. The soldier spoke in an unusually gruff, scratchy voice, as though he had a fifty-a-day cigarette addiction. 'This isn't shutting. Help me pull it shut before we lift.'

Grumbling, a couple of Eleanor's sentries left the seats next to her and went to add their weight to the task.

'Come on, throw your backs into it. We don't want this opening on us at a thousand feet.'

Outside, the engines' buildup continued as fan jets rotated faster.

Suddenly the door swung open and the guard who had called for help booted the two soldiers in the back, sending the escort tumbling, yelling, out of the door. Then the guard slammed the exit shut. He tossed his helmet onto a nearby chart table and banged on the cockpit's sealed anti-hijack door. When the door opened, Eleanor saw Sister Mee in the pilot's position, Sister Rae sitting in the copilot's and — even more shockingly

— Bex Crawfield filling the navigator's position. The guard who had booted out the pair of soldiers onto the airstrip below pulled away his balaclava, revealing Alasdair's flushed features below. The soldier still sitting sentry next door to her peeled his black balaclava away. *Ian!*

Eleanor could hardly believe what she saw. *Of all the stupid . . .* 'What, was that your big-boy voice, Al?'

'No, it's my "We're getting out of here" voice.'

'Why?' shouted Eleanor, dazed by the sudden turn of events. 'It wasn't enough that I get myself exiled to the Vigil's private Guantanamo Bay beach resort? You're all going to find yourself fitted with orange straightjackets for busting me free now, too.'

'Shut up and listen for once,' called Bex, their aircraft rising on four jets of flames, shuddering as two engines swivelled to forward thrust, before powering the transport away into the sky.

'*This* is your why,' said Alasdair. He waited for Ian to unlock Eleanor's chains. Then he pulled a tablet out of his backpack and turned the screen towards her. 'I cleaned this imagery up from your spectacles' cam footage.' Eleanor stared at the playback from her own glasses. It was the Aztec temple during the final cave-in, Diane clinging on for dear life as her handhold on the rock disintegrated, the cavern folding in on itself. Diane fell. The footage slowed to frame-by-frame analysis. Diane was struck by tumbling rocks, the limpness of her body indicated she was mercifully unconscious for her entombment. That was when Eleanor saw it. A shadow flashing through the air, emerging from one of the lower level tunnels exposed by the rupture, a silhouette leaping straight through the avalanche of soil and rock. The shadow collided with Diane mid-air, seized her, hit the exposed tunnel on the other side and rolled away clutching her comatose body.

Alasdair tapped the rolling silhouette, visible for a mere millisecond before the sea of falling soil filled in the rupture and blocked the view. 'Motion analysis pegs that as a demi-gog.'

Eleanor rubbed life back into her wrists where the chains had secured her. 'Why on earth would one of those monsters bother saving Diane?'

'We're high-value assets to the Reds,' said Alasdair. 'Same as the vampires are to us. They work hard to capture us, torture us, roll up our networks. Try to extract the locations of Vigil bases and safehouses, the identities of our staff. Whether agents have family members who can be kidnapped and used as leverage, so those fighting on our side can be turned.'

'The same nest who stole the coins captured Diane,' said Ian. 'That means wherever the Judas Purse is, it's also where Diane is being held and interrogated.'

Eleanor didn't know if the relief she was feeling was for her insane rescue, or for the fact she hadn't got Diane killed back inside the temple. *Yet*, a dark voice reminded her. *You haven't got her killed, yet.* 'And *this* is your plan? You're crazy. You have to show this video to the Vigil, beg them to deploy a heavy rescue force.'

Ian flashed Eleanor a grim look. 'We did. John told me that Diane's capture is regrettable, but the chances are she's already broken under interrogation, told the Reds everything and been thrown to the nest as supper. The director said he's too focused on saving humanity from the second Cuban Missile Crisis to devote resources to side-missions.'

'Old timers can get like that,' said Bex. 'So busy reliving their glory days they can't see the future clearly.'

Eleanor flashed the woman a distrustful stare. 'And how come you're here, California?'

'Harriet wasn't happy with us cutting and running on Agent O'Hara. We never leave a soldier behind - that's not an official rule, but like, it really should be. The boss told me to tell you that you need to decide if you're in the cracking heads business or the cracking wise business, and not to mess up this time.'

It's the trust business I'm having problems with. How very convenient Dirty Harriet sends you to help me out. Just like back in the Aztec's zombie Disneyland . . . and look how well that ended for us. 'So we're it? Just the six of us to save Diane?'

Sister Mee turned around in her pilot's seat. Eleanor caught a glimpse beyond the cockpit windows - they were skimming low over the sea now, well below radar tracking. 'Saving your friend's life is your job. My mission remains unchanged . . . dealing with the Judas Purse. Those blood-cursed coins cannot be allowed to remain in the Sidhe Antiqua's possession.'

'And I'm your best chance of finding the Judas Purse in time.'

'Precisely. We're flying towards the Yellow Sea region. As we approach closer, are your senses recovered enough to home in on where the coins are guarded?'

'If you're asking me if I'm mission-fit here, the answer is yes. I'll find your damn coins for you.'

'Good. The Black Pope has dispatched emissaries to the Moscow Patriarchate. Certain resources are being tasked to us from a military base inside Yakutsk.'

Certain resources? Eleanor wasn't certain she liked the ominous sound of that. Whatever was on its way, she doubted it was squirt guns filled with holy water blessed by the Russian Orthodox Church.

Sister Rae snorted with delight. 'Kind of military base that doesn't officially show up on any bleeding map.'

'Yeah, well, at least *you're* fully recovered, sister,' said Eleanor. 'I can see that. We going to be relying on Russian Special Forces for this gig?'

Sister Mee shook her head. 'You mean the Spetsnaz? No. Scutum Dei is deploying its own elite force to the area . . . the Knights Solomon. Their presence will be more than adequate for our needs.'

Eleanor snorted. 'The *what*? Sounds like something out of a Monty Python movie.'

'You think?' said Sister Rae. 'Look, mate, I don't know if the Knights Solomon give the bloodsuckers the willies, but I can tell you one thing, those troops bloody well scare the black bonnet right off of my noggin.'

Given that the ninja nun was basically a human chemical explosive perfectly willing to go Kamikaze should things go sideways for her and her fanatic friends, Eleanor wasn't sure if she should be glad the Black Pope's pet killers were on their side, or anxious that they could be counted as allies.

Sister Mee, it transpired, had found and disabled the plane's tracking beacon prior to takeoff. So as long as their aircraft remained in stealth mode, they could land in front of the White House without the Secret Service shooting them down. Eleanor moved into Sister Rae's seat up in the cockpit, the better to play her part as a compass to hunt the coins. After the plane put the US East Coast's Urban Radar Zone behind them, their craft started climbing for height until they reached 50,000 feet. With all four engines manoeuvred into forward thrust configuration, their wings reconfigured for supersonic flight. The explosions of breaking the sound barrier sounded like yanked soda can tabs inside their insulated cabin. They accelerated north over Alaska and the polar ice cap, before navigating south-east, heading towards Northern China, drawn to the Judas Purse by Eleanor's instinct - even if every iota of Eleanor's instinct was screaming to head in the opposite direction and never stop flying. But the world was too small for them to escape what was coming. There was no hidey-hole deep enough, no bolt hole distant enough. Eleanor's mind knew this, but the hammering heart clutched in a vice inside her chest told her to heed her fears. To heed her terror. All in all, an excellent way to be too distracted to admire the pole's impressive white wastes, the icebergs and snow sheets and a seemingly endless sea, followed by barren mountains where Genghis Khan's hordes had once swept aside the most advanced civilisation of their age. She stretched her legs for a few minutes, examining the Arctic survival gear and weapons Ian had packed into the plane's hold. Then Eleanor ate from a microwaved ration pack — lasagna with tomato that tasted too sweet to be natural — before settling into the cockpit again. The plane kept to its course, using stealth mode to carefully keep a healthy distance from the naval fleets patrolling the Asian coastline, dozens of air patrols roaming the skies from their carrier groups, both sides patiently waiting for the enemy to pull the trigger on the end of the world.

After a while, Eleanor began to feel the tug of sleep pulling at her eyelids. She tried to resist it and her head suddenly jerked up in response to find . . . *What?* Eleanor no longer sat inside the jet's cockpit. She stood in the centre of a sandy road, a handful of men and women tramping along the route in open leather sandals - travellers wearing simple robe-like clothes that ended above the knees, dyed orange, white and brown and held in place by rope-style belts. Eleanor blinked in astonishment. This was no dream - too vivid. *But it's daylight and we were flying into the night? Hot here, too. It should be the depths of winter in Asia.* Yet on this road, Eleanor could smell the juniper trees' pungent odour, taste the dust from the road, hear braying from pack animals further down the road. The path wound its way across a rocky slope, cavities further up the rock lending the hillside the appearance of leering skull faces. Cries sounded from around the bend, wailing from a good few people. *Where am I?* Eleanor cautiously approached the sounds of human misery. *That isn't a healthy sound.* Nothing pleasant was dragging such a noise out of a crowd's collective throat. Her fellow travellers on the road didn't look Asian if she was any judge. *Am I on one of the mountains outside Teotihuacan? But how could I end up back in Mexico?*

A woman in a pale green robe came walking towards Eleanor, bearing a wooden pole with two pottery-like amphorae balanced on either end.

Eleanor tried to stop the woman in the dirt track. 'Where is this place? Where am I?

The peasant replied in a language Eleanor didn't recognise. Not Spanish, but a few seconds after the words were spoken, their meaning arrived with her. Eleanor touched her spectacles. No, it wasn't the computer inside the frames translating.

'Golgotha, lady. You are walking to Golgotha. This is no place for a fine woman to tarry.'

'You understand English? Wait, I don't know where Golgotha is? Are we in Mexico?'

But the traveller was striding away in the opposite direction.

Eleanor's glasses suddenly sprang to life, a warning scrolling across the lens. *Unidentified energy emission. Unidentified energy emission. Maximum scale superseded.*

'No kidding.' Eleanor muttered to herself. 'What the hell is going on here? Where's everyone else from the plane? How did I end up here?' She walked around the crest of the hill, gasping as she came across the source of the wailing. A small crowd of people held their hands up beseechingly towards the air on the slopes below her. They were humming, praying, lamenting. And in front of them, a line of wooden crosses bearing the nailed bodies of human victims. 'Dear God - that's barbaric!' *What is this, a brutal punishment dished out by the drug cartels to informers?*

That was when Eleanor saw them. Soldiers behind the wooden crosses, standing straight and watchful, clutching spears. *It can't be!* They wore a uniform she recognised - but only from watching too many TV episodes of *Spartacus: Blood and Sand*. The Roman Legion. *This ain't Mexico. This ain't even Kansas or Oz!*

Someone shoved his way through the crowd of mourners, scrambling up the slope and stopping, swaying in front of Eleanor as he surveyed the light traffic along the track. He might have been a handsome man once, bearded with tanned sharp aquiline features. But now he appeared pale and ill, his face's features swollen as though he was running a fever,

The man glanced desperately at Eleanor. 'He should have fought them. Fought back. He was meant to destroy the Romans! I was promised!'

Eleanor glanced down at the bulging cloth money bag

clutched in the man's fingers, waves of pain emanating from it making her recoil. *The purse, the coins!*

'You have to forgive me. I was promised!' The man shouted before sprinting off down the road.

Judas Iscariot. No. This can't be real. And why should he ask me to forgive him? This can't be happening.

And if that was Judas, then one of the crucified over there was . . . 'No. No, this can't possibly be real!' One of the crosses stood higher than the others, the figure hanging there familiar to her from a hundred altars.

Two old men followed Judas out of the crowd to watch him flee the execution. 'Those coins are cursed. Blood money for a fool.'

'Perhaps the blood is on us all, Luke.'

Eleanor looked up at the sky. It was darkening. A solar eclipse appeared to be under way. 'Can I see him?'

'You do not belong here. He doesn't want you to see him like this. Go home, daughter.'

'It is finished,' said Luke.

Eleanor grabbed the front of the man's white robe. 'I want to *help.*'

'It is good to help, daughter. But for you, it must be another time.'

The pain inside Eleanor's head swelled and the two men clutched her as she stumbled and fell. *Those damn coins.* She touched her nostrils with her fingers, drawing then back stained crimson. *A nosebleed.* The combat glasses flashed an alert status again. *Unidentified energy emission. Unidentified energy emission. Maximum scale superseded.* She shut her eyes. This pain was like ice daggers stabbed into her mind. Eleanor opened her eyes. She was back on the floor of the cockpit, Sister Mee and Ian kneeling by her side. The senior nun wiped blood away from Eleanor's nose with a white cloth. A first aid kit sat open on the deck behind her.

Unidentified energy reading nullified, the words scrolled across Eleanor's specs. *Safe limits restored.*

'What—happened?' coughed Eleanor.

'You tell me,' said Ian. 'You collapsed out of your chair. Then all our flight deck instruments started going nuts like we were flying over the Bermuda Triangle or something.'

'I was concerned we had flown into an EMP blast,' said Sister Mee. 'That nuclear missiles had begun detonating across the globe.'

'But—'

Ian shook his head. 'No, the U.S. fleet is still at high alert, but there're no nukes flying yet.'

'I think it's because we're following the coins,' said Eleanor. 'The Judas Purse is trying to stop me.' *And maybe there's another power intervening to make sure we still have a fighting chance.*

'You're well enough to track the coins down?' asked Sister Mee.

'Do we have a choice?'

Sister Mee squeezed Eleanor's shoulder and helped her back into the co-pilot's position. Eleanor's head still throbbed, but she ignored it. Their aircraft powered ahead, Eleanor doing her damnedest impression of a homing pigeon; even if she was heading for a home her gut told her to avoid at all costs. They flew until the aching blackness of the Judas Purse grew all-consuming.

'The coins are close,' said Eleanor, finally. 'Can't you feel them pulsing below us? Is it really just me?'

'Yeah, it's all about you,' said Bex, glancing out of the cockpit window. She switched the view on the navigation screen, a GPS marker flashing their position on the map's scrolling landscape. 'That's North Korea down there. We're not far inland from the coast. This region is called *Kilchu.*'

'North Korea. Why am I not surprised?' said Sister Mee. 'The Reds have subverted the entire benighted land for two centuries. A corrupt ruling family with all the mafia politics that accompany a hereditary dynasty. A closed society. Peasants disappeared at the click of any official's fingers, never to be seen again. The entire nation is practically a country-sized canteen for the vampires and their foul servants.'

Bex stared out of the cockpit. 'The landscape's dark below. Like, no lights. No towns.'

'The North Koreans don't generate enough electricity to keep their street lamps and buildings lit after nightfall. Most cities run black after sundown,' said Ian. He called Alasdair over. 'Find out exactly what's down there. Use every database we have taps for, even if we have to burn our feeds tunnelling in - NSA, the Pentagon, the MSS.'

'Been a while since I hacked into the Ministry of State Security,' mused Alasdair. 'I wonder if the Chinese ever dug my last worm out from their mainframe?' Alasdair sounded as if he was joking, but Eleanor could hear the strained weight behind his words. How little time Diane had left before she finally broke and was tossed to the monsters as an afterthought... as an after-dinner snack. No, it didn't take long for Alasdair to uncover what they needed, even with the relative lag in the aircraft's satellite connectivity. He completed his hack, then skim-read the fruits of the raid. 'There's an irony for you. Most of what the Chinese hold on Kilchu came from breaking into U.S. government servers. The Pentagon keeps a set of Ultra-level classified files on this zone. Seems the North Koreans constructed their version of the NORAD Cheyenne Mountain Complex below Kilchu back in the nineties. A secret underground city purpose-built to keep safe the regime's highest-ranking members. The North Koreans think we don't know about the place, but the Pentagon's off-the-books stealth station tracked its construction from orbit.'

'What, we have a secret space station up there and nobody thought to send me the memo?' asked Eleanor.

'A hardened subterranean city? Kilchu sounds like the perfect place to survive the Third World War,' observed Ian.

Eleanor tapped the GPS screen. 'Sure it is. You maybe know someone looking to start a major nuclear conflict? I'm willing to bet this Party Palace contains electricity, hot water and every other mod-con for the ruling elite.'

'I believe we have successfully located their nest,' agreed Sister Mee. 'I'll place us in a holding pattern. Give the Knights Solomon time to drop into position.'

'How near are they?' asked Alasdair, clearly trying to suppress his panic over any delay to their rescue.

Sister Mee pointed out of the cockpit. Eleanor just caught the shimmer of electronic ink across a fuselage, masking the giant jump jet pulling ahead of their plane. 'Agent, they've been ghosting above us for the last two hours.'

The nun settled their stolen transport down outside a forested area, every treetop streaked with snow. Eleanor caught no glimpse of the city on the way down; but then, that was probably the point of building a secret bunker complex in the first place. They dressed in warm winter clothing for the environment outside, selected weapons, made sure their specs held the download for the Korean language, then exited via a ramp at the back of the aircraft. The group dispersed in a tight military pattern, checking for any sign their uninvited arrival had been spotted by the locals. There were none. All was silent. Eleanor noted their plane's fuselage had turned white, snowflakes drifting from the sky spattering the camouflage as its digital skin compensated for the snowfall. She noted the accompanying troop transporter was larger than their jet, before its active matrix camouflage also slowly adjusted to blend in with the winter landscape. Landing first, its troops had disembarked before them. Eleanor carefully picked her way up a low rocky slope and before they reached its top, spotted where the Knights Solomon had taken up position. Figures knelt in a line spread out along the incline. They wore white cloaks with a small red cross marked on the spine, crouching silently as though meditating or praying. Sentinels guarding this cold landscape. As she drew closer, she noticed that their capes concealed camouflage jackets in Arctic warfare pattern and a veritable armoury of heavy machine guns, rifles, pistols and grenades. A mixture of male and female soldiers among the company. Despite the difference in their faces — obviously a mixture of nationalities — the soldiers all shared a common cast; big, heavy-set and grim, like a hard-faced weight-lifting team arrived visiting for the North Korean Olympics.

Eleanor walked up to the nearest group of the Black Pope's

elite troops. 'We're heading in that direction. You coming with?'

None of them bothered to reply to her question; as silent as menhirs inside an ancient standing stone circle.

Well, that's just plain rude. Eleanor turned to Sister Mee. 'They don't say much, do they?'

'Their order has taken a vow of silence,' explained Sister Mee. One of the force turned and his fingers flickered using sign language. Sister Mee replied with a few quick gestures.

'What did he say?' asked Eleanor.

'Nothing you want to hear,' said Sister Mee.

Not a compliment, then. They must watch us blundering around in the snow and think it's amateur hour here.

Ian, Bex, Alasdair and Sister Rae joined the rest of the group at the top of the slope.

The lens of Eleanor's combat specs misted up. She removed the pair and rubbed them clear. 'Why aren't these goons moving forward, sister?'

'The Knights Solomon are not here to help us fight our way into the Kilchu complex,' said Sister Mee, regretfully. 'They're here to make sure nobody gets out of the city.'

There's a big "but" left unsaid somewhere in there. 'And why the heck would they do that?'

'The knights are waiting for the GOAB,' said Sister Mee. 'There's a modified Antonov An-225 in the stratosphere and that's what the plane is flying down here.'

'The GOAB? I thought that was an urban legend,' said Alasdair, kneeling in the snow, examining the landscape with a pair of night-vision binoculars.

'No, it exists. They only built the one, but it certainly exists.'

'What the hell are you two talking about?' asked Eleanor.

Alasdair pointed up to the clouds, speaking in hushed tones as though he was discussing the big guy himself. 'GOAB - it stands for *Giga-scale Ordnance Air Blast* bomb. Nicknamed the "Grandmother of All Bombs" inside the Kremlin. Five hundred tonnes of death, the largest non-nuclear conventional explosive ever constructed.'

'Oh, we'd gladly nuke this whole region,' said Sister Mee. 'Nuke Kilchu five times over. But with most the world's atomic-tipped cruise missiles currently sailing up-and-down the coast with safeties off, we can't risk an unannounced radiation flash triggering the Red's war for them.'

'And this big-ass Russian bomb will do the job?' asked Ian. 'Destroy the Judas Purse, even inside their hidden bunker city?'

'The trick won't be the Judas Purse surviving, it will be *us* surviving,' sighed Sister Mee.

Alasdair slipped his binoculars away. 'It's a thermobaric weapon. The bomb will generate a two-mile blast radius of total destruction, causing a 9.7 earthquake on the moment magnitude scale. It won't just smash the bunker complex, it will liquefy the very bedrock. I presume that's the cover story, here? You're going to cause the world's largest earthquake and blame the devastation on the Amurian tectonic plates slipping.'

'Quite so. You have less than two hours to locate Diane, free her and escape the blast radius,' said Sister Mee. 'The bomb is en route and its detonation cannot be called off or cancelled. Not if his Holiness the Black Pope himself was inside Kilchu sipping tea with the President of Russia and the leaders of the G8 serving sandwiches. Come what may, the coins and this region of North

Korea will be blown all the way back to hell.'

'So glad we brought you along,' muttered Eleanor.

'Biggest bomb ever,' laughed Sister Rae. 'Knights Solomon on the ground to make sure nothing escapes alive. You mug. It's like Christmas come early out here.'

'Your speechless killers will let us pass back through their execution zone, though?' asked Bex.

'You're half-dead already, ain't you? What you care?' said the British nun.

'Like, I heal fast, but not *that* fast,' muttered Bex.

'She's half alive and I'm hundred percent kicking,' said Eleanor. 'Not to mention Diane O'Hara trapped in Redsville across there.'

'Let's have a pop at the Reds, then,' said Sister Rae. 'Better than standing out here in the cold, waiting for Jing-Jong-Merrily-on-High and his wicked vampire overlords to try to scarper away with the coins.'

Yeah, better than that, thought Eleanor. *But not by much.*

'Our orders are to remain on post here,' pointed out Sister Mee, 'and ensure the Knights Solomon maintain the perimeter's integrity.'

Sister Rae indicated the AX50 long guns carefully being set up in the snow on snipers' tripod mounts by the hulking soldiers. 'Doesn't need two of us for babysitting. And I never was very good at blindly taking orders.'

Sister Mee shook her head, sadly. 'No, you never were. Go with God, sister.'

The other nun clicked back the safety on her machine pistol. 'Going with God, but dispatching a few filthy rascals back to Hell where they belong.'

Sister Mee tapped her watch. 'Time is not your friend. Move quickly.'

They needed no further urging. Alasdair used a ground penetrating radar device to lead them down the slopes and through the forest in the valley below until they came to the top of a concealed air-vent. It looked like a natural outcrop of rock rising between a stand of trees. On closer inspection, the icy outcrop transpired to be a cylinder of moss-covered moulded concrete, camouflaged brown and green to blend into the landscape. When Eleanor placed her head over the grille protecting the top she felt a flow of warm air from below, heard the distant hum of fans carrying away stale air.

'This is our best bet to break inside unopposed,' said Alasdair. 'There's a phony village beyond this forest called Musudan-ri. Most of its farms and barns are fake - they're actually storage buildings, garages and security checkpoints leading down into the complex.'

Eleanor inspected the metal grille. 'Did your hacked Chinese spy files give any indication of how large their bunker city is?'

Alasdair raised his hand and gave it an uncertain flutter. 'Big enough, I reckon.'

'So what's the grand strategy here, then, girls?' asked Sister Rae. 'We grab any randoms we chance across in the corridors, put a bullet in their heads one-by-one until someone blabs the location of Agent O'Hara's interrogation facility?'

'That's a lousy plan,' said Eleanor.

'It's bloody simple, though. Simple works. Let's not over-complicate things, eh?'

'I like the sound of it,' said Bex, approvingly. 'It's gnarly.'

'Well, you can take a lot more damage than the rest of us,' said Ian.

'Damn straight,' agreed Eleanor.

'You make it sound like a bad thing.' Bex sounded proud. She did a little pirouette in the snow. 'With the Bexster, almost everything is a flesh wound!'

Eleanor winced to herself. *The Bexster, give me a break.*

'We don't need to shoot the staff,' said Alasdair. He worked a counter-measures unit through the grille to deactivate the alarms protecting the vent. 'I copied Diane's RFID code from the Vault's security systems.'

'Her *what* code?' asked Eleanor.

'There's a 0.05mm-sized short range encrypted radio-frequency identification chip injected into the calf muscles of Diane's left leg. It's passive, no energy source, but the Vault's sensors can ping it and get a reply. It's how we know you're *you* inside New York Central, and not some shape-changing Red or one of the other Sidhe Antiqua races trying to infiltrate the Vigil.'

'What, you mean you chipped me *too* like I was no better than a stray dog?'

'You. Her. Me. Your RFID chip is no larger than a speck of dust,' said Alasdair. 'Undetectable even under a full body examination. What did you think all that prodding and poking was about back in medical?'

'I don't know. Maybe keeping me healthy and alive after surviving the bite? Maybe not violating most of my constitutional rights?'

'I'm sure you were given flu jabs, too. But the point is, Diane will be *real* glad she got a chip. We can't get a read on her location from up here with the bedrock blocking the signal. But once we're inside the city proper, we'll be able to ping Diane's RFID and home in on her location.'

Ian yanked the ventilation grille away from the concrete with Eleanor's help. They both peered down the shaft.

'It's narrow,' said Ian. 'We can climb down, but we'll need to stow our rifles up here to squeeze through.'

'Oh, that's just bleeding super,' said Sister Rae, in a voice that indicated it was anything but.

'You'll have your moly-sword,' said Ian. 'And subterfuge will serve us better than a full-on commando assault. Once we're in the city, just act like you belong there.'

'I really don't,' said Sister Rae, but she broke out the grappling gear from her backpack all the same.

It's going to be a long climb, Eleanor sighed to herself.

21

~ THE END OF THE WORLD ~

It seemed to take an age to descend through the ventilation shaft into the North Korean bunker. Every second lost deactivating sensors and alarms, halting fans and using their grappling equipment was time they didn't have to spare. But eventually, the party touched bottom. Ian kicked out a grille and the group crawled out into an antiseptically clean white corridor with coloured markings along the wall that could have belonged to a slightly dated hospital. Thankfully, there was no sign of any of the bunker's staff, here. Eleanor examined a sign painted in Korean script along the wall, her glasses translating the message into English. *Level Five. Route 34B. Security Clearance Eight+.* It left her none the wiser.

Shortly after Eleanor emerged in the bunker, her spectacles displayed a red icon next to the letters *GM* in the corner of her field of view. 'Anyone else getting this? What, there's an army of genetically modified mutants down here?'

Alasdair chipped in. 'I have it too. GM means Geiger–Müller reading, as in Geiger counter. It's an abnormal rads warning. Abnormal, but not dangerous at this level. Must be how the North Koreans are powering their city: a small-scale nuclear reactor. Makes sense. They could survive off-grid for seventy years down here without needing to truck in extra fuel.'

'Won't blasting their reactor to pieces release a mushroom cloud and trigger a shooting war off the coast?'

'That's not how nuclear piles work,' said Alasdair. 'When the GOAB detonates, what isn't disintegrated or liquefied will be left buried in a very deep but only mildly radioactive grave.'

'That's got to be worth seeing,' said Sister Rae, 'but not up close, eh?'

'Which way?' asked Ian.

Alasdair consulted his scanner. 'The signal is faint bordering on non-existent; that's an issue with short range transmitters.'

'So, which way . . .?'

Alasdair pointed down one of the corridors. 'That direction I think.'

Eleanor sniffed the air, trying to pick up any trace of Diane's scent. She winced as a bolt of agony struck her between the ears and attempted to run her brain through a mangle.

Ian steadied her. 'Are you alright? Suffering from increased radiation?'

'No, it's the Judas Purse again. Those antique Roman coins are playing some really bad Disco inside my skull every time I reach out to try to track Diane.'

Eleanor closed her eyes for a second. She was being battered by pulses; far worse now than when she had stood inside the Aztec temple. Attempting to locate Diane was like standing in the middle of a hurricane trying to pick up the sound of a distant radio. She stopped trying and they pushed on, passing through an area filled with steel tanks and pipes that were probably part of the air recycling system. They didn't encounter anyone, but occasionally they heard voices drifting down the corridors. In one section of the complex they passed a chamber sealed off by a transparent wall. On the other side of the glass lay ranks of tables, hundreds of human bodies wearing white gowns stretched out across cots, caught in a web of drips, feeds and bleeping life support monitors. Sedated, but alive. Just.

'Well, at least we're in the right place,' said Alasdair, indicating the comatose bodies on the other side of the glass. 'This is one of the Reds' food supplies stores.'

'It's horrible,' said Eleanor, disgusted. 'Can we help them escape?'

Ian shook his head sadly. 'This is the standard set-up inside every nest we've rolled up. Even if we tore those prisoners off their drips, they'll be in no condition to escape for days. Most of them have been kept in medical comas for months, maybe years. Half of those healthy enough to survive the reawakening process will be left psychotic from their time in captivity.'

'Casualties of war, either way,' snarled Sister Rae. 'Poor flipping bleeders.'

Eleanor stared through the glass. *A warehouse of the dead.* 'I wish—'

'Me too,' said Ian. 'But not here, not today.'

Yeah, not today. So, how many other innocents will die down here, today? Cleaners and maintenance staff, locals forced to work inside the bunker city with not an iota of choice in the matter. Accept the job, rather than the one-way ride to a concentration camp if they refused. And all Eleanor could do was make sure Diane wasn't added to the butcher's bill.

They rounded a corner and Alasdair slowed, tapping the side of his tracking unit. 'That's weird . . . ?'

'What is?' asked Eleanor.

Alasdair sounded worried. 'Now that we're getting nearer to Diane, I'm picking up a Doppler effect from her chip.'

'Like the kind of effect you might get if said chip was shifting around in the gut of a demi-gog?' asked Bex.

Eleanor felt a flare of anger at the woman's lack of tact. 'Oh, that's nice.'

'Only saying what everyone here must be thinking.'

'Actually, I don't know what this is,' said Alasdair, confused.

'Let's just track Diane's signal to source,' said Ian. 'We'll worry about what we do or don't find after we arrive where Diane is being held.'

Eleanor checked her watch. Time was draining away from them. Only a little over an hour left to break Diane free and escape the deadly blast radius. Crossing the corridors they passed a door containing a small porthole-sized window. Eleanor peered through. On the other side was what looked to be a cloakroom, dozens of silver suits hanging from hooks with transparent box-like hoods resting on the shelves above.

'We must have broken in close to the reactor,' said Alasdair, glancing inside. 'Those are power plant workers' radiation suits.'

'We can use the uniforms,' said Ian. 'They'll make us look a lot less like tourists.'

Bex appeared uncertain. 'Silver is the new black?'

'To hell with fashion sense. Staff worried about rad leaks won't be too keen to stop us for a chat,' said Alasdair.

'I guess that's totally rad,' said Bex.

'And you never exactly had much fashion sense back in the world, anyway,' teased Eleanor.

Ian shrugged. 'Thanks for pointing that out, but you're the one wearing an orange boiler suit under your parka.'

'You got me there, Mickey J.'

They tried the door and finding it unlocked, entered, then donned the silver suits, pulling them on over their clothes. Bex was, at least, right about one thing . . . they weren't going to win any fashion awards inside the garb. They resembled extras from a cheap sixties sci-fi movie. Each chest bore a black bar-code strip rather than a fashion house's logo. Eleanor felt hot and uncomfortable, her vision restricted by the hood-like helmet - albeit suitably camouflaged for a bunker city designed to survive World War Three. *Of course, if our next problem is surviving a full-scale nuclear conflict, then we'll have failed in more than just rescuing Diane.* Alasdair lifted a spare suit off the rack for Diane to use when they freed her.

After leaving the suiting area they arrived at a busier section of the bunker city, a two-lane tunnel with pedestrian walkways on either side, electric carts humming along its roadway in a variety of configurations - vehicles with plastic bucket seats holding passengers, others resembling the kind of specialist works vehicles you might find rumbling down mine passages or crossing airfields. To access the tunnel they had to pass a checkpoint with a cluster of bored guards seated behind a security station. The soldiers chain-smoked cigarettes while a laptop sat open on their worktop, a bootleg DVD in its drive playing a Chinese fantasy movie. A colourful pair of warriors were literally running over treetops, exchanging fierce flurries of sword cuts between each other.

One of the guards grunted, halted the group and picked up a bar-code scanner. He ran it across the line on Ian's chest, then scanned the others in the group, leaving Bex and Eleanor until last. The soldier scrutinised the results on his screen, then barked again in Korean. Everything these people said sounded angry and hostile.

Eleanor's specs translated. 'Where are you going, engineer?' Her spectacle's whispered a reply in Korean into her ear-buds while displaying the English meaning across her lens. *A potential leak. We need to inspect the cooling pipes.*

Ian had obviously received the same phrase. "Jamjaejeog in nuchul. Ulineun paipeu leul geomsa haeya," he squawked, trying to inject the same level of distemper into his words.

'Hah.' The guard made a dismissive gurgle which needed little translation, adjusted his loose-fitting khaki uniform and waved them away, his eyes already drifting back to the medieval swordsmen dancing above the forest. Eleanor hoped the soldier had a decent collection of films. Should war break out, he was going to be stuck underground for a very long time - unless the Reds ran out of their supply of unwilling blood donors first.

Out on the tunnel system's walkway, the party chanced across a motor pool recessed in a cavernous garage. Dozens of transports to choose from. After investigating, it transpired the vehicles ran with electric engines and button-start ignitions. No hot-wiring required. So they borrowed something that resembled a stretch golf cart with five seats on either side, Ian driving it whining and jouncing through the subterranean two-lane roadway while Alasdair called out directions, following the pulses - ever stronger - towards Diane's location.

'We need to step it up,' called Eleanor, checking the time. 'This city won't exist in an hour.'

'I've seen faster bloody milk floats,' agreed the nun.

'We'll get her out in time,' insisted Ian, as if just saying it would make it true.

Alasdair's portable scanner led them down a side-tunnel

and a long corridor which terminated in a steel door. Red Korean characters stencilled on the door translated as "Political Reeducation Holding Centre Five". If that meant what Eleanor thought it did, then they had arrived at the right place inside the complex.

Eleanor blinked as they pushed open the vault-like door, entering the centre. It looked less like a prison and more like an animal rescue centre; cages constructed of toughened transparent glass and racked on multiple storeys inside a warehouse-sized cavern. Less like prisoners, more like zoo exhibits.

'That's a lot of reeducating,' said Eleanor, her eyes running across hundreds of transparent cells.

'Yeah,' said Bex. 'Like semaphore year for battery hens.'

Angry shouts drew Eleanor's gaze to a guard post where three heavy-set warders emerged, arms furiously waving at the "engineers". *Visiting rights obviously aren't a priority, here.* Sister Rae strode towards the guards, raising both gloved hands placatingly. As she got closer she pulled her box-like hood off her head and tossed it at the nearest man. The guard caught the helmet and stared in surprise at the sister as she triggered her moly-sword, stepped forward and gutted the soldier, swinging the blade around her head in a high arc to slice out the throats of the other two thugs. All three tumbled dead to the floor. Her intricate swordwork had been near perfect. Less than a second to strike down three lives.

'Well, those muppets weren't going to let us just walk out with your chum, were they?' said the nun, cutting Ian's protests short. She patted down the corpses, searching for key cards to open the cells. Sister Rae found what she was looking for and tossed the key-chain to Ian. 'Move it, Yankee-Doodle!'

Ian and Alasdair clambered up the stairs, heading towards the first level of cells. Ian turned to the rest of the team. 'Bex, cover the entrance into the prison. Anyone enters, you chop them into pieces. The rest of you spread out and check the cells for Diane.'

Luckily, there weren't many prisoners held inside the complex - this place was obviously intended for use under full occupancy when the entire regime and their entourage of countless thousands were sheltering out the worst of a nuclear winter. They found Diane stretched limp on a cot inside a glass cell on the second level. The team clustered on the gantry until they unlocked the door. Its transparent door slid open with a touch of the key-card on the lock plate. Alasdair practically fell inside, rolling the agent's body over on her plastic mattress, desperately searching for signs of life.

'Diane?'

'I had faith,' spluttered Diane, bruised eyelids flickering open. The young agent looked lucky to still be alive, her eyelids heavy, weariness etched across every line of her face as though she had aged a decade in captivity. Eleanor suspected that few of the woman's injuries had been sustained escaping entombment in the Aztec temple. Only sleep deprivation mixed with truth drugs, beatings and physical torture could do that to a body; even a form as resilient as someone who had survived the Cure.

Alasdair held Diane as tight as he dared. 'You were never lacking in that department.'

'No,' said Diane. 'I had faith *you* would come for me. That you would never give up on me.'

'Of course, I would never give up on you,' said Alasdair, 'not if I lived to be a thousand. We need to leave fast. Do you think you can walk a little? We've parked an electric cart outside the prison.'

'I can't even feel my legs.' Diane gestured towards an intravenous drip in the corner, rubber pipes coiling out through a tiny hole in the clear ceiling. 'They've had me wired up to that filth for my stay here.'

Alasdair scooped the woman up in his arms. 'We'll get you into a radiation suit. If anyone stops us on the way out, I'll tell them you were injured in a reactor accident and we're driving you to decontamination.'

Bex coughed from just outside the cell. 'You're so going to have a problem with that!'

Eleanor turned. Bex held her hands high in the air, the moly-blade still clutched in her right hand. The steel gantry outside the cell stood crowded on either side by a small legion of demi-gogs clutching rifles and machine guns, weapons raised and pointed towards the cell and the agents inside.

Eleanor's fingers twitched, readying her moly-sword to decapitate Bex. *I can slay you before the demi-gogs gun us down.* 'Bitch! You called these monsters down on us.'

'I wouldn't try gutting Agent Crawfield,' growled a familiar voice. The demi-gogs moved aside and a figure stepped out from the Reds' ranks. *No, that's impossible!* Guy Drew flourished an RFID scanner. 'You'd be slicing up the wrong woman. You weren't the only ones to copy the team's chip codes from New York Central. Lordy, but you have to love the Vault's security system!'

Ian swayed on his feet in shock. '*Guy* — but you — you were blown to bits trying to defuse the bomb!'

The old man shrugged. 'Heck, I didn't have enough time to start slicing wires and praying for the best. Just long enough to sprint out of the tunnel and grab the Judas Purse, though. After that, I had the Reds to help me avoid the temple cave-in, same as Agent O'Hara here. Although the Reds had slightly different motives for saving my ass.'

Eleanor couldn't believe her own eyes. This was the cause of Alasdair's Doppler signals while tracking down Diane. Another chip faintly answering the pulses, a chip they had never counted on broadcasting inside the city. 'You? *You* were the traitor all along?'

'Only doing what I needed to do to survive, kid. Retract your blades and throw your swords down to the floor.'

Eleanor stared at the ranks of demi-gogs, weapons aimed at the team, the creatures converted and hungry, itching for a chance to feed on them. The team could go down swinging, but they'd go down all the same. Bex angrily tossed her blade to the floor, followed by the rest of the group. Eleanor reluctantly relinquished her sword too. Sister Rae yelped as one of the demi-gogs stepped back from her, withdrawing a syringe it had used to inject the nun's neck.

'A little something to ensure you don't go Kamikaze on us,' said Guy. 'The chemical trigger for those nasty liquid explosives inside you is just urine now.'

The nun glared with hatred towards Guy. 'I don't need my explosives to murder you. I'll bloody snap your neck for this, you turncoat.'

'Sure you will, sis. Just waiting for a chance to meet the nest's Top Cat, intending to blow yourself and the big boss to bits, right? Well, you'll get your chance to meet the Master of Masters. He's curious to see who it is stupid enough to think they can break into his city and steal the Judas Purse out from under his nose. He's grown pretty attached to the coins. Some might say a little too attached.'

Eleanor felt a brief shock of realisation. The Reds hadn't cottoned on yet to the Grandmother of all Bombs about to be dropped on their ass. Guy believed Diane was a sideshow to the team's real mission: stealing back the coins from the damn vampires. She glanced at Ian and he met her eyes. *No, we're not saying anything about the bomb, are we?* No chance for the Reds to escape from the city. This might be the team's tomb, Eleanor's tomb, but it would also mean the end of the Judas Purse and the Reds' ability to super-charge their scheme to halt human civilisation's ascendance.

'How did you jokers even track the coins here?' Guy swung his pistol at Eleanor. 'Let me guess, your migraines, right? I always knew there was something hinky about you and your powers. That cock-and-bull story you fed us about what really went down in the back of the Keeper's store.'

'Go to hell,' spat Eleanor.

'Yeah, well your headaches are going to get a lot worse. You've piqued the curiosity of the Master of Masters. That's not a healthy place to find yourself.'

'Why?' cried Ian. 'Why - what made you go over to the Reds?'

'You live long enough and a little of the Reds' immortal worldview begins to rub off on you,' said Guy. 'People stop looking like people and start resembling mayflies. Here today, gone tomorrow. You see the same mistakes being made over and over again and can't do anything to stop 'em. Boom, bust, then boom again. War after futile war, all the violent monkeys tearing each other apart for a little extra territory and the bragging rights of calling themselves head ape. The Reds want a return to the feudal system? We're practically handing that to the vampires on a plate anyway. A fraction of one percent of the population grabbing ninety-nine percent of the world's wealth. Computers and robots stealing the last remaining work and making the rich even richer, while everyone else is left to fester and fight over the scraps of the world's dwindling resources like a plague of locusts. Our population swelling beyond all sane limits, just waiting for a random strain of swine flu to mutate strong enough to make us extinct. You know the only real difference between the Reds and the humans feeding off our people? Under the vampires' rule, there'll still be an Earth left in a couple of centuries' time. Not a greenhouse hellhole like Venus or a dead planet like Mars. Because that's the only legacy our grandchildren were getting from us.'

Eleanor could hardly believe what she was hearing. Guy wasn't telling them the true reason for his betrayal, he couldn't be - she could feel the lie in her bones. *He's lying, he has to be. What we're doing in the Vigil has to mean something. Because if it doesn't, then they might as well all be better off dead.*

'Like, you've lost it,' said Bex, 'You're totally psyched, old man.'

Guy indicated the ranks of armed demi-gogs surrounding them. 'Nope, Agent Crawfield. Right now, I reckon *you're* the ones who have lost it.' He waved his pistol barrel down the corridor. 'Let's find out by how much, shall we, kids.'

***

Eleanor and the others were marched through the bunker city, ending up in a massive factory hall stripped of its production line and given faux-homeliness by scattering expensive carpets, rugs, tapestries, flags and even an intricate wooden throne, although the latter was no medieval antique, not if the German eagles and swastikas carved into the oak were any indication. The team were dragged into the chamber down a sweeping set of stairs, a small legion of vampires and demi-gogs at their rear, all hissing how much they would enjoy feasting on the agents. It wasn't much consolation to Eleanor to know she would probably be incinerated long before it came to that. Eleanor couldn't see the Judas Purse, but she guessed from the hammering inside her skull that the cursed coins were somewhere here. And in the centre of the chamber, waiting behind a large desk, the creature who no doubt sat on that throne, trying it out for size every now and then. Portly, pale-faced and pallid. He looked like a cop close to retirement who had gone to seed on the job.

'What is this, a garage sale of Nazi regalia?' quipped Eleanor. 'I'm not buying.'

The vampire rose up from behind his desk. 'How fortunate, then, that I am not selling. You stand in the presence of Gebhard Truchsess von Waldburg, although I have worn so many other names throughout history. I was private secretary to the Fuhrer, once, hence my sentimental attachment to our glorious past.'

Yeah, you strike me as the sentimental type. 'How about asshole?' said Eleanor. 'You ever wear that name?'

'Ah, the freshness of youth,' sneered von Waldburg. 'Young, stupid and naive. Stupid enough to think you can break inside *my* realm and steal *my* coins.'

'Well, when you're passing through Mordor . . .' said Sister Rae. 'Nicking the Precious and poking you in your evil sodding eye seemed like a stand-up plan at the time.'

'On your knees!' yelled one of their demi-gog guards. 'You befoul the presence of the Master of Masters!' A flurry of blows pistol-whipped the team down onto the chamber's hard concrete floor.

'That's better. So those who are last now will be first, eh, sister? The whole world shall soon kneel before me - at least, the few among the herd I permit to survive their long overdue culling.' The Master of Masters pressed a button on his desk and a section of the wall retracted, revealing a glass-walled chamber with a desert vista on the other side. But it wasn't the desert that grabbed Eleanor's attention. It was the truck-sized ants straining up towards the viewing gallery, antennae twitching as their huge razor-sharp mandibles attempted to crack the armoured glass. 'Let us see if you still think yours is such a fine plan after you have been properly introduced to my pets. Poor beasts. They haven't fed for the longest time. My fault, alas, so preoccupied have I become prodding and poking China and America towards a final conflict.'

'You won't spark another world war,' cried Diane. 'We're better than that, now.'

'Ah, the other little God-botherer speaks. Well, I suppose if we had cut out your tongue, Agent O'Hara, your interrogation would have proved more work for us. Always placing your faith in all the wrong things. Your pathetic race will never outgrow war, poverty and pestilence. The last man to break inside the Nazi base at Antarctica and steal one of the Judas coins is here now working for me. What does that tell you about human nature?'

'That you'd be better off hiding your skanky ass under the polar ice?' said Eleanor.

'Hollow threats. Even your own agency doesn't wish you alive anymore,' smiled von Waldburg without a trace of warmth. 'Mister Drew has been kind enough to keep on monitoring the Vigil's communications for us. You idiots have lethal-force arrest warrants issued against you by your organisation - a wise move when dealing with rogue abominations. Your last ditch presence here isn't even an officially sanctioned Vigil mission, is it?'

'Yeah, I'd say you're all well and truly off the reservation,' noted Guy.

'Spoken like a true cowboy.' Von Waldburg paced behind his desk. 'What little power you abominations possess has been stolen from the Sidhe Antiqua, from my kin. Your cure, your high science and your filthy half-breed kind are about to be erased from history. Left as an unsung and unmissed footnote. All that will remain will be the hunters, our prey and the herd's terror. Back to business as normal.' A section of the steel desk slid open and the Reds' ruler lifted out a casket. The same wooden chest Eleanor had glimpsed inside the Aztec temple. 'This is as close as you fools will get to fulfilling your goal.'

As the chest emerged, Eleanor clutched her head, pain inside her skull dialled up to a synapse-shattering agony.

'Fascinating,' laughed the Master of Masters. 'I have never heard of such a poisonous reaction to the coins.' He glanced to the top of the stairs as another Red appeared. It was the female vampire who had fought them at the Swiss museum, a young woman walking by her side. 'Figchen. Just in time, as always. Your sly double agent has served me up another little gift. A team of Vigil outcasts arrogant enough to think that they could steal my exquisite prize away from me.' He tapped the chest containing the Judas Purse. 'Spend a few hours torturing these young abominations. Use that fine set of skinning blades I gave you for your three-hundredth birthday. Do attempt to keep the pups breathing until their interrogation is completed. My ants are fussy eaters - they prefer hunting live food, rather than having haunches of dead meat tossed to them.'

The female vampire arrived at the bottom of the stairs. 'And we wouldn't wish to disappoint your murderous mutants, would we?'

'Ah, Sophia Augusta, you so rarely disappoint your master. Your brought me a new Judas from the Vigil, an agent willing to sell out the original Judas's gift to the world. You have made your master happy beyond words.'

Sophia bowed somewhat warily towards the prince of her kind.

'No, you would never betray me, would you, Figchen? Through the ages, I have always been able to rely on you.'

'Always, master,' said Sophia.

'Of course. Our young guests will benefit from having their imaginations stimulated before they are tortured,' said von Waldburg. 'A demonstration of both the coins' power and my pets' appetites will serve to loosen their tongues.'

'Ever the sadist,' said Sophia.

'Sadist? No, figchen. Merely the thrill of the chase,' said von Waldburg. 'I still feel its rush. As fresh as though I was newly turned.' He clicked his fingers at his demi-gogs. 'That last batch we received from the prison camp . . . they appeared healthy enough to make for a little sport.'

His guards unlocked a door in the wall and the Master of Masters walked through and disappeared from view. After a minute, two portals opened on the far side of the desert vista. Von Waldburg appeared nonchalantly through the first doorway. The giant ants swivelled and stampeded towards the prince. For a moment it looked as though they might devour the vampire, rushing him, but the giants skittered to a stop, sand from the dunes splattering the man's body His mutant pets bowed head, thorax and abdomen towards him, like tank-sized cats presenting themselves for stroking. Von Waldburg triumphantly reached out and rubbed each black armoured skull in turn, his voice amplified by speakers inside the enclosure and carried into the throne chamber. The monstrous creatures' antennae quivered in delight at their master's close attention.

'You see? The power of possessing the coins makes me unstoppable. Foolish outcasts, how did you possibly think you could stop me? Before I took the Judas Purse, these ungrateful little beauties here would have torn me in half. Now they worship me. But don't let their subservience fool you. Let me demonstrate their true nature to you, red in both mandible and claw. . .'

A howl of fear sounded from beyond the other entrance, the sight of demi-gogs with electric prods driving a group of prisoners out into the open. As soon as the rag-wearing North

Korean peasants were shoved through, the door sealed shut and the prisoners stumbled through the orange sands, yelling in terror when they saw the ranks of giant ants bowing low before von Waldburg.

The vampire raised his hands under the enclosure's hot artificial lamp light. 'Take your supper, my malevolent lovelies, you deserve it! Your new queen feeds you well!'

Doubled over in agony, Eleanor held onto her terrible pain to distract her from the horrific sight that played out before them, the ants breaking position around the vampire and loping after the human sacrifices; their latest meal. Heads lashed forward, mandibles snapping, and human bodies splattered across the sands, the giant ants dragging their prey below ground and disappearing as each bloody victim was chased down. With each desperate twist and turn of his prisoners, the vampire yelled advice to his killer beasts as though they might actually heed him. Von Waldburg watched the last few prisoners pursued across his artificial arena, giggling as happily as if he was watching puppies capering around him.

The vampire prince slapped his thighs happily as the last fingers disappeared flailing below the blood-stained sands. 'Such a brief diversion from my duties' burden. Almost as enjoyable as forcing cattle to fight each other to the death with the promise of life for the last animal standing.'

'I prefer more active participation in a hunt, myself,' said Sophia, watching the Master of Masters stride out of the enclosure. 'Spectator sports never were to my taste.'

Ian struggled to reach Eleanor, but the demi-gog guards held him back. 'You toss me back my moly-sword and we'll make it an even fight,' snapped the agent.

Sophia shrugged in amusement. 'I said I enjoyed the hunt. Nobody said anything about making it a *fair* hunt.'

As Eleanor writhed on the floor she felt something happening to her, a force slowly intruding from outside her body. Filling her with something unnameable and inexplicable. A growing warmth which seemed to shield her from the pain, bringing her a faint reprieve from the agony, before converting into a series of shivering palpitations, like glugging freezing cola on a burning hot afternoon. *What's happening to me? Why me?* Then Von Waldburg reappeared back inside the throne chamber. He crossed to the chest containing his prize and locked the coins securely inside his desk again. Eleanor moaned in relief as her misery dwindled. *The safe has to be heavily armoured.* Her torment diminished to manageable proportions.

'Better, girl? You should spend a little longer playing with this curiosity, Figchen. Agent Drew believes the girl managed to murder the Keeper. A feat even my people couldn't achieve. If you find anything of interest to us, you may keep the girl alive as a second human pet for a while.'

Sophia's companion glanced coldly towards Eleanor. The young woman obviously didn't relish being supplanted as the mistress's house cat.

'Best not to feed the ants too much at once,' continued the vampire prince, 'it makes them torpid and lazy. And who knows, these young abominations should yet make a most excellent dessert.'

'I'm a little crunchy,' glowered Eleanor.

'We will discover exactly what you are,' said Von Waldburg. 'I do not tolerate mysteries. Time to peel yours away, one layer of skin at a time.'

Dismissed, the prisoners were shoved roughly back up the stairs in the company of Sophia, the young girl, Guy and a large escort of demi-gogs.

'After you skin them,' asked the young girl, 'will you make me a handbag out of their hide?'

'Of course,' smiled Sophia, indulgently. 'But you should retire to my quarters for a while. This will be blunt, boring work and I wouldn't wish to splatter these abominations' innards over your clothes. I am certain it will prove annoyingly difficult to secure fresh Alexander McQueen dresses after war breaks out.'

Eleanor sagged, dispirited on the top of the steps, her legs turning to jelly as the realisation of their fate finally sunk in. *This is the end. There's no chance of escape for me.* The best Eleanor could hope for was a sudden end to her torture when the Russian's monstrously large bomb detonated above her head.

22

~ NUKEM STYLE ~

Eleanor watched the vampire woman run her fingers across a range of razor sharp scalpels and other evil-looking surgical equipment spread across a steel tray. Sophia reached out and patted Ian's trouser leg encouragingly, the agent secured like Eleanor to an operating table under the interrogation chamber's surgical bright light. The vampire glanced towards Guy standing sentry over the exit. 'Who do you think should go first? The boy or the girl?'

'You can't allow this to be done to us,' Eleanor appealed towards Guy.

'You wanted to die a clean death, you should have stayed in the States and waited for the nukes to start flying,' shrugged Guy. 'I'd put a bullet in your heads as a mercy, but that crazy old coot of a blood-sucker back in the throne chamber would add me to his giant leaf-cutter ants' diet if I dared cross him.'

Sophia lifted the spectacles off Eleanor's face while she struggled on the operating table. 'No need to record this for posterity. The Vigil knows what befalls all abominations we capture.' Rather than selecting one of the terrifying devices from the tray, the female vampire seized Eleanor's forehead tight with both her hands. For a moment, Eleanor thought the monster would try to crush her skull, but that misapprehension vanished as she felt the vampire pushing, forcing her mind inside Eleanor's. Against Eleanor's will, she felt memories start to surface, bubbling out from within her. The Red was unpicking her mind! Eleanor lashed out with the force of her will, driving the vampire back, neurons ablaze as she burnt the invading freak with every iota of her fibre. Sophia stumbled back, a brief look of rage distorting her face before being replaced by astonishment.

'Very impressive,' said Sophia. 'Nobody has ever resisted me like that before.'

Eleanor wished she could take a shower, wash this ancient devil woman's stench off her. 'First time for everything.'

'I wonder if your curious abilities include the ability to grow back key parts of your anatomy?'

Eleanor spat at the vampire. 'I guess your abilities never included growing a sense of humour.'

'There's a reason why I prefer to question subjects in pairs,' continued Sophia. 'I am saving your friends in the theatre next door for my later amusement. Alasdair and Diane appear quite close if I am any judge of character. I can exploit their weakness. A pity the nun doesn't have anyone she values inside the city. Not even herself. The zealot will just have to watch me carve up your half-zombie comrade. Dissecting Bex Crawfield will take a tediously long time, so I need to shake a tail questioning you.' Sophia lifted a device off the steel trolley that resembled a blowtorch. 'There's also a good reason my tool of choice is a short-range laser cutter taken from an automobile production line robot. It possesses the advantage of cauterising wounds as it cuts, which means my subjects rarely die of blood loss without answering my questions. You see, not all of us have an aversion to the fruits of your people's perverted science.'

And one of those fruits is about to turn this underground city into molten lava. Eleanor had lost all sense of time, now; but she was fairly sure they had run out of enough of it that there was zero chance of escaping from the hellish bunker.

Sophia activated her cutter's laser blade.

'Leave her alone!' yelled Ian, struggling against his table's restraints.

'You misunderstand my intentions towards the girl. *This* is the reason I interrogate subjects in pairs,' smiled Sophia. She swung the device towards Ian's operating table and the agent screamed as she neatly severed Ian's left hand, his severed limb falling to the cell's floor with a sickening slap. 'There, I've left you your right hand. Consider that a small professional courtesy.' Sophia swivelled back towards Eleanor. 'You want to make it two-for-two? Or perhaps I should continue a little slower with the boy .. . say, one finger at a time?'

'What do you want from me?' screamed Eleanor, trying to drag her eyes away from Ian's smoking stump, bound to the table, the agent writhing in agony at his sudden slicing.

'Allow me inside your mind,' said Sophia.

'Be careful what you wish for,' hissed Eleanor.

Guy bent down, picked up Ian's severed hand before dropping it in a metal bin, tutting. 'You want my advice, I'd cooperate a little more, here.'

'Don't let her probe you if you can resist,' moaned Ian. 'She can go to hell.'

'I'm sure I'll get there on my own, one day. But long after you are both dust. One of *my* abilities,' said Sophia, 'the talent to penetrate the minds of animals and poke around. A talent you would share if you had sprung from my lineage, rather than that of Contessa Calogera.'

Eleanor's eyes narrowed. 'That was the Red who bit me?'

'A conceited old hag who usually overestimated her abilities as well as her usefulness to the Master of Masters,' said Sophia. 'Calogera wouldn't have lasted five minutes against the Keeper. Which rather begs the question, how did you?'

'Beginner's luck.'

'Luck is a lie told by fools to excuse their failures. Allow me access to your mind.' Sophia moved the laser cutter close and Eleanor's eyes were drawn to her hand. Eleanor prayed the vampire believed she was mesmerised by the deadly hissing white blade of focused light, rather than the creature's expensive gold Breitling Ladies wristwatch. Eleanor caught a glimpse of the time on the dial and tried not to show relief on her face. *It doesn't matter what this monster takes from my memories. We're all dead in a few more minutes. The largest bomb on the planet is about to run our atoms through a whisk with the world's molten mantle.*

'Time to make your mind up, young lady,' said Sophia. 'You can keep your oath to the Vigil, or you can allow me inside your mind and I'll leave your companion with five fine fingers and ten toes.' Sophia seized Ian's strapped-down arm with his remaining hand and started working his fingers like she was playing Five Little Piggies. 'Do you really need that last thumb? Let's see . . .'

'You never got around to your counter-interrogation training, kid,' Guy said to Eleanor, 'so I'll tell you the most important thing you would have learnt. Everyone talks in the end. How this ends is up to you.'

Eleanor's resolve finally cracked. 'Don't hurt Ian anymore. Please. I'll let you inside.'

'No,' pleaded Ian. 'NO!'

'Excellent,' said Sophia. 'I knew you would see sense.' She rested the laser cutter on the tray next to the steel scalpels, then seized Eleanor's forehead again tight with both hands. The creature's palms felt like ice, but the pain growing in Eleanor's skull wasn't from the cold. Eleanor tried not to resist the vampire, as hard as her passivity proved, the Red's unholy power grinding into her mind like a dentist's drill. The creature's presence was disgusting, intrusive, like allowing a bucket of slugs to slide wriggling through Eleanor's mind.

'Good, don't fight it,' commanded Sophia, 'let me pass inside.'

Unbidden, the vision of what Eleanor had glimpsed at the Crucifixion rose out of her, the vampire's violation of her prisoner faltering, confused by the ancient scene replaying. *How can this be?* projected the vampire. *This is not possible. You could not have been there.*

You ever work it out, drop me a postcard, thought Eleanor.

More, ordered Sophia, burrowing deeper inside Eleanor. *Show me everything.* Sophia battered past Eleanor's defences, Eleanor suppressing her natural reaction to vomit this entity out of her soul. The vampire reached to caress Eleanor's powers, trying to gauge what her prisoner was capable of, the range of the abomination's gifts. *There is something within you,* growled Sophia, *that it is not of us. But if not us, then what?* As Sophia probed, fresh visions came tumbling out from Eleanor — spilled like blood from a dagger wound — impossible and unknowable things, a jumbled storm of phantasms, futures and pasts and possibilities branching out. Both of them tumbled, lost among a multiverse both so complex and simple that to confront its fundamental paradoxes burnt like a horizon of exploding suns. Yet, the fieriest star of all was Eleanor. Her mind burning and roiling as what couldn't be contained splintered free of her weak mortal human shell. *My turn.* Eleanor lashed out at the vampire, giving the monster a little of what she had received; rejoicing as she slapped aside Sophia's mental defences like damp tissue paper. *Let's see what you're made of.* The Red flailed in outrage, but couldn't stop Eleanor sweeping through the halls of her monstrous mind like a barbarian horde sacking a city. *Yeah, what's sauce for the goose is sauce for the gander.* A stream of memories from the creature's long existence swirled around Eleanor, as unwanted and foul as Eleanor's fever-tossed glimpses of the Countessa's foul history. A burning high sun above the pyramids, the crunch of snow in icy forests, human prey running and falling, blood and feeding. And somewhere amidst it all, a tiny baby crying. Eleanor lost sight of that hideous second life, what had been released inside her swelling too strong to control. Eleanor tried to master her wild outpouring, but instead found herself riding the energy uncontrollably, surfing a sea of raw immensity. Out of that roaring gale emerged one coalescing vision that the two of them tried to latch onto, vampire and human both, like drowning shipwreck survivors flailing for a single life raft.

Von Waldburg's twisted ant farm habitat, Joanna shoved forward, lurching across bronze-coloured sands, screaming in raw terror as giant mutants rose out of the dunes, eager to rip apart this trespasser intruding across their territory. Punishment, the girl's punishment for the ultimate transgression of the vampires' racial laws.

'No!' yelled Sophia, releasing all contact with Eleanor's mind, the vampire stumbling back and almost falling across Ian's table. Guy rushed up to the vampire woman. 'What is it? What did you find inside the kid's brain?'

Eleanor could hardly hear their words, mere vibrations of air now as her mind tumbled out of infinity, buffeted by what the vampire had released within her, power and energy without limits, a universe of dancing futures and particles closing, narrowing back to the lumpen present. To... *here*. The present.

Sophia shoved Guy towards the interrogation room's exit. 'Joanna's life is in danger . . . the throne room, *now*.'

Both interrogators sprinted out, leaving their two victims still strapped and shocked at the speed of their tormentors' exit; Eleanor tried to gain control of the splintered present, reorient on just this raw reality.

'Did the Red catch a glimpse of the super-bomb?' groaned Ian, the arm containing his severed stump trembling uncontrollably in shock. 'Is that why she and Guy sprinted away so fast? She was shouting something about Joanna?'

Eleanor tried not to throw up while she yanked desperately against her restraints. *Too strong. Designed to contain us.* 'Nope. That Russian bomb is going to come as a really unpleasant shock to her on a couple of levels. Joanna is Sophia's so-called human pet . . . she's not anyone's house cat, though. The girl's really the Red's daughter - not to mention Guy's child.'

Ian almost choked. 'That — just can't be possible,' gasped Ian, his face a definition of bewilderment. 'Reds are totally sterile. They pass on genetic material by converting humans into their kind, a virus quickening through the generations. If a vampire already has human offspring when they're turned, they're expected to hunt their children down and murder them. Loyalty to their nest and race has to be utter and complete.'

'Yeah, I saw that. Their vampire mind-suck-shtick is a two-way street,' said Eleanor. The agent felt her powers swelling within her, their unholy resonance magnifying in an almost infinite loop, fed by her desperate fear of their fast approaching destruction. Eleanor's powers fully unleashed by the vampire's violation of her very soul. 'I poked around in the ice-lady's noggin while she raided my head. Sophia dug up an ancient Egyptian amulet which allows Reds to suppress their vampirism and fake as a full human for a year. Naughty old Sophia was meant to use the ability to infiltrate NATO and kick off a war against the USSR. Instead, she fell for Guy and got in the family way. Joanna was the result. They both thought that they had kept the Master of Masters in the dark, but the old monster became suspicious and confirmed Joanna's parentage after testing pet-girl's DNA. Now the King of the Fangsters believes he's about to leave humanity huddled as pushovers inside the radioactive ruins, he intends to punish Sophia for her transgression. The whole human kid thing is a biggie in their culture, isn't it? That was my vision - what Sophia saw. Joanna getting served by the big boss as an appetiser inside the mutant ant farm!'

'Good riddance and bon appétit,' grunted Ian.

'Vampire lady cut and ran too early,' said Eleanor, shaping the power burning through her veins, barely restraining it from incinerating every cell inside her body. 'If Sophia hung around a few seconds longer, she would have glimpsed what I saw at the end. *A future, at least, a slim shot at a possible one.* 'Close your eyes.'

'Why?' croaked Ian.

'Because this is probably going to kill us both,' said Eleanor, 'so it's kind of traditional.'

***

Sophia skidded to a stop, banging her fists in frustration against the armoured glass of the ant farm. *Too late.* Below, Von Waldburg had emerged inside the artificial desert vista, dragging Joanna screaming and flailing behind him. The vampire prince had a pair of demi-gog soldiers following him, one carrying a large professional-grade video camera and the other a telescopic sound mic.

The Master of Masters sensed her presence, looked up and made a cheery wave up towards the viewing gallery. 'Figchen! Now you have spoiled my surprise for you. What a pity. I was going to force you to watch the recording of your little abomination's death each and every day until I tired of your treacherous presence.'

Guy arrived beside Sophia, panting from the exertion of sprinting after her. 'Please, don't do this! I passed you the Judas Purse . . .'

'Should the mule master express undying gratitude towards a beast merely for bearing his load? No, agent. The coins were always my true destiny. One way or another, I would have taken possession of the Judas Purse. But what you chose, Sophia Augusta, what you chose is beyond the pale. Casting away your perfection, copulating and giving birth like a grunting animal. I made you! You should have passed on our lineage through bite and blood. Instead, you betrayed your master and your species and for what—' he yanked Joanna around and forced her to her knees—'for *this*? This squealing pathetic little prey animal. I would feed on her, but your taste flowing through her veins sickens me to my very core.'

The leader's heavily armed guards flooded into the chamber behind Sophia and Guy. Sophia sensed her own demi-gogs responding to her urgent summons, but they were massively outnumbered by Von Waldburg's loyalists and the ranks of North Korean serfs subservient to him.

'Save Joanna,' Guy begged Sophia, listening to their daughter's pleas for mercy in desperation.

No more time. Orange sands stirred in front of the Master of Masters, ebony-armoured mutants ants emerging from their deep subterranean tunnel system.

'You cuckolded me for a filthy sub-human!' yelled Von Waldburg. 'An abomination who once hunted our kind for the Vigil. You treated me like a mortal fool, Sophia Augusta, and for that sin, you will relive my vengeance a thousand times. I shall replay this foul little creature's death every day for you; every day until you beg for the mercy of a clean beheading.'

Behind Sophia the leader's forces closed in, readying firearms and blades. Sophia hardly cared if they took her alive now, her gaze fixed on Joanna's terrified attempts to break free of the old monster's iron grip. Guy attempted to reach the passage down to the sands, but the master's demi-gogs seized him, holding him struggling and cursing in their claws.

'For you, agent, I have other plans,' sneered Von Waldburg. 'My little Figchen shall be starved of all human sustenance. How long, do you think, before she grows hungry enough to turn on you and rip you to pieces? She is in possession of an iron will, my fine blood-child. She could last two months before she is hungry enough to lose self-control and devour you.'

'I would have given Joanna the gift,' begged Sophia, knowing her pleas were useless even as she gave voice to them. 'When she was of age. Joanna could have been as a granddaughter for you . . . a guardian of your legacy.'

'You wanted to give birth to the same abomination *twice*? You pollute my presence with your filthy perverted longings. Now witness your reward for your betrayal of me . . . '

Sophia reached out with her power, trying to engage the emerging beasts; three giants. Sophia tried to force her way into their consciousness, but the mutants were too primitive to reason with, let alone control without the unnatural power of the Judas Purse behind her. *Hate and hunger and the chemical twitching of base hardwired instincts.* They skittered forward, massive mandibles clacking like chainsaws. Von Waldburg raised his hands to the air in the manner of a jubilant prophet. 'Cut her head off, my giant lovelies, rip her limbs away one by one. Then drag her bloody carcass beneath to feed your larvae.'

Sophia looked on in horror, fear turning to confusion as the monstrous ants swarmed past Joanna's quivering form. They ignored the girl, heading towards Von Waldburg and the two camera crew filming behind him.

'What is this?' yelled the vampire prince. 'Consume the little abomination. I control the Judas Purse. You are mine to command. Sever this abomination's head from her filthy shoulders. Scatter her bones to line your nest!'

Guy watched the vampire prince back uneasily away as his pets menaced him. 'What is—?'

'It's not me,' said Sophia, shocked. The female vampire felt the ants' waves of raw hate towards this false queen, this usurper who had captured the mutants and imprisoned them and regularly tormented them here. They were no longer obeying the Master of Masters. It was as though the Judas Purse had lost all of its power. *But that can only happen if the curse is lifted. And only one family, the descendants of one foul lineage has the ability to erase it … the blood whose execution cursed the coins in the first place.*

Von Waldburg swivelled and raced towards the exit, shoving the camera crew back before the pursing mutants. His act of cowardice was almost enough to reach the tunnel's open doorway, but the ants possessed six long legs to the vampire's two, and one overtook him from behind, mandibles snapping shut around his torso even as his palms clasped the exit's edges. There was an explosion of blood as the Master of Masters was sliced in half, followed by a far greater detonation as his long stored energies erupted, an immortal made mortal after an unnatural age. The sandstorm of orange dust cleared to reveal Joanna limping away down the corridor.

Sophia remembered the impossible vision she had glimpsed inside Eleanor's mind. Two of the false saviour's disciples greeting the girl on the mountain. 'You do not belong here, daughter.' *Daughter.* Not just any customary greeting, perhaps, but a resemblance the pair had spotted and mistaken for some other child's? Eleanor, rolling in agony in the throne chamber in front of the artifact as though it was pure poison. *The girl was the damn poison! She's bled our prize of all of its power, as surely as attaching jump-leads to a battery.* Burning angels, still slowly shifting their best pieces across the board, the game of ages played exactly as intended.

'Clever,' Sophia whispered in admiration, as she turned and punched her fist through the nearest demi-gog's windpipe. Most of the nest had folded in agony to the floor, all connection to their master severed by his disintegration. Guy seized a machine pistol from the nearest demi-gog, opening fire on the loyalists, shell-cases clattering to the ground as he emptied the magazine. Sophia side-stepped a North Korean soldier's bayonet, breaking his neck as she danced. 'Oh, you clever, clever ethereal bastards.'

That was when the bunker's air-raid sirens activated, shaking the throne chamber with their shrill warning.

Damn. It appeared it wasn't just the angels who had outmanoeuvred the vampires today.

***

Eleanor ignored Ian's yells. She wasn't sure if he was screaming out of concern for her, or pain from the growing heat inside the interrogation chamber. Maybe it was his shock from seeing her naked now all her clothes had burnt to ash against her skin. It was hard to hear him over the screech of the air raid warning sirens. The city had been designed to survive a nuclear attack, but not what was about to slam down from the heavens. *I can't halt now. If I slow down, we'll all be melted when the Russian's Big Boy's Toy hits this place.* Instead, it was her torture table that was melting - quite literally - the agonising overload of energy coursing like napalm through her veins.

'You have to stop,' shouted Ian, 'you'll burn yourself to a crisp if you don't stop this!'

Eleanor couldn't reply properly - her throat filling with super-heated steam from the accelerated particles spinning around her flesh. *Concentrate, girl. Focus. Just you and the table. The steel softening like butter, the carbon-reinforced manacles turning to gas.*

Your flesh acting as a conduit for this hell-storm of yours, holding it in check.

'Please,' begged Ian, 'I can't live if you-'

His voice grew dim as the table began to bubble around her head, spitting molten metal across the floor. *Just a little bit longer.* Eleanor's flesh took the power, shaping it, leeching energy to regenerate her body even as it disintegrated around her, a sudden fizzing as the nearly indestructible polymer yarn of reduced graphene nanotubes composing her restraints hit their limit at the surface temperature of the sun. She rolled off what was left of the deformed table and hit the bare concrete floor, her feet leaving scorch marks as she faltered for a second. Her body glowed as she pulled the mist of gaseous steel floating inside the torture room towards her, covering her modesty with a jump-suit of silk-thin metal, protecting Ian from second-degree burns at the same time.

'How? What are you?' stammered the agent.

'Unlocked.' Eleanor slapped the prisoner release button under Ian's table, the black restraints retracting at speed like a seat belt. 'And now so are you.'

Ian half-slid, half fell, off the table, banging into the abandoned cart full of surgical nasties and torture implements. 'You look like a superhero in that silver suit.'

'Yeah, Hot Girl: The Molten Mistress. We got to cut and run, or we're all going to be molten and not in a good way.' She shut her eyes for a second, feeling the Russian super-bomber with its super-sized payload seconds from release above them. *Too late.* She pushed Ian aside. 'Stand back!'

'But-?'

'This is the cut…' Eleanor raised both hands and poured what was spinning around inside her against the wall. Basic reinforced concrete, but it might as well have been soggy cardboard as the material near instantly vapourised in the pounding, a smoking round hole leading to the interrogation chamber next door. She slipped through and caught the demi-gog guard running towards her, tossing him against the wall hard enough to leave another hole. Somewhere in the stratosphere, a bombardier was caught mesmerised by the target release icon sliding across his head-up display, the bomber's targeting computer loading the final wind-speed and live weather readings into the GOAB's targeting packet. But the world's biggest bomb was so massive it hardly needed guiding - it was like dropping a building from the sky. Hell, it was like dropping the Death Star. Eleanor felt the aircrewman's satisfaction, saw the cramped confines of the bomber through his helmet's visor, tasted the recycled oxygen in his rubber mask. This beast was the only weapon of its kind and he had been trusted to drop it on this vital secret mission. Target match. Releases snapped back and raw gravity took its course.

Ian rushed through the hole after Eleanor, his eyes casting madly around the torture tables containing Sister Rae, Alastair, Diane and Bex. Even Bex couldn't survive what was dropping whistling towards them.

'Release them,' barked Eleanor. 'World's biggest hammer is about to hit us.' She struck Diane's release button first, leaving her struggling free for a second, sprinting across to Alasdair's table. Ian did the same for Sister Rae and Bex, the nun rushing to the door, checking through its porthole-like window and yelling back towards them. 'Soldiers incoming, too. A company's worth. Local mugs, not Reds.'

Ian sprinted to a steel cabinet against the wall, his remaining hand skimming over the scalpels and blades, looking for the sharpest, meanest stick he could find to wave at a platoon or two of vampire-corrupted North Korean fanatics.

Eleanor tracked the spinning bomb's descent through the bombardier's sights. *Twenty seconds to air-blast.*

'Bar the door,' ordered Eleanor, then had second thoughts. 'Actually, sister, stand back.' She raised her fists and poured energy into the two doors - not enough to blast them off their hinges, but as an emergency spot-weld, it'd pass.

'Bleeding heck!' shouted the sister, moving cautiously back from the hissing hot doors. 'A little warning.'

Fifteen seconds to air-blast.

'We're sealed inside,' warned Ian sounding distraught, adrenalin kicking in, giving him a pharmaceutical grade blast of cornered animal terror.

'Nearly sealed,' said Eleanor, swivelling towards the hole in the wall she had entered by, giving the ceiling enough of a blast to bring an avalanche of rubble down across it. Outside the chamber, the guards had grown bored of trying to open the torture room doors the normal way, a burst of heavy machine-gun fire as they tried to shoot their way inside, steel buckling under the onslaught. 'Now we are.'

Ten seconds to air-blast.

Eleanor assisted Alasdair in levering Diane off the operating table.

'Nice suit,' said Bex, grabbing a handful of scalpels.

'This season's look - melted torture table.'

Sister Rae, still by the doors, sounded resigned rather

than panicked. 'Shit, they're bringing up an RPG. What kind of paranoid nutters keep a rocket launcher for use inside an enclosed bunker?'

Five seconds to air-blast.

'To me!' shouted Eleanor. 'Everyone in close: group hug-close.'

Three seconds to air-blast.

'You picked up teleporting as a power?' asked Ian, halting before her, the others sprinting over near enough to touch her as the door's viewport shattered under machinegun fire.

'I wish.' As powers go, she truly wished she possessed that ability, rather than a bucket full of crazy. *I need perfect timing, here. Anything else would be instant death.* She moved her hands, began dividing her energy in two, shaping the first half into a sphere around them. A perfect ball of energy. A shield. It didn't have to last long. Just long enough for the second part of what she was summoning, here. Eleanor tried not to be distracted by the reinforced glass of the door port shot out under heavy machine gun fire, the whoosh of a rocket propelled warhead exiting its launcher, tiny, tiny, compared to —

Detonation.

Five hundred tonnes of explosive death airburst above a fake village in North Korea. One second the village was there, then it wasn't, as any ground in Kilchu that hadn't turned to gas liquefied, a shockwave force spreading down and out that hadn't been felt on Earth since a rogue asteroid murdered the dinosaurs. Liftshafts which could carry small regiments instantly vapourised, huge artificial tunnels and underground facilities filled in by half a mile of bedrock flowing sideways at hypersonic velocities. And somewhere inside that hell of subterranean destruction, a tiny bubble of energy, almost crumpling under the impossible onslaught despite an eerie power desperately renewing the sphere's surface integrity. Hardly enough of Eleanor left over to send a blistering lance of energy piercing downward towards the Earth's core. If there was one benefit of suffering inside the middle of a live GOAB explosion, it was that the bedrock was already so utterly shattered by the shockwave that it couldn't resist a volcanic sinkhole suddenly being drilled into it. If the Amurian tectonic plate could have voiced a sentient thought right then, it would have been, 'Sure, why the hell not?' as it splintered and released a thousand bars of magma pressure through a very focused hole driven down by Eleanor. Then her bubble of close to collapsing protective energy wasn't static anymore. It became a cannonball surfing a volcanic eruption through the world's biggest earthquake, courtesy of the planet's largest bomb.

Eleanor allowed herself a high-pitched groan, barely vocalised, the feedback loop stealing energy from outside and reinforcing her sphere holding her — clutching them all — as tight as amber-sealed insects. Up. Out. That was the second advantage of liquefying the landscape — once solid ground parted like an ocean vomiting out a surfacing submarine, then a fast flying sub blown into the sky, giving Eleanor an interesting new problem — how to reinforce her sparkling sphere strong enough to survive the impact of landing. Sharp cold air, filled with debris from the smoking, burning crater below. They struck the forest they had passed through earlier with the velocity of an artillery shell. Half the forest - the closest half facing Kilchu -

had already collapsed from the bomb blast and ensuing quake, but then they collided with the half that still endured. Eleanor used the thunder of splintering trees as an air-brake to slow them to non-lethal speeds; trunks cracked, trees that had stood for centuries turned into matchwood. No more feedback loop to suck away the explosion's own power, though. Holding the sphere together under the shocking force of this punishment was all on Eleanor. Carving out their own passage through the icy green cathedral for mile after mile. They rolled and screamed inside the ball, all stabilising forces shed in her agony, the sphere fast losing coherence, the forest striking her now as much as the shield. Smashing. Cracking bones. Bruises. Pain. Then they were free of the trees, ploughing through snow-drifts beyond, the ball of energy melted away back to wherever it had emerged from inside her soul. Cold. Fierce cold. Eleanor steel suit creaking around her as she rediscovered her mortality. Bodies lay scattered in the winter wilderness around her. Whimpering, so still alive. Eleanor tried to crawl forward but found she could hardly lift her broken, shivering fingers. Her body possessed no more energy, no more strength. She was spent, an empty vessel barely conscious enough to feel the waves of pain spreading across her now feeble body.

There was a soft crunching of snow as a line of cloaked giants crossed the valley towards her. One of the Knights Solomon glanced over Eleanor and across what was left standing of the forest, observing fountains of volcanic fire lighting up the night sky orange. Rocks the size of cars - once reinforced concrete bunker material - hurled skyward, popping and exploding at this distance like mortar volleys. The soldier's military order had observed their vow of silence for half a millennia, but now, at last, the vow was broken.

'Well, *shi—*'

23

~ EPILOGUE ~

Monica Morton hadn't expected to flee terrified for her life during a supposed afternoon educational visit. But then, she hadn't exactly been expecting to see her classmates fall flailing and screaming when the staff showing them around the remote Flaming Gorge Dam turned into a pack of monstrous fanged beasts. The hideous creatures had set upon the children like hungry wolves, the memory of flashes of blood, yells and horror unable to leave Monica's mind as she stumbled away, near catatonic in shock. Some of the creatures were tracking her down the access tunnel, the passage she prayed led to the top of the dam and a slim chance of surviving this nightmare. The penknife Monica clutched in her sweaty right hand was sharp enough to peel the orange in her backpack, but as far as monster-slaying went, she knew it was going to prove entirely inadequate to the task of killing what was chasing her. She would have fled faster, but her body was burning, her head dizzy. Her unnatural hunters' unholy howling grew louder and louder, pursuing her, panicked, around the corner. That was when she ran into three more of them in the shape of two young women and a man.

'Like, I got this,' said the blonde with a Californian accent. She stepped in front of Monica who plunged her penknife into the young woman's gut. It had thrust into her stomach right up to the hilt, but the woman glanced casually down at the blade as though it was merely an unexpected splinter of table wood. 'Really? That sweater's a Fendi. You paying for a new one?'

'You're bleeding,' said the boy, pointing at the wound on Monica's neck.

It took a moment for Monica to realise he was talking about her, not the blonde she had just tried to gut with her pen-knife. Another second and she realised that none of these people possessed the oddly distended faces of the things attempting to consume her. So these freaks weren't with the pursuing monsters? 'One of the dam's staff tried to … to eat me.'

The second young woman drew out a pen-sized steel hilt and a long silver blade seemed to fold out of it. She sliced the air and the cut of its edge sounded like a hissing snake. 'Yeah, that do happen. Al, one survivor to extract here, stat. Diane, prep for cure.'

Down the corridor, the eerie howling was swelling. Monica felt sick, and not just because they were all about to die. Something awful was happening to her body, eating her out from the inside. Nothing should feel as sick as this. 'They're coming to kill us!'

'Balls to the wall, kid. Business as usual.' The young woman touched the side of the spectacles she was wearing and Monica heard a faint buzz coming from the frames - an earphone set into its side. 'One-mile exclusion zone set. Okay, Harriet. We're nearly in close contact, give us a few seconds and these Reds are Alpha Mike Foxtrot. Anything tries to blow this joint that isn't Vigil, that's what the warm sticky goo inside the Cav's flamethrowers are for.'

'They're monsters!' cried Monica as the howls echoed louder, almost on top of them.

'And we're what keeps monsters awake at night,' grinned the woman. 'But only the ones lucky enough not to bump into us down a dark passage.'

The blonde yanked Monica's penknife out of her body and dropped it to the floor with a disgusted expression on her face.

'It's totally time for the Bexster Bash.'

'We *really* got to work on a new catchphrase for you,' sighed the second woman.

'Actually, Eleanor, I kind of like it,' said the young man.

'That's because your taste never matured from thinking Ultravox was the height of musical expression.'

All three of them ran around the corner as Monica clutched onto the wall, swaying from the unnatural fever burning through her. The howling grew louder, followed by the hissing of blades, and then there was quiet. The silence might have been from Monica falling to the floor, half-passing out.

But it wasn't.

FINI

THANKS

A special thanks to all my Apprentices, students and test readers, who proved that a little back-seat driving doesn't have to be a painful experience.

Those thanks include, but is by no means limited to...

Aether James, Alex Duvall, Alice Bennett, Alicia Drinkwater, Alison Burcombe, Amy Milham, Angel Bradley, Angela Ho, Annie-Budgie Mills, Arietty Powell, Becky Garcia, Ben Shepherd, Benjamin Sharpe, Bláithín 'BumbleBee' CCR McGuiness, Brody Sommers, Carlson Z Whang, Carrie Evans, Chaojidage, Chermain Galloway, Ciara Watson, Dominique Gould, El Presidente Michael, Ella Kitching, Ellen Olsen, Emily Felstead, Emily Tang, Erin Rose, Ethan Dowley, FShore800, Gabrielle Lucas, Garlic Bread, Georgia Cook, Gibson Nevill, Grace Burkhart, Grace Shaw, Harry Fortescue, Holly Tolhurst, Incman7, Iola George, Jeevanjit Singh Kandola, Jess_Marvelite, Jessie Taylor, Jina Lee, Joan Kanyago, Joel Francis, Julia Hill, Julia Mae Gammon, Karen R. Conner, Kate Power, Kiara Swaby, Lady Acacia, Laura Porteous, Lauren Aspoas, Levia Yee, Lucas Rylar, Lucy Cole, Luke Wyeth, Madison Wong, Marissa C., Maryam Malik, Max Church, Maya Cumberbatch, Meg Maguire, Michael Sidorenko, Morola Olugbile, Nathan Hubert, Olivia Baker, Owen Marsh, Pegamoosicorn, President Anna Babriecki, Ravtej Singh, Reece Cornhill, RH_Burns, Rhys Monkley, Samantha Young, Samarah Irving, Saphron Brookes, Sarah Carrasco, Sebas, Selina Bean, Shakira Gawne, Shannen Johnson, Spencer Bilyeu, Steven Judge, Sumaiyaa 'Maya_Herondale' Khan, Taylor Hall,

Taylor McAmis , The Other, Thomas Neill, Tom Wayerworth, Vishmi Liyanage, WhovianAtHogwarts, Wynter_The_Storm. Aditi the Llama, Alex Hopkins, Alexander Grant, Alfonso Murray, Alison Joseph, Alma Gill, Alyssa French, Andres Aguilar, Angel Burns, Anita Morton, Anthony Herrera, Arlene Alexander, Arthur Rowe, Arturo Allison, Bernadette Brooks, Bernice Hopkins, Betsy Drake, Bitesized_Journalist, Bobbie Garcia, Bonnie Holloway, Brad Mason, Bradford Willis, Brian Singleton, Brooke Roberson, Bryant Smith, Carla Sherman, Cary Crawford, Chester Ford, Chester Kelley, Christian Robertson, Christina Murphy, Claire Bennett, Clarence Hardy, Clark Schmidt, Claudia Mathis, Clay Osborne, Cockle_Echo, Cody Vaughn, Cornelius Park, Courtney Knight, Cowbird Supernova, Curtis Larson, Dallas Gill, Dan Jennings, Daryl Baker, Dave Norton, Dave Rivera, Denise Gregory, Diana Webster, Domingo Thomas, Doug Banks, Duane Sandoval, Dwayne Bradley, Eddie Warren, Edgar Carpenter, Edwin Ballard, Elaine Morales, Elena Briggs, Elizabeth Stokes, Ella Strickland, Ellis Craig, Elsa Curtis, Emilio Norris, Enrique Hodges, Erin Hines, Ethel Cain, Ethel Ramos, Eula Russell, Felipe Nunez, Felix Lawrence, Fernando Daniels, Francis Schultz, Franklin Hammond, Fred Hernandez, Fredrick Ray, Garry White, Gary Neal, Gary Singleton, Genevieve Collins, Geoffrey Higgins, Georgia Maldonado, Geraldine Page, Gerardo Mccarthy, Gilberto Turner, Gloria Curry, Grace Allen, Grady Valdez, Grant Mack, Guadalupe Bishop, Gustavo Hall, Hattie Fuller, Heidi Cobb, Henrietta Carroll, Iris Grant, Irma Barton, Isabel Anderson, Jackie Gomez, Jaime Gilbert, Janie Mendez, Jason Hodges, Jean Huff, Jeanne Ramirez, Jessie Ellis, Jimmy Garrett, Joe Lyons, Joel Abbott, Josie Hampson, John Benson, Jordan Santos, Juana Hanson, Judith Leonard, Justin Peters, Kathleen Nash, Katie Burton, Katrina Mccormick, Kellie White, Kerry Bradley, Kevin Walsh, Kim Richards, Kristine Gardner, Lance Phelps, Latex Lagan, Laura Rose, Leigh Dunn, Leo Gordon, Lila Miller, Lillian Griffith, Lisa Hamilton, Lola Torres, Lonnie Weber, Loretta Byrd,

Lowri Clarke, Louis Collier, Luis Carpenter, Luis Joseph, Luther Mclaughlin, Madeline Eaton, Magnetotail Gaff, Mamie Wallace, Manuel Mack, Marcella Powell, Marco Gardner, Margaret Morris, Margie Gomez, Marie Long, Marion Miller, Marion Parker, Mark Young, Marshall Long, Marta Santiago, Martha George, Matthew Perkins, Maurice Schwartz, Melanie Newton, Melissa Owen, Melvin Burgess, Meredith Bates, Miguel Edwards, Miranda Fletcher, Molding Striker, Molly Thornton, Monica Blake, Naomi Jacobs, Nathan Horton, Nathaniel Ramsey, Nettie Guerrero, Nick Tyler, Nicolas Young, Noel Thompson, Omar Lyons, Panicky Conniption, Pete Carson, Phil Manning, Phillip Peterson, Rachel Robbins, Ramona Rodgers, Regina Hill, Reginald Knight, Rex Brock, Rhonda Bryant, Richard Roberts, Rick Hayes, Ricky Vargas, Roderick Poole, Rodney Graham, Rolando Hines, Ronald Curtis, Roshni, Roxanne Moss, Roy Wade, Sally Anderson, Saul Barnett, Sean Flowers, Seth Brooks, Shannon Duncan, Sheila Richards, Shelly Elliott, Shivangi Sharma, Sidney King, Simon Stevenson, Stacy Becker, Stewart Rogers, Susan Hamilton, Susie Byrd, Tara Richardson, Taylor Bass, Terrell Goodwin, Toby Moran, Tom Owens, Tommie Buchanan, Tommy Holland, Tonya Sandoval, Traci Graves, Wendell Parker, Wesley Garner, Wesley Hoffman, Whitney Patterson, Wilbert Reid, Wilfred Pratt, Willie Doyle, Woodrow Harper, Writer@Twitchy, Yvonne Obrien.